Just Like in the Movies

HEIDI RICE

One More Chapter
a division of HarperCollins*Publishers*
The News Building
1 London Bridge Street
London SE1 9GF

www.harpercollins.co.uk

HarperCollins*Publishers*
1st Floor, Watermarque Building, Ringsend Road
Dublin 4, Ireland

This paperback edition 2021
1

First published in Great Britain in ebook format by
HarperCollins*Publishers* 2021

A catalogue copy of this book
is available from the British Library.

ISBN: 9780008372583

Set in Birka by Palimpsest Book Production Ltd, Falkirk Stirlingshire

Printed and bound in Great Britain by
CPI Group (UK) Ltd, Croydon CR0 4YY

To my mum and dad whose perfect date night, once upon a time, was watching a double bill together at the National Film Theatre on London's South Bank. He loved esoteric foreign language dramas and she adored glamorous Hollywood musicals – so I'm not really sure how they ever got together, but I'm very glad they did.

To my husband Robin who took me on a first date to see Dead Calm which gave me a great excuse to cuddle up with him because it was really bloody scary. Good call, Rob. To Catri who is my best mate thanks, mostly, to our shared love of James Dean and Thelma and Louise.

To the Coronet cinema in Notting Hill Gate where my love of the movies began ...

And to the Everyman Screen on the Green in Islington, where I had my latest movie-going experience almost a year ago now. I hope I get back there soon, to watch lots more movies with the people I love.

Prologue

Live in the moment, and try not to die while doing it.
Matthew Aloysius Devlin

Ruby Graham stepped out of the tube at Hammersmith Broadway on a Thursday morning in March and adjusted her sunglasses to quell the headache detonating in her frontal lobe.

Commuters barged past her, cutting through the pedestrian traffic with the grim determination of First World War squaddies leaping from the trenches.

She forced herself to move, instead of standing like a dummy at the tube entrance – causing a pavement pile-up was not going to bring back her soul mate or unbreak her heart.

I miss you so much you daft old sod, why did you have to die?

She sniffed down the sob cueing up in her throat as she headed along Shepherd's Bush Road.

No more tears, Ruby, all they do is make you look like a badger.

If she tried hard enough, maybe she could hear Matty

laughing at himself and the ridiculousness of being struck down with congestive heart failure in his flat above The Royale Cinema, instead of dying while cliff diving in Acapulco, or motorbiking across the Sahara desert or participating in one of the many other 'marvellous adventures' that had made up his life.

She dug her iPhone out of her pocket and reread the email she'd received the day after Matty's death. The email she'd ignored in the last ten days while getting the million and one things done that came with an unexpected death. Unfortunately, she couldn't ignore it any longer, because the appointment was today.

She lowered her sunglasses to double-check the address.

Peter Ryker, Solicitor, Ryker, Wells and Associates, 121a Shepherd's Bush Road.

She stopped at a doorway jammed between a kebab shop and a florist and pressed the bell for the first floor.

The muffled ring drilled into her skull and she cursed her lemon-tini binge at yesterday's wake for the five hundredth time since she'd woken up in Matty's tiny flat above The Royale an hour ago amid a pile of debris worthy of Glastonbury.

Note to self: catastrophic hangovers and grief do not make great bedfellows. Especially when you still have the reading of the will to get through.

The intercom buzzed and she whispered her name, so as not to wake the sleeping dragon that had only been temporarily tamed by the cocktail of extra-strength painkillers she'd found in Matty's medicine cabinet.

She climbed the narrow staircase to the first floor, praying on each creaky tread that Matty hadn't lined up too many shocking reveals for this afternoon's entertainment. Given Matty's addiction to showmanship and the fact he appeared to have stage-managed the reading of the will scene from *The Grand Budapest Hotel*, she wasn't holding out too much hope.

Ruby's stress downgraded when she reached Peter Ryker's office to find an open airy space, the clean lines of the modern furniture highlighted by the comforting view through the Victorian bay window of Brook Green – and no sign of Ralph Fiennes anywhere. Ryker stood when she entered and came from behind his desk. A slim man in his fifties, he wore an expertly tailored slate-grey suit, his warm smile contradicting his conservative appearance.

'Miss Graham, thank you so much for coming.' He shook her hand in a firm grip, the easy confidence in his manner matched by the cosy chestnut brown of his eyes.

Ruby's lungs squeezed, Ryker's paternal smile reminding her of Matty – and everything that would be missing in her life from now on.

No Matty to make her laugh at some daft exploit from his youth. No Matty to pore over the relative merits of *Easter Parade* versus *Monty Python's The Life of Brian* for The Royale's Good Friday screening. No Matty to share a spiced caramel latte with while they debated the next quarter's schedule of gala events. No Matty to be there for her when she needed a shoulder to lean on. Or a person to tell her they were proud of her. Or even a hopeless romantic with Cupid delusions who insisted on trying to fix her up with guys *he* fancied, most of whom turned out to be gay.

She dragged in a breath past the boulder in her throat that had taken on asteroid proportions during yesterday morning's service at the Golders Green Crematorium. Time to stop fixating on the prospect of her life with no Matty in it and concentrate on the irony that she was even going to miss those terrible blind dates Matty had been fixing her up with ever since she'd turned twenty-one.

'Sorry, if I'm a bit late,' she managed to mumble to Ryker.

'Not a problem.' He touched her arm as he let go of her hand, the welcoming smile faltering. 'And let me say, I'm so sorry for your loss. Matty was such a character, I'm sure we'll all miss him immensely.'

She nodded as her eyeballs began to sting and the asteroid in her throat head-butted her tonsils.

Ryker indicated a chair on the left side of his desk. 'Why don't you take a seat so we can begin.'

Remembering her sunglasses, she slipped them off and stuffed them in her bag.

She and Matty had never discussed what would happen in the eventuality of his death for the simple reason that he had been fit and healthy and only in his early fifties – and neither of them had known he had an undiagnosed heart condition. Because it was, well, undiagnosed. She choked down the asteroid, which was expanding again. That Matty had written a will at all was news to her when she'd gotten Ryker's email.

But whatever the will contained, her only objective now was to keep The Royale open for business. The small, and only slightly dilapidated art-house cinema in north, north

Notting Hill had been Matty's life and his legacy – and it was all she had left of him.

She crossed to the chair Ryker had indicated as he stepped behind her to close the office door. But as she shifted round to place her bum on the seat, she stiffened and bolted upright.

The trickle of blood still left in her head flooded into her cheeks as she spotted the man sitting in the chair behind the door.

His striking blue gaze flicked over her, the assessment both dispassionate and yet disturbingly intimate.

'Luke Devlin,' he said, and nodded.

The curt introduction struck her low in her abdomen. Even his voice sounded like his famous father's – the deep American accent enriched by the sandpaper quality that had had the media dubbing Rafael Falcone 'the voice of sex' nearly half a century ago.

'Rube ...' She cleared the rubble in her throat and attempted to introduce herself again, preferably without a helium squeak worthy of Minnie Mouse. 'Ruby Graham, pleased to meet you,' she murmured.

Although she wasn't pleased to meet him. What was *he* doing here?

She'd spotted him yesterday at the back of the crowd in the crematorium. Even then, with his face downcast and his shoulders hunched, the resemblance to the man who had fathered him was striking enough to make Ruby catch her breath.

That had to suck.

But now the likeness almost made her swallow her tongue. Not easy with an asteroid in the way.

It had been Matty's dying wish that Ruby invite his long-lost nephew to his funeral, one of several dying wishes he'd whispered to her from the gurney as they waited to wheel him into surgery. But Ruby was fairly sure he'd only done it at the time to be melodramatic. Matty had always been a drama queen, no way would he have missed the opportunity to milk a possible dying wish scenario. But he'd never met Luke Devlin, having been estranged from this man's mother, his sister Helena, since before Devlin was born. Ruby had only sent the invite because, well ... it had been a dying wish for goodness' sake, intentional or not. She'd never expected Luke Devlin to show at Golder's Green Crematorium on a rainy Wednesday morning. Especially as she hadn't even been able to find an address for him, so had been forced to send the funeral notice to his mother's agent.

Wasn't the guy a property magnate in Manhattan?

Yesterday, he'd looked supremely uncomfortable, probably because he'd been hit on by half the congregation – after all, most of them were massive film buffs – then left without a word. The whole experience of burying her best friend had been so surreal and overwhelming, Devlin's appearance had just been one other piece of weirdness Ruby hadn't had a chance to process properly ...

But she was processing it now, like a data analyst on crack.

She searched her memory banks for what she knew about the guy.

But her head was still too fuzzy with grief to remember anything coherent about Devlin. Just that he was rumoured to be the love child of Matty's sister, renowned stage star

Helena Devlin, and actor Rafael Falcone. Helena had always been coy about admitting who had fathered her oldest son – he had a couple of half-siblings, a brother by a Maine fisherman and a sister by British director Hal Markham whose parentage she hadn't been nearly so coy about. Helena had been notorious in her day for having three love children by men she hadn't married, children she had then proceeded to drag around the globe with her and shove into the full glare of the media spotlight. But all three of them had faded from the gossip columns as they'd grown up. Luke in particular was famous for being a bit of a recluse – which had to explain that dark frown.

But if he liked to keep out of the limelight, why had he attended Matty's funeral? Matty's death had been mentioned in the tabloids, even if it only got a couple of column inches, simply because of his association with Helena, who had hit 'national treasure' status last year, after a decade in the wilderness, with a Tony-winning role in a revival of *Gypsy* on Broadway. Ruby hadn't spotted any photographers, but there was always a chance one might show up for a Where Are They Now? angle. Getting a photo of Falcone's son, his only known progeny, would be a major coup.

Devlin acknowledged her with a slight inclination of his head, sweeping the thick wave of expertly styled hair off his brow when it threatened to slide down his forehead.

She dragged her gaze away and forced her knees to bend. Her bum hit the cool leather seat just as the rod in her spine collapsed.

Luke Devlin was here on Ryker's invitation. He had to be.

Which could only mean one thing. Devlin was attending as his mother's representative. Had Matty left The Royale to his sister? After all, Helena and her three children were Matty's only living blood relations.

Ruby had always considered herself Matty's family, but she wasn't his *real* family. And while he'd refused to speak to his sister for thirty-something years, and never met any of her children, Ruby had never once heard Matty say a mean thing about Helena.

Matty must have been planning to make some grand gesture of reconciliation from beyond the grave. Although he had probably intended to do it when he was ninety, not fifty-one. It would totally fit with Matty's sense of the dramatic. She could just imagine him savouring this scene as he dictated the terms of his legacy to the solicitor. Either that or he'd had a crush on the debonair Ryker and had needed a reason to see him.

Panic combined with the grinding pain in the pit of Ruby's stomach and turned the asteroid into a lump of radioactive waste. She'd been so busy making funeral arrangements in the last ten days and coming to terms with the great empty space in her life which would never be filled, she'd had no time at all to properly consider her future and the future of The Royale.

Was she about to lose her home and her job as well as her best friend? Because The Royale *was* her home, not only did she spend more waking hours there than she'd ever spent in her tiny flat in Maida Vale, the Art Deco cinema had been the home of her heart ever since she was twelve years old, and Matty had caught her sneaking into a Saturday matinee of *The Magnificent Seven* and offered her a job selling popcorn and ice creams in the foyer on weekends. She had quickly made herself indispensable, Matty's expansive friendship and The Royale's glittering fantasy world providing a sanity-saving escape from the chaotic council flat in Bayswater she shared with her mother, and her mother's endless parade of inappropriate boyfriends.

'Right, let's get started,' Ryker said with forced enthusiasm as he sat down behind his desk.

He opened his laptop and began to talk, but Ruby couldn't hear a word, his calm sensible delivery washing through her like acid. A spot beneath her right earlobe prickled, far too aware of the man sitting behind her.

And to think she'd woken up this morning, the day after cremating her best friend and soul mate – and the only man she had ever loved – while rocking the killer hangover from hell, convinced her life couldn't possibly get any shittier.

No such bloody luck, Rubes.

PART ONE

The Wizard of Oz (1939)

Ruby Graham's verdict: *I want to live in Oz, where danger is defeated by friendship and solidarity, charlatans are exposed, your dreams are always in glowing Technicolor and you can get a pair of absolutely stunning ruby slippers simply by landing a house on a hag!*

Luke Devlin's verdict: *Flying monkeys? Seriously?*

Chapter 1

'Could you run that by me again,' Luke Devlin murmured, concerned he had entered an alternate reality. Or been hit over the head by a two-by-four. Because that's what his head felt like at the moment, as if he'd been sideswiped by a piece of lumber, the way he had been during his first major rehab job in Queens a decade ago.

'Certainly, Mr Devlin,' the urbane lawyer said in his cut-glass British accent without even flickering an eyelash. But then Luke would hazard a guess that these guys were trained to tell people insane shit while pretending it wasn't totally nuts. 'Which section do you want me to run by you again?' the lawyer asked.

'The part about the movie theatre,' Luke said over the choking sound coming from the girl sitting next to him, which was starting to worry him.

She'd started spluttering the minute the will had been read. He'd already been kind of disturbed by her colour when she'd entered the room. He never knew people could actually turn green, but her pale skin had a definite tinge when she'd lifted her sunglasses and spotted him. The way she'd jolted then winced suggested to him his uncle had been given one hell of a wrap-party after the cremation he'd attended. Thanks to his mom, he was trained to spot a bitch of a hangover from thirty paces.

'Yes, please could you repeat that bit,' the girl said, her voice hoarse with stress.

So, she'd been hit by a two-by-four as well.

'Of course, Ms Graham.' The lawyer shuffled through the pages on his desk, which constituted The Last Will and Testament of Matthew Aloysius Devlin, and read the relevant chapter again in the dry-as-dust tone that, unfortunately, didn't make his estranged uncle's bequest sound any less batshit crazy.

'The residue of my estate, and most specifically The Royale Cinema, is to be shared equally between my dearest friend Ruby Elizabeth Graham of Flat 22c Carmel Estate, Maida Vale High Road, London W9 1DZ and the son of Rafael Falcone, Luke Marlon Devlin of Devlin Properties, 10 West 12th Street, New York, New York 10015.'

'Matty left me half of The Royale?' The girl had finally stopped choking. But instead of looking pissed – which Luke would have expected, seeing as she'd obviously gone above and beyond the call of duty to be entitled to a much bigger share of the guy's realty – the girl simply sounded stunned.

Luke wondered what she was stunned about. That her sugar daddy had only left her half of the theatre, or that he'd left the other half to some guy he'd never met? Because he knew both of those things were stunning him. That and the weird decision in the will to only mention that Luke was

Falcone's son instead of the much more relevant fact that his mom was Matthew Devlin's sister. Thanks to his own face, and his mother's gossip-hogging decision never to confirm or deny publicly who Luke's father was, his parentage was easily the worst-kept secret in Hollywood – but what the heck did Falcone being his old man have to do with his mom's brother? He hated not having all the facts. And he hated unscripted surprises even more.

He'd only come today because he had time before his meeting in Canary Wharf and his mom had started mugging him with emojis as soon as he'd turned his cell back on this morning. He was supposed to be here as her representative, at the lawyer's request. No way had he been prepared for this, though, and he didn't like it. He'd spent the whole of his childhood dealing with the slings and arrows of his mom's outrageous behaviour, now he was going to have to deal with his uncle's freaky shit from beyond the grave – not to mention the lady in red who was now gaping at him with red-rimmed, luminous-green eyes which matched the colour of her hangover.

Luke shifted in his seat, feeling vaguely uncomfortable under that stunned gaze – which was also weird. He didn't know this girl from Adam. He hadn't asked for a part in this melodrama. And he was well used to people gaping at him, because they'd been doing it ever since he hit puberty and the striking resemblance to his father had made him the focus of a spotlight he'd never chosen and done every damn thing he could to avoid.

But there was something about the way she was gaping at

him that felt different than all the other invasive stares he'd become immune to over the years. For once, the light flush on her apple cheeks, the brutal smudges under her eyes and the stunned distress making her expression even more transparent and vulnerable than it had been at the cemetery, seemed to be actually directed at him – instead of the phantom of a long-dead and wildly over-rated movie star.

'Yes, he did, Ms Graham,' the lawyer confirmed. 'As I said, he also had several other bequests and stipulations. He would like to have his ashes scattered over the Serpentine in Hyde Park. And he wants you to have the exclusive use of the flat above the theatre.' The lawyer shuffled through some more pages, and the girl's gaze shifted away from Luke and towards Ryker.

A tiny drop of moisture slipped from the corner of her eye when she blinked. The lawyer continued to outline the myriad weird clauses in the will again, as the tear slid over her cheekbone and down the side of her face. Just as the drop curled under her chin, she brushed it away with the tissue screwed up in her fist.

Luke tore his gaze from her profile and evened out his breathing to release the tightness in his ribs, annoyed at becoming momentarily transfixed by the track of her tear. He wasn't one of those guys who got freaked out by a woman's tears – or anyone's tears, for that matter – because he'd learned at an early age every possible way crying jags and assorted other histrionics could be used to manipulate your emotions. He considered his cynicism one of the upsides of having an award-winning actress for a mother who found it all but impossible to separate her real life from the roles she played. But there was something about that solitary drop and the indignant way it had been wiped away, that bugged him.

He shook off the observation, and the unfamiliar moment of empathy.

There was no point in contemplating the depth of Ruby Graham's grief, because it would only make this situation more melodramatic – and they were already heading towards Argentine telenovela territory.

'Let me get this straight,' he said, interrupting the lawyer's flow of bequests to what Luke guessed had to be the other employees at the movie theatre. 'I've now got a half-share in this movie theatre in ...' He hesitated, trying to recall the address the lawyer had mentioned. 'Where is this place, exactly?'

The lawyer opened his mouth, but the girl interrupted him.

'The Royale is the premiere independent art-house cinema in Notting Hill,' she said, her voice jagged with indignation. 'Well, North North Notting Hill. It's on Talbot Road opposite the Tesco Metro. We're open seven days a week, for a mix of first showings on weekends and a collection of classic retrospectives during the week. We run screenings for homeless families and school kids in conjunction with the council, an apprenticeship programme for under-25s, and a matinee club for local pensioners. We're an essential part of the community but we also host gala nights – our last one sold out in three hours.' She gulped in a breath, before continuing. 'In short, The Royale is a West London institution and has been ever since Matty bought the derelict Art Deco cinema in 1988 and stopped it from being flattened and turned into a petrol station.'

All he'd wanted was an address, but the fierce passion as she gave him the low-down on the movie house made it clear the place was a lot more than just an address to her, so he didn't bother cutting her off. Once he'd heard the words Notting Hill, though, his mood had brightened. The fancy area of West London was one of the prime property locations in the realty capital of Europe. Owning a half-share of anything there would be worth a fair chunk of change – and a movie theatre would surely have a large footprint.

'How many seats?' he asked.

'Excuse me?' she said, blinking at him like a baby bear cub who had just come out of hibernation and wasn't sure where she was. Obviously, her long-winded speech had taken it out of her.

'How many seats have you got at West London's premiere art-house institution?' he asked again, attempting to get a handle on the building's dimensions.

'One hundred and twenty. We had to take out twenty-five seats five years ago to open up a bar at the back of the auditorium – which Matty installed to increase our revenue.'

She deflated then, the green tinge becoming more pronounced. He could see the headache in her eyes, but stifled the unwanted sting of sympathy. Her hangover was her business, but the movie theatre was now his, or fifty percent his. He didn't like the apologetic look when she mentioned the words "increase our revenue". He had a sixth sense for good business investments – and crummy ones –

and he was already getting the impression The Royale was the latter.

'How's that going? The revenue?'

She straightened, re-inflating herself with an effort, but he caught the hesitation and the flicker of something – which had all of his crummy investment antennae going on to high alert.

'It's going very well, thank you,' she said.

Yeah, right. He wasn't buying it.

'So you're in profit? You're not running at a loss?'

She nodded, but that luminous-green gaze slipped away from his as she did so.

'What was your turnover last year?' he asked.

'I don't know the figures.' She propped her chin up and glared at him, but the bright flush highlighting the sprinkle of freckles over her nose didn't make her look any more convincing. 'Matty handled the books. But I'm sure Mr Ryker will let you know all the details of The Royale's finances once the will has been finalised.'

He heard it then, the snap of resentment he'd been expecting earlier. She was pissed now. He ignored the pang of something resembling admiration at the show of indignation. It certainly was not his business she seemed to have a bigger attachment to a failing movie theatre than she did to the chance to cash in on what sounded like a lucrative property portfolio.

'I guess so.' He shrugged and switched his attention to the lawyer. 'When do you think that will be?' He was heading to Europe tomorrow for a series of meetings but he could swing back through London on his way home a week from Friday.

He had no pressing business in Manhattan that couldn't be postponed. And he had to admit he was intrigued now. Despite what the girl seemed to think, he wasn't here to cash in on a legacy he hadn't earned. If the business was making a profit and keeping her and her friends employed, he was more than happy to be a silent partner.

If, on the other hand, it was a failing business, which had debts he would have to finance as a part-owner, then he was not prepared to inherit fifty percent of that liability. The last remnants of being broad-sided by a two-by-four finally faded as the reason for Matthew Devlin's batshit bequest became blindingly obvious, once again confirming Luke's lack of faith in human nature – and surprise bequests from relatives you'd never met. That had to be why the old guy had left him a half-share of his estate – because he knew Luke was a successful businessman with a large pool of investment capital at his fingertips. Matthew Devlin was obviously as much of a mercenary romantic as his sister. The cunning bastard had probably figured if he named Luke in his will, he would be able to coerce him into stepping in and helping finance his vanity project and keeping his girlfriend solvent, based on some erroneous concept of kinship. That wasn't gonna happen, because Matthew Devlin's cunning will strategy had miscalculated by one important degree.

Luke did not do sentiment, in business or in his private life. And he had more than enough liabilities already when it came to family. Keeping tabs on his kid sister, bailing his reckless younger brother out of scraps and handling the fallout whenever their mother went rogue was all the bullshit responsibilities he needed in his life. He was not about to acquire any more – especially from people he didn't even know, and wasn't closely related to, no matter how luminous their eyes, or how genuine their tears.

'I can email you all the financial projections for The Royale's business later today,' the lawyer said. 'The accountancy firm are working on them now. Obviously, finalising the estate will take a little longer, as Matty's was an unexpected death. As the executor, I can ...'

'Not a problem,' Luke cut in, before the guy could launch into another long list of details. He now had less than an hour to get to Canary Wharf for the meeting he'd set up with some venture capitalists from Delhi to make this detour to London at his mother's insistence worthwhile. 'You can reach me at The Grant on Park Lane until tomorrow if you need to speak to me in person.' Standing, he fished his wallet out of his jacket pocket and slapped his business card on the lawyer's desk. 'Otherwise, email over the financials when you have them. Are we done here?'

'Well, yes, I suppose so,' the lawyer said, looking flustered for the first time since Luke had walked into the room.

Leaning across the desk, Luke shook his hand. Then, as he turned to offer Ruby Graham his hand, she shot out of her seat, her freckles beaming out of her flush-like spotlights.

'Wait a minute. That's it? Where are you going?' she demanded.

He shoved his now redundant proffered hand into his pocket. 'I have a meeting in Canary Wharf in ...' He glanced at his watch. 'Fifty-eight minutes.'

'Can't you cancel your meeting? Surely sorting out Matty's final wishes is more important than any meeting?'

Not to me, he thought, but didn't say. Her lip was trembling, and while he was totally, one hundred percent immune to women's tears, he did not want her to start bawling or he'd miss his meeting.

'We won't be able to figure anything out today,' he said, keeping his voice firm and impersonal, so as not to set her off. Luckily, he was an expert at dealing with women on the verge of a nervous breakdown. *Thanks, Mom*. 'Once I've gone over the financials, we can talk about what we're going to do next.'

'What do you mean, what we're going to do next? We're going to run The Royale ...' Her throat constricted as she swallowed. 'Together,' she added, the word propelled on a torturous puff of breath. 'It's what Matty would have wanted.'

Yeah, but Matty's dead.

It's what he wanted to say. What he *would* have said if he wasn't trying to diffuse the situation instead of have it blow up in his face. And if he hadn't watched that damn tear track down her cheek and disappear into a wad of damp tissue.

'I'll be back in town Friday next.' At which point he could only hope she would have gotten herself under control. 'We can talk then.'

'Um, yes, okay.' He was surprised to see her brighten. But also grateful. At least she wasn't going to have her nervous breakdown today. 'That could work.' Her mouth tipped up in a smile, which looked remarkably guileless for a woman who had shacked up with a guy twice her age just to get her hands on a half-share in a movie theatre. 'If you come to the cinema, we could introduce you to the true wonder of The Royale and everything you've inherited,' she finished with a flourish.

He didn't give a damn about The Royale, or the wonders of what he had inherited. But her enthusiasm for the place was obvious, and a lot easier to handle than her grief, or her enmity, or her detachment from reality, so he gave her a curt nod.

'My assistant will be in touch,' he said.

He didn't want to go to the theatre. Why would he? The movie industry had caused him nothing but trouble his whole life. And he knew exactly how fake the wonders of everything associated with the movies were. Plus, he should know by next week what the bottom line was with the place, so he could communicate his plans over the phone or, better yet, via email through his administrative assistant. Right now, he had somewhere else he needed to be, so he headed for the door.

By Friday next, he should have all the facts at his fingertips – so he could explain to Ruby Graham in words of one syllable what was and was not going to work for him, crummy business ventures-wise.

As Devlin walked out of Ryker's office, Ruby was still processing the flicker of distaste that had shadowed his expression when she'd suggested he come to The Royale. He had exited stage left before she'd gotten enough of her wits back to realise she could not let him leave – not before getting a much firmer commitment from him than, "My assistant will be in touch".

After spending most of her life getting fobbed off by pretty much everyone except Matty and her friends at The Royale, Ruby was getting much better at spotting a con job when she saw one. Like her mum, when she swore she would never hook up with another creep again while getting dolled up to head out to Pete's Wine Bar so she could hook up with another creep; or the school careers' counsellor who had been *so* enthusiastic about Ruby's determination to become a film director, before sending her on a ton of interviews for minimum-wage jobs in retail; or the baby-faced decorator who had charmed her into paying him an upfront deposit last year with all of his convincing talk about how he could repaint The Royale's foyer on a shoestring, only to disappear from the face of the earth as soon as he'd pocketed the fifty quid from petty cash.

A dizzying rush of purpose and determination – which had been conspicuous by its absence ever since Matty's death – flooded her bloodstream.

'Mr Ryker, I have to go, too,' she said, swinging her bag over her shoulder. 'If you could email me all the details of the Will that would be terrific.'

'Certainly, Ms Graham,' Ryker said, but his words were lost in the buzz of adrenaline as she shot out the door after Devlin – frantic to stop him and get some kind of actual commitment.

She clattered down the stairs and burst into the street. Devlin stood on the pavement fifteen feet away, about to step into a black cab. She almost missed him because he'd donned a green baseball cap, which totally clashed with his dark blue Tom Ford suit. *How odd.*

'Mr Devlin?' she shouted and waved. '*Wait!*'

His head snapped round and he paused. 'Ms Graham, don't shout out my name.' Although his face was obscured by the baseball cap, she could hear the frown in his voice as she jogged towards him. She ignored it. She was on a mission here, a mission that suddenly seemed crucial to the survival of her home and her business.

Her business.

It took her a moment to recalibrate her breathing.

Well, half of her business, as the other half was Luke Devlin's.

I own half of The Royale now.

I won't let you down, Matty. I swear on the ruby slippers. I'll keep our dream alive. Even if it means stealing Luke Devlin's broomstick.

Okay, perhaps that was a bit much.

Luke Devlin was certainly a lot hotter than the Wicked Witch of the West. That said, he had a pinched look on his face by the time she reached him that would have rivalled Miss Gulch's sour expression after being savaged by Toto.

'Please, I need to talk to you, it really won't take long,' she said, a little breathless – either from her mad dash to catch him, or Devlin's phenomenal bone structure. Because even with his face obscured, his resemblance to a movie star whose poster had been pinned on her bedroom door all through her teenage years was so striking it was breath-taking. Literally.

'Here, mate, you getting in or not? I haven't got all day,' the cabbie said with typical London taxi driver *savoir faire*.

Devlin directed his frown at the driver. It was all the opportunity Ruby needed.

'If you could just hear me out,' she begged unashamedly. 'You can get another cab in a minute. This really won't take long and there's not too much traffic this time of day, you'll get to Canary Wharf in no time.'

Which was a massive whopper.

Traffic was always horrendous in London and Canary Wharf was the other side of the city, but even with a broomstick handy Luke Devlin would be unlikely to make his meeting in time now, anyway; plus, some things were more important than his punctuality – keeping Matty's dream alive being right at the top of that very long list.

He swore under his breath, not impressed with the delay, and rude enough not to bother hiding it, but then shouted to the driver.

'I'm out.' He slammed the door.

The cab sped off, leaving them standing on the pavement alone together – give or take the usual flow of commuter traffic.

'You've got five minutes,' he said, glancing at his iWatch as she imagined him starting a mental countdown. 'What is it you wanted to discuss?'

What had she wanted to discuss? *Crap!* She had absolutely nothing.

She'd had some vague notion he might agree to go for a coffee, so she could come up with a plan, but she didn't even bother suggesting it, because she sensed that would just piss him off more.

Thoughts of broomsticks and ruby slippers and Miss Gulch on her bike and Matty and The Royale swirled around in her head, making her feel as frantic and confused as Dorothy inside the tornado – until the elements spun into a semblance of an idea, which ejected from her mouth.

'You're going to be back in town next Friday, right?' she said.

'That's the plan,' he replied.

'That's fabulous and so fortuitous. Because that just happens to be the evening we're kicking off Matty's Classics season.' *Or rather, it is now*. 'And I wanted to invite you to the opening event. We're doing a themed evening around *The Wizard of Oz*.' Watching the musical masterpiece together had always been one of her and Matty's favourite traditions. 'There's going to be fancy dress and themed cocktails and we're sourcing a singalong version of the film,' she continued, embellishing the lie, aware that her five minutes were ticking down. Except it wasn't a lie. Because really what better way to commemorate Matty than to show some of his favourite films at The Royale? The more she thought about it, the more it made perfect sense. 'You must ... you absolutely *must* come along as our guest of honour. Not only will you be able to see what we do, you can get to know a bit more about your uncle. Everyone at The Royale adored Matty, he was the centre of our universe.' She swallowed around the asteroid. 'And *The Wizard of Oz* was one of the films he loved best.'

Devlin hadn't said anything, and what she could see of his

face wasn't even radiating emotion, let alone enthusiasm, so she went for broke.

'If you need, I could source you a costume, so you can get into the spirit of the thing.'

It was the wrong thing to say, she realised, when a muscle in his jaw tightened and twitched.

'Something low-key and totally cool ...' She backtracked furiously, racking her brains to think of one single character in *The Wizard of Oz* who didn't dazzle and sparkle. 'Maybe you could come as Uncle Henry?' Perhaps Luke Devlin was more of a sepia personality than a Technicolor one. 'Or ... one of the farm hands in Kansas before they turn into the Lion, the Tinman and the Scarecrow?' That rigid jaw did not look like a yes, but perhaps it was a maybe? If she could get the right costume.

'I don't do dress-up,' he said.

So not a maybe. Definitely a no.

'That's absolutely fine,' she said. 'Not everyone wears a costume.' Another whopper – The Royale's singalong evenings were legendary, and the one she had just invented would be even more so, because every single person there would be celebrating Matty's life and legacy with the same passion Matty had showed every one of them during his thirty-one-year career as their favourite cinema proprietor. Matty hadn't just built a local art-house cinema with The Royale, he'd built a community of like-minded people who needed the glittering fantasy world he had created to escape their humdrum lives just like Dorothy when she landed in Oz.

'I'm sure they'll be other people there who aren't in

costume.' Perhaps she could bribe Errol their projectionist to come in civvies so Devlin wouldn't stick out like a sore thumb. It was probably better for health-and-safety anyway to have Errol not wearing tons of flammable fabric near their ancient 35mm projector – and Errol had once pointed out the distinct lack of black people in Oz, so there was that.

'You could just watch the movie with us,' she finished, struggling not to deflate completely.

'I saw the movie as a kid,' he said. 'The flying monkeys freaked me out.'

'You didn't like it?' she asked, unable to keep her own jaw from heading South. Had she ever met anyone who didn't love *The Wizard of Oz* – apart from Errol, and at least he had a good reason? And how could Matty's own flesh and blood not adore it?

'If you're busy that day, we can reschedule ...' he began, and glanced at his iWatch again, losing interest. 'Or I can email once I've checked out the financials,' he added, pulling out his phone.

'No, really, it'll be fine,' she interrupted. 'I'm sure I can make some time to speak to you that evening. I've seen the movie a thousand times already.' She totally couldn't make time. She needed to be in the auditorium on Friday night for the gala singalong screening of *The Wizard of Oz* that she'd just invented. She wanted to see the movie she and Matty had loved again, to sing her heart out to all the amazing tunes – well, all except *King of the Forest*, the song no one ever remembered the words to because it was the only dud. This gala screening, and Matty's Classics season in general, was going to prove to everyone who loved The Royale that even if Matty was dead, his spirit lived on.

But that would all be academic, if she couldn't get her new co-owner on board.

And really, what better way was there to do that, than to get Luke Devlin to sit through *The Wizard of Oz*. To give the movie that had freaked him out as kid another chance. And thus persuade him to give The Royale a fighting chance, too.

It was clear she had her work cut out getting this man to buy into The Royale's mission, but surely this was a good strategy to start with? How could anyone sit through the most hopeful movie ever made, and still worry about The Royale's bottom line?

'It would mean so much to me if you would come,' she said, desperation starting to war with her determination. 'Please, Mr Devlin, if you won't do it for me, would you do it for Matty?'

It was a cheesy line. But then Matty had been the king of cheesy lines. And sometimes cheesy worked, if it was delivered with one hundred percent conviction. Right now, Ruby was sure her life depended on Devlin agreeing to come to the screening, so she could show him The Royale in all its glory, so her conviction was one thing she was not faking.

He let out a soft sigh and shoved his phone into his pocket. 'Okay, sure, email my assistant the details and I'll be there.' He tugged out his wallet and handed her the same card he'd handed Ryker.

'Thank you, Mr Devlin.' She took the card, running her

thumb over the embossed lettering, so relieved even her catastrophic headache dimmed a little.

He stuffed two fingers in his mouth and whistled. She
jumped, but two seconds later a black cab pulled up to the
kerb – just like in the movies.

People actually did that?

He opened the door, as if he had expected nothing less,
then glanced over his shoulder. 'But no publicity, of any kind,
I don't want anyone to know I'm coming. And no costume,
you got that?'

'Absolutely.' She saluted him with his card, ready to sell
him her first-born if he asked.

He jumped into the cab without another word. The vehicle
sped off, belching out a burst of exhaust fumes.

Ruby watched the cab disappear into the rush-hour traffic,
reminded of the Wicked Witch of the West cackling mania-
cally while writing "Surrender Dorothy" in mile-high letters
over the Emerald City with her broomstick.

She tucked Devlin's card into her backpack.

*You're not surrendering anything, Dorothy. Not without a
fight.*

Chapter 2

'I cannot believe Rafael Falcone's son is coming tonight. Or that he owns half of The Royale. That's so extra,' Jacie Ryan, Ruby's assistant manager, announced while shovelling green popcorn into a green-striped paper sack.

'Believe it,' Ruby murmured. Jacie's stream of consciousness about Devlin's visit was starting to fray her nerves. 'But keep your voice down, no one is supposed to know.' She wasn't entirely convinced their secret guest of honour was actually going to show. He'd been due here about twenty minutes ago according to the email she'd had from his PA confirming his attendance.

The foyer was packed with people, all dressed to the nines in their best Oz paraphernalia – from Munchkins to Tinmen to Brynn, the owner of Brynn's Babes, the bar round the corner, who had gone all out and looked magnificent as Glinda the Good Witch of the North, complete with pink-sequined frock and a crystal crown. *The Merry Merry Land of Oz* rang out on The Royale's tinny sound system on a loop, and people spilled out of the auditorium where Brynn's master of mixology, Cameron, and Gerry, The Royale's barman, were busy serving Rainbow-coladas, Emerald-aritas and Munchkin Mojitos.

Ruby had gathered her six-person staff and as many helpers as she could muster eight days ago to put together tonight's event in record time. To do it, she'd called in every favour she had ever been owed and several she hadn't, basically bribing, begging and borrowing her way across West London with the ferocity of a Kansas tornado.

To be fair, The Royale looked awesome, as a result. The peeling paint and crumbling cornices were disguised with enough glitter and fairy lights to make the place visible from space and Jacie had even managed to source a gold runner at a knock-down price in Shepherd's Bush Market to double as the Yellow Brick Road and cover the worst of the wear on the threadbare carpeting.

Emerald City, eat your heart out.

He has to show. Please let him show.

The whole Royale community had put so much work into making tonight's event a success – everyone from the drag queens at Brynn's Babes, who had made some spectacular costumes, to Agatha, a local primary-school teacher who had gotten her pupils to make papier-mâché flowers and vines and corncobs to decorate the lobby, to Errol, their projectionist and Jacie's granddad, who'd roped in the ladies from his local church with their famous Goat Curry and Plantains and Rice and Peas recipe to serve after the show at five pounds a pop and raise funds for the church's homeless shelter.

Tonight was going to be epic, but it would all be for nothing if Devlin didn't put in an appearance as promised.

'Good luck keeping it a secret once he shows,' Jacie said. 'Remember how he got mobbed at the cremation? His resemblance to his old man is freaky.'

'I know,' she said, even though she had barely registered Luke's appearance at Matty's funeral because she'd been way too busy being poleaxed by grief.

The sharp edges of that awful day and the week before it had blurred in the last eight days, the unbearable pain of losing Matty shoved to the edges of her consciousness while she got stuck into Operation Get Luke Devlin Invested In The Royale with a *Wizard of Oz* Extravaganza. But now that all the work was done and the only thing left to do was enjoy the event, and wait for her co-owner to appear, Ruby had begun to second-guess her whole strategy.

'Perhaps I should have warned people?' she murmured.

Devlin had stipulated that no one was to know he was coming. The man obviously had an issue with being recognised, she realised, recalling that clashing baseball cap. But perhaps it would have been wiser to prepare everyone for the arrival of Rafael Falcone's doppelgänger rather than respect Devlin's wishes.

Devlin's father was a movie super star whose films had set a billion hearts fluttering in the seventies and eighties and could still do so today whenever they ran a season at The Royale. His brooding image graced T-shirts and advertising hoardings and posters in student dorms. The bad boy with the face of a god. A hot god. All lean chiselled lines and moody intensity, with a crystal-blue gaze that had the power to make most women and some men pant by proxy. The actor had become a cultural icon as enduring as Elvis and Marilyn and Jimmy Dean and had only become more iconic since his untimely suicide sixteen years ago.

Rafael Falcone was a legend to most of the people here tonight. And Luke Devlin looked *exactly* like him. Hadn't she had breathing difficulties herself when she'd first clocked that remarkable face up close in Ryker's office?

'I thought you said he said not to tell anyone?' Jacie whispered, as she handed over packs of green popcorn to a bunch of Gen Xers kitted out in red wigs and green jackets and leggings.

Were they supposed to be Munchkins, or citizens of Oz, or leprechauns, because it was hard to tell?

'He was very specific on that score,' Ruby confirmed once the leprechaun-Munchkins had moved off. 'If he got mobbed at the funeral, I guess that explains it. But there's a good chance the same thing might happen tonight and I don't want to make him uncomfortable.'

'Make who uncomfortable?' Gerry their barman – who was dressed as a rather chunky Scarecrow – joined them behind the concession stand.

'Nobody,' Ruby said, starting to panic in earnest. What if she had made a terrible mistake? Not warning everyone of Devlin's arrival?

Jacie tapped her nose piercing. 'It's top secret, Gez, but I think you'll be wowed by our guest of honour tonight – when he turns up.'

'*What* guest of honour?' Gerry asked, his eyes sparkling

with curiosity, because he was a much bigger star-stalker than Jacie. 'I didn't know we had one. Shouldn't we have put it on the posters?'

'He's shy,' Jacie said.

At the exact same time, Ruby shouted, '*No, we should not have put it on the posters!*'

Gerry and Jacie stared at her, as did a couple of the Generation X leprechaun-Munchkins who were still munching popcorn nearby.

'He doesn't like publicity,' Ruby added, whispering this time. 'He's not a proper celebrity.'

He's just the spitting image of one.

The anxiety began to build in her throat.

Telling Jacie about Devlin's planned appearance at the event had seemed like a good idea when they were getting ready in the upstairs flat in their Dorothy outfits – Ruby channelling Judy and Jacie channelling Diana Ross from *The Wiz* because they were also screening the Motown classic in deference to Matty's opinion that it was one of the most underrated musicals of the Seventies.

After keeping the news of Devlin's visit secret for over a week, Ruby had been about to burst. But should she have told Jace about Devlin's new status as their co-owner? Had she raised Jacie's expectations to impossible proportions? Not to mention her own.

Then again, she hadn't told Jacie the whole truth – that Devlin now controlled the future of The Royale, and this extravaganza was actually one giant schmooze initiative that might backfire spectacularly.

'Who *is* this guy?' Gerry said. 'The *actual* Wizard, because you're blushing, Rubes. I can see it through your make-up.'

'He's only Ruby's biggest crush ever.' Jacie laughed. 'Sort of.'

Not anymore, Ruby wanted to say ... right after she'd strangled her assistant manager. It was true that she'd once idolised Falcone. But Luke Devlin was not his father and being reminded of all the fantasies she'd once spun about Falcone were not going to help with her panic attack.

'O. M. G. I am super excited now. Is he a Jake Gyllenhaal lookalike?' Gerry asked, as if they were having a Guess Who game.

'Wrong crush,' Jacie said. 'And better than a lookalike, practically the real deal.'

Before Gerry could ask any more probing questions, the 'Take Your Seats' bell sounded from the auditorium.

'Oops, I forgot,' Gerry said. 'Errol said he's all cued up, so we can start the screening.'

Follow the Yellow Brick Road chimed in over the sound system and some of the customers started singing along in the corner, while others clapped and whistled. The music stopped as planned and Brynn – aka Glinda – stepped on to the green podium they'd set up near the entrance to the auditorium.

'Hello, fellow Citizens of Oz,' Glinda announced in all of her glory. 'Before we start the screening, I wanted to call up our darling Dorothy – the Judy Garland variety ...' Glinda winked at Jacie, who toasted her with a sack of popcorn. 'To say a few words,' Glinda continued, 'about the launch of

Matty's Classics season, and our Wonderful Wizard Matty who went to the Great Emerald City in the Sky last month.'

A hush descended over the crowd, then everyone started applauding.

Ruby grabbed the toy Toto she'd left under the counter, tucked it under her arm for emotional support and made her way through the crowd.

Devlin hadn't turned up. She tried not to feel devastated. It might even be for the best. Even so, dejection slowed her steps as she crossed the Yellow Brick floor runner and the crowd parted, the moisture in their eyes and the shaky smiles making her heart bobble.

It doesn't matter. I'll find another way to schmooze Devlin. This night is about Matty.

Stepping on to the podium, she waved Toto to silence the applause.

'Hi, everyone. I didn't want to say much, just that you're all so, so welcome. Thanks to everyone in our movie-mad community who helped make tonight happen. I can't actually believe Matty isn't here with us.' She gulped to soothe the raw spot which had settled on her tonsils again for the first time in a week. 'But I know he's here in spirit – probably dressed as a Horse of a Different Colour to finally finish off all the leftover paint from last year's Royale Pride float.' Everyone laughed. 'Don't forget, this is just the *first* film in the Matty's Classics season. We'll be organising more gala evenings over the coming months and celebrating Matty's life by screening some of his favourite movies.' Her breath got trapped as the enormity of the task facing her – which she had happily buried in manic preparations for a week – began to scrape at the raw spot.

I will keep The Royale open. I will keep The Royale open. I will, I will, I will. Even if it means landing a house on Luke Devlin.

'So, keep an eye out for details of the next Matty's Classics movie on our Facebook page, our Instagram and Twitter accounts and the local—'

She stopped talking abruptly as a tall figure dressed in black, even down to his baseball cap, slipped through the double doors at the front of house and joined the back of the crowd in the foyer.

The raw spot grew as the bill of his ball cap lifted and that startlingly blue gaze locked on her face.

He came. He actually came.

People's heads swivelled round, trying to locate the reason for Ruby's sudden silence. She coughed, struggling to recall what the heck she had been saying.

With his shoulders hunched, his hands buried in his pockets and that baseball cap tilted back over the top half of his face, Devlin was doing his best to be invisible.

Was that why he had arrived so late?

'So, my fellow citizens, let's Follow the Yellow Brick Road to Oz,' she managed, while she really wanted to shout, at the top of her lungs: "*Pay no attention to the man standing at the back of the foyer!*"

But it was already too late. A few people at the front of the crowd clapped, while others entered the auditorium, but the bulk of the crowd's attention had shifted to the back of foyer and the whispers began.

'Bloody hell, is that Falcone?'

'He's dead. Who hired the Falcone lookalike? He's worth every penny.'

'It's his son, remember he was at the cremation.' This from Glinda whose voice was so rough with awe, it was as if she were about to start levitating.

Devlin really should have followed the dress code if he wanted to remain inconspicuous, Ruby thought, as she stumbled off the podium and shoved her way towards the muscular figure in black standing out like a sore thumb in a sparkling sea of green and assorted other primary colours.

'I should take a selfie and put it on our Instagram account,' Jacie piped up as she joined Ruby in her trek across the foyer. 'It'll be great for business.'

'Not sure that's a good idea,' Ruby cautioned, feeling like Dorothy wading through a field full of drugged poppies – the crowd and the deep sense of foreboding closing in around her.

She got as far as Gerry who was standing a foot from Devlin, looking more awestruck than Glinda. '*He's* the guest of honour?' he hissed in a theatrical whisper that Devlin had to be able to hear. 'Oh. My. Can I say hello to him?'

'*No!*' Ruby said, attempting to muscle Gerry out of the way. But their bulky Scarecrow wouldn't be budged.

'Hello, Mr Falcone— I mean, Devlin.' Gerry launched himself forward, breaking through the exclusion zone around Devlin that had been created by the industrial strength back-the-fuck-off vibes pumping off him. 'I'm Gerry,' he said grasping Devlin's hand. 'I didn't get a chance to introduce myself at the funeral,' he continued, pumping Devlin's fingers as if he were trying to win an arm-wrestling contest. 'It's so wonderful to see Matty's nephew here. It's not often we have a *bona fide* celebrity in our midst. Would you like an Emerald-arita?'

Oh, shit. Gerry was hitting on him.

'I'm good, thanks,' Devlin said smoothly, managing to extricate his hand.

Ruby side-stepped Gerry, but before she could get close enough to rescue Devlin, Jacie shoved past her.

'Hi, I'm Jacie Ryan. It's so sick that you're here at The Royale.'

Ruby winced as Jacie grabbed the hand Gerry had only just released.

'And we're even more excited one of Matty's own family will be part of our fam now,' Jacie said, then reached inside the pocket of her floaty pink Seventies skirt.

The blood drained out of Ruby's face.

Please, Jacie, please don't …

'Hope you don't mind if I take some shots for our Instagram account?' she asked whipping her phone out.

'I'd rather you …' Devlin began, but before he could issue a cease-and-desist notice, Jacie – who was their social media guru as well as the assistant manager – had positioned her iPhone and snapped off about twenty shots.

The sound triggered the rest of the crowd, and suddenly, Devlin's exclusion zone was history. Everyone poured forward en masse like Munchkins waking up to the joyous news the Wicked Witch was dead. They shouted greetings, tried to shake his poor abused hand, and congratulated him on his stunning resemblance to 'a cinematic icon of the first water' – this last compliment from Beryl, the septuagenarian head of the pensioners' club and their matinee cashier who'd had a crush on Falcone about twenty years longer than Ruby.

It was a bloodbath. Instead of the buoyant, beautiful introduction to the glowing fabulousness of The Royale Ruby had anticipated, she was watching a reboot of *The Wizard of Oz* as directed by Quentin Tarantino, the carnage in agonising slow-motion.

Why had she thought inviting Devlin to their first Matty's Classics gala evening would be a good idea? Why hadn't she at least briefed everyone on the proper etiquette when greeting this guy? He'd said he didn't want any fuss. She should have known this would be their reaction. She knew most of these people. And she loved them. But not one of them knew how to behave when getting the chance to meet a long-dead cinematic icon made flesh.

Having Luke Devlin walk among them was like witnessing the Second Coming of Christ ... but with much better hair and cheekbones.

Devlin's body language was still screaming 'back the hell off' and his frown had become catastrophic. But when his gaze connected with Ruby's over the heads of the Munchkin mob, instead of fury, or distain, what she saw was panic.

Then he mouthed something at her, and she didn't have to be a lip-reader to understand it.

Help!

Jolted out of her trance, Ruby clapped her hands above her head.

'Everyone, chill the hell out!' she shouted in her best Arnie-as-*The Terminator* voice.

The crowd turned as one, shocked into silence – which was precisely why she kept Arnie for special occasions.

'Mr Devlin is not here to fulfil your Falcone fantasies,' she said, striding past Jacie and Gerry to get to their guest of honour and grip his forearm. The flex of sinew beneath the expensive cashmere of his sweater had her Arnie voice taking a detour into Annie territory. 'Mr Devlin now owns half of The Royale. And if we don't want him to shut us down, we need to treat him with respect.'

'Who said anything about getting shut down?' Jacie's mouth fell open in horror.

Balls, that was too much Arnie and not enough Annie, because the Munchkins – who weren't known for their lack of drama – were all staring at her as if she'd just reanimated the Wicked Witch of the East and helped her wrestle the ruby slippers off Dorothy.

'It's okay, Jace,' she said. 'Everyone. Everything's great. Errol's waiting to start the movie, so I think we should head into the cinema,' she added hurriedly, scrambling to take the tremble out of Gerry's bottom lip – and the shock out of everyone else's eyes.

'Mr Devlin, would you like to join me?' she asked, cutting through the crowd towards the auditorium, keeping a firm grip on her guest's elbow, despite the goose bumps ricocheting up her arm. His forearm beneath the cashmere was quite spectacular. 'We have a seat for you at the back – where no one is going to bother you,' she said casting an evil eye over everyone they passed.

'I'll bet,' he said, raising a sceptical eyebrow. The panic had gone, if it had ever been there in the first place. She must have imagined it. He didn't look like the type to get freaked out by a load of overeager film buffs.

'No, really,' she said. 'Are you still happy to stay?' she added, not wanting to give him a choice, but knowing she had to.

She waited for his reply, aware of the silence, as if the whole theatre was holding its breath. But thank god, no one said anything. And no one approached him.

He nodded, finally. 'Yeah, I guess so. I'm here now.'

It was hardly a fulsome endorsement, but she'd take it.

She led him into the auditorium and to one of the two-seater sofas right at the back, which she had reserved for them both. The rest of the audience filed in behind them. Every single one of them stared at him while trying to look as if they weren't staring at him.

He took the seat nearest the wall and ignored the attention.

The house lights went down at last, cocooning them in darkness, and the film's opening credits began, accompanied by the opening bars of the overture.

'Would you like a drink? On the house,' she whispered as everyone finally found their seats and stopped whispering and glancing their way. 'We have several wonderful themed cocktails ...'

Perhaps one of Cameron's Munchkin Mojitos would redeem the evening – after all, they were super-delicious.

'A beer will do, if you have one,' he said, his striking features cast into harsh lines by the sepia light from the screen.

'I'll be right back.' She shot off past the bar, which bar staff were busy clearing as quietly as possible for the start of the movie, and into the kitchen alcove behind.

'Shit, Ruby, what's going on? Is he going to shut us down?' Jacie wedged herself into the small space next to her.

'No. No one is shutting down The Royale,' Ruby replied. She grabbed a bottle of Camden Hells lager from the fridge, and popped off the cap. *Not ever.*

She peered round the bar at Devlin. His body language screamed indifference as he watched Dorothy hound Auntie Em and Uncle Henry about the imminent arrival of Miss Gulch and her plan to eviscerate Toto.

Dorothy was scared and anxious and about to run away to save her dog. Ruby knew how she felt. If only she could run away, too.

She reached for the pitcher of Emerald-aritas Gerry had put in the fridge for after the screening and poured herself a generous glass. She was going to need something stronger than a beer to get through two hours of watching Devlin watch this movie while praying for a sign he was falling under its spell ... or had at least forgiven her for the Munchkin mobbing in the lobby.

'Could you to do me a massive favour, Jace,' she murmured to her assistant manager, who was also eyeballing Devlin.

'Sure, what?'

'I'm going to sneak Devlin up to Matty's flat during the end credits of this movie' – the entrance to which was conveniently situated in the foyer – 'so he can leave via the flat's fire escape before anyone spots him and we don't get a repeat of what happened when he arrived.' Perhaps she had imagined his panicked look, but she wasn't taking any chances.

'But everyone will want to meet him,' Jacie said, still not getting it.

'I know, but he doesn't want to meet them. Not yet, anyway.' She could only hope that one day he would, but that wasn't going to be today.

She should have laid the groundwork for his appearance tonight and she hadn't. She wasn't going to make that mistake again.

'So, what's the favour?' Jacie asked.

'Could you handle everything down here till I've gotten him safely out of the building? Create a distraction if you have to. Get Glinda and Gerry to help you.'

'I suppose, but they'll be pissed off they missed him.'

'They'll get over it.' Her top priority had to be ensuring Devlin survived his first night at The Royale without any lasting trauma – so they got a second chance to impress him at a later date.

Judy Garland launched into her signature tune on screen, but her rich contralto voice was soon drowned out by the audience. The Royale's vintage movie nuts belted out 'Over the Rainbow' as if their lives depended on it, just as they had at Matty's funeral.

Emotion clogged Ruby's throat and she joined in the chorus with Jacie.

Devlin wasn't singing, she noticed. But he *was* still watching. He'd stayed, when he could have done a runner. That had to count for something.

She lifted her drinks, ready to join him on their sofa.

'One other thing, Jacie,' she said as she passed her friend. 'You need to delete the photos you took of him. And make sure if anyone else took any they delete them, too. And tell everyone they must not under any circumstances post anything about him being here online or on social media.' She hadn't seen anyone else taking photos, because they'd all been way too busy harassing Devlin, but she needed to be sure.

'You're kidding?' Jacie said, having to raise her voice over the singing. 'Nothing at all, but ...?'

'I'm serious,' she said. 'The Royale's future may depend on it.'

'I thought you said we were okay?'

'We are ...' Or at least she hoped they were. Matty had always handled the books, and somehow found a way to keep them in the black each month. But she knew they couldn't have been making much of a profit, or Matty would have found money to pay for all the repairs which had built up over the years. The Royale had always been Matty's dream but she'd realised in the last week, once she'd started functioning again, that Matty hadn't spent any money on the cinema's infrastructure in well over a decade. His flat, which she'd moved into this week, was just as dilapidated and he'd stopped going on his 'marvellous adventures' years ago, too – which could only mean one thing. Matty had been broke, which meant The Royale had to be struggling as well. She hoped the stress of keeping the place running on limited funds hadn't contributed to his heart attack, or she'd be absolutely gutted with guilt as well as grief. 'I'm sure we're okay,' she said, taking another sip of her Emerald-arita. 'But if we could get Devlin to invest in the cinema's future we could finally get the thousand and one things done that Matty and I have been talking about doing for ages.' Such as repainting the foyer, sorting out the dodgy plaster near the stage, buying a new sound system, and that was just for starters. 'Devlin owns half The Royale now, and he's loaded.' Which she knew because she'd done some Internet research over the last eight days, in between killing herself and everyone else to turn The Royale into the Merry Merry Land of Oz. 'Which means schmoozing him to within an inch of his life, and not pissing him off. He's a private guy, let's respect his privacy, okay?'

Jacie's mutinous look dissolved as the final bars of the song faded. But then she shrugged as Miss Gulch arrived on her bike to snatch Toto.

'Fine,' Jacie whispered. 'I suppose I can forego five million likes on Instagram, if schmoozing Devlin means getting carpeting in the lobby that doesn't smell like my armpits after V Festival weekend.'

Ruby gave Jacie a kiss on the nose. 'Thank you, Jace, you're awesome.'

'I know, now go schmooze him into a new carpet, Dorothy,' her friend said.

'No problem, Dorothy.' Ruby took another fortifying sip of her cocktail and headed towards Devlin's sofa with their drinks just as the real Dorothy and her little dog escaped through a window.

I do believe I can schmooze Devlin into investing in The Royale. I do. I do. I do.

Two hours later, Ruby wasn't even convincing herself anymore.

Devlin had sat through the whole movie, drunk his beer, declined another. And said nothing. Not one thing. He hadn't even moved much. And there had certainly been no singing, of any description – even during the many renditions of 'We're Off to See the Wizard', which was the catchiest song known to man. The constant stream of people heading past them to the toilet, then back to their seats during the screening probably hadn't amused him much. Because he must have figured out that either The Royale's clientele had some serious bladder issues or he was still the night's star attraction.

It hadn't amused her much either.

Obvious much, guys?

That said, Devlin hadn't shown any signs of distress from the constant eyeballing, either, *and* he'd survived the flying monkey scenes without flinching, so she'd taken that as a positive. Maybe Matty's movie favourite had started to grow on him, a teeny tiny bit? Even if the nosey parkers in The Royale's audience hadn't.

He hadn't objected when she'd suggested they head up to the flat so he could avoid the crowd once the film finished.

But as she entered the flat's living room behind him, she couldn't shake the thought that tonight's schmooze offensive had been a bigger disaster than the tornado.

Thank god she'd cleaned the fallout from the Glastonbury wake off the carpet.

Devlin would have looked out of place in Matty's front room – decorated in Matty's flamboyant shabby-chic style to disguise the twenty-year-old paint job and the aging furniture – but for the giant framed poster from *Boy Blue*, Rafael Falcone's debut film, that hung above the fireplace.

Falcone's image – all brooding angst and dramatic cheek-bones – in tones of blue and black stared down at them both. The resemblance was striking, and would probably have freaked Ruby out more, if she hadn't bypassed the Toto-en-route-to-the-abattoir stage of anxiety an hour ago.

She took a moment to observe Devlin with his hands stuffed into the back pocket of his black jeans, but instead of noticing the similarities between the two men, she noticed the differences.

Luke Devlin was taller than Falcone and leaner, his rangy build that of an athlete rather than a boxer. And his features were unmarked. He didn't have the bump on the bridge of his nose Falcone had gotten in a barroom brawl in Burbank, or the famous crescent shaped scar next to his left eye which legend had it the star had acquired during a knife fight in his native Bronx. But the look in Devlin's sky blue eyes, the dark rim around the irises the only thing he appeared to have inherited from the Devlin side of his bloodline, was just as moody.

'Would you like a quick cup of tea before you go?' she said, forced to break the stony silence. 'We should probably wait a few minutes before you make your getaway, so Jacie can distract everyone from your disappearance.'

'No tea,' he murmured. 'But thanks for the getaway plan.'

His gratitude seemed grudging at best, but Ruby decided to take it at face value.

'They mean well. They're just a bit—'

He raised an eyebrow as if daring her to state the obvious.

'Overawed by your resemblance to Falcone,' she finished.

The awkward silence which followed made her wonder if she had made another major *faux pas* by commenting on the likeness.

'Yeah, I got that,' he said. But then he raked his fingers through his hair. And let out a weary breath.

His gaze flicked up to the oversized poster, then flicked away again. And she noticed the tint on his cheeks.

I wonder what Falcone was like as a father?

The thought popped into her head unbidden. She shoved it straight back out again. Just because she'd spent years wondering about what her own dad – aka the invisible deadbeat – might be like. And may even have fantasised on occasion about having Falcone as her father, it did not give her a connection with this man.

But weirdly, the thought calmed her down a little, regardless.

'What did you think of the film this time around?' she forced herself to ask, when his gaze met hers. 'Still freaked out by the flying monkeys?' she added, trying to push past her anxiety and smile.

'No,' he said. 'It was a cute movie.'

Cute? Hadn't he been moved at all?

'But what did you think of the message behind the movie?' she asked.

'Cute, too. I guess. What do you think happened to the

yappy dog, because I'm guessing the bitchy neighbour was still gonna get it destroyed?'

Huh? That was his takeaway? That Toto was doomed? 'I'm sure Toto would have been fine,' she said.

He didn't look convinced.

'Auntie Em and Uncle Henry would have been so pleased to have Dorothy back, I'm sure they would have done everything they could to save Toto second time around,' she said. At least if they were discussing the movie there was still hope to—

'Maybe,' he said and shrugged. 'Have you checked out the financial report?' he asked, cutting straight to the chase.

She swallowed the rest of her argument in defence of Toto's continued well-being.

'Umm, no, not yet.' Ryker's email with the report from the accountants attached had only arrived in her in-box yesterday and she'd been too busy with preparations for tonight. 'Is it bad?' she asked, her heart shrinking to the size of a ball bearing at the look he was sending her. More pitying than patronising could not be good.

'It's not good,' he said.

Oh shit. Oh shit. Oh shit.

The ball bearing sunk into her abdomen and began to ping about as if it were stuck in a pinball machine.

'You're running at a loss,' he added.

'How much of a loss?'

'Enough of a loss to require my uncle to borrow heavily to keep this place open over the last ten years at least,' he said.

Oh, Matty. Why didn't you tell me?

'How much did he borrow?' she asked, the guilt constricting around her tonsils.

'A lot.'

'Perhaps, if we got the theatre's operating costs back into the black,' she said, hopefully, 'we could start paying off the loans?'

'Doubtful,' he said. 'The bulk of the repayments – totalling close to two million pounds sterling – become due in three months.'

Two million pounds?

Shock reverberated through her. How on earth had Matty managed to borrow that much?

'Perhaps we could find an investor,' she said, hinting desperately. *Like maybe a millionaire property magnate from Manhattan who now owns half the theatre.*

They still had options, surely. If she could just get him to—

'Maybe, but I'm out,' he said, slicing through the last of her happy thoughts, right down to the bone.

'What do you mean you're out?' she said, but she already knew, she could see it on his face.

'I get that this place means a lot to you,' he said with a sigh. 'But if your lover figured I was going to bailout a failing business on his behalf, he got that wrong. My best advice is to sell.' He let his eyes skim over the shabby room, while Ruby tried to stop herself from hyperventilating. 'With the money you'll make from the sale of the property you can pay off the debts, start a new business and still give all the people working downstairs a very generous severance package.'

Severance package? Sale? What the actual fuck?

The terrifying words pinged about in her head with the pinball, rattling her brains and her equilibrium. But only one word of his devastating speech hit the jackpot.

'Matty wasn't my—' She stopped. Breathed. There were so many things she wanted to say in that moment – all the things she had loved about Matty, all the many things she was going to miss, even the things she hadn't loved so much – but she'd need an Oscar-winning scriptwriter, a dose of Xanax and the wonderful wonderful Wizard of Oz's gift of the gab to deliver it coherently. So she said the one thing that seemed the most important for him to know. 'Matty was my boss, and my friend, and my soul mate and my kindred spirit ... and I loved him to bits. But we were never lovers.'

'If you say so,' Devlin said, the cynical edge in his tone digging into her stomach.

Then the grief grew like a clump of nuclear waste, pushing out through her lungs, seeping from her pores, and the inky blackness exploded.

'He was gay, you stupid—' She cut off the expletive, the inky blackness flattened by a dark tide of sadness. 'He was gay.'

But that wasn't who Matty was. He was so much more than just his sexuality. And this man knew none of it. Not one thing about him. Even though they were blood relations and he now owned half of Matty's dream. A dream he didn't even want.

'He meant everything to me,' she murmured in the most reasonable and non-hysterical voice she could muster while her heart was shattering into tiny shards of agony. 'And you didn't even know him. So if you don't mind, I'd really appreciate it if you would make an effort to at least fake regret while telling me you think I should destroy his legacy.'

Luke stared, the hairs on the back of his neck doing the mamba as he watched Dorothy – or rather, Ruby Graham – hang on to the flood of grief-stricken tears with a dignity he had not expected.

Next time perhaps try sugar-coating the bad news, you dumbass.

Another solitary tear escaped, melting the ball of rouge highlighting her cheekbone, before she swiped it away.

'Hey.' He held his palms up, in the universal sign of surrender.

Please don't cry.

But to be fair she didn't look like she was going to just cry, she looked a whole lot more devastated than that.

For the first time in a long time, it occurred to him he'd misjudged his approach. Then again, he hadn't planned to come into the theatre all guns blazing. He knew how to close a deal, for chrissakes.

But having his father staring down at him from a poster the size of a Times Square billboard had only exacerbated the fallout from the unwanted blitz when he'd arrived. His palms had been clammy, his heartbeat struggling to slow down from warp speed, and his stomach had twisted itself into a giant pretzel in the lobby before the show.

The onset of physical reactions, which he thought he'd

conquered years ago after a ton of therapy, had been a devastating reminder of the similar incidents he'd had to endure as a kid when his mom had happily paraded him about as Falcone's Mini-Me.

He hadn't had an anxiety attack since he was eighteen, not even close, because he hadn't associated with people in the movie business for almost that long whom he wasn't related to. And the construction business was not generally packed with people who gave a crap about some has-been movie actor who had killed himself sixteen years ago.

But it had spooked him to know those symptoms were still there, ready to tackle him to the ground again at a moment's notice if he wasn't careful. The therapist had told him as much, why hadn't he listened?

Perhaps it was that knowledge though, that hunted feeling, that gave him a weird sort of empathy with Ruby Graham's battle to contain her distress.

'Don't cry,' he said, aware of the tortured breathing making her breasts look even more impressive against the gingham bodice of her Dorothy costume.

Look away from the rack.

He raised his gaze and connected with her luminous-green eyes, awash with tears. But then to his shock, she did as he told her. Biting into her lip, she broke eye contact to stare at the poster of his old man he'd been busy ignoring.

'Shit, shit, shit,' she whispered. 'I bloody swore I wouldn't do this and now I've done it anyway.'

'Done what?' he asked, although he wasn't sure she was talking to him.

She scrubbed her cheeks with the back of her hand. 'Gone the full drama queen.' Flags of colour lit the sprinkle of freckles visible on her cheeks under the smudged make-up.

'If you think that's going the full drama queen,' he said. 'You don't know enough drama queens.'

She huffed out a hoarse laugh. 'Believe me, I know one of the very best.' She swallowed convulsively, then dropped her chin to stare at her hands, which were clenched into fists in her lap. 'Or rather, I knew one of the best.' She gave her cheeks another swipe, even though no more tears had appeared. 'Why do you have to talk about dead people in the past tense?'

Unease gave the pretzel in his stomach an extra twist. Sharing was not his strong suit – especially with strangers.

'I don't want to talk about Matty in the past,' she said fiercely, saving him the headache of thinking up a sympathetic reply. 'As if we lost touch somehow, or he isn't my best mate anymore. It feels weird and wrong and callous.'

Somehow he doubted she had a callous bone in her body.

She dragged in a tortured breath and let out a jagged sigh. 'Death really bloody sucks, doesn't it?'

Her grief felt so raw and real, he found himself actually struggling to find an answer for her, even though she didn't seem that aware of his presence anymore.

'I'm sorry I never got to meet him,' he managed at last, surprised by the words.

Matty Devlin, however colourful, sounded way too much like his mother – and one Oscar-worthy drama queen in his life had been more than enough. But he was here to crush

Ruby's dreams, as much as his dead uncle's, toughing out *that* unvarnished truth seemed like enough for her to handle today.

She lifted her gaze and studied him, and he had the unprecedented urge to squirm.

'No, you're not,' she said at last, but then her wide lips tilted on one side in an almost smile. His heartbeat stumbled – which was strange, because he didn't appreciate being figured out so easily. 'But thanks for lying,' she added, not sounding offended by his inability to lie convincingly. 'I'm sure Matty would have loved to have met you, so he's probably doing a snoopy dance right now if his spirit is still hanging about ...' She ran her open palms down her dress. 'Which I certainly hope it is.' She glanced around the room. 'You hear that, Matty? I'm expecting a full on haunting worthy of Hill House or I'm going to be really disappointed in you.'

Her gaze glided back to meet his as she flicked one thick braid over her shoulder. 'Sorry,' she said, the sheepish smile endearing. 'You probably think you've landed in Oz.'

You haven't seen my mom hit peak Helena Devlin.

He swallowed the too revealing retort.

'Not really,' he said. Despite that one errant tear, and the weirdly hot Dorothy costume, Ruby Graham was pretty much the most forthright and restrained person he'd ever met. Of course, that wasn't saying a whole hell of a lot, if you considered that apart from his work colleagues, sense and sanity didn't run strongly in his list of close acquaintances.

But still, he had to give her credit for her honesty – and her lack of unnecessary drama in the face of extreme circumstances.

'You're grieving,' he added, surprising himself even more with this demonstration of his previously untapped share-and-discuss skills. 'Feeling shit and behaving like a nut job goes with the territory.' *I know*. 'Or so I'm told,' he finished, yanking himself back from that piece of over-sharing.

He had no experience of the true ravages of grief, because he'd made a point of protecting himself from the kind of pain this woman was going through ever since he was fourteen by the simple expediency of keeping close relationships to an absolute minimum. And while a shrink – or his mom in fake-shrink mode – would have a field day with that, it worked for him.

She nodded. 'I suppose,' she said, not sounding convinced. 'Although I really wish I hadn't given you the impression I can't even run a *Wizard of Oz* extravaganza without bursting into tears.'

She hadn't burst into tears, even though she'd had more than enough provocation, but he didn't think pointing that out would help him get back to where he needed to be so he kept his mouth shut. He doubted whatever she was going to say would change his mind about what needed to happen next, but he was willing to hear her out. Something he had planned to do before he'd been ambushed by the Falcone For Pope brigade in the lobby.

Negotiations were his strong suit.

'I want you to know I'm absolutely committed to making this business more profitable,' she said, the determination in her voice making the short hairs on his neck bristle again. Annoyingly. Sentiment, however well intentioned, had no place in a business negotiation.

'I had a feeling our finances weren't great,' she continued. 'Obviously I didn't know how bad they were, because Matty was always super cagey about that and now I know why.' She took an unsteady breath and he waited for her to continue her spiel. 'Because he was trying to protect me.' The wobble in her voice was quickly controlled. 'But I've got lots of ideas to improve our revenue. Ideas that Matty wasn't keen on because he felt they compromised The Royale's mission as a community cinema—'

'Exactly how keen on these ideas are you?' he cut in, because he could hear the defensive tone. Coming up with ideas to solve a financial crisis were all well and good, but if you weren't one hundred and one percent committed to them they wouldn't work.

She straightened in her chair, her expression going flat and direct. 'I'm keen on anything that will allow us to stay open for business,' she said, which was a non-answer if ever he'd heard one. But at least the defensive tone was gone.

'Okay,' he said.

'*Okay?*' she asked, her brows launched up her forehead. 'Okay, as in you'll help me keep The Royale open?' she added, jumping way ahead of herself. But the hope in her voice made it tougher than it should have been to set her straight.

'No, okay as in, you don't have to pay the money straight away,' he said.

'I don't ... I don't understand,' she said, her crest-fallen expression telling him she did understand, she just didn't want to.

Hard truths were his stock in trade. But he could feel the blip in his heart rate when he gave it to her straight.

'At a conservative estimate, this place is worth upwards of five million pounds sterling. It's got a large footprint in a prime market location. It's had listed buildings status for over two decades.' Something his uncle must have angled for to save it from ever becoming a gas station. 'Even though the London market is slowing down, a developer would snap it up.' He'd taken a good hard look at the dimensions, and done some calculations on his iPhone while he'd sat in his rental car on the street outside and waited for the right moment to slip into the theatre unnoticed – which had turned out to be the wrong moment. 'They'd have no problem getting planning approval because this area needs housing. And even if they only redeveloped into apartments to rent instead of buy you're talking at least six units, possibly eight. That's a good six-figure profit margin.'

'But it's a cinema. I don't want to sell it.' Her expression became mulish. 'I understand you would make a nice tidy profit if we do sell but I ...'

'Stop right there.' He held up his hand. The remark had been guileless, and it really shouldn't matter to him one damn bit whether this girl thought he was a freeloader anyway, but somehow it did. 'This isn't about the profit I can make. I'm not interested in taking anything out of this place. Like you say, I didn't know my uncle and I wasn't expecting this wind-fall. I sure as hell don't need it. I'm quite happy to have my share used to pay off the debts when the sale goes through.'

'You ... You are?' There was that hope again, shining too brightly in her eyes.

He was through pandering to it. 'But that's not gonna solve

your problem if you don't sell. Because if you don't sell you're gonna have to come up with a couple million on your own, and that's at a conservative estimate.'

'What happens if we can't manage to pay all of it?' she asked, the hope in her face crucifying him. She just wasn't getting the fact this was a lost cause.

'Matty borrowed the money against the property, so if you don't cough up in time, the bank will foreclose and you lose the place anyway for less money.' He stood up, suddenly keen to get out of the theatre, and away from the pointless hope in her eyes.

'But perhaps if we could find an investor, someone willing to loan us the money?'

'You'll need to get it back in the black to make it attractive to an investor,' he said, because he had a sneaking suspicion she still saw him as a possible sugar daddy in this scenario. 'I figure it'll sell pretty damn quick once it goes on the market,' he said, trying to stick to the script and not get side-tracked by the grief hovering round the edges of the room like a bad smell, or the misguided hope in her eyes. The Dorothy outfit – complete with pop socks and ruby slippers – wasn't helping, because now she looked younger and cuter and even more naïve than she had on the sidewalk outside Ryker's office. 'Like I said, I reckon a developer will snap it up if you put the right price on it,' he added, the desire to soften the blow still festering in the pit of his stomach, alongside the pretzel. 'If you want to take it to the wire you could give yourself two weeks on the market to sell it, giving you the maximum amount of time to turn this gig around, bring the business into profit and find that extra investment to cover the debts so you don't have to sell up ...' He glanced at his iWatch to confirm today's date and do a quick calculation. 'Which gives you until around June twentieth, before you have to make that choice.'

'But if I sell I'll be closing a community institution that's been going since 1988 and all my staff will be out of a job?'

She sounded so forlorn, all he could do was nod. 'Yeah.'

He dug his business card out of his pocket, then scribbled down his cell number on the back. 'You can reach me on that number if you want to discuss the details.'

Not that there was really anything left to discuss.

She seemed to get that, taking the card with trembling fingers.

He shoved the pen in his back pocket. 'Do you think it's safe for me to get out of here now?'

She trapped her bottom lip under her teeth, still staring at his card, then looked up. 'There's a fire escape at the end of the corridor,' she said, pointing down the hallway. 'It's probably safest to slip out that way.'

He nodded. He needed to get out of here. But his stomach twisted into a pretzel again at the sight of her in her gingham dress and white blouse, her thick French braids tied with blue ribbons and her round green eyes mistier than Judy Garland's as she sang about rainbows and lemon drops.

'I'm not flying back to Manhattan until late Monday night, if you want to speak to me in person,' he said.

'Thank you ...' Her face flushed and she smiled – and he

realised he'd made a tactical error. He didn't want to give her false hope.

He dismissed the ripple of unease as he made his way down the hall. If she contacted him on Monday he could screen the call – and let his assistant Gwen handle it.

He'd given the situation to her straight; those were the facts.

He hadn't created this situation – an undiagnosed heart condition and bad financial planning had done that. So why should he feel responsible? If his uncle had been any kind of a businessman, or had the foresight to plan ahead, he could have found more tax efficient ways to borrow against his business, or found an investor instead of bankrolling the place with loans. But the guy hadn't expected to die in his fifties. So they were gonna have to suck it up, lay the blame for this crummy situation at fate's door and deal with it.

But as he headed down a hallway lined with framed film posters – none of them featuring Falcone, thank Christ – and photographs of Ruby and the guy she had loved, he heard the faint sound of gulping sobs behind him.

The pretzel in his stomach rose up to press against his larynx.

She'll get over it.

He climbed out the window and down the fire escape, then jumped into the alleyway behind the theatre. Once Ruby Graham had a cool two million plus in her pocket and no ties or responsibilities to worry about, she'd be able to see the other side of this rainbow. Surely.

Chapter 3

'**I** can't believe he's so heartless. How can he be Falcone's son?' Jacie rubbed Ruby's back as they sat hunched together on the sofa in Matty's flat.

Somehow or other, Ruby had managed to get through the weekend without freaking out completely over what Devlin had told her after *The Wizard of Oz* screening.

But when Jacie had appeared ten minutes ago with a bottle of Prosecco to toast finishing the schedule for Matty's Classics' season they'd put together, Ruby had blurted out the whole sorry mess to her assistant manager – on pain of death if she repeated it to anyone. And Jacie had begun pouring the Prosecco. Because what else was there to do?

'I'm not sure how his genetic make-up has anything to do with it,' Ruby murmured, taking a judicious sip. After her lemon-tini binge at the wake and one too many Emerald-aritas on Friday night she had been avoiding alcohol ... but she needed something to lift her spirits. And drown the terror which had been lurking in her gut ever since Luke Devlin had disappeared down her corridor after delivering his death blow to The Royale.

'But Falcone did emo so well, his empathy bleeds off the screen,' Jacie said, knocking back her own glass and refilling it. 'His son seems to have had a heart by-pass.'

That was acting, Jace.

Ruby bit back the retort, because it wasn't Jacie's fault they had to find two million pounds plus in three months.

She burped. But surely all was not lost ... *yet?*

'He was pragmatic about our financial situation, but he wasn't completely heartless,' she said, clutching at straws. 'He told me I could call him, perhaps he just needs to be persuaded this is a good investment?'

Okay, that was a bit of a stretch, even for Ruby's usually boundless optimism.

From the look on his face after he'd told her he would be in London until tonight, she suspected he'd instantly regretted the olive branch.

'You think?' Jacie asked, lifting an eyebrow almost as sceptical as Devlin's. 'I wasn't getting the impression he could be persuaded during the screening. He didn't even join in any of the songs.'

'Yes, but maybe he's just not the singalong type,' Ruby said. 'He seemed fine about the flying monkeys at least.'

'Why wouldn't he be fine about the flying monkeys?' Jacie's eyebrow arched even higher.

'Apparently they freaked him out as a kid.'

'So he's been a dick for a while,' Jacie said, her disillusionment making her grimace. 'He so does not deserve that beautiful face.'

From the way Devlin had glanced once at the *Boy Blue*

poster then avoided eye contact with it, Ruby didn't think he considered having his father's beautiful face to be much of an asset, but she decided against pointing that out to Jacie.

There was a story there, she was sure of it. But she didn't think he'd appreciate her asking him what it was. And anyway, she did not have the time to get side-tracked. She had a two million-plus pound hole to fill in The Royale's finances or Luke Devlin was going to sell the theatre out from under them.

'It's nearly five o'clock. Are you still planning to scatter Matty tonight?' Jacie asked.

Crap!

Ruby's gaze shot to the plastic urn on the bookshelf she'd picked up from the undertaker's that morning. How could she have forgotten about Matty's ashes.

I'm so sorry, Matty.

Guilty heat worked its way up her neck.

If only forgetting about fulfilling Matty's request to scatter his ashes after the park closed was the sum total of how she was about to fail him. Somehow, presiding over the destruction of the community institution he'd created and watching it get converted into six or possibly eight rental units would be so much worse.

'Yes ...' She walked to the urn and lifted it off the mantel. It felt far too light.

How could such a robust, larger-than-life person be reduced to something so small and insubstantial?

'What time does it get dark tonight?' she asked.

Jacie checked her weather app. 'Sunset's at six twenty-six.

So you'll probably want to wait until seven to be sure the park police don't stop you.'

'Good thinking,' she said.

Was that why Matty had requested she scatter his ashes on the Serpentine after dark? After all, he'd always told her she needed to live more on the edge.

Don't be so tediously law-abiding all the time, snookums. Imagine how dull Louise would have been if she hadn't blown up that trucker's rig? And Thelma if she hadn't robbed that convenience store? Just for starters, Thelma wouldn't have gotten to shag Brad Pitt.

She had pointed out that Brad had stolen all of their money and Thelma and Lou had ended up driving off a cliff. But tonight, perhaps Matty was right.

Sneaking into the park and scattering his ashes seemed like the perfect way to say goodbye to him. She very much doubted it would actually be illegal, but she almost wished it were. A little danger – coupled with a little Prosecco – could only help take the edge off all of her other worries.

She stuffed the urn into her backpack. 'I should probably get going. Matty was fairly specific it had to be done no less than two hours after sunset.' What that was about she had no clue, she'd racked her brains for the possible film reference but hadn't been able to come up with one.

Jacie stood. 'Are you sure you don't want me to come with you?'

'Yes, I'm sure.' Matty had been specific about that, too. No one but her and Luke Devlin were supposed to be in attendance.

She tugged on her jacket. 'Could you cash out the box office?' she said. 'After the evening screening starts? I should be back to lock up before the final curtain.'

Luckily she had tons of time, because tonight's film was *The Lord of the Rings: The Return of the King*, which lasted well over three hours thanks to its twenty-five endings.

'Sure thing, I'll see you tomorrow.' Jacie handed her the Prosecco bottle. 'Here, finish the Dutch courage.'

Ruby chugged the final sip from the bottle.

'And don't worry, we'll figure out something,' Jacie added.

'Yes, we will,' Ruby said, buoyed by her mission and the Prosecco. Not necessarily in that order.

It was only after she'd left the theatre though and made her way towards the tube that she had a realisation worthy of Donald Duck and his light bulb.

Bollocks. Matty had wanted Luke Devlin there, too. Probably all part of the in-joke she didn't get. But if Matty wanted him there, she had to at least try to get him there. She'd planned to suggest it on Friday, but she'd never gotten the chance.

He'd given her his number even if he didn't want her to use it. And maybe, just maybe, the chance to see him again would shake something lose – like his squishy side, or a fabulous investment plan to save The Royale.

After trying his number twice though, and getting switched to his voicemail her plan had begun to unravel. As she headed to Ladbroke Grove station, the name of the hotel on Park Lane he had given Ryker over a week ago echoed in her head in his deep voice.

The Grant.

Turning from the tube station, she hopped on a bus heading to Marble Arch. Why she had remembered the name of the hotel he was staying at a week and a half ago she was not going to examine too closely. Plus he might not be staying there on this trip.

Frankly, guilting Luke Devlin into coming with her to scatter his uncle's ashes tonight was almost certain to be another failure. But she was going to give fulfilling this dying wish her best shot.

Not least because there was the distinct possibility she might be forced to deny Matty the one dying wish he would have wanted the most – to keep The Royale open.

'Could you let Mr Luke Devlin know I'm here?' Ruby asked the receptionist in the lobby of The Grant, attempting to sound authoritative. The hotel's steel and glass interior design was everything Ruby would have expected of a high-end Mayfair watering hole for billionaire businessmen – sleek, soulless and defiantly impersonal.

Intimidating much?

'Certainly.' The receptionist sent her a benign smile and picked up the in-house phone. 'Who should I say is calling?'

He's actually here. Perhaps this is a sign.

'Um, Ruby Graham,' Ruby replied, a tickle of anxiety working its way past her Prosecco buzz.

The woman nodded, keyed in a number and then spoke into the phone.

'Mr Devlin, Ruby Graham is in the lobby and wishes to

see you.' The woman smiled beatifically at Ruby obviously listening on the other end. 'Yes, Mr Devlin, she's here in front of me.' The woman frowned. 'Um, yes, sir, she can hear me talking to you.'

As the conversation continued for a moment, Ruby realized she'd been right. His offer to talk to her had been fake news back at The Royale.

The receptionist covered the handset's mouthpiece. 'Mr Devlin would like to know if you could contact him tomorrow?'

What? After he's checked out? I don't think so.

'Could you tell him it's super urgent and involves his uncle's ashes,' she said. She reached into the backpack and pulled out the plastic urn to punctuate the surprise reveal. 'I have them with me.'

'Oh, I see,' the receptionist replied, a light flush appearing through her expertly applied make-up. Clearly, having human remains brandished at her wasn't a regular occurrence.

The receptionist relayed the information. There was a long pause and then she nodded.

'He's in the penthouse suite on the sixteenth floor. Room 1601.' She directed Ruby to the bank of elevators on the other side of the reception area. 'He said to go right up,' she added chirpily.

I'll just bet he did.

'Okay, thanks.' Hefting her backpack, Ruby headed to the elevators, her Prosecco buzz now no more than a discordant hum.

He'd tried to give her the brush-off. That moment of connection back at the flat had all been in her imagination. Devlin was as mercenary as she'd tried not to assume. No way in hell was she going to be able to persuade him to change his mind about investing in the theatre – which made her mission here somewhat redundant.

The weight of the urn in her backpack became heavier.

She patted the pack. 'It's okay, Matty. I'll ask him if he'll come tonight. If he says no, at least we tried. Right?'

He's going to say no, so there's no point in getting stressed.

But she *was* stressed, as she got to the end of the corridor on the sixteenth floor and tapped on the door marked Penthouse Suite.

The door opened a few seconds later. And there he was, in all of his glory. His dark wavy hair mussed, as if he'd been running his fingers through it. That devastating gaze locked on her.

'Hello, Ruby,' he said, sending her a quizzical look. 'What's this about my uncle's ashes?'

The last of her wishful thinking evaporated under his inscrutable gaze. So he hadn't been listening at Ryker's office when this dying wish had been mentioned? She had to admit a lot of what had been said that day had gone over her head, too, but it wasn't really an excuse, given that he hadn't been poleaxed by grief at the time like she had.

'I ... I need to ask you to do something.' She cleared her throat which was now drier than a Groucho Marx one-liner. 'With Matty's ashes.'

He frowned, the suspicion clear in his gaze. 'Right, okay, but I need to pack.' He directed her into the suite. 'Come in, we can talk in the bedroom.'

A few seconds later, she stood in the middle of a palatial bedroom with a staggering view over Hyde Park. She could even see the corner of the Serpentine Lake in the distance. It wasn't quite dark yet, the orange and red of the sunset made all the more resplendent by the pollution haze that hung over the park.

But it wasn't the stunning view that was getting all of her attention.

Don't look at the bed.

The only problem was that meant looking at Devlin himself, who was busy wedging a neat stack of – crap, were those boxer briefs – into an expensive leather hold-all. He had his toiletry bag on the bed, next to a ream of papers, and a laptop, which he proceeded to stuff into the hold-all, too.

Why was she not surprised the man packed his luggage the way he did everything else? With ruthless efficiency.

He wasn't wearing any shoes and dark wool socks peeped out from under the hem of his jeans.

Ruby gulped. Why did this whole scene feel stupidly intimate?

'So, what do you need?' he said, still packing.

The impatience in the tone snapped Ruby out of her sock-induced coma, a forceful reminder that Luke Devlin was all business, even if she had caught him packing his smalls.

'In his will, Matty requested I scatter his ashes on the Serpentine; you can see it from here.' She pointed to the body of water in question, disconcerted when he stopped packing and gave her his full attention. She patted her backpack. 'I've got them with me now. He wanted you to come, too.'

'Are you serious?' he said.

Anxiety turned to annoyance in the pit of her stomach. Did he think she'd made it up? Why would she do that? Unless ... Her mind stalled. Did he think she was coming on to him? The arrogant ... She took a steadying breath.

Don't lose it. Stay focused. And as unemotional as he is.

'You possibly missed that part of the will reading when you walked out to go to your very important meeting in Canary Wharf,' she said, not quite able to keep the hint of bitterness out of her tone.

His gaze flattened and she knew he hadn't missed the implication. That he'd been more interested in his business meeting than the final wishes of a dead man. But he didn't seem remotely phased – or guilty. Just more proof, if she needed it, that Jacie was right – he *had* had a heart by-pass.

'Are you sure that's legal?' he said at last.

'What?' she asked, confused.

'Scattering human remains on public land?' he said. 'At the very least my guess would be you'd need a permit.'

Ruby stared at his formidable frown for two very long seconds, completely nonplussed. 'You're not serious?'

'Of course I'm serious, have you researched it?' he replied, as if she were a person with severe learning difficulties.

'No, I haven't researched it,' she said slowly, so he would understand the significance of what she was doing here.

'Then there you are,' he said, and turned to zip up his hold-all.

'I don't need to research it,' she continued, the buzzing in her ears turning into a maelstrom. 'It was Matty's dying wish.

76

I couldn't give a toss if you need a permit or not. Or whether or not it's legal. I'm doing it tonight because that's what Matty wanted. I stopped by to invite you along because for some unknown reason you mattered to Matty and he obviously wanted you to be part of his final farewell.' Although that impulse was looking increasingly bonkers. The man appeared to have about as much empathy as the Wicked Witch of the West or one of her flying monkeys. Something Matty must have been wholly unaware of, or he would never have left his nephew half The Royale, or put her in this impossible situation.

Devlin straightened, and stared her down past that prominent nose. And for the first time since she'd met him, she detected a real emotional reaction from him. Unfortunately, the reaction wasn't guilt, it was irritation.

'Uh-huh,' he said. 'Because I so want to get arrested on my last night in London? Was that your thinking?'

'We won't get arrested. That's ridiculous. At the most we'd probably get a caution.'

'Yeah, well, thanks but no thanks. You go scatter my uncle's ashes all you want, but you can leave me out of it.'

Ruby clutched the backpack, wishing, for a moment, she could get out Matty's plastic urn and dump the contents on Devlin's perfectly styled hair. What a prick. Unfortunately, that would be a disservice to her best friend, who did not deserve to get scattered over a dipshit like Luke Devlin.

'Fine, I will,' she said. 'I'm fairly sure Matty wouldn't have wanted you along anyway if he'd ever actually met you.'

She marched to the door, ready to make a dignified exit. But then something twisted inside her. The same something which had got her in trouble age fifteen, when she'd told one of her mother's boyfriends to get his hand off her bum, and again at age sixteen when she'd waltzed out of her maths GCSE exam after signing her name 'Miss Couldn't Care Less About the Sum of the Hypotenuse' on the top of the paper. The same something that had come to her rescue two weeks ago when Matty had collapsed in front of her holding his left side and she'd had to pull herself together and call an ambulance before she went totally to bits. It was what her mum had once called her Arsey Gene. The gene that told her now, she needed to get the last word in here, if for no other reason than Matty's wishes meant something. And this sod didn't get to piss all over them with his snotty attitude.

She paused at the door. 'But before I leave, I've got something to say to you.'

He sighed. 'Don't tell me, this is the big parting speech? How about you get it over with fast because I've got a plane to catch in three hours.'

She hesitated, momentarily taken aback by the biting sarcasm in his tone. Good grief, how did anyone get to be so jaded? Or so much of an insensitive dickhead? She swallowed, bolstering her courage and calling on her Arsey Gene, which seemed to have momentary malfunctioned on being introduced to his Couldn't-Give-a-Shit Gene.

'I don't know who you think you are,' she launched into her speech, only to have him interrupt her.

'But I'm sure you're about to tell me.'

'And I have absolutely no clue why Matty gifted you half of a cinema that he adored and which you clearly could not give a single toss about ...' She continued riding roughshod over the cynicism in his tone.

Doesn't matter Rubes, pearls before swine, kiddo.

'But that cinema, and more importantly that man, meant everything to me.' For one horrific moment, she could feel her eyes stinging and sunk her teeth into her tongue to force back the tide. Steadying her breathing and bringing the moisture back in-house she carried on, somewhat vindicated when Mr Snotty didn't interrupt her again. He seemed momentarily struck dumb in the face of her emotion – clearly he was one of those guys who thought a woman's tears had the power to slice off his testicles – well, good, all the better to flail him with.

'Matty was kind and generous, an amazing teacher and a really bloody good laugh, and even when he was dying he knew how to bring down the house. And people meant something to him. People and making them feel good. Which was why he poured so much love and passion into a movie house that never made any money. Why he took me under his wing when he really couldn't afford an assistant. And why I'd dance naked through Hyde Park scattering his ashes over the nearest policeman if that's what he'd asked me to do. And why you can't lift a finger to him, with your two-thousand-dollar suit and your pricey haircut and your humungous bank balance and your sexy cologne.' *Shit, did I just say sexy cologne?* She breathed in a breath of said sexy cologne – sandalwood with hints of orange. Sod it, at least she was honest. 'And that huge stick stuck so far up your bum I'm surprised it doesn't give you lock jaw.'

She finally let out the breath she'd been holding.

Well, that had certainly wiped the cynicism off his face. The frown had disappeared, to be replaced with ... well, nothing.

Mr Snotty had turned into a sphinx. She'd struck him dumb with her big parting speech. Just like Sally when she finally came clean about her feelings for Harry.

Not that she had any feelings for this jerk other than disgust. However much he might look like the man who'd fathered him.

'Have a nice flight, Mr Devlin, and a nice boring conventional life,' she said, all politeness. 'I'll be in touch with your assistant in the next quarter with your share of the profits from The Royale.'

And there would be profits, even if she had to work double shifts and open the cinema to the events management company who had been knocking down their door for the last year. If they had to close their doors in three months' time she intended to keep Matty's dream alive to the bitter end.

Because she had a heart. And however bruised and battered it felt right now, however fatally wounded, as she marched out of Devlin's suite, she knew it had to be better than having no heart at all.

Shit!

Luke listened to the outer door of the suite slam shut and carried on packing.

Do not go after her. This is not your issue. She's fine. She'll survive, even if she does get busted. They'll take pity on her. She's grieving. She may also be hammered. You have a plane to catch. You do not have time to give a shit.

But his hands began to shake as he unplugged his phone charger from the wall and stuffed it into the bag's front pocket.

And the look on Ruby Graham's face, all fierce and furious and heartbroken, made his heart crash into his tonsils.

This is not your mess to fix.

He shouldn't have deliberately tried to antagonise her. It had seemed a good strategy when she'd walked in with her urn. He'd figured it was by far the best way to persuade her he really was the emotionless property developer he appeared to be. He didn't want to give her any more false hope. But he had been way too convincing. So convincing he felt like a Grade A asshat right about now.

Ruby Graham had just had her life kicked into touch.

And yeah, the theatre was not his mess to fix. And she needed to know that. But maybe this side mess was?

Swearing furiously under his breath, he found his boots, stamped them on, then charged out of the hotel room after her. Whipping his cell out of his pocket as he headed down the hall, he texted his assistant Gwen to rebook his flight for tomorrow morning.

He knew he was going to regret this. But he couldn't let Ruby Graham go out into the night alone, to scatter her best friend's ashes, looking as if she'd just been punched in the stomach.

Because the person who'd punched her in the stomach was him.

Chapter 4

'Bugger, bugger, bugger.' Ruby's toes slipped on the rain-slick railings as she slung her hand over the bar and heaved. Her upper body strength was non-existent though, and two seconds later she was dropped back on to her feet on the wrong side of the park gate. For the tenth time. She was never going to get into the Serpentine section of the park. Why hadn't she thought this through? The bloody gated area was over eight-foot high. She should have bought a step ladder.

'Fuck a duck!' she murmured, feeling defeated. And hating it.

'I certainly wouldn't advise that or you're sure to get busted.' The laconic comment – in a far too familiar American accent – gave her such a shock she let out a small shriek.

Luke Devlin stood behind her looking solid, and steady and smug.

'If you've come here to gloat, go ahead,' she managed, having lost all sense of decorum in her abject misery. 'Then you can piss off.'

All she'd wanted to do tonight was finally lay Matty to rest, the way he'd wanted, the way he'd asked her to. Why couldn't she even achieve that much without making a tit of herself? But then she seemed particularly adept at making a tit of herself in front of Luke Devlin.

But Devlin wasn't laughing, she realised, as he tilted his head to one side and studied her. 'I'm not here to gloat. I'm here to apologise.'

'What for?' she asked, because there were about a million and one things she could think of.

Why did he have to be so detached? So unfeeling? So pragmatic? So broad and solid and hot? Okay, scratch that last bit, *so* not the point.

'For making this even harder for you than it needs to be,' he said.

He actually sounded sincere – and just like that her righteous anger deflated like a popped party balloon. Unfortunately, the anger had been keeping all of her misery at bay fairly effectively, which happily rushed in to the fill the vacuum.

'Apology accepted,' she said, turning back to the railings and ignoring him. 'Now you can piss off,' she added under her breath.

She gripped the railings again with numbed fingers and heaved herself up. She struggled and slipped and cursed and battled with the gate for a further two minutes, which felt like ten years, all the while assuming he'd pissed back off to his hotel and his flight.

But then the dry voice reverberated down her spine. 'Why don't you just dump the ashes in the park?'

She slumped against the railing, her forehead connecting with the cold slippery metal, perilously close to tears.

'Because that's not what Matty wanted. He specified the Serpentine.' She pushed her finger through the locked gate at the dark expanse of water beyond. 'Which is through there.' She still hadn't figured out why Matty had asked for this particular ritual to be carried out. But she was too numb and disheartened to care about figuring out the why. Suddenly, all the things she wasn't going to be able to do for him anymore – like laugh at his rubbish jokes, make the popcorn to his lemon-tinis, or keep The Royale afloat – loomed large around her. This was one thing she refused to fail at, or compromise on.

She glanced through the gathering dusk at the road that ran through the park and the bridge in the distance that stretched over the lake – illuminated in waves by the headlights of passing cars.

'Perhaps I could scatter them from the bridge?' she thought aloud.

Getting over this bloody gate was not going to happen. And the thought of having to come back tomorrow with a stepladder felt too overwhelming.

'Not a good idea,' said Mr Pragmatic and Emotionless from behind her.

Why hadn't he buggered off already?

'There's a lot more ashes than you think, it takes forever to scatter them. And you'll be super exposed there.'

She let go of the railings and turned. 'You've done it before?'

'Sure,' he said, frowning. 'I scattered my old man's ashes.'

'You scattered Falcone's ashes?' she whispered, the thought – that she was standing less than a foot away from a person who had such an intimate connection with her cinematic idol – so shocking and yet epic she completely forgot to be pissed off with him.

'Yeah. My mom asked me to.' His shrug was stiff and unyielding and defensive, not unlike the look on his face when he'd sat under the *Boy Blue* poster in Matty's flat on Friday night. Yup, there was definitely a story here and it didn't look particularly Walt Disney. 'And it took forever.'

She leaned against the railings to study him. Absorbing the strange situation she was in – standing outside the Serpentine in the almost dark, trying and failing to scatter Matty's ashes with a man who was Rafael Falcone's son. The son of the icon she had idolised through all of her lonely fatherless teenage years. His face a facsimile of the poster she'd had pinned to the door of her childhood bedroom so she could gaze at it while she fell asleep to the sound of her mum shouting at her latest boyfriend, or banging the bed against the wall in the bedroom next door in rhythmic thumps.

Maybe it was the Prosecco and the heartache talking, but it all suddenly seemed so surreal. 'This is so bloody weird.'

'What is?' he asked, his frown deepening.

'You sound just like him in all of his movies, you know?'

It was the wrong thing to say. She knew it instantly because his gaze became wary and tense, where before it had been pragmatic.

'So I've been told,' he said, not sounding remotely impressed with the observation. What *was* the story? Because she was exhausted and down-hearted enough to wonder about it now

– mainly so she didn't have to wonder about how she was going to scale an eight-foot high gate.

'You've been *told*?' she said, not even attempting to hide her astonishment. 'You don't know? Haven't you watched any of Falcone's movies?' Surely he must have. His father had been one of the greatest actors of his generation. If not *the* greatest. Hailed as the successor to Brando and Dean and on par with De Niro and Pacino. A rare talent who had blazed across the screen like a comet, captured the zeitgeist and the hearts of millions, won an Oscar, been nominated for several more, changed the face of screen acting and then faded and died far too soon.

'No,' he said, the cutting tone slicing through her Falcone reverie like a machete.

'Why not?' she asked. 'They're all brilliant. Well, apart from *The Tangri-La*, but that was just a blip. And he was your father, Luke,' she added, going the full Darth Vader. But seriously, this man was the only child of a legend and he'd never even seen any of his father's movies? It felt like a crime, somehow, a crime against everything she and Matty had held dear.

Instead of answering her perfectly valid question, though, his frown eased and he tucked his hands into the back pocket of his jeans. His lips curved in a cynical half smile as he tilted his head to one side – studying her in a way that didn't feel entirely complimentary. 'Funny, I didn't spot you for one before now. But I guess it goes with the territory.'

'Spot me for what?'

'A Falcone nut,' he said, his tone dripping with sarcasm.

'Never ceases to amaze me how many of you there still are, even sixteen years after the old ham died.'

Old ham? What the fuck?

Ruby's tongue swelled, her outrage on behalf of movie lovers everywhere choking her.

'Well, of course it amazes you,' she replied. 'How could you possibly know how cool and incredible he is? I mean was?' she corrected herself, feeling oddly flustered. She knew Luke Devlin had none of his father's brilliance or sensitivity, but this whole scenario felt a bit too close to Mia Farrow's predicament in *The Purple Rose of Cairo* when Jeff Daniels had literally stepped out of a cinema screen and invited her to Egypt. Surreal, Ruby decided, didn't even begin to cover it. 'Especially if you've never actually bothered to watch any of his movies?'

'Uh-huh! And how would you know what a self-absorbed asshole he was,' came the lookalike Falcone's deadpan reply. 'If you never actually met him?'

'Your father was an asshole? *Really?*' The mossy green eyes widened, Ruby's avid curiosity making them even more luminous than usual. And Luke wanted to kick himself hard in his own ass.

Never engage, never discuss. Not with the Falcone nuts.

How had he forgotten the law he'd laid down when he was a thirteen years old? Ever since the last time he'd sat in the lobby of his mom's LA mansion, on a sunny Saturday morning, with his soccer boots on and his heart bursting with excitement and pride and a foolish sense of hope that this time would be different. Sure the great Falcone would have to show eventually, because he'd promised Luke on the phone only the day before that he would.

But then he'd waited ... and waited ... for two endless hours, while the Falcone nuts amassed by his mom's gate – also waiting – shouted at him to ask when his father was arriving.

It was the last of the many no-shows. And after that he'd finally had the sense to tell his mom he didn't want to schedule regular meet-ups with his father anymore. On the rare occasions he did show, they had to sneak around and do everything in secrecy anyway – to avoid the paparazzi and the Falcone nuts. He'd rather be playing with his friend Mitchell down the block. Or even his hyperactive kid brother, Jack. Hell, he'd almost rather kick a ball about with his toddler sister, Becca, who was only just out of diapers, than be caught dead waiting for a man again who half the time – no, three-quarters of the time – never bothered to keep his promises. And when he did ...

He pushed the bitter memories aside. Yeah, definitely not going there. Especially not in front of a Falcone Nut. Time to change the subject.

He glanced past Ruby at the eight-foot high gate. 'Move aside,' he murmured, because getting arrested for dumping the ashes of some guy he didn't know seemed like a much better option than reminiscing about his asshole of a father.

Ruby dutifully stepped back and he ran at the gate. Grabbing hold of the top bar he strained the muscles he'd first begun developing years ago at Harvard, flung his leg over the top, scrambled up and over and landed heavily on the other side – luckily, without breaking anything.

The rattle of the gate didn't drown out her astonished shout.

'How did you *do* that?'

'Excellent upper body strength courtesy of Varsity crew,' he said, as he shoved his hands through the railings and formed a stirrup. 'Now it's your turn. I'm not getting arrested on my own.'

'We won't get arrested,' she said, as she puffed out her chest, grabbed the bars and stuck her muddy boot into his palms.

He boosted her up and she managed to get her foot over the top but was then perched precariously on the gate, her legs dangling.

'Bloody hell.' She leaned forward, trying to steady herself, he guessed, so she didn't tumble off headfirst. 'It's a long way down.'

'Don't look.' He grasped her ankle, above the boot. Her short skirt had ridden up. Damn, he could see ... He squinted into the darkness. Not nearly enough. 'Bring your other leg over,' he instructed. A nearby street light was shining on her cascade of curls like a spotlight. He'd noticed a cop when he'd headed into the park after her. And while there didn't seem to be anyone about now, if the cop chose to do a tour of the park they'd both get busted.

'But if I do that I'll fall off,' Ruby squeaked, sounding a lot less sure of herself. Clearly, she wasn't a habitual felon.

'I'll catch you.' He placed his hand as high as he could reach on her thigh, to reassure her. *Mostly*. The muscle bunched and quivered beneath his fingers. Ruby worked out. Either that or managing a movie theatre was more strenuous than he'd thought. Because her thigh felt toned and warm and hot as hell.

'Really?' She peered down at him, still holding the gate in a death grip, but the look on her face – wary but full of hope – sent a ripple of sweetness through him to go with the heat. *Not cool.*

'Ruby, get down here! Now!' he demanded, trying to concentrate on his impatience instead of that damn ripple.

The commanding tone worked because seconds later he had his arms full of warm, breathless woman. Her scent – citrus and roses – filled his nostrils as his face was covered by a cloud of hair. His hands grabbed a hold of something soft and fleshy as he staggered backwards, struggling not to drop her on her butt while her giddy shriek deafened him.

After a few major wobbles, and some hand and limb adjustments, at last they stood, safe and reasonable steady, together, a few feet from the edge of the water – her head buried against his neck, her hair making his nose itch and her arms wrapped so tightly around his shoulders she was close to strangling him.

But weirdly, he didn't care.

'You okay?' he asked, enjoying the soft, pliant weight of her way too much.

She lifted her head. The shadows cast by the trees and the dying light made it impossible to see her expression, but her delighted chuckle gave him all the answer he needed. 'Yes, thank you.' Her peppermint-scented breath whispered across his mouth as she sighed. 'Did you learn how to catch in Varsity crew, too?'

'Nope,' he said. 'That would be shooting hoops with the college basketball player who shared my dorm room.'

Although he couldn't see it, he could hear the smile in her voice when she replied. 'Upper body strength *and* great hand-eye coordination. Who knew a university education could be so useful?'

Was she hitting on him? It sure sounded like it and it occurred to him he should put her down now. He certainly didn't want to encourage any flirting. It also occurred to him that he really didn't want to put her down.

He flexed his fingers on her soft flesh, inhaled the fierce, floral scent that clung to her hair one last time, then forced himself to let her go. He held on to her waist a nanosecond longer than was strictly necessary but then she stepped back. Her face caught the light of the street lamp. A wrinkle had formed between her brows, and her eyes were even wider than usual.

If she had been flirting, she already regretted it.

'I guess we should get this over with,' she said with a sigh, as she smoothed her little skirt down and then hauled a large plastic container out of her pack.

She sent him a weary smile and he watched the dark cloud of grief settle over her again. 'Really, thanks for doing this with me. It means ...' The words choked off.

He sunk his hands into his pockets, uncomfortable again. Emotion really wasn't his thing.

'Where do you think we should do it from?' she asked.

He turned, to examine the layout of the lake, or what they could see of it in the dark. There was a building on one side that he guessed housed some changing rooms, a wide path that circled the lake at the water's edge and a small jetty which led out to what looked like a bathing platform. 'You think you can make it out there in the dark?' he asked, pointing towards the platform. 'It'd probably be best to scatter them as far out as we can get. That way if there's blowback, he won't end up on the grass.'

'Good thinking, Batman,' she said, the plucky tone like that of a GI about to jump off a landing craft onto Omaha Beach. 'Matty definitely would not want to end up getting stepped on by the Serpentine Ladies' Bathing Club tomorrow morning,' she added, marching off towards the jetty with her container.

He followed, preparing to stand back and give her space to say her final goodbye. But after she had unscrewed the lid and dropped it on the backpack, she turned towards him, the container clasped to her chest.

'Do you know the words to "Somewhere Over the Rainbow"?' she asked. 'You didn't sing along during the screening, but I just wondered if you might know the words anyway?'

'I guess,' he said, because didn't everyone know the words to that song?

'It was Matty's favourite show tune.' She paused and gulped in a breath. 'He liked to hum it while he was doing difficult or scary stuff, such as The Royale's VAT return or skydiving over the Grand Canyon. He said it made him feel brave and bold and happy no matter what. Would you ...' She sniffed. 'Would you sing it with me while I scatter his ashes?'

'Sure,' he said.

She smiled at him then, the curve of her lips sad but genuine and his throat became kind of tight.

Then she began to sing.

She had a rich, melodic, pitch-perfect voice which trembled over the lush, true notes of the tune. He joined in the choruses he could remember about bluebirds and chimney tops as the grey remains of the uncle he'd never met – but now kind of wished he had – swirled into the air and spread out over the glassy surface of the lake.

The final notes of the song died as the last of the ashes sunk beneath the dark water. They stood in silence together, the intermittent swish of rain-slicked tyres and the rumbling hum of engine noise from the cars on the bridge the only sound.

He swallowed to dislodge the raw spot in his throat.

Her breath hitched, loudly. And he braced himself.

But she didn't cry, or sob, or crumble. She simply stared at the water, drew in another sharp breath, then whispered. 'Bye Matty, you silly old sod. I love you to bits. And I always will.'

Two seconds later, they got arrested.

PART TWO

About a Boy (2002)

Ruby Graham's verdict: *A coming-of-age movie featuring
some top tips on how to survive life:*
1.) If you're an island (even Ibiza) the FOMO you feel is real
*2.) If you're just not that into your family or they you,
find a new one*
3.) Never enter a school talent show with a Roberta Flack song
*4.) If you're a massive wanker make sure Hugh Grant plays
you in the movie, because then at least you'll be a hot
massive wanker.*

Luke Devlin's verdict: *Suicide is a really crummy thing to do
to your kid.*

Chapter 5

Hendon Magistrates' Court was not the most salubrious place to be spending a morning, especially if you'd had to fly all the way from New York for the privilege, Ruby thought miserably. She watched Luke Devlin arrive in the crowded ante-chamber flanked by an elegantly dressed older man wearing a gown but no wig, a younger man in a pin-striped suit busy talking on his mobile and a woman in ice-pick heels, her arms laden with file folders.

'Looks like he's brought the cavalry with him. Surprised he bothered to come all the way from Manhattan,' Jacie whispered in her ear.

So was Ruby, really. She'd assumed when she'd last seen Luke Devlin getting into a taxi on Kensington High Street, after they'd been booked at the Hyde Park police station by a particularly eager young officer of The Royal Parks Police, that she was never going to see him again.

All things considered, he'd taken the arrest surprisingly well. Or she'd assumed he had, because he'd barely spoken once the officer had apprehended them.

Devlin's gaze landed on her from across the room and he

gave a terse nod of greeting. Then he ignored her, as he listened to the man in the robes, who had to be a barrister.

'Perhaps we should have bought a legal team, too?' Jacie said. 'I thought this was just a formality.'

'What legal team?' Ruby murmured. 'We don't have one and we can't afford to get one. And it *is* a formality, as I'm pleading guilty and falling on the mercy of the court.'

'You can't go to prison can you?' Jacie hissed.

'No, it's only a misdemeanour.' Or at least she had assumed as much, not really understanding any of the charges listed on the paperwork the police officer had given her over three weeks ago. How was singing 'Over the Rainbow' disturbing the peace? Maybe she'd been a little off-key – but it was hard to remain on pitch when your heart was shattering into a billion pieces.

Perhaps she should have checked what permits were needed to scatter ashes, and waited to do it in the daylight. But that's not what Matty's will had asked her to do. And she refused to feel bad about carrying out Matty's wishes. She didn't even feel bad about the inappropriate shivers which had sprinted up her spine when Luke's deep voice had joined hers, or that his hands had closed over her bum when she landed on top of him after taking a header off the gate.

Although she did feel bad about delaying Luke's departure and then dragging him back to London and into court three weeks later. Any hope she'd had of persuading Devlin to invest in The Royale to help cover their debts was surely deeper in the duck poo than Matty's ashes now.

When the clerk finally read out their names – a whole

hour later – the inappropriate shivers had turned to guilty recriminations.

She really hoped she couldn't be sent to jail for singing 'Over the Rainbow' off-key in a Royal Park. She had their gala screening of *About a Boy* – the next film in Matty's Classics season – to host this weekend. And they had all been working their bums off over the last three weeks to get The Royale into profit again. She and Jacie had gone over the accounts each evening, trying to find savings that didn't involve cutting any staff jobs and they'd discovered quite a few. But there was still more to do. She did not have time to do time.

She filed into the court beside Jacie. But Luke didn't meet her gaze this time, and her heart plunged even further into her chest cavity.

He probably hates you now.

The overly bright fluorescent lighting and an abundance of blond wood in the décor made the courtroom look like a cross between an IKEA showroom and a Dickens novel, but nowhere near as intimidating as *In the Name of the Father*, which Ruby had been braced for. The three average-looking people – two men, one woman – who sat behind the high bench at the front of the court weren't even wearing gowns or wigs.

Ruby was actually a tad disappointed. She'd been hoping for an experience to at least make this calamity worthy of a decent anecdote. But the setting and the participants – apart from her fellow defendant – looked decidedly ordinary.

She scanned the faces of the three magistrates as the usher led her past the long table where the prosecutor and the defence solicitor sat. But as she stepped into the box, her gaze snagged on the rotund elderly man in the middle of the bench.

It took a moment, but as the court proceedings began, and the clerk read out the charges, recognition finally struck.

Benjy?

Could it possibly be him? She'd only exchanged a few pleasantries with the man, and he looked much more austere in the dark blue three-piece suit, but she was positive he was one of Matty's friends and a semi-regular at the Pensioners' Club matinees each Wednesday run by Beryl.

A small smile lifted his hangdog face as he obviously recognized her too, but then he coughed into his hand and the smile dropped as he launched into his opening spiel.

Clearing his throat, he shuffled the papers on the bench in front of him. 'Minor criminal damage and trespass, is it? I see you've pled guilty to the charge, Ms Graham. Is that correct?'

'Yes,' she murmured. 'I didn't want to waste any more of everyone's time. I am sincerely sorry.'

'Can I ask what you were doing in the park after dark, Ms Graham?'

She nodded, feeling marginally less like Oliver Twist thanks to his avuncular Mr Micawber tone. 'I ...' She glanced over her shoulder to find Luke sitting at the back of the room with his legal team, waiting for his turn. 'We. Myself and Mr Devlin were scattering Matty's – I mean Matthew Devlin's – ashes ...' The friendly neighbourhood asteroid that had been jammed in her throat ever since Matty's death scrapped over her throat. 'As per his wishes. I persuaded Luke to come with me. It was all my fault, I'm willing to accept full responsibility for the—'

'Thank you, Ms Graham.' Judge Benjy said, lifting his hand and she faded into silence. 'I'll confer with my colleagues now to pass sentence,' he added.

After a short deliberation with the other two magistrates on the bench, Judge Benjy delivered his verdict in the same warm tone she remembered from Matty's wake, when he'd been telling a story about the time Matty had toppled backwards off The Royale's float at Notting Hill Carnival because he'd sewn way too many diamantes into his fairy wings.

'Given the extraneous circumstances. We think a sixty-pound fine is sufficient. You have sixty days to pay, Ms Grahame – if you have significant problems paying you can make arrangements with the courtroom clerk.' The gavel came down on the bench, making Ruby jump.

'Would Mr Devlin like to step into the dock?'

She was led out of the dock.

Oh, thank you, Judge Benjy.

Sixty pounds was doable. All she had to do was raid her LA trip fund and forego her bi-weekly treat of a spiced caramel latte from the local coffee shop for the foreseeable future.

She took a seat in the viewing gallery at the back of the court, assuming Luke would get a similar treatment. Like her, he entered a guilty plea via the barrister in his legal team. He was only here for a sentencing hearing, too. A sixty-pound fine would be nothing to him.

Should she offer to pay it, though? On a matter of principle? After all, he'd been there helping her. And somehow, much to her astonishment, he had made the whole experience better.

He had literally caught her when she fell off the gate. And his deep voice had added resonance and comfort to the chorus of 'Over the Rainbow'. Her throat began to ache again. Plus, she needed to keep him as sweet as possible if she was going to have any hope at all of saving The Royale.

But as the case progressed it appeared neither Judge Benjy – nor Luke – had read the script.

'I see Mr Devlin that your solicitor has already made two requests that you be excused from today's sentencing hearing?'

'Your Honour, Mr Devlin runs a multi-national construction company and lives and works in Manhattan. He has had to fly here especially for this hearing. He was only in London to attend the funeral of Mr Matthew Devlin and the reading of the will. His business responsibilities have already been severely—'

Judge Benjy held up his hand to silence the barrister. 'So we understand. But he has pled guilty to the charge, has he not?'

'Yes, Your Honour.' The barrister stepped in again.

'Did you know your uncle, Mr Devlin?' Judge Benjy asked.

Ruby did not have a good feeling about the magistrate's tone.

Luke's solicitor and his barrister conferred with each other, probably not liking it, either.

'Mr Devlin, perhaps *you* would like to answer the question?' Judge Benjy said.

'No, Your Honour, I did not know my uncle,' Luke replied. 'Although I don't see how that's relevant,' he added. 'Or how it's any of the court's business.' The insolent tone had Judge Benjy's brows lifting.

'Well, now, I'll tell you how it's relevant,' said Judge Benjy, all traces of Mr Micawber well and truly gone. 'If you did not know Matty Devlin, why precisely were *you* breaking into The Serpentine Lido to pollute the lake with his ashes?'

Because Matty asked him to. And so did I.

The answer reverberated in Ruby's head. But instead of giving himself a get-out clause, Luke shrugged. 'It seemed like the right thing to do at the time.'

'I understand you have inherited half of The Royale Cinema in West London but are considering selling your stake in it?'

Ruby's throat closed. Who had told Benjy *that*?

But instead of defending himself, again Luke seemed keen to dig himself in even deeper. 'That would be correct, because I'm sure as hell not planning to inherit its debts.'

Judge Benjy liked that answer even less, his cheeks reddening and his eyes narrowing to slits. 'I see.'

He bent his head to have a whispered discussion with his colleagues on the bench. After an endless five minutes, he cast his gaze directly at Luke. 'Given your vast wealth, Mr Devlin, and your somewhat cavalier approach to the laws of trespass in our Royal Parks and the legacy of the community institution you have inherited, I feel that a fine will not suffice on this occasion.'

'But, Your Honour, Mr Devlin has entered a guilty plea and is not on trial for—' The barrister tried to intervene but Benjy, the hanging judge, was having none of it.

'Mr Grayling, please sit down. You can dispute the sentence at a later date, and certainly not before it has actually been bestowed,' Benjy said, clearly enjoying his role as a hokey arbiter of justice who wouldn't have looked out of place in a Steven Spielberg movie.

The barrister sat down.

'Mr Devlin, I sentence you to three hundred hours of community payback at The Royale Cinema on Talbot Road, North Kensington. Given your construction skills and the cinema's lengthy list of on-going repairs, I'm sure you can find a way to make yourself useful.'

The barrister jumped back up. 'But, Your Honour, that's outrageous. Mr Devlin has a business to run in Manhattan, this punishment far outstrips the offence for which—'

'*Mis-ter* Grayling, sentence has been passed. If you wish to appeal it, you can do so.' Judge Benjy's gaze slid back to Luke, who was showing no emotion whatsoever that Ruby could see. Although his shoulders looked rather tight.

He had to be furious. But he could have been a lot more accommodating and a little less arrogant.

That said, why had Judge Benjy gifted them with Luke's community payback? They weren't a public institution.

They did do some gratis outreach work for the local council by running non-profit screenings for schools in the area and the senior citizens – but they'd never had a community payback order made on their premises before.

'Mr Devlin half-owns the cinema, Mr Grayling,' Benjy added, going the full Judge Dredd now – all pomp and circumstance and taking no prisoners. 'I can't imagine why he'd object to basically working for himself to improve facilities that have been enjoyed for decades by our local community.'

Grayling opened his mouth, but Benjy slammed his gavel down. 'This sentencing hearing is closed.'

Ruby stood, shocked by the verdict.

Should she go to Luke, and apologise for the arrest ... again?

Her gaze connected with Luke's as he stepped down from the dock. The barrister and solicitor surrounded him, talking at him in furious whispers, but that pure blue gaze remained fixed on her.

The tense expression on his face wasn't hard to read.

He *was* furious, but when he broke eye contact to walk out of the courtroom with his legal team, she had the strangest feeling it wasn't her he was furious with.

Terrific, you've just managed to turn a cluster fuck into a cluster fuck-tastrophe.

'Mr Devlin, I assure you this sentence will not stand. We can appeal it. The magistrate clearly had prior knowledge of your situation, which suggests a conflict of interest, and we can—'

'It's okay, Grayling,' Luke interrupted the stream of outraged legalese that was costing him five hundred pounds an hour. That had been his first mistake. Hiring a Queen's Counsel to argue a misdemeanour case in Civil Court. And then letting his jet-lag and his extreme irritation – from that weird jolt of awareness at seeing Ruby Graham again – get the better of him. He probably deserved the damn slap. He had behaved like an arrogant asshole. The magistrate had spotted it, even if no one else had.

Or rather his fifth mistake, he corrected as he watched

Ruby and her selfie-snapping friend from *The Wizard of Oz* night, disappear down the corridor towards the clerk's office. Ruby was dressed in another of those shorty dresses with the biker boots she'd been wearing three weeks ago in the Park. He jammed his hands into the pockets of his suit pants, the memory of inadvertently grabbing her ass as she dropped into his arms way too vivid, the weird jolt of awareness coming back for an even weirder encore.

No, his first mistake had been to follow Ruby to the park thinking he could fix her grief when he didn't even know her.

His second had been to engage in a conversation with her about a man who meant nothing to him and meant so much to her.

His third had been to help her scale the gate, discovering exactly how glorious her ass was in the process.

And his fourth and final mistake had been to indulge in a halting chorus of a cheesy eighty-year-old show tune while Ruby stood beside him, scattering her best friend's ashes, the tears she was unwilling to shed causing her to tremble over every single note.

1

Because now he felt invested. And responsible. In a way he hadn't felt since he was a kid and he'd walked into the en-suite bathroom in his old man's townhouse in Montecito and found—

'I'm going to do it,' he said to Grayling and Janet Abernathy, the solicitor, blanking the picture in his head which was only going to turn this cluster fuck-tastrophe into a cluster fuck-mageddon. 'The sentence ... I'm going to do it,' he added, because both Grayling and Abernathy were momentarily dumbstruck.

'You really don't need to do that, Mr Devlin,' Janet Abernathy pitched in first. 'It's a fairly simple process to get it overturned. All we need do is show that your business interests will suffer if you're forced to stay in London for any length of time. And a magistrate's court simply does not have the jurisdiction to compel a US citizen to—'

'I have both US and British citizenship,' he said. 'And I can rearrange my schedule.' Gwen was going to love him when he gave her the good news. He'd have to give her an even bigger bonus this December. 'To make sure my business interests don't suffer, there's always the Internet, and I can fly home on weekends, right?'

'Well, yes,' Janet murmured. 'Community payback orders only apply outside the hours of work if the subject is employed.' Her gaze intensified. 'In fact we could negotiate a lengthy time frame to complete it, so you would only have to return for a weekend every couple of months. Or perhaps we could offer a donation in lieu of your time on—'

'Nope, I don't want to do that,' he added, surprised to realise it was the truth.

Throwing his money around had already made him look like enough of a dick and he wanted to get this over with – stringing it out for months would only increase his contact with Ruby of the Lush Ass and Sad Eyes and that probably wasn't a good idea. Plus, the theatre had less than three months left in business now, if his financial calculations were correct. 'I'd rather just do the time.'

It's what he'd always done to make cluster fucks go away: bury his head in work – the harder and sweatier and more time-consuming the better. This would be the first time he'd be doing that to fix a cluster fuck of his own making, so at least it had novelty value. Plus, it was years since he'd had to get his hands dirty on a job. And even longer since he'd strapped on a tool belt. From the snapshot he'd got of The Royale while he was being mobbed by the Falcone for Pope brigade, it needed a lot of work. The cornices were crumbling, the carpets were wrecked, the paintwork looked as if it had been done by a five-year-old and the light fixtures, even in the lobby area, hailed back to the days when Judy herself had been a bright young thing and drug addiction, burn-out and an untimely death had all still been years ahead of her.

He was a code certified electrician, knew enough about plumbing and roofing to fix any major problems, and had more than enough experience as a painter, decorator and carpenter to handle anything the old building had to throw at him. And while he'd never met his Uncle Matty, after singing a few off-key choruses of the guy's favourite show tune, in a weird way he felt like he owed him. Something. Working on his uncle's movie theatre ought to get that out of his system before they had to sell the place.

Plus, he had once loved getting his hands dirty.

And he'd missed it. Luckily, he had no major projects launching globally at the moment. And when was the last time he'd taken any vacation time? A genuine break? Not only that, but the greatest plus of all, he'd be an ocean away from the biggest drama queen in the Western World for four whole mental-health-cleansing weeks while she was rocking her grief-stricken dying swan act over the untimely demise of the brother she hadn't spoken to in thirty years.

Cowardly yes, but what choice did he have? He'd gotten into this fix by helping out Ruby Graham, so now he was going to have to help out Ruby and her movie theatre to get out of it again. There was a certain freaky kind of logic to that, too. And he loved logic. And heck, if he did the work he'd be increasing the property's potential profit when they had to sell the place.

When you looked at the sentence that way, it was almost a win-win.

He tensed at the memory of holding Ruby Graham's warm weight in his arms, her fresh spicy scent filling his nostrils and the weird jolt of awareness that had freaked him out a moment ago, then released a careful breath.

This decision had nothing to do with Ruby, or her toned thighs, or her full, firm breasts, or her sweet sensual voice catching on the words of that dumb song. This was about owning his own shit after a couple of dumb decisions, bad mouthing a judge for no good reason, paying a debt to his Uncle Matty and getting the heck out of his mom's orbit.

He didn't owe Ruby a thing – especially not after getting himself arrested and slapped with a community service order on her behalf – and the weird jolt would go away as soon as he got stuck working in her theatre.

He tugged his iPhone out of his pocket after bidding goodbye to Grayling and Abernathy, who still looked shell-shocked.

Join the club, guys.

'Hey, Gwen,' he said when his ultra-efficient administrative assistant picked up on the first buzz. 'I've got good news and bad news,'

'Hit me with the good first,' she said in a suspicious growl, because Gwen Calhoun was nobody's fool.

'You're not going to be seeing much of me in the next four to six weeks.'

'Damn, that actually is good news!' she said, because Gwen – who had been with Devlin Properties ever since the days when their office was a trailer on a construction site in Queens – had never learned how to respect her boss. 'What's the bad news?'

'You get to overhaul my schedule for the next month and locate me an apartment within walking distance of the Talbot Road in West London.'

'London as in *England*?' Gwen asked, the suspicion back with a vengeance.

'Correct. I just got ordered by a judge here to do three hundred hours community payback. AKA court-ordered community service.'

'In *England*? You have got to be kidding me?' Gwen said, because she did not mince her words either. 'How the hell did you manage that, Dev? You a badass in disguise?'

'Apparently. Go figure, huh?'

Gwen's deep forty-a-day chuckle rasped down the phone line.

Well hell, good to know someone is being entertained.

Chapter 6

'Did someone speak to Benjy about Luke and his involvement with The Royale?' Three hours after her date with Hendon Magistrates' Court, Ruby raked her team with a beady eyeball of doom worthy of Thanos in *Avengers: Endgame*.

The staff were having a meeting in Matty's flat to discuss the final prep for the talent show they were running in the lobby before the screening of *About a Boy* on the coming Saturday but first she needed to know what the heck had just happened in court.

Yes, Luke had been mouthy and irritable, but he was probably jet-lagged. And she wasn't sure he had deserved to get shafted like that.

Three weeks ago, he'd stood beside her stoically through the whole ordeal in the police station without making one word of complaint, or casting any blame. He hadn't even said 'I told you so', which would certainly have been within his rights because he had warned her they might get arrested. But more important than the arrest, he'd been there when she had needed someone. Not just to help get her over that gate physically, but also metaphorically. He'd stood beside her in the dark and sang a song he probably didn't like so she could scatter Matty's ashes without falling to pieces. And for that, he deserved better.

She'd had nearly a month to review the whole Titanic mess while waiting for their day in court, and there was one thing she'd figured out. Beneath Luke Devlin's arrogance, his don't-give-a-damn superiority and that mile-wide anti-sentimental streak there lurked a man of integrity. And that had to count for something.

Most of the team uttered denials, or looked confused but then she cast her beady eyeball on Beryl who had remained suspiciously silent.

It had to be her. Beryl knew Benjy much better than the rest of them, and she had voiced her dismay that Luke wasn't going to save The Royale with his vast wealth, ever since the details of the will had become common knowledge among the staff ... which was approximately twenty-four hours after she had sworn Jacie to secrecy on the matter.

Note to self: never trust a person to keep a secret, no matter how convincingly they fake the butter-wouldn't-melt look.

'Was it you, Beryl?' Ruby asked.

'I may have mentioned it in passing at the last Pensioners' Matinee,' she murmured, looking sheepish. 'I didn't know Benjy would be on the bench today. That was just surprisingly fortuitous,' she added. 'But I can't say I regret it after the way Luke Devlin has treated us.'

'But, Beryl, he didn't do anything wrong,' Ruby said. 'He was only there to support me.'

'That's not the point,' Jacie chimed in. 'I'm with Team Beryl on this. I'm glad Benjy got creative – instead of just giving him some derisory fine. He's Falcone's *son* and he couldn't care less about an institution which has idolised his father and everything his father stood for, for a generation. I mean, what's he ever done to honour the guy's legacy? Absolutely nothing. He's never even admitted they're related! It's like he's ashamed of Falcone. His own *son*.'

How would you know what a self-absorbed asshole he was, if you never actually met him?

Luke's grudging comment echoed in Ruby's head.

She had no idea what Falcone had done to his son to make him call him an asshole. But however much she idolised Falcone the movie icon, she had to believe Luke about Falcone the man. Because while she didn't know much about Luke, she did know he was stoic, and guarded and almost pathologically pragmatic. He didn't do emotion, fake or otherwise, or he would have made much more of a fuss about being dragged off to Hyde Park police station and then dragged back to Hendon Magistrates' Court three weeks later.

If Luke said Falcone the man was an asshole, he probably was.

But she could see Jacie wasn't interested in listening to that explanation. And Ruby wouldn't have repeated Luke's comment about his father anyway. Luke's relationship with Falcone was personal and private.

'He owns half the theatre and he won't step in to save it,' Jacie added.

'Well, he made it clear he doesn't intend to profit from it,' Ruby replied. 'There's still a chance *we* could save it.'

'We've got to find two million quid by the end of June,' Jacie said, sounding exasperated. 'Those odds aren't exactly in our favour.'

'I know.' Ruby sighed, because to be fair, Jacie had a point.

'I think a major charm offensive is in order when Luke Devlin comes to work off his community payback,' Beryl chirped up. 'If anyone can do it, you can, dear.'

Beryl's rheumy grey eyes shone with a faith in Ruby and her charm capabilities which made her want to weep. 'It seems to me Benjy has gifted us with an opportunity that we'd be foolish to waste,' the older woman finished.

'I very much doubt he'll be working off his community payback, Beryl,' Ruby replied gently. Surely his sharp suited legal team's first objective would be to get the ruling over-turned?

A pang of regret squeezed her ribs at the thought of never seeing Luke again, which was as delusional as everything else about this ridiculous mess.

'But what if he does?' Jacie said, her eyes sparking too now. 'Quite apart from the repairs he could do, that's three hundred hours of prime bonding time Benjy's bought us. You never know, he might fall in love with the place despite himself.'

'Are you actually serious right now?' Ruby said, wondering when she had stopped being the only cock-eyed optimist in the village.

'Hey, I know it's a long shot,' Jacie said, clearly warming to Beryl's idea as the spark became a glow. 'But with three hundred hours, you could totally Marcus him, Rubes. I have faith in you.'

'*Marcus* him?' Ruby said. 'What are you even talking about?'

'You know, Marcus, the dorky kid who shows Hugh Grant's shallow wanker in *About a Boy* that the Will Show is actually an ensemble drama. We need Luke Devlin to become part of our ensemble drama, ASAP, if he's gonna fork up two million quid to save us.'

'Strictly speaking, it isn't Nicholas Hoult's Marcus who turns Grant's Will Freeman into a good guy,' Claire their main cashier said, ever the film pedant. 'It's Rachel Weisz remember, because he wants to shag her.'

'No, that's much later in the movie, at first he wants to shag the nice Irish neighbour lady with the baby, so he pretends to have a kid.' This from Imran, one of their bar staff who was even more pedantic than Claire about movie trivia.

'What about the school talent show?' Gerry countered. 'That's when Will *really* turns into a good guy because he can't let Marcus survive that humiliation alone.'

'Yes, but—' Claire began again.

'Can we stop talking about Hugh Grant and all the women he wants to shag in *About a Boy*,' Ruby interrupted the game of film-buff-one-upmanship. 'This isn't a movie. And Luke Devlin's not Hugh Grant ...'

Except ...

She sat down heavily in an armchair, her mind racing. Beryl and Jacie's idea was insane ... Wasn't it?

Even if Luke didn't find some slick way to wiggle out of the community service order, or have Benjy arrested for being a bent magistrate, what were the chances he even knew what an ensemble drama was?

He'd helped her out at the Serpentine when he didn't have to, but that had been under duress.

Her gaze fell on the posters Beryl had brought with her for the talent show they were arranging to go with their Matty Classics' gala screening of *About a Boy* on Saturday.

Hugh Grant's Will had been a hopeless cause, too – his inner ensemble drama buried under a whole movie full of super sarcastic voice-over narration – but Nick Hoult's nerdy bullied Marcus *had* eventually inducted Will into his alternative family. And it had only taken him an hour and forty-one minutes. The Royale would have three hundred hours to work on finding Luke Devlin's sentimental side.

'Admit it, there's a chance it could work?' Jacie said, interrupting Ruby's racing thoughts.

'It's a super slim chance,' Ruby said, but for the first time in weeks, the tightness in her chest eased.

Maybe it was a super slim chance, but it was also their only chance …

The flat's bell chimed the opening bars from Barbra Streisand's 'Memories', making all six of them jump and interrupting Ruby's desperate burst of hope.

'Can you get that, Tozer?' she said to the forty-something unemployed theatre dresser who Errol had taken on as an apprentice projectionist four months ago to help out when his arthritis was playing up. Tozer had been sitting glumly in the corner of the sofa during the whole debate, probably contemplating the possibility of being out of work again in a few months' time.

'It might be the supplier from Gourmet Snacks,' Ruby

added. Yet another person she owed money to. 'If it is just sign for the order,' she said. 'And tell him I'll transfer the money I owe him on Friday.' Once she had established some cashflow from the ticket sales for their *About a Boy* event. Hopefully.

Tozer nodded and left.

Ruby was still trying to get her head around all the possible ramifications of Luke's community service order while Beryl joined the how-many-women-did-Hugh-Grant-attempt-to-cop-off-with-in-*About a Boy* debate, when Tozer popped his head back round the apartment door.

'Ruby, it's him,' he hissed. 'He's down in the foyer. He wants to see you.'

'Who?' she asked, but she was pretty sure she already knew who because a Mariachi band had started a set in her abdomen.

'Luke Devlin, the Falcone Reboot, who do you think?' Tozer said, but his sarcasm was not matched by the vivid blush setting fire to his cheeks.

Jacie bounced up. 'No way? Already. He's keen.'

Gerry swore softly. 'Keen to tell us where we can shove our repairs, more like.'

'Calm down,' Ruby said, even as her own *About a Boy* fantasies took a hit. Had Luke come to tell them he wasn't doing the community service? That had to be it, why else would he have turned up here so quickly. 'Let's find out what he wants first.'

After getting everyone to promise to stay put so she could scope out the Luke situation in private – which earned her a 'you go, girl' from Beryl – she took the flat's stairs to the lobby area.

As she opened the door, she spotted Luke with his back to her, crouched in the corner by the main entrance, checking out the peeling paintwork.

The Mariachi band jiggled her tonsils.

She cleared her throat. 'Luke, hi.'

He swivelled on his heels, then stood. The air thickened. He really was stupidly gorgeous, even when he was frowning, like now.

'Hey,' he said and walked across the threadbare carpet, his long legs in dark jeans eating up the space as he sucked what was left of the oxygen out of the foyer.

Until he told her he was nixing the community service order, there was still a chance he might do it, however slim. But Ruby wasn't sure that was the only thing making her stupidly grateful to see him again, as she became a bit giddy from lack of oxygen.

'I'm so glad you're here,' she said. 'I wanted to say yet again how sorry I am about everything that happened at the Serpentine.'

Even though she wasn't *that* sorry ...

As her gaze took in his fit figure and that incredible face, it occurred to her she wouldn't be at all sorry to see Luke Devlin in a tool belt.

'The community service order was a bit harsh,' she said. 'But ...' She swept her hand out to encompass the plasterwork he had been examining. 'As you can see, we could totally use your help around here.'

'I noticed,' he said, the stern twist of his lips not all that encouraging. 'Tell me something, did you know the magistrate?'

'Absolutely not,' she said, as the guilty flush spread across her collarbone. Being sorry not sorry about the community service order didn't make her a more accomplished liar, unfortunately.

'Funny that, because the sentencing had inside job written all over it.'

'I beg your pardon?' she said, trying to channel Jacie's butter-wouldn't-melt face, but from the heat threatening to blow her head off, probably getting Guilty McGuilt Face instead.

'The magistrate. It was like he was channelling the judge from *Mr Deeds Goes to Town*. You know, not even pretending to be fair or impartial.'

'You've seen Frank Capra's Depression-era comedy starring Gary Cooper and Jean Arthur? Isn't it amazing?' she said hoping to deflect the conversation from Benjy Gate before her cheeks burst into flames. 'I have to say, I did not have you pegged as a vintage movie buff.'

'I'm not.' He shrugged. 'But I was force-fed that stuff as a kid because my mom thought Capra and Spielberg could teach us more about life than Darwin and Shakespeare.'

It wasn't exactly a ringing endorsement of the art form she adored, but the dry admission might be a positive. Perhaps a tiny chunk of Matty's movie-loving DNA *had* been passed on to Luke, after all.

The door to Matty's flat creaked open behind her and

Luke's oxygen-stealing gaze jerked above her head. The line of his lips hardened.

'Hello, Mr Devlin,' she heard Gerry's voice say, and swung round to see all the staff – who were supposed to be holding tight until she'd got the low-down on Luke's community service – crowding into the foyer.

So much for the No Interruptions on Pain of Death promise they'd given her.

'We just wanted to say, we're all really sorry you got slapped with three hundred hours of community service here,' Gerry said, having obviously been elected Liar in Chief. 'But we're really looking forward to working with you.'

'Thank you, Gerry,' Ruby replied, wanting to die inside, because Gerry was an even less convincing liar than she was.

'Are you going to duck out of it?' Jacie asked, cutting straight to the chase as always. 'Because this place belongs to you now, too, and it needs the TLC like, yesterday.'

Oh, for the love of …

'Nope,' Luke replied. 'I'm gonna do the time.'

'*Really?*' Ruby gasped.

Everyone was holding their breath, all eyes on Luke. The hard line of his lips hadn't moved. Was he joking? She couldn't tell.

'Isn't three hundred hours of your time extremely valuable?' she asked, then wanted to shoot herself. What was she doing? Trying to talk him out of it?

'My time's not cheap,' he said. 'But your friend is right, this place could use the work.'

'Jacie's our assistant manager,' Ruby said. 'Jacie meet Luke. Luke meet Jacie,' she added, introducing them formally.

Jacie and Luke nodded at each other as the Mariachi band in Ruby's stomach began mainlining coke.

'Don't look so concerned,' Luke said, and she spotted a quirk at the corner of his mouth. Not a smile, exactly, but not entirely stony faced. 'The Capra Nut Magistrate wasn't wrong about my construction skills.' He glanced over at the vintage refreshments counter and the ticket booth. 'Luckily, the place looks structurally sound. I'll get some surveys done to check that out first, but I can schedule at least a hundred hours of work in here alone once we know there aren't any nasty surprises waiting for us.' He cast his constructor's gaze over the foyer, which looked a lot more shabby than chic in the daylight streaming in from the theatre's glass frontage. 'You've got the beginnings of wet rot in the wall over there.' He pointed to the corner he'd been inspecting when she arrived. 'I'll have to hack back the top layer, most of which has already blown and install some damp proofing before I replaster and redecorate.'

'That ... that would be incredible.' She hadn't doubted his construction skills for a second; what she had doubted was his willingness to do something she had assumed he could easily get out of. But she was not about to correct his assumption any more than she was going to look this gift horse in the mouth. Having Luke here for three hundred hours, getting stuck into all the repair jobs she and Matty had neglected over the past decade free of charge, wasn't just a gift horse, it was a gift unicorn.

Not only could they use the repairs, but there would be a Devlin in the theatre again.

'Is there a bar around here with low lighting where we can talk without an audience?' Luke said, kicking the Mariachi Band back up to coke speed.

Low lighting? Was he coming on to her? But just as the question threatened to torpedo the last of her lung function, Luke's gaze flicked to her staff. The wary glance reminded her of the look he'd sent the poster of his father three weeks ago.

Whoa, girl!

She gulped down a steadying breath. Of course, he needed low lighting so as not to be harassed by any lingering Falcone nuts.

'Absolutely. Jacie can you finish off the meeting while I take Mr Devlin to Brynn's ...'

'We can handle Hugh Grant, dear,' Beryl – who was supposed to be deaf but suddenly seemed to have better hearing than Sandra Bullock in *Bird Box* – said loudly. 'You go on and have a nice time with Mr Devlin, I'm sure there's lots you need to discuss.' The twinkle in Beryl's eye was bright enough to illuminate Greater London.

So much for discreet, then.

'Okay, thanks everyone.' Ruby grasped Luke's arm, ignoring the renewed buzz in her fingertips as his forearm flexed.

All the better to cure wet rot with, she determined.

Five minutes later, they walked into Brynn's Babes, the bar owned by their legendary local drag artist, Brynn Da Mood for Love. Round the corner from the cinema, Brynn's had become a local hang-out for Matty and The Royale's staff over the years and offered Royale customers two-for-one themed cocktails with daft names like Bridget Jones's Daiquiri and Slumdog Martini. Luckily, it wasn't happy hour yet, and the only clientele were a couple of tourists soaking up the local atmosphere.

'Take a seat,' Ruby said as she perched on one of the bar stools. 'What's your poison? It's my shout,' she added, as Brynn's partner Thérèse approached to take their order.

'I'll buy,' Luke said, then had a brief conversation with Thérèse about the beers on draft before settling for a bottle of Sam Adams.

'Really, you don't have to pay for the drinks,' Ruby began. 'I feel like we owe you—'

'Ruby, just order a drink,' he said, riding roughshod over her objections, but the quirk of his lips had practically become a smile, so she didn't take offence.

'I've got a flight to catch tomorrow morning,' he added. 'And I don't want to miss another.'

'Oh, okay, absolutely,' she said, quickly ordering a lemon-tini, because it was Matty's favourite and right now she needed some Matty courage. Thérèse walked off to get their drinks after sending Ruby a conspiratorial wink.

'I'm sorry to keep you, you could just email me about anything you need to ...' she continued.

'Relax, Ruby,' he said. 'I was kidding about the flight.'

'Oh, I see,' she said, deflating. 'So what did you want to discuss?'

Thérèse slid her the lemon-tini. As Luke paid for the drinks and thanked Thérèse, Ruby tried not to chug the fortifying cocktail in one go.

'We need to work up a schedule,' he said. 'I can come by to hammer out a checklist of work that needs doing but I have to return to New York for a few days to rearrange my schedule first.' He stroked his thumb down the side of the beer bottle, creating a trail in the cold droplets clinging to the glass, but his gaze remained fixed on her face. 'How does Saturday sound? Then I can start work Monday.'

'That would be beyond wonderful,' she said, suddenly struggling to resist the urge to fling her arms round his broad shoulders and hug him.

He was actually genuinely serious about helping to repair The Royale. Surely that had to mean he might be softening towards West London's Premium Art-House Institution? And even if it didn't, it would give them time to work on him. Work *with* him, she corrected, trying not to get fixated on his shoulders.

Don't hug him Rubes, you don't want to scare him off.

Although Luke Devlin didn't look like the type to be easily scared off by serial huggers, she wasn't taking any chances.

'What time is good, on Saturday?' he asked, tugging his iPhone out of his pocket and making the cashmere of his sweater stretch across his chest.

'Oh, any time you can make it we'll be available ...'

He frowned, looking up from his phone 'Seriously? You don't have screenings that day we should work around?'

Yes, they did. The fortuitousness of the date struck Ruby like a bolt of lightning.

Just Like in the Movies

Saturday night was the *About a Boy* Talent Show Gala. The second film in Matty's Classics season.

It was a sign. She had to get Luke to that screening, because as her staff had pointed out ten minutes ago, it had to be a much better Get Luke On Board bet than *The Wizard of Oz*.

As much as everyone at The Royale had always adored the Judy Garland classic, the film had obviously been far too cute and sweet and idealistic to pierce Luke's anti-movie cynicism. Surely the caustic Hugh Grant Brit-com would be much more Luke's thing? Snarky and witty, with even the cheesy moments played for laughs, *About a Boy* also had the huge advantage that the only song in it was a piss take of Roberta Flack's 'Killing Me Softly'.

'How long do you think the checklist will take to hammer out?' she asked, as guilelessly as she could while she was frantically working out the logistics. If they moved the talent show to after the screening, she should at least be able to get him to watch the movie. He'd probably rather claw out his eyeballs than watch a talent show. Even if he didn't stay for the gala, the movie was the important thing, with all it's wonderful messages about not being an island and making your own family. The Royale was Ruby's family, if she could just plant the seed in Luke's head he didn't have to be an island anymore like Will in the movie, they could start to—

'A couple of hours,' he said. 'There's a ton of stuff that needs work. I'll arrange to get the surveys done first, but as I said, the structure looks good to me. They made these old buildings to last.'

'Five o'clock would work for me,' she said, hoping the guilty heat fanning out across her neck wasn't visible in the bar's low lighting.

'That late?' He sounded unconvinced. 'I can make it earlier. I'll be getting a red-eye from New York.'

'No, really, five's good, it'll give you time to rest after the flight.' And would ensure he was in the theatre when the screening started at seven. 'Where will you be staying? At The Grant again? I could send Gerry round to pick you up?' Gerry was the only one of them who had a car.

He sent her a suspicious look. And the flush intensified.

Dial down on the eager. For crap sake, he'll think you're hitting on him.

'I can walk over,' he said. 'My assistant is renting me a space in Notting Hill for the duration.'

He was hiring a flat in Notting Hill? The rent on a studio flat in one of London's most sought after neighbourhoods would cost him three grand a month at least.

'That's ... *Really?* You're hiring a flat for a whole month.' *Just to come work at The Royale?*

Visions of Hugh Grant's superfly noughties pad in *About a Boy* sprang to mind. *More* than three grand a month, because she doubted Luke Devlin would be living in a pokey studio flat.

'It's a house,' he said without looking up, busy tapping the details into his phone's calendar with his thumbs. 'On a street called Chepstow Villas. It was the only rental Gwen could find at short notice,' he finished.

A *house*? On *Chepstow Villas*? Quite possibly *the* most expensive residential road in the whole fricking country?

Those Georgian piles were enormous. It would cost him an absolute fortune to hire a house in Chepstow Villas for a month. He wouldn't get change from *twenty* grand.

Ruby gulped her lemon-tini to stop her heart exploding out of her chest with anticipation and astonishment as realisation struck.

Luke Devlin was already invested in The Royale. He just hadn't figured it out yet.

'That's incredibly generous of you,' she said, barely able to speak around the emotion threatening to close her throat.

His thumbs paused on the iPhone. She bit into her lip to keep the wave of gratitude below tsunami proportions.

'Generous how?' he said.

'To be renting a house in Chepstow Villas so you can help us,' she qualified. Was he being modest? That was so ... *sweet.* The tsunami built again. 'While you're here, I mean. That's above and beyond the call of duty.'

The blank look on Luke's face turned into a frown. 'I'm under court orders, remember.'

'I know but ...' *You could totally have got out of that.* 'I just mean, that's going to be expensive. And we really appreciate it.' *Don't give him ideas again Ruby. Be cool. Pretend like it's no biggie.*

'I'm not paying for it personally; it's a company expense. I'm going to be doing other work while I'm in the UK – I figure I can schedule in three to four hours a day tops at the theatre because we'll have to work around your screening times and I'll need to clean up each day before you open up.'

'Oh, yes, of course,' she said, not buying his qualifications for a second.

Luke Devlin might want to be all business. He might not even realise what was happening here. But The Royale's magic was already working on him, a little bit.

She took a moment to study him in the half light. That fall of hair that had dropped back over his forehead, the lean lines and perfect angles of his face, the square jaw, and the dimple in his chin. Luke Devlin was breathtakingly handsome, but it occurred to her she didn't even notice the physical similarities to his father anymore. Had it been their 'Over the Rainbow' duet, their arrest, their day in court, or the thought of the weeks ahead while they worked together that had turned him very much into his own person in her eyes?

'Ruby, you do get that nothing's changed,' he said, carefully. 'That me doing this *court-ordered* community service to help you fix up the theatre isn't going to magically find you two million bucks to fill the black hole in your finances?'

Her lungs squeezed tight, the question suspended in time as she wondered if he was really as clueless about what was going on here as he was making out. Unlike his father on a movie screen, with Luke it was impossible to tell what he was really feeling.

'Of course,' she said. 'Absolutely.'

Maybe Luke didn't get it yet. But he would, or she wasn't the smartest film buff in West London – with a string of classic movies chosen by a maestro to indoctrinate him with.

She took a sip of the lemon-tini, only to find her glass

empty. How had she finished that so quickly? 'I should probably get back to the theatre,' she said reluctantly.

She needed to start plotting with her co-conspirators how
they were going to get him to stay for *About a Boy* on Saturday
night. And then figure out which of Matty's other Classics
might be useful to show Luke the healing power of cinema.

'Not so fast,' he said as she got up. 'There is one other
thing.'

'Yes?'

Anything, anything you want.

'It can't get out, that I'm working at the theatre,' he said.
'Gwen has already briefed our press team, they're putting out
the story to anyone who wants to know that I'm in Alaska
on a fishing trip. Luckily for us, the press in the UK don't put
reporters at Hendon Magistrates' Court, so we're good there.
And when I'm working I'll make sure I stay as low-key as
possible while the place is open. I've got a lot of experience
at being invisible so that shouldn't be a problem.' His brows
lowered again and she realised this was another aspect of his
life she'd never considered.

Why had it never occurred to her how tough it must have
been to keep under the radar with Falcone's face? But as she
looked at him now, she thought again that he didn't look
like Falcone anymore. Not to her. Not at all. He looked like
Luke.

'So the only other possible leak will be you and your staff,'
he continued. 'I'll need you to promise me they won't release
the information to anyone. Not to any of their friends and
acquaintances. And definitely nothing on social media. No

photos, no Instagram, no Facebook, Twitter, TikTok. Nada. Get it?'

'Yes, of course.' Even if she had to cut out everyone's tongue and chop off their fingers, she would make sure no one broke Luke's cover. The Royale would become a safe haven for him, no matter what, the way it had always been for her.

'I swear, no one who doesn't have to will know you're here.' She stroked her fingertip over a spot on her left breast.

At The Royale, we look after our own, Luke. And we're making you one of our own … whether you like it or not.

Chapter 7

'Once I've hacked away the blown plaster I can re-install the damp proofing then replaster and repaint here, too.' Luke knelt down at the edge of the old theatre's stage to knock against the wall, getting a series of hollow thuds. He glanced over his shoulder at Ruby. 'Write this whole area down.'

'Right.' She bent over her clipboard, puffing upwards at the curls that had escaped the top knot she'd tied her hair into.

The aggravating and now far too familiar pulse of awareness had Luke concentrating harder on checking the plaster in the auditorium.

The woman was cute and fresh and homely, there was nothing hot about that. Maybe this was the result of his jet-lag. He'd had a quick doze at his rental in Chepstow Villas and ended up oversleeping. Not like him. He was still groggy after the seven-hour flight from JFK, and the texts he'd been fielding all afternoon from his mom, who had already figured out the fishing trip in Alaska story Gwen had given her was a crock.

Not good.

He'd been questioning himself ever since about why exactly he'd spent the last three days handling a whole heap of bullshit so he could make this happen without screwing up his business.

All the answers he'd given himself on Monday at the Magistrate's Court still held.

The theatre could do with the work.

He owed his uncle ... something.

He'd missed working with his hands.

He needed a break from his mom in Greta Garbo mode.

But now he was here, back in the theatre, doing a punch list of all the repairs and decorating needed to bring his uncle's movie house back to its former glory – or at least back to a place where it could be sold quickly – the answer he hadn't wanted to acknowledge, hadn't even consciously admitted to himself until now was staring him right in the face.

Ruby Graham – and the weird jolt, not to mention the desire to see her again and check up on her – had also been a factor in his decision to do the community service.

The thought would be funny, if it weren't so fricking annoying. But it was hard to deny she had snagged his attention.

'How do you think I should list this area?' she asked from behind him. 'West of the stage?' She gave a nervous chuckle. 'That sounds like something John Wayne would say.'

'Nah, it's better to draw a grid.' He straightened, walked the two steps towards her, took the clipboard out of her hands – and got a lung full of her fierce, floral scent for his troubles.

He let his gaze glide over the notes she'd been jotting down for two hours as they assessed the work needed together.

'Ruby? What the heck is this?'

The notes and diagrams she'd drawn on the work sheet – with a smattering of doodles and movie quotes thrown in for good measure – were totally unintelligible.

Her cheeks pinkened and she made a grab for the board. 'It makes sense to me.'

He whipped the board away. 'Uh-huh ...' Lifting the list above her grabbing hands, he read one of the barely decipherable squiggles aloud placed next to the list of supplies he'd asked for and what looked like a cartoon robot. 'Smell. The. Glove?'

'It's to remind me to order the eleven litres of primer you asked for.'

She reached to grab the board back. The pulse of awareness became a shudder.

Sweet Jesus, ignore it.

'What has smelling gloves got to do with primer?'

'It's a perfectly obvious reference to *This Is Spinal Tap*,' she said. Her face had gotten even pinker. Had she felt that shudder, too?

So not good.

'*Spinal Tap?* You mean the movie about a rock band?' He vaguely remembered watching the old mockumentary in college and laughing his ass off, but he'd been wasted at the time so he wasn't sure it counted.

'The numbers all go to eleven,' she said in a dead-on imitation of one of the British guys in the band. 'Get it?'

'Yeah, weirdly.' The laugh rumbled up his torso but he held it at bay. 'What's with the robot guy?' he asked, pointing at the scribbled drawing next to the quote. This he needed to hear.

'That's Optimus Primer, to you,' she announced. 'From *Transformers*. The first film with Shia LaBeouf, not the sequels, obviously.'

The laugh burst out before he could stop it.

It was like breaking a seal, because suddenly his chuckles matched hers. Their spontaneous laughter echoed round the empty auditorium and felt good in a way he hadn't felt in a while. Not since a couple of years back in Rome, when he'd shared a brew with his kid brother while they both coughed up a lung over the latest random bullshit to befall Jack on his travels.

'That's nuts, but yeah, I get it,' he said as the laughter faded.

She smiled and took the clipboard from him. 'Precisely,' she said. 'Do not mock the method in my madness,' she added primly as she tucked the board back under her arm.

Her cheeks were still that pretty shade of pink, highlighting the freckles.

'Do you have a movie reference for everything?' he asked, genuinely intrigued.

'Pretty much,' she said, without an ounce of embarrassment. 'Movies are like life, if you look hard enough. A good movie can allow you to walk around in someone else's shoes and also help you escape your problems, at least for a little while. That's why I love them.'

It was the sort of naïve woo-woo crap his mom had used

to justify the bad decisions she'd made throughout his child-hood. But coming from Ruby, her expression bright with sincerity – and not fake sincerity either – it sounded kind of profound.

It was still bullshit, of course. He'd seen the damage that kind of crap could do, especially to those poor suckers left to pick up the pieces when others doggedly invested in the dream and refused to face the reality. He'd seen the man behind the curtain – to borrow a quote from Ruby's favourite movie – and he knew the guy was a faker, a charlatan, a cheat.

But Ruby believed it. She wasn't faking her optimism or her wanderlust to manipulate him, the way he suspected his mom had for years. And there was something endearing in that, however crazy.

'Did you ever want to direct movies? Or be in them?' he asked, because he was curious. Pretty much every movie fan he'd ever met – and with his face he'd met a lot of them – had a secret ambition to be either the next Tarantino or Bigelow or the next J-Law or RDJ. If you bought into the hype, why not go for the gold star while you were at it?

'I certainly never wanted to act,' she said.

'But you did want to direct?' he prompted.

'For a while,' she said. 'Matty encouraged me to do some classes in film production at the local adult education institute after I left school. I think he was worried I might be hiding my light under a bushel.' She pushed her bangs out of her eyes and he could see the sadness at the mention of his uncle's name. 'But I was rubbish, every idea I came up with was derivative.'

'But that's how the industry works – especially in Hollywood. Every movie is made on the back of another one,' he said.

'Perhaps, but the truth was, I also discovered I wasn't really interested in making my own movies. I was happy just to run this place with Matty. Maybe it lacks ambition but this has been my ideal job since I was twelve and I make no apologies for that.'

An ideal job he was going to do nothing to save. He stifled the pang of guilt.

So so not good.

'Ruby, can we start letting people in now, we've only got twenty minutes before the screening starts?'

He turned to see Ruby's assistant manager Jacie standing by the door.

'Yes, thanks, Jacie. Where's Gerry and the bar staff?' Ruby asked in a weirdly studied voice, as if she were making a point of asking a question she already knew the answer too.

'Right here, Ruby.' Gerry, the bar guy, popped out from behind the assistant manager, then him and his crew filed in and starting prepping behind the bar.

'That's my cue to scram,' Luke said, pulling his ball cap out of his back pocket and slapping it on. He glanced at his watch, they'd been at it for close to two hours. He hadn't had a chance to look over the lobby yet, but he had more than enough chores to be getting on with. Chores he was actually looking forward to.

He couldn't save this place for prosperity, but it was a beautiful old building, and maybe if he got back some of its past glory in a couple of months Ruby could get a good price for it. Or better yet, find an angel investor who was as sold on the magic of the movies as she was.

'You want to translate your notes and email me the list of supplies we talked about?' he said.

'Why don't I do that now?' she said, clutching the board as if her life depended on it. 'My office is upstairs in Matty's flat. I could type it out and maybe we could do some of the ordering online.' Her gaze flicked backwards and forwards from him to the customers making their way into the auditorium.

'Just email me the list, I can source the materials and pay for them.' He had no intention of billing her or the theatre. From the state of the place he suspected the cost of materials would bankrupt them.

'You're going to pay for the supplies?' Ruby said, misting up like she had when he'd revealed he was renting a house nearby. 'Even though you already paid for all those surveys?'

'I got the surveys done through a company account. And I can write off the expense against my tax liability when we sell the place,' he said, hoping to direct her back to the big picture.

The hope in her eyes didn't even falter.

He figured he'd done his best. Ruby was an optimist, no question about it. All he could do was keep giving it to her straight. If she chose not to believe it, that was her issue.

People were starting to line up at the bar to order drinks. He recognized some of the folks from the last movie night. A lot of the audience were wearing nerdy knitted beanies like the kid on the movie poster in the lobby and the kind of twenty-year-old gear he guessed went with the theme.

He resisted the urge to shudder. People around here must really love dress-up.

'I'll see you Monday,' he said. 'I'll start early so I can pack up before the first screening.'

Ruby nodded, enthusiastically. 'As early as you want to come is good with me.'

'If you want to get some keys cut, I won't need to disturb you,' he said.

They'd already had a discussion about how best to fit the work round the theatre's schedule. Luckily, The Royale only did matinee screenings twice during the week, so he could work until five on the other days. One thing he did not want to do was impact on their revenue. He also wanted to keep his contact with Ruby to a minimum. She was too cute for her own good. And while cute had never attracted him in the past, those weird jolts and pulses whenever he was around her meant he wasn't going to push his luck.

'Will do, although you won't disturb me at all.' She beamed those misty green eyes at him again then glanced round at the dimly lit auditorium. 'I cannot wait to see this place get the love and attention it deserves. At last. And from a Devlin no less.'

Love was way too strong a word, but he let it go. Why piss on her parade when he didn't have to?

'Can I head out that way?' he asked pointing to the exit door at the side of the stage.

He wasn't concerned about getting harassed again, everyone

was keeping a respectable distance as they made their way to their seats – give or take a few curious stares. Ruby had assured him The Royale community wouldn't break his cover. And he believed her, because while Ruby looked like a pushover in a lot of respects – with her misty eyes and her freckled nose and her movie-mad philosophy of life – he knew how fierce she could be too, after having her ream him out over his refusal to scatter his uncle's ashes.

'Actually, it's alarmed,' Ruby said, but her gaze flicked away when she said it. Was she lying? Why?

'Okay, I'll head through the lobby, see you around.' He shoved his hands into his pockets, ducked his head and prepared to make his way through the crowd.

But then her fingers landed on his arm. 'Luke, wait.'

He shot a look at her hand, annoyed by the ripple of awareness that shot up his arm.

She lifted her fingers immediately, making him regret giving her the death stare.

'Would you ... would you let us pay you back for the materials, and everything else you're doing?' she said, so earnestly he was forced to stand still and listen.

'I told you, Ruby this is business, I can ...'

'Not in money,' she butted into his explanation. 'We'd love to have you as our guest of honour again, for tonight's Matty's Classic. And for the other Matty's Classics screenings while you're in London. You know, so we can thank you for helping us out. When you really didn't have to.'

'I got ordered to by a magistrate's court,' he pointed out, but she rode roughshod over the comment.

'It would mean so much to us all to have a Devlin in The Royale again.'

Please say yes, please say yes, please please please say yes.

Ruby watched the muscle jump in Luke's cheek.

He wanted to say no. That much was blatantly obvious. And she was pretty sure he'd figured out her little ruse to trap him here until the show started.

But he didn't say no straight away. He simply levelled that inscrutable stare at her, as if he were trying to gauge what was really going on.

She attempted to look as guileless as she could – not easy when her heart was beating so hard she was surprised she hadn't passed out.

Luke was a cynical man. He didn't believe in the magic of the movies, or their power to transform lives and people.

But Luke was also the man who had sung a show tune and gotten arrested for an uncle he'd never met. And the man who had relocated to London for a month or more to help fix a dilapidated cinema he planned to sell. He had also laughed at her Optimus Primer joke. Which meant Luke Devlin was not a completely lost cause.

Just like Hugh Grant's Will Freeman.

If an egocentric dick like Will could discover his warm and fuzzy side with a little help from a nerdy kid and his hippie mum, then Luke could discover his warm and fuzzy side, too.

She held her breath waiting for his answer, not entirely sure anymore that getting Luke to discover his warm and fuzzy side so she could get him to help save The Royale was the only thing at stake.

'What's the movie tonight?' he asked.

Ruby's breath gushed out so fast she felt dizzy.

Of course saving The Royale was the only thing at stake here. This wasn't about getting to sit next to him again for the duration of another movie, it couldn't be. She refused to be that desperate.

'*About a Boy*,' she said. 'Matty loved it. He always said Hugh Grant was at his hottest playing complete and utter bastards.'

'Never heard of it,' he said, but the muscle in his cheek had unclenched.

It was enough for Ruby to start feeling light-headed again. 'Well then, you're in for a massive treat.'

'Do I have to sing? In the Talent Show?'

So he'd noticed the posters in the foyer announcing the after show entertainment? She had a moment of panic, how to reassure him that was not a requirement?

But then his lips curved. He was joking.

She got breathless again; Luke Devlin really was gorgeous when he smiled. And even more gorgeous when he laughed, she'd discovered a few minutes ago.

Although he was most gorgeous when he ran his long tanned fingers over the skirting board to test for woodworm, she decided. She would probably have a spontaneous orgasm when she saw him in a tool belt

Ruby flushed at the arbitrary thought.

Earth to Ruby. You and Luke are not going to be a thing.

He was not and could never be her type. When it came to dating, she didn't do hot and solvent, she only did geeky and dysfunctional. And she would hazard a guess she was about as far from his type as Hugh Grant.

But that didn't mean she couldn't admire Luke Devlin in a tool belt – on a purely aesthetic level.

'Not unless you really want to,' she said, smiling back at him.

'I can't promise I can make any of the other screenings,' he said, the stern tone not as convincing as it had been.

'But you'll stay for this one?' she asked, the light-headedness becoming euphoria.

'Sure, I guess it can't do any harm.'

'That's so wonderful, Luke.' She led him to their sofa in the back row, and gave Gerry and Jacie, who were watching from the bar, a thumbs up behind his back. 'You have no idea how much this means,' she gushed as they took their seats.

Because it could mean everything.

As the lights went down five minutes later, and Hugh Grant's Will Freeman started spouting off about how cool his empty life was, Ruby sent up a silent prayer.

Over to you, Will. This is our chance to show Luke what family can mean – even to cynical loners. So don't fuck it up.

But as she sat beside him, it was actually quite hard to concentrate on her – and Will's – mission and not the industrial strength hotness vibes pumping off him.

'How's it going? What does he think of the movie?' Jacie hissed, waylaying Ruby on her way back from the loo.

The film was nearly over and the tension had taken its toll on Ruby's bladder. The school talent show – which was part of the film's finale – was in full swing on screen. Will and Marcus sharing an uncomfortable duet of 'Killing Me Softly' had been Ruby's cue to make a dash for the loo for a tension-busting pee. Sitting next to Luke and gauging his every reaction was hard work, not least because he was not a demonstrative man, and she'd become more than a little addicted to his gruff chuckles, which had a rough, rusty quality to them that only made them more precious. Until the scene in the middle of the movie, when Will and Marcus and the Irish Lady with the baby who Will wanted to shag walked in on Marcus's mum after she'd made a suicide attempt. At which point everything had changed ...

And Ruby had actually started to feel sick.

'Good, I think,' Ruby whispered, trying not to stress about it. 'He's laughed a couple of times, which is a big improvement on *The Wizard of Oz*.'

But who wouldn't laugh at *About a Boy*? It was a very funny film which had stood the test of time. Will Freeman's self-serving laddishness was infectious – you couldn't help liking Will because he was so self-aware about being a selfish tosser and so unapologetic about it too. Will's studied immaturity had also made him the perfect person to understand Marcus – a thirteen-year-old boy with a suicidal mum and no cool points whatsoever.

But the more of the film they watched together, the more she became aware of the massive flaw in her strategy to use *About a Boy* as a way to soften Luke up.

The notion she could put the kernel of an idea into Luke's head, that family could come in all shapes and sizes, and that being rich and cynical could make your life poorer – had been delusional at best, and manipulative at worst. Especially as there were a lot of things about the movie she'd forgotten, or never realized in the first place.

After watching it with Luke, those omissions had become glaringly obvious.

First off, she'd realised Luke's personality wasn't that close to Will's at all. Luke might be rich and cynical, but no way would Will have helped her over that gate or done something as cheesy as sung 'Over the Rainbow' with her, or gotten arrested, not unless he was trying to get into her pants – which Luke categorically was not.

And that was without even factoring in the massive misstep she'd made getting him to sit through the suicide attempt scene. That scene had taken on a different significance when she'd noticed Luke's reaction. He'd immediately tensed, then his expression had become rigid, he'd disappeared to the toilet and she'd been scared he might not come back. But when he had, there had been no more laughing.

Why hadn't she remembered that scene? And figured out the hideous significance it might have for Luke? She'd hurt him, and that had never been her intention.

'That's fabulous,' Jacie whispered, hearing what Ruby had wanted her to hear, instead of the devastating truth – that by getting Luke to watch this movie, they might well have triggered extremely painful memories they had no right to trigger.

'We can start the schmooze offensive big time next week,'

Jacie added. 'Who'd have thought a knob like Will Freeman would help save The Royale.'

'I'll take Luke out by the fire exit once it finishes and everyone's left the auditorium,' Ruby said.

'Why don't you ask him to stay for the talent show?' Jacie said. 'Now we've softened him up we should go in for the kill.'

'I don't think so,' Ruby said firmly, controlling the urge to snap at Jacie. It wasn't Jacie's fault Ruby had forgotten about the bloody suicide scene. Or that she felt super-guilty now for trying to use Luke. Jacie didn't know Luke, not the way Ruby did. Ruby was the one who should have nixed the whole idea in the bud of trying to manipulate Luke into investing in The Royale with the help of a bloody movie. Instead she'd encouraged her staff to believe they could exploit his generosity in agreeing to do the community service. And not even just to save The Royale, but because she had gotten vicarious pleasure out of having him there beside her in the darkness.

'Ask Errol not to turn up the lights until I've gotten him out of here,' Ruby said.

The least she could do was protect Luke from prying eyes and get him safely out of the building before anyone approached him.

Then she needed to make sure he was okay. And that the scene with Marcus's mum hadn't brought back too many traumatic memories for Luke of his father's suicide when he was only fourteen.

He killed himself. Because he was a careless, selfish bastard. It wasn't your fault. Get over it.

145

'Thanks for the movie, it was cool,' Luke managed round the bitter taste that had been lingering in his mouth for over an hour.

He pushed open the exit door – which apparently wasn't alarmed after all – and took a deep breath in, his first deep breath for over an hour. Even tinged with the aroma of rotting garbage from the nearby dumpsters and the pungent scent of urine, the lung full of night air was enough to loosen the vice which had a stranglehold on his ribs.

'I'll see you Monday,' he said to Ruby, who had followed him out into the back alley.

'Yes,' she said, holding the heavy metal door open so she could slip back inside.

But as he pulled his cap out of his back pocket, she murmured. 'Luke, I'm so sorry. I totally forgot that scene was in the movie.'

The vice clamped tight again as her eyes darkened with compassion and regret.

She knows? What gave me away?

He thought he'd held his shit together. Something he'd become an expert at as a kid. Ruby Graham, though, was more observant than most people.

He didn't say anything, because he couldn't. Instead he concentrated on putting on his ball cap and evening out his breathing. Again.

Should he pretend he didn't know what she was referring to? Talking about it would only make him feel more exposed. More humiliated.

But how could he pretend he didn't know, when *everyone*

knew what had happened to his old man. It had been plastered all over the world's press for weeks when it happened. And every year since they still held vigils on the anniversary of his father's death in Falcone's old neighbourhood in the Bronx. He knew because he filed the invite he got sent by The Falconios in the trash every year. Last year, the damn anniversary had even gotten its own hashtag trending on Twitter.

Ruby only knows what everyone knows. There is no need to freak out.

Ruby was a Falcone nut, all she knew was that his father had killed himself. The familiar anger seared his throat. He swallowed to soothe the raw edge.

You're not angry anymore, remember?

He was an adult now. What was the point in being angry with a dead guy? And so what if Falcone had been a crummy dad? A lot of people had crummy fathers, like both the asshat and the kid in the movie he'd just seen. Plus, his mom had spent a fortune on therapy to help him get over the fallout from that godawful day.

'It didn't bother me,' he said, determined to mean it as he adjusted the cap. Or at the very least to get Ruby to believe he meant it. He'd revealed more than enough about himself to this woman already, and it made him super uncomfortable. Why had he done that? 'No need to be sorry. I liked the movie, it was pretty funny,' he added, which wasn't completely a lie. Up until that bombshell moment, he had been enjoying it.

What bugged him was the scene had been a trigger, when it shouldn't have been. Since when did movies freak him out? He'd known since he was a little kid they weren't real.

Unlike Ruby, who bought into all that woo-woo crap, he knew how movies faked emotion. The moment when the nerdy kid found his mom collapsed on the couch was just a clever plot device used to shock the lead guy into giving a shit about someone other than himself. The guy had been enough of an asshole – albeit a hilarious one – to need dynamite to blast him out of his own orbit, so it made total sense the writers would need a big shock moment to make that happen. Hence the mom's suicide attempt.

Freaking out about a plot device was beneath him.

Ruby nodded. 'Okay, I'm glad.' She didn't look convinced by his denial.

'I'll see you Monday,' he said, then realized he was repeating himself.

She smiled, the sweet sunny expression making the damn vice squeeze his ribcage again. What was *with* that?

'I'm looking forward to it,' she said. 'Let me know if there's anything you need me to do beforehand.'

He nodded, and tipped his hat, then walked away.

He didn't look back once. Although he found himself listening for the sound of the heavy exit door slamming shut as she went back inside.

But the sound never came.

PART THREE

Brokeback Mountain (2005)

Ruby Graham's verdict: *I can't imagine anything more painful than loving someone so passionately your whole life and yet never being able to say it out loud. Not even to them. Jack and Ennis are like a modern-day Romeo and Juliet, and the poison that destroyed them was the secret they were forced to keep.*

Luke Devlin's verdict: *No one should have to hide who they really are. Or who they want to be with. That sucks. But I wonder if Jack and Ennis would have been better without Brokeback Mountain, because all it did in the end was screw up both their lives.*

Chapter 8

'Bollocks!' Ruby shrieked as she shot out of the shower, the water turning from warmish to freezing the second after she'd dumped a ton of shampoo on her hair. *Naturally*.

She grabbed a towel from the pile on the vanity, and folded it around her body, then wrapped a hand towel around her head to keep her soapy hair out of her eyes.

She did not have time for this today. The Royale's LGBTQIA+ weekender was kicking off in approximately eight hours and she had about a million and one things to do – not the least of which was checking the print that had finally arrived for the Matty's Classics screening of *Brokeback Mountain*, due to finish the weekender tomorrow.

Luke would be arriving in half an hour and she wanted to present him with Professional and Efficient Ruby not Wet and Wild Ruby – she'd even ironed the pencil skirt and blouse she usually wore to see the bank manager, especially for the occasion.

He'd started the repairs in the auditorium four days ago now, arriving each morning at seven on the dot, and then packing up and cleaning everything away in time for the first screening each day. She and Jacie and Gerry and the rest of the theatre's staff had been tasked with being as friendly as possible and making sure he had everything he needed – including coffee and food – but he had declined all offers. To the point where she'd been forced to tell everyone to back off.

The schmooze offensive wasn't working, all it was doing was making her feel more guilty about it. She hadn't managed to even talk to him properly since the disastrous screening of *About a Boy* – when she'd managed to traumatise him by mistake.

She stomped out of the bathroom, opened the door to the stairs down to the foyer and shouted: 'Gerry, call Mehmed, and tell him the boiler's on the fritz again.' She scowled, wiping the soap out of her stinging eyes. Mehmed was a retired plumber who lived round the corner, he didn't charge an exorbitant call-out fee and would accept free cinema tickets in exchange for his efforts to keep the aging boiler in Matty's flat functioning. Only problem was, she wasn't sure he'd come this time as he'd been adamant a month and a half ago when he'd called round just before Matty's funeral that the flat needed a new boiler – even though she'd been adamant they couldn't afford one.

'Tell him I think it's a different problem,' she lied smoothly. If she could just get him here, he would surely find a way to work his plumber magic one last time.

Gerry's reply was muffled, but sounded like. 'I'll try.'

Shivering, she walked into the flat's tiny galley kitchen and switched on the kettle. She could wait for ten minutes for Mehmed to get here. If he didn't turn up in that time – which was highly likely – she'd just have to rinse her hair in the sink again. But she was having a cup of tea first to gird her loins.

'Bloody boiler.'

She was still swearing furiously and shivering in her towel two minutes later between sips of her fortifying cuppa when she heard footsteps on the stairs.

She dropped her tea on the counter and dashed into the flat's living room. 'Mehmed, that was quick! Thanks so much for—'

Her greeting cut off. Because it wasn't the seventy-something retired plumber who stepped into her living room.

'Luke!' Fire blazed from the top of her towel-clad head to the tips of her scarlet-painted toenails. 'You're early?' she croaked, so mortified she was surprised she hadn't incinerated on the spot.

'Gerry said you had a heating emergency,' he murmured.

Not anymore, she thought, as his gaze snagged on her bare legs, and the whole body blush hit fifty thousand degrees centigrade.

Crapola! She was completely naked under her towel, which felt like the size of a napkin under that hot blue gaze. Did it even adequately cover her bum? Which, let's face it, needed more coverage than usual after the binge-eating she had been doing for six weeks to stave off her grief.

Ruby's law: while other women waste away in mourning, I gain ten pounds.

She scooted the back of the towel down with her free hand, while keeping her other arm locked over her breasts, so as not to give Luke even more of a peep show.

'Do you want to show me where the issue is?' His deep voice reverberated in the hot spot between her legs where the full body blush had settled.

Yes, please.

'Ruby? Where's the boiler?' he asked, the demand in his voice startling her.

She shook her head, trying to kick out the erotic visions which had stalled every last one of her brain cells. Visions of Luke, looking hot and buff and helpful, sorting out the overheating issue between her thighs.

'Yes ... Absolutely.' She coughed, attempting to dislodge the frog in her throat which was making her sound like Ennis Del Mar on a Marlboro bender. 'It's right through here,' she finished. But as she lifted her arm to indicate where the boiler closet was, the towel slipped. She grasped the hem, fumbled with it and then wriggled and jiggled everything back into a respectable place ... or rather, as respectable a place as it was possible to get to when she was butt naked under a napkin in front of the hottest guy in London and blushing like a menopausal nun.

She fled down the corridor towards the closet, trailing her lust and her mortification behind her – while convincing herself she had totally imagined the answering flash of heat in those ice-blue eyes. Because that way lay humiliation. Humiliation of the he-doesn't-fancy-you-you-only-think-he-does-because-you-fancy-him variety. And she had been there enough in school and later while using Matty's terrible blind-dating services to know what a dangerous place that was – not just for her ego, but also for conducting a working relationship with Luke.

How many times had she broken cover with boys at school and then had to sit next to them in chemistry class for the rest of eternity – knowing they thought she was a loser, or a nerd, or worse?

She could not afford to go there with Luke. And neither could The Royale.

The bitter memories of her loser school days helped to douse the flames still flickering between her thighs as his footsteps followed her down the hallway.

After trekking to Siberia and back they finally arrived at the boiler closet.

'It's in t-t-there,' she stuttered, as a violent shiver racked her body.

'Hey, you're freezing.' Before she had a chance to object, he'd doffed the checked shirt he wore over a black T-shirt and threw it over her shoulders. It was still warm from his body, the scent of sandalwood clinging to the brushed cotton as she inhaled. Another shiver hit her, but this one had nothing to do with the chilly flat.

'Go get dressed while I take a look,' he said, opening the closet and ducking inside.

She made a hasty retreat before she could make an even bigger tit of herself. But as she arrived at her bedroom door, she sneaked a peek over her shoulder.

All she could see of Luke was his long legs and exceptional backside as he bent forward to examine the boiler. A brand new collection of inappropriate erotic visions sent another hot flash through her body.

Look away from the man booty.

She darted into her bedroom.

Objectification is bad.

She repeated the mantra to herself while throwing on her underwear and some sweats – because there wasn't much point in donning the newly pressed pencil skirt and blouse hanging on the back of her door, seeing as the good ship Professional and Efficient had already sailed into an iceberg. Or rather a volcano.

'Is it fixable?'

Luke glanced over his shoulder at the quiet question. And let out a breath.

Thank the Lord. She was fully clothed. Although even with her flushed skin now swamped in baggy sweats, he could have sworn the sight of Ruby Graham's bountiful curves barely contained by a towel the size of a postage stamp was going to be tattooed on his retinas for all eternity.

He swallowed heavily, unfortunately it didn't do a damn thing to budge the lust still jammed down his throat.

'Not without some parts.'

Her face lit up like a Christmas tree. 'But with the parts you could fix it?'

'I figure I can jerry-rig it so it'll work – but I can't guarantee it'll last.'

'Oh, thank you, that's wonderful. You're a genius,' she said. 'I really really appreciate it.'

'I haven't fixed it yet.'

'Yes, but I know you will.' How the heck did she know that? Were there no bounds to this woman's optimism?

'What do you need? In the way of parts? I'll go get them now,' she added breathlessly.

He let his gaze drift to her head. 'Shouldn't you figure out your hair first?'

Her hand touched the towel wrapped round her head. 'Balls. I forgot. I suppose I'll have to rinse it in cold water after all. The hot water cut out just after I'd dumped the shampoo on it. Would you believe it? Perfect timing all round.'

She tugged off the towel, revealing a wet soapy mass of chestnut curls and the scent of roses drifted towards him. The scent he remembered from when he'd had his hands full of her at the park.

'Bummer,' he murmured.

'Exactly,' she said. 'Why don't you write a list of the things you need while I go do the water torture.'

But as she headed past him, his hand shot out of its own accord and snagged her wrist. 'Wait up. Why don't you heat some water in a pan and I'll rinse it for you?' The minute the offer popped out, he knew it was a mistake.

'*Really?* That would be beyond wonderful.'

He dropped her hand, the sensation sprinting up his arm making the ulterior motives for his generous offer crystal clear. He wanted to sink his fingers into the fragrant mass and find out if it felt as soft and silky as it looked.

Devlin, you dirt bag.

'Or you could do it yourself. Up to you,' he said, giving her an easy out, in case she didn't want his questing fingers testing the silky softness of her hair.

'Honestly, it would be much less of a mess if you did it,'

she said, the light in her eyes not entirely guileless anymore. 'If you don't mind, that is?'

'I don't mind,' he said, following her into a kitchen the size of shoebox.

Seemed like he and Ruby were on the same page. He wasn't entirely sure what page that was, but for once he decided not to get hung up on the small print. Offering to wash her hair was not the same as asking her to drop her postage stamp and let him caress all those bountiful curves until she begged.

He watched her fill a kettle and find a plastic basin and a measuring jug. She hunted up another towel and half-filled the basin with cold water. When the kettle boiled she mixed the hot water in with the cold, then wrapped the towel around her shoulders and bent over the sink.

'Just fill up the jug from the tub and tip it over my head,' she said, her voice muffled by the hair she had swept over her forehead.

He picked up the jug and dipped it into the warm water.

Surely, they couldn't get into too much trouble? He'd never fantasised about washing a woman's hair before, so how erotic could it really be?

The memory of Ruby's breasts pressed against the postage stamp towel echoed through him but he quashed the memory as he rested his thumb and forefinger on her nape below the hairline. Her neck muscles trembled beneath his fingertips – and the jolt of awareness sped up his arm, arrowed down through his torso and shot straight into his crotch with the speed and accuracy of a heat-seeking missile.

Answer: when it was Ruby Graham's hair he was washing, erotic enough to give him an instant woody.

Don't purr.

Ruby chewed on her lip to stop the moan of pleasure coming out of her mouth as Luke's strong firm fingers massaged the base of her skull. Warm water flooded over her head and his caressing fingers moved up her scalp.

Pleasure rippled through her in eddying waves. The heavy weight in her abdomen sunk, making her clitoris purr along with the rest of her body.

His massaging fingers migrated all over her skull, finding the tightly packed muscles behind her ears, the supremely sensitive skin on top of her head, releasing the frown on her forehead.

Just kill me now.

The flowing water only made the sensations more acute as Luke awakened nerve endings that had been in a coma for a very long time.

Perhaps forever.

The five guys she'd slept with – since losing her virginity in the back of Stan McCormack's dad's Skoda Octavia age seventeen – had never made her feel this good when she was actually having sex with them. Not even close.

His magic fingers threaded through the short curls at her nape. She bit her lip hard enough to taste blood, but couldn't choke off the orgasmic sob or stop the full body shiver of pure unadulterated joy.

His fingers paused. 'Are you okay?'

'Absolutely,' she rasped, her voice husky enough to lead a bobsleigh across the North Pole.

'You sure you're not cold?' he said, the magic fingers still withholding their orgasmatronic powers.

Are you bloody kidding me? If I get much hotter I'll spontaneously combust.

'No, no, not at all.' She knew she protested way too much but seriously, if he stopped now she might have to beg. Getting her hair washed by Luke Devlin was the best thing that had happened to her in months. And definitely the best thing *ever* to happen to her sex-wise.

Even though it wasn't supposed to be sexual.

She probably ought to feel guilty that she was exploiting him and his magic fingers and his kind offer to rinse her hair for her own erotic pleasures. But she could feel guilty about it later. Much much later, maybe after she'd had a one-on-one with her vibrator while reliving it first.

He ran his fingers over her scalp, while pouring another dose of the now cooling water over her head. Bliss rippled over her skin and reverberated in her torso, releasing a flood of warmer moisture between her legs.

The moan of pleasure would not be denied this time.

'Ruby? Are you *sure* you're okay?' he said again, but she could hear the rasp of amusement this time.

Did he know what he was doing to her? Was he doing it deliberately?

The thought ought to have mortified her. But she was way past the point of no return now, on her voyage to erotic nirvana. So instead the mocking, self-satisfied tone had the opposite effect, making the heavy weight pulse and ache in her abdomen.

'I'm fine,' she croaked. 'In fact I'm better than fine. I'm ecstatic,' she added, because there wasn't much point keeping it a secret. 'You have a rare talent. You could make a fortune in tips at a women's hair salon.'

'Good to know.' He chuckled, the sound decidedly smug now but all the hotter for it. Lifting the towel she had round her shoulders, he plopped it on her over-sensitized head and gave it a vigorous rub. 'All done,' he said as he let her go.

'Seriously?' she asked unable to keep the pout out of her voice. 'Are you absolutely positive you didn't miss any? It's important to be thorough.'

I begged. Sue me.

'Yeah.' The deep laugh from behind her was its own reward.

What was it about Luke Devlin's rough, rusty laugh that made it even more erotic than his magic orgasmic fingers?

She straightened and turned, taking hold of the towel he'd abandoned as she swiped the now thoroughly rinsed hair out of her face.

He stood with his hip propped against the counter, taking up most of the space in the flat's tiny kitchen, watching her. He had his arms folded over his chest which added even more definition – as if they needed it – to his spectacular pecs and the smooth bulge of his biceps beneath the black T-shirt. The sparkle of mockery only made the pure iridescent blue of his irises more vivid.

'One hundred percent, sure?' she asked, flirting shamelessly with him, because what the hell? He was beautiful and beyond fit and in her kitchen and she didn't have anything else pressing to do right this second – other than save a failing art-house cinema from catastrophic debts. 'I would hate for you to do a half-arsed job and lose out on the impressive tip I was intending to give you.'

His lips quirked, but then he unfolded his arms and ran his thumb down the side of her face. 'Don't tempt me, Ruby,' he said, the wry amusement all the more compelling because the sparkle of amusement in his eyes had faded. 'I've been sporting a boner the size of the Empire State with your name on it for the last five minutes.'

The hot spot between her thighs ignited.

'Don't look,' he said, gripping her chin and holding her head up, just as she went to check out the veracity of his statement.

She tried to wriggle free. 'No fair,' she said, but he held firm. 'I need to see the evidence.'

She managed to jerk her chin out of his grasp, but just as she attempted to dip her gaze, he stepped into her personal space, bracketing her waist and pressing his hips to hers to hide himself from her view.

'Ah, I see what you mean,' she gasped, as the ridge in his jeans imprinted itself on her belly. She could feel every solid inch of him – and there were a lot of inches. Her chin rose so she could meet his gaze as she settled her hands on his lean waist to complete their clinch. He smelled as glorious as he looked. Of salt and spice and sandalwood and juniper berries with an added hint of wild rose shampoo. 'I'd say those proportions are longer and thicker than the Empire State though ...' She tilted her head to one side, considering. Then rolled her hips to get the full measure of him, loving the outline of his strident erection – and rejoicing in the thought that she was the cause of it. 'Perhaps more New World Trade Center,' she mused.

He groaned. 'Jesus, quit it,' he said as she went for a second pass. His hands clamped down on her hips, preventing any more movement down below. 'Who knew? Under that cute-as-a-button exterior, you're a badass,' he said.

He sounded tortured. Her joy increased.

'And your point would be?' She flattened her palms on his pecs, and then let them run riot over the planes of muscle and sinew – which quivered.

Result.

He swore. But with his hands full preventing her hips from moving she had him at her mercy, so why not torture him some more because ... *Cute!* He'd called her cute as a button. When she wasn't cute as a button or anything else, she was a flirty dirty badass. And boy was she proving it.

'Damn. Ruby, don't, I'm not kidding.' He leaned back and her palms paused. 'You need to stop, before this gets out of hand.'

The tortured rasp of his breathing and the desperation in his voice had her lifting her hands, and shoving them behind her back – not easy when his hands were still clamped on her hips.

She could still feel his erection pulsing against her midriff, but what had been hot and joyful and empowering a moment ago now felt the opposite.

When was she going to stop exploiting this man?

Touching without consent wasn't sexy. Ever. She owed him an apology.

'I'm sorry, Luke, I was just teasing you. I ...' She raked her hands through her damp hair. Horrified by her behaviour.

What was *wrong* with her? He'd rinsed her hair and she'd turned into Ruby the rampaging ho. There was absolutely no excuse for it.

'I wasn't going to ...' She shifted, so uncomfortable now her throat closed. 'I wouldn't have taken it any further. I promise. You can let me go now, I absolutely *won't* check out your boner.'

Or salivate. Definitely no salivating. Under any circumstances.

Shame filled her at the salivating still going on in her knickers as he lifted his hands from her hips. She stepped back as far as she could go before her back hit the fridge, and forced her eyeline to remain level with his face to keep her promise.

His skin was flushed and taut. His expression ... Shocked? Disgusted? Wary? Angry? It was impossible to tell. But he had a right to feel all four and more.

For crap sake, Ruby, you just molested him.

How was an apology ever going to compensate him for that?

'I feel terrible, Luke. I don't know what got into me,' she said, but the explanation was lame at best. Because she knew exactly what had got into her.

Forget exploiting and objectifying him, she'd wanted to devour him – his unfortunate physical response like a red rag to her rampaging ho pheromones.

'Will you ever be able to forgive me?' she asked, more

sincerely sorry than she had ever been about anything in her entire life – even agreeing to go all the way in the back seat of Stan McCormack's dad's Skoda Octavia.

'Forgive you for what?' Luke asked, still so horny it was hard to concentrate, because every last drop of blood had left his brain close to ten minutes ago.

But while he was struggling to shift his brain back into gear, one thing he had figured out was that he'd screwed up somewhere, badly, because Ruby looked as if she'd just run over a puppy. Instead of cute and delicious and hotter than a chilli tamale. She'd scrambled out of his arms so fast when he'd let her go that he'd wondered for a second if the lava pouring through his body had scorched her.

Jesus, Devlin, get real, you didn't turn into the Human Torch, it just felt like you did.

'For ... for molesting you,' she murmured, dropping her chin and looking away.

'*For what now?*' he asked. Did she say molesting? Or was his hearing now as compromised as every one of his cognizant brain cells? It must be, because that made no sense.

But then she lifted her head, stared directly at him and he could see the cloud of fresh guilt shadowing her bright green eyes.

'For attacking you, Luke. I got completely carried away. And I feel absolutely awful about it. Especially after traumatizing you last week during the *About a Boy* screening.'

He let the comment about the screening go. Why she felt responsible for his dad's suicide he had no idea. But ...

'Attacking me?' he repeated her words like a dummy, but he couldn't seem to get his blood-deprived brain cells – or what was left of them – to engage with the massive disconnect that had just occurred.

She thought she had attacked him? Molested him? Was she for real?

'Yes, I ...' She stuttered to a halt. Her chin dropped to her chest again.

Goddamn it, she was actually serious.

'Ruby ...' He tucked a knuckle under her chin brought her gaze back to his. 'You didn't do anything wrong. And you sure as *shit* didn't molest me.'

The shadows brightened. 'Are you sure?' Her brows puckered and the shadow darkened again. 'But you begged me to stop? You sounded tortured.'

'Only because I was enjoying it too much,' he said. 'And I wasn't begging.'

He had totally begged, but he was more than emasculated enough by her insistence on taking the blame for something that had been entirely mutual.

At least her misplaced guilt and the mention of his dad's suicide had managed to wilt the New World Trade Center of boners, he thought ruefully as he dropped his hand from her face. Touching her was not a good idea. It had already gotten him in way over his head.

'How could you be enjoying it *too* much?' she asked, the guileless look back, and no less captivating. 'If it was consensual?'

Because I was within seconds of shooting my load in my pants.

'Ruby, it was consensual, will you just take my word for it,' he snapped, frustrated with her now as well as himself.

But damn, this was the freakiest conversation he'd ever had in his life with a woman – and they hadn't even got to second base yet.

Not that he wanted to, he told himself. But he couldn't even convince himself of that anymore when she wetted her lips and his dick started to perk up again.

She blinked at his curt tone. 'Okay, if you're sure.'

'I'm sure. In fact, I'm one hundred and ten percent sure.' Why did he have to keep stating the freaking obvious?

'But then why did you stop me?'

Seriously? They were back to that again? 'Because I was about two seconds away from tugging off your sweats and burying the New World Trade Center of erections deep inside you.'

She flinched – he would guess at his nasty potty mouth – but he resisted the urge to apologise for it. He needed her to know exactly how close he'd come to losing it. So it wouldn't happen again.

Because what had been dirty fun had quickly become ... well, he wasn't even sure what it had become it had happened so fast, but he'd never experienced anything like it before, her touch like a torch paper setting light to his libido. The slow burn was his usual style with women, not hot, hard and horny. He guessed that was probably because he'd spent longer in Ruby's orbit in the last week than he had with most of the women he'd dated.

'Oh.' Her tongue darted out to lick her lips, which was not

helping him in his battle to keep the blood flowing in the right direction.

'Yeah, oh.'

Now she was starting to get it.

Or so he thought, until her brow puckered again.

'So why didn't you, then?'

Oh, for ... 'Because you and me, Ruby, that's not happening.' On that point, he was definite – he'd given it a lot of thought since ... well, since inappropriate thoughts about her had become a regular occurrence. He wasn't even sure when that had happened, but he needed to stop pretending it wasn't happening because then he did dumb things like offering to rinse her hair.

He couldn't sleep with Ruby because their relationship was complicated enough already. His libido would just have to get with the programme.

'But why not,' she said. 'If we both want to?'

Damn but she was persistent. 'That's just it, I don't want to. Not with you.'

'Why not with me? Is there something wrong with me?' She looked offended, and that had not been his intention. So what else was new? 'Am I so unattractive all of a sudden?'

'You know damn well you're not,' he said, not sure if she was fishing for a compliment, or simply trying to piss him off. Either way it was working. 'But that's the whole problem, I'm here for a month, six weeks tops, and I don't need the complication.'

'It doesn't have to be complicated. It's just a biological urge.' She sounded like she meant it. Maybe she did, or thought she did. But she was kidding herself, and he wasn't that easily fooled.

Ruby Graham was a romantic. But unlike his mom, she was also the real deal.

The sort of woman who probably teared up watching cheesy movies, but who wouldn't cry when her heart was breaking. The sort of woman who believed in fighting for hopeless causes, and would happily risk arrest to make a dead guy's dying wish come true.

'Whatever,' he said. 'I'm not indulging my biological urges with you. You're too nice.'

'I'm too ...' Her face screwed up in horror. Okay, he'd upset her now, as well as offending her, but what choice did he have? 'I'm *not* nice,' she sounded appalled. 'I'm a badass, you said so yourself.'

'I wasn't thinking straight when I said that.' Hell, he hadn't been thinking at all. But he was thinking fine now – give or take the odd rush of blood from his brain – and if he couldn't let her down easy, he would just have to let her down hard. 'Don't push me, Ruby, or we'll have to call this whole arrangement off. And I don't want to do that. *Do you?*'

Her face fell and he saw the moment the fight went out of her. 'No, I don't.'

He hooked his thumbs into the front pockets of his jeans, hunched his shoulders, feeling vaguely guilty for putting the defeated look into her eyes. Which was dumb. He'd given it to her straight. He didn't hook up with women who were likely to misconstrue sex for something else. Especially if he was in danger of misconstruing it for something else, too ...

He already liked Ruby, too much. She made him laugh, she seemed genuine, boning her would create problems he did not need.

'You want me to write you that list now?' he asked.

'Just tell me,' she said. 'I've got a very good memory.'

He reeled off the list of things he needed to jerry-rig her boiler, all business again. Unfortunately, he didn't feel all business, as she headed off to purchase the stuff he needed, and he headed down to the theatre's basement to get his tools.

But he'd get there, eventually, he reassured himself – especially if he didn't make the mistake of offering to rinse her hair again any time soon.

Chapter 9

'Luke the Builder's buns are a work of art are they not?' Jacie whispered theatrically as she gazed past the bar at the back of the auditorium to where Luke was busy up a ladder finishing off the repair work on the auditorium's cornice. 'Everything they say about men in tool belts is true,' Jacie purred, as she helped Ruby polish the bar for the start of the LGBTQIA+ weekender in four hours.

'Stop objectifying his arse, Jace, it's so uncool,' Ruby hissed, trying and failing not to glance in Luke's direction herself.

Her scalp bristled from the memory of his fingers circling her skin that morning as he reached forward to mould the last of the filler into the cracks on the cornice.

The man was fitness personified. Seriously, it wasn't fair. Then again, she deserved every ounce of sexual frustration she was suffering from. Maybe if she hadn't molested him this morning after he did her a favour – two favours if you counted his miraculous ability to get her boiler working again – her hormones wouldn't have been in a hot mess ever since.

'Stop being such a killjoy,' Jacie hissed back. 'He can't hear us, and anyway, you've been objectifying those buns of steel, too. I've seen you.'

Ruby swallowed down her retort and sprayed some more polish. Jacie wasn't wrong, and arguing about it with her would just make her think about Luke's buns more and she'd been thinking – and watching – them enough already.

'Hey Ruby,' Gerry appeared from the lobby area, juggling the large mailing box which contained the Brokeback Mountain print and the handset from the phone in the ticket office. 'I'm just gonna take this up to Errol, you wanna check it with us?'

'Sure,' Ruby murmured, although she wasn't sure watching Jack Twist and Ennis Del Mar get hot and bothered in a pup tent was really going to help with her hormonal problem. 'Why have you brought the phone in?'

'Oh, yeah, I forgot.' Gerry placed the parcel full of film reels on the bar. 'There's a lady on the phone asking for the manager of The Royale.' He placed his hand on the mouthpiece. 'I didn't catch her name but she sounded important.'

'Thanks, Gerry.' Ruby took the phone while stifling a sigh.

Important-sounding ladies on the phone could mean one of two things, neither of them good: the bank was calling to harass her about their debit bank balance, again, or one of her suppliers wasn't prepared to wait any longer to get their invoice paid.

'Hello, this is Ruby Graham, I'm the manager of The Royale,' she said into the receiver.

'Ruby, hello, it's so wonderful to finally speak to you at

172

last.' The crisp British accent echoed down the phone line. 'I've been meaning to call you for days.'

'Hi, that's ... thanks,' Ruby said feeling overwhelmed while also completely nonplussed. 'It's wonderful to speak to you, too ...' *I think.*

Ruby's fingers tightened on the handset.

Whoever this woman was, she wasn't calling from the bank or Tasty Treats Gourmet Popcorn, which ought to be good. But Gerry was right, she sounded very important, so important Ruby felt intimidated. Not only that, Ruby recognized that commanding crystal-clear voice, but she couldn't quite place it. Did she know this woman? She didn't sound like the sort of woman you would forget.

'There's no call to thank *me*, my dear,' the woman said with a deep throaty chuckle that sounded even more disturbingly familiar.

Good grief, was sexual frustration now messing with her cognitive skills, too?

'In fact, I believe I am the one who should be thanking *you*,' she added.

Why? Ruby wondered as the strange conversation strayed even deeper into *The Twilight Zone.*

'I ... I see,' Ruby said, although she didn't see at all. 'Could I ask who I'm speaking to? I'm afraid my ...' She struggled for a more upmarket sounding title for Gerry than barman. 'My colleague didn't catch your name.'

'Yes, of course, my dear. Silly me.' The woman gave another smoky chuckle, that finally pierced through the fog of confusion.

173

Was this ...? Surely, it couldn't be? Could it?

'My name's Helena Devlin, darling. I'm Matty's sister,' she added, not that there was any need to clarify that announcement.

Oh. My. Fucking. God.

I'm talking to an actual Broadway legend ... And Rafael Falcone's lover ... And Luke's mum.

'I ... Wow. Hi. It's ... it's such an honour to be talking to you,' Ruby stuttered, almost dropping the phone, pleased she'd managed to stop herself from saying anything completely inane out loud.

She really ought to have recognized the voice immediately. Apart from the fact that Helena Devlin was a stage legend, Ruby had seen *every one* of her movies, and she'd watched her debut, *One Summer in Sorrento*, about thirty times. It was the film the then twenty-two-year-old British ingénue had starred in opposite Rafael Falcone. The film that had kicked off their tempestuous and famously short-lived affair. The film that had effectively created Luke, Ruby realised, as her gaze tracked back to the buns of steel across the auditorium. With his earphones in as he applied the last of the plaster he was oblivious to what was going on.

Both Jacie and Gerry were staring at her expectantly, obviously wondering what had gotten her so flustered.

'No, dear, it is *I* who am honoured,' Helena Devlin announced, sounding more sincere than Halle Berry giving an Oscar acceptance speech.

'*Really?*' Ruby asked. 'Oh? Why?'

'Because I understand you've managed to persuade my son

174

Luke to take leave of absence from his construction firm. Which, believe me, is no small feat. I've certainly never managed it.'

'You … you haven't?'

Helena laughed again, the rich throaty sound making Ruby feel as if she were the most amusing and erudite person on the planet – which seemed unlikely seeing as she was struggling to string a sentence together.

'My dear Ruby, I can't even manage to persuade him to stop by for a ten-minute mimosa break before curtain-up.'

Helena sounded more amused than offended by her son's lack of attention, but Ruby still felt the sting of guilt. And the need to explain herself. 'I really didn't persuade him to come to London. He was sort of forced to,' she said. 'To complete a community service order.'

'*Really?*' It was Helena's turn to sound incredulous. 'A community service order?' she added, sounding intrigued. 'My goodness, what on earth did he do to acquire that? I've never met anyone more boringly law-abiding than my eldest progeny in my entire life.'

My eldest progeny?

Ruby swallowed down her own incredulity as Jacie started flaying her arms about wildly – obviously losing patience with having the identity of the mystery 'important lady' caller revealed.

'Well, we got arrested, about a month ago,' Ruby winced. 'Which was entirely my fault. I asked for Luke's help and, even though he told me not to do it, that it might be illegal, I wanted to do it anyway.' The whole sorry saga began to spill out of Ruby's month. Luke had not been to blame and she really didn't want to get him into any more trouble, especially with his mother. 'And, well ... The Royal Parks police weren't very impressed. Although I still think the young constable who arrested us was a bit over-enthusiastic. I mean, there was no one else about. And it had been Matty's dying wish to have his ashes scattered at the Serpentine. And, I actually think our rendition of "Over the Rainbow" was quite tuneful, considering.'

She finally stopped to draw breath. And realised she could hear Helena chuckling down the other end of the phone line. Not a sarcastic laugh, but a genuine, heartfelt full-bodied inclusive laugh – as if Ruby were part of the joke, not the butt of it. Ruby's anxiety faded a little.

'My darling, that is simply priceless,' Helena murmured. 'I don't know how you managed to get my Luke singing a show tune while scattering my brother's ashes in a park and then getting him arrested but, however you managed it, I salute you. And I'm sure Matty would have adored you for it, too ...' She paused. The rich amusement in her voice had faded when she continued. 'But then I'm sure you know that, if you knew Matty well, and it sounds as if you did.'

'Yes, I did.' Ruby's throat began to clog. This was so surreal, to be talking to Matty's sister about him. The sister he hadn't talked to in more than thirty years. She wondered if Matty would see this conversation as a betrayal. After all, he'd had a thirty-something-year-old feud with this woman. But as soon as the thought occurred to her, she dismissed it. On the very few occasions Matty had mentioned Helena, or spoken about her, he had never seemed angry with his sister, more sad and disappointed. Ruby had no idea what had caused their long silence, she'd always sort of assumed Helena must have instigated it, but now she wasn't so sure. Maybe it was some silly disagreement that they'd never had a chance to resolve.

'I did know him. I loved your brother a great deal,' Ruby found herself saying as the familiar tears leaked out of her eyes. 'Matty was my best friend for a long time. And he always will be.'

'I know that feeling, my dear,' Helena said, her voice rough with sympathy and understanding. 'He was my best friend, too … once. And I've missed him more than you can imagine over the last thirty-one years. What fools we both were not to bury that hatchet a long time ago. And now I will never have that chance. I feel devastated about that. I'm so glad that, while I was foolishly holding on to my pride, he had someone like you to look after him.'

'I didn't look after him,' Ruby said, her voice broke as the tears she thought she'd finally gotten a handle on over the last few weeks started to strangle her again. 'He looked after me.'

The strange *Twilight Zone* conversation continued, but the ball of grief that had made Ruby feel wretched for so long, didn't feel quite so wretched as Helena spoke to her about her brother. Ruby could hear the raw edge of grief in the actress's rich resonant voice – a voice that had entertained kings and presidents and seduced a movie icon – and Ruby realised for the first time she was speaking to someone who understood the full extent of how hard her life was going to be without Matty.

Every morning when she woke up, for a split-second, she would believe Matty was still alive, but then the truth would slam into her again, and shove her into the deep bottomless pit which she would have to drag herself out of to function.

And no one else truly understood how deep and black and all-consuming that pit was. Because no one else had ever depended on Matty or loved him, or enjoyed his cheesy taste in movies or his daft exploits or his ridiculous sense of humour as much as she had.

But as Helena spoke, Ruby realised even if Helena hadn't talked to her brother in over thirty years, Helena understood about that bottomless pit, how cold and black and ugly and unforgiving it was, because she had been in it a great deal longer.

Ruby sniffed and chuckled weakly, turning her back on Jacie and Gerry who now both looked appalled, while clinging to Helena's voice and the distinctive rasp of emotion in it she recognized from *One Summer in Sorrento*. The tears flowed freely down her cheeks, as she listened to a wonderful anecdote about Matty from forty years ago.

Helena Devlin knew. Helena Devlin understood.

And for the first time in months, Ruby felt less alone.

Luke pressed the last of the plaster into the damaged moulding with his fingertips while The Strokes banged out 'Last Night' on his ear buds. The raw angry lyrics fit his mood as he wiped his fingers on his overalls and reached round to pluck the moist piece of cloth from his tool belt. Plastering of this sort was hard sweaty precision work, but The Royale deserved the care he was giving it. He'd never seen such intricate moulding in a building of this sort. And concentrating on the plaster-work and The Strokes' date night disaster song was keeping his mind off Ruby and their boiler date that wasn't from a couple of hours ago.

But as he stretched to wipe the last of the residue, a tug on his overalls startled him so much he almost toppled off the ladder. He whipped out an ear bud to find Jacie the thea-tre's assistant manager standing below him. The troubled look in her usually lively brown eyes had him swallowing down the swear word about to bounce off his tongue.

'What's up?' he asked, because something was clearly up. From the few interactions he'd had with Jacie he knew she liked checking out his butt and didn't make any secret of it, that she was nosey and more than willing to hold a grudge against him for not stepping in to fund the theatre. But he also knew she was Ruby's fiercest defender.

'It's Ruby,' she said without any preamble. 'I think she's having a breakdown talking to your mother.'

'Huh?' The tension in his gut he always got when his mother was mentioned had him tightening his grip on the ladder.

'Helena Devlin, your mother,' Jacie said, as if she were talking to a dumb toddler. 'She's on the phone to Ruby right now and Ruby's in floods of tears. I've never seen her so weepy. Not even at the hospital when they told us Matty was gone.'

'Fuck!' Luke jumped off the ladder, ignoring the wobble

in his knees and marched across the auditorium towards the woman he'd been trying to ignore for the last two hours. Jacie scrambled after him.

Ruby stood with her back to them both, her shoulders hunched and trembling. Gerry sat next to her on a bar stool looking even more troubled than Jacie.

Ruby had changed into a pair of skinny jeans and a Pride in London T-shirt, Luke noted. The heat pulsed in his abdomen, as it did every time he got within a few feet of her, but he ignored that, too.

So not *the damn time.*

What was his mom playing at? What the hell was she saying to Ruby to make her cry? And how the heck had she gotten this number? The only two people he'd told his true whereabouts to were Gwen and his kid sister Becca, who he'd given the information to in case of a family emergency. And Gwen was a rock.

Becca? You didn't? You're a dead woman.

He tried to dial down on his fury with his kid sister. He of all people knew how hard his mom's probing was to resist when she went the full Spanish Inquisition on your ass. But as he touched Ruby's shoulder, she glanced round, and the fury lanced through him again.

Nope, Becca was definitely going to have to die.

The freckles on Ruby's cheeks were raw, her eyes dazed with sadness.

'Hey, what's up, are you okay?' he said, even though the question seemed kind of redundant, because she was clearly not okay.

Despite all the damning evidence to the contrary, she bobbed her head, still clinging to the handset. 'I'm ... yes ... I'm talking to Helena.' A wobbly smile lifted her lips that only made him madder. 'I mean, I'm talking to your mother about Matty.'

It was all the evidence he needed. Resting his hand on her shoulder, in a vain attempt to relieve her trembling, he lifted the phone out of her fingers. 'Can I speak to her?'

'Yes, of course.' Ruby handed over the phone, the flash of colour backlighting the moisture on her cheeks.

Becca wasn't the only one who was going to die now.

'*Mom?*' he barked into the mouthpiece.

'Luke, my darling, it's so wonderful to hear your—'

The fury surged. 'I'll call you back,' he interrupted the effusive greeting. Did she really think he was going to let her get away with this? 'But don't you dare call this number again or there will be consequences. Do you understand?'

'Luke? What are you—'

He dropped the phone and clicked off the handset. Then clicked it on again to block any return calls. He knew his mom: consequences – especially unspecified ones not written in blood – weren't an effective deterrent. And getting a busy signal when she was intent on contacting someone was the one thing guaranteed to drive her nuts.

Deal with it, Mom. While I deal with the fallout from your latest emo-bomb.

He dumped the handset on the bar.

'*Luke!*' Ruby's waterlogged eyes had gone wide with shock. 'Why did you speak to your mother like that?'

'Don't worry, it's how we roll,' he said, cutting off that line of conversation, because the last thing he wanted to do was discuss his dysfunctional relationship with his mom, or give the woman who had put that sad look in Ruby's eyes a single extra ounce of attention.

Ruby wasn't a crier – she was tough and tenacious and brave. She didn't do fake emotions. But his mother made a living out of them. And Ruby was a babe in the woods when it came to dealing with his mother's particular brand of emotional manipulation.

Keeping his hand on her shoulder, he leaned past her to grab a couple of paper napkins out of the dispenser on top of the bar. He dabbed her cheeks. 'Now, tell me the truth – are you okay?'

A new wave of tears flooded over her lids and she gave a little hiccup. Then she shook her head.

'I guess not. I'm sorry, it's silly, really,' she said, taking the wad of napkins from him and scrubbing her own cheeks. 'I didn't mean to make such a scene,' she added, tangling the damp tissue in her fingers. 'It's just so hard sometimes. I miss him so much. But it was nice to talk about Matty with your Mum, really it was. I think she's the only person who misses him as much as I do.'

'Uh-huh.' He nodded back, struggling to sound sympathetic while the fury choked him.

So his mom had called the theatre to share reminiscences with Ruby about a guy she hadn't contacted in thirty-one years? Like hell. He had no idea what his mom's true motives were, but he wasn't buying the let's-share-our-pain one for a second. He'd have to deal with that melodrama another time though, because first he had to take the devastation out of Ruby's eyes.

'Could you use a hug?'

The flash of shock at his offer made him feel like an asshole.

It was true, he wasn't a natural-born hugger, but he did make important exceptions. Like when Becca's hamster had been eaten by the ginger tom his mom was starring opposite during the shoot of a low-budget kids comedy in Spain, or when his brother Jack's dad Bill – who they had all adored – had died tragically during a storm at sea off the coast of Maine ten years back, or when his mom had won her second Tony a year ago. Although he really wished he hadn't made an exception on that occasion when the stolen shot of the two of them backstage had been juxtaposed with clinch shots of his mom and Falcone in their only movie together and gone viral as a creepy, vaguely incestuous meme with the tagline 'Helena Devlin: Being only as old as the man you feel'.

His mom, of course, had adored that meme. '*I do love to be current.*'

'You don't mind?' Ruby said, clearly concerned she would be taking advantage of him again.

And he wanted to kick his own ass for making her scared to touch him that morning.

'Nope,' he said, spreading his arms wide and tugging her into his body.

She stepped into his embrace, tucked her head under his chin and ran her own arms around his waist to hug him back. Her fingers trembled as she clung to him. The silent shudders while the last of the storm battered her, had his heart rising into his throat. He rubbed her back and racked his brain for something to say, that might alleviate at least a little of her grief.

But really what was there to say? Her loss was huge. She hadn't just lost her best friend, she was about to lose her job and her home. Not for the first time, the thought of loaning her the money she would need for the debt skimmed through his consciousness. But he forced himself to let it pass by and land back in the box marked Bad Ideas.

He was entangled enough in this situation already. And loaning her the money might solve the immediate problem, but it would only create more problems down the line. He was going to be gone in four weeks at the most – after checking the repairs that needed doing, he'd decided to extend his stay through the end of May – but come June 20th, Ruby was still going to have a stark choice.

He couldn't replace his uncle as her guardian angel, he just wasn't cut out for the job.

The shuddering finally stopped as the storm passed. Ruby's deep sigh against Luke's neck sent a cloud of her scent – floral sin and rose shampoo – into his nostrils. His hands tightened on her lush curves, before he forced himself to let her go and step back.

She looked at him through tear-gilded lashes. 'Thank you, I think I needed that,' she said, the embarrassed heat in her face, and the honesty and integrity in her gaze only making her more luminous.

'You're welcome,' he said. 'You want to take a break for the rest of the day?' he asked. 'I'm sure me and the rest of the crew can handle the clear up.'

'No, I'm good. Really, I am,' she said, sounding much more sure now. She glanced around the auditorium. 'And I love seeing this place get the care it deserves.'

He dismissed the guilty pang that wrapped around his ribs.

'Why don't we start watching *Brokeback Mountain?*' Gerry said, holding up a reel of film. 'Errol can thread it up in no time. Do you want to join us, Luke?'

Luke frowned. Was the guy serious? Wasn't that movie a tragedy? Didn't the cowboys die at the end?

But before he could say anything, Ruby had pasted a brave smile on her face. 'You know, Gerry, I think that would be an excellent idea. Matty adored that movie, even though he said it was a gay movie for straight people, it always made him cry. And I'd love to have a chance to clean out my sinuses over a sad movie for a change.'

As Jacie stepped up to give her a hard hug, Luke stepped away.

'Luke, if you want to stay, we'd love to have you,' Ruby said.

'Sure,' he said.

She was being kind to Gerry by humouring his asinine suggestion. She couldn't really want to watch a movie about lovelorn cowboys while she was feeling like shit. So he'd stay and watch it with her. Make sure she didn't get too shaky again.

It was the least he could do – after his mom had played fast and loose with her grief. And later today, after he'd let his mom stew in her own juices for a while, he was going to call her back, and give her hell for screwing with Ruby's karma. And his own.

'Mom, seriously, what the hell were you thinking?' Luke kept his voice low and even.

He had finally relented and called his mother's cell from the phone in his house in Chepstow Villas after he'd order in some take out and eaten it. It was close to eight p.m. UK time so he'd left her stewing for over six hours, it still didn't feel long enough.

'Darling, I don't know what you mean.' *Yeah, right.*

'Ruby Graham is grieving, she scattered her best friend's ashes barely two months ago,' Luke added, his voice rising as the memory of Ruby's tear-streaked cheeks blasted back into his memory and made him mad all over again. 'Her emotions are shaky at best, she does not need you calling her out of the blue, playing the heartbroken sister and driving her emotions off a cliff.'

He'd been forced to sit through one of the most tragic films ever made to keep an eye on Ruby that afternoon. To her credit, she'd been a rock during the three-plus-hour endurance test as they watched Jake Gyllenhaal and Heath Ledger act their asses off. But he'd been watching her like a hawk before he'd headed out, for any signs of a wobble, and he'd seen her chin tremble more than enough times to know Ruby's tough-it-out routine had been an act.

Ruby was still shaky, still devastated, still way too close to the cliff-edge for his liking. And he planned to get it through his mom's skull that she was not to contact Ruby and freak her out again.

'But I *am* the heartbroken sister,' his mother replied. 'And all I did was talk to her about Matty. It was good for us both. You may find it easy to close off your emotions, but not everyone else can do that,' she finished, sounding hurt.

Yeah, he wasn't buying that either.

As usual his mother was avoiding the actual problem to take a detour into yet another conversation about his 'withholding issues.'

'And how was it good for you, Mom?' he asked, changing the subject right back again. He was pretty good at playing the deflect-and-rule game, after all, he'd learned how from a master. 'You actually want me to buy you gave a crap about Matthew Devlin when you had refused to speak to him for over thirty years?'

'I didn't refuse to speak to him, he refused to speak to me,' she said, still sounding hurt. 'For a very good reason. I did something unforgiveable.'

So what else is new, Mom?

'Whatever,' he said, already bored. The details of his mom's feud with his uncle had jack shit to do with him. And while it was super rare for his mother to admit culpability for anything, he still wasn't buying the contrite routine. 'Just don't call her again.'

'But I wanted to visit The Royale when I'm in town,' she said. 'I'd love to meet Ruby. She sounds adorable. And I wanted to talk to you both about—'

'Wait up. Wait a damn minute,' Luke cut in as every one

of his freak-out vibes freaked out. 'Did you just say you're coming to London?'

Hell, no. This could *not* be happening. He thrust his fingers through his hair, the mild headache caused by the emo-fest this afternoon morphing into an all-out migraine.

'I'm going to be in London next week,' she said. 'I'm doing my one-woman show at the National in June for a limited run. They had an unexpected gap in their schedule. I found out about it, made the suggestion to my agent, he talked to *Gypsy*'s Broadway producer, and the general manager at the National. It just seemed so fortuitous. I'm celebrating thirty-five years in the business this year and I wanted to come back to my home town during our break on Broadway. Especially when I discovered my first-born was in town, too. We start rehearsals in a couple of weeks.'

No. No. No.

Luke could feel his break – which had already gotten more confusing than he would have liked – turning into the massive fuck-mageddon he'd been trying to avoid.

'You're not visiting The Royale, or meeting Ruby.'

'But I wanted to talk to you both about ...' she began again.

'You're not listening to me, mom, I'm not kidding, if you show up at the movie theatre, I will cut you out of my life for good.' It was extreme, but then extreme was the only language his mom understood.

His palms were starting to sweat, his heart punching his rib cage. He wasn't even sure why he was so dead set against Ruby and his mom getting together. He just knew it would not be good. For all of her self-absorption, his mom could be pretty damn intuitive, and he didn't want her intuiting anything about his friendship with Ruby.

'Luke, you don't sound well, are the anxiety attacks back?'

'Not yet,' he growled. But they soon would be if she didn't listen to him. He didn't want her here. He could feel the box he'd spent his childhood trying to escape folding in around him.

Holding his hand over the mouthpiece he forced himself to breathe. And count. The way the CBT therapist had trained him to do as a fourteen-year-old when these dumb attacks had started.

In. One, two, three. Out. One, two, three.

'If you really don't want me coming to The Royale, I won't come,' she said.

'Good.' *In. One, two, three.* 'Don't.' *Out. One, two, three …*

'But I wanted to tell you about something. You *and* Ruby. It's about Matty. And me. And your father.'

In. One, two, three. 'You're not meeting Ruby.' *She doesn't need this shit any more than I do. Out. One, two, three …*

Whatever nonsense his mother had to impart, he was not dragging Ruby into the drama. She had enough drama in her life already.

'Okay, just you then. I suppose you can tell Ruby. Perhaps you could come to my hotel for lunch next Friday …' She paused then added. 'Assuming you're sure you don't want me to pop into The Royale, instead?'

The counted breathing had slowed his pulse down to frigid. 'That's blackmail, Mom.'

'I know, dear,' his mother said without an ounce of remorse. 'But how else am I supposed to get you to come see me?'

Chapter 10

The following Friday at noon, Luke walked into the lobby of the Mayfair Grand, London's most prestigious and exclusive six-star hotel. The old-world elegance of marble, mahogany, gilt-edged mirrors and expensive flower arrangements were a reminder of the thousand and one similar high-end hotels all over the globe he'd stayed in as a kid when his mom's career had hit the heights. The latent anxiety of running herd on his daredevil brother and kid sister – and attempting to stop them wrecking the joint – while his mom was either 'resting' or 'doing lines' added to the low level hum of anxiety which had been sitting in his stomach since the week before.

He didn't have time for this. He needed to get back to The Royale. He had some more detail work he wanted to finish on the moulding before the matinee kicked off at four.

His mom was getting exactly thirty minutes for her heart-to-heart.

He approached the concierge desk and tugged the ball cap he was wearing lower. 'Hi, I'm here to see Helena Devlin in The Queen's Suite.' *How appropriate.* 'Could you tell me how to get there?'

'Of course. Who shall I say is calling?' The distinguished older man asked picking up the house phone.

'She's expecting me, could you just give me the directions.' He wasn't giving a name. It was bad enough his mom was making him show his face in the West End at a hotel renowned for its VIP and celebrity clientele. As it was he'd turned up a half hour ahead of schedule in case she'd arranged a reception committee.

'Certainly, sir, once I've informed Ms Devlin of your visit. I'm afraid it's hotel policy,' the man replied, his eyes widening a fraction as Luke met his gaze. Apparently, there was no need to give the guy his name, but the man was obviously well trained enough not to comment.

After dialling his mother's suite, and informing her 'her guest' had arrived, the concierge covered the receiver. 'Ms Devlin has suggested you meet her in The Salon Grill for lunch.'

'Tell Ms Devlin, I'll meet her in her suite or not at all.'

If you think you're getting another viral meme from this visit, Mom, you're on crack.

The concierge conferred with his mother, and then gave him directions to the suite. Finally.

When he knocked on the door five minutes later, his palms were damp. He rubbed them on his jeans.

His mom opened the door with a flourish. Dressed in one of her multi-coloured silk lounging kaftans, her feet bare, her toenails painted mailbox-red, her defiantly raven hair wrapped in a matching silk bandana and her still virtually unlined skin devoid of make-up she looked as if she were about to open a production of *Woodstock the Musical*.

'Luke, my darling boy,' she said, throwing her arms around him in an extravagant hug and surrounding him in a cloud of patchouli perfume as she air-kissed him on both cheeks. 'What a wonderful surprise, you're early!'

'Yeah, surprise,' he said, playing along half-heartedly, as he gave her a brief hug, kissed her cheek and stepped into the room to slam the door behind him. 'What did you need to talk to me about, I haven't got long.'

'Luke, will you stop it with the grumpy attitude.' His mother chastised him. 'I haven't seen you in months. Come in and sit down – I thought I could order us up some lunch.' She sent him a blinding smile over her shoulder as she wafted into the Suite's elaborate lounge area which had an impressive view over Green Park.

Luke wasn't impressed.

'And you can tell me all about Ruby,' his mother added. 'I love her already and I haven't even met her.'

Ah-ha, so that's what this is, the perennial probe into my love life.

'No lunch, I haven't got time. But I'll take coffee, if you've got it.' He felt himself relax a little as he sat down on one of the suite's matching leather sofas. His mother's intrusion into his private life was nothing new. 'And, FYI, Ruby and I are not dating,' he added, getting straight to the point. Telling her the subject of Ruby was off-limits would only encourage her curiosity; better to simply nip that line of enquiry in the bud.

'Which is precisely what makes her so intriguing,' his mom replied, not having her bud nipped in the least. 'She sounded so sweet and adorable on the phone,' she added as she fired up a state-of-the-art coffee machine on the sideboard.

'You can be intrigued all you want, we're still not going to be dating any time soon,' he said. 'She's not my type. Way too sweet and adorable,' he added, with a theatrical shudder.

His mother laughed, the deep throaty laugh he had once adored as a kid because it usually meant she was about to spring something fun on them – like a spur-of-the-moment trip to Disney World, or VIP tickets to see the Yankees in the play-offs, or a road trip to Maine so they could hang out with Bill Newman, Jack's dad, for the summer. But he'd learned to like that laugh less and less as he grew older and discovered the fun almost always came with a price. A price which he would usually be forced to pay.

'*Touché*,' his mother said. 'But I believe the fact she's not your usual type is another thing which makes her so intriguing. Is she pretty?'

Stunning.

The thought echoed in his head, as the memory of her a week ago with wet hair and a saucy smile echoed in his groin. And of the days since, whenever he'd bumped into her at the theatre. He'd spent far too much time in the last seven days watching her go about her business each morning, usually while humming a show tune, as she held her grief in check.

'She's okay, I guess.' He shrugged. 'If you like wholesome.' *And built and hot and honest and smart and brave.*

'Hmmm, I see,' his mother said, her eagle-eyed gaze not buying his indifference. 'Funny that for such a wholesome girl she managed to get you arrested.'

'She didn't get me arrested. *I* got me arrested. And it was only a misdemeanour.'

'A misdemeanour that got you slapped with community service that you've relocated to London and rearranged your whole schedule to accommodate. And you're still speaking to her. In fact, you're not just speaking to her ...' She ladled fresh coffee in the machine and flicked on the switch. 'Don't think I didn't notice how you rode to her rescue last week when your big bad mother started harassing her with her over-sharing.'

'She was crying. I needed to close it down. You know how tears freak me out.' Not true, but he wasn't above using his mom's fake-shrink shit against her. 'And I agreed to do the community service because it was a court order, and The Royale needs work – most of which is cosmetic, luckily – before she can sell it.'

His mother's hand jerked, splashing milk over the two china cups she'd laid out on the sideboard. 'Why is she selling Matty's Cinema?'

'Because we have to. It hasn't been economically viable as a business for over a decade, and there are a ton of debts to pay,' he said, glad to offer up the information if it would shove his mom off the topic of him and Ruby. Weirdly, though, he'd heard the distress in his mother's voice when she'd mentioned her brother's name and for once, it didn't sound like an act.

'*We?*' She wiped the milk off her fingers. 'Why we? Did Matty leave a share of the cinema to you?'

Shit.

He'd been busted, giving up information he hadn't intended

to give up. But what surprised him was his mother had jumped so quickly to that conclusion thanks to his slip, that was spooky intuitive, even for her ... unless ...

Maybe she knew more about her brother's bequest and the reasons behind it? Hadn't she said something last week on the phone, about a story she had to tell him and Ruby about Matty and her and Falcone? He shook off the moment of curiosity.

Whatever story she had to tell – and he was sure it was a doozy because his mom's stories always were – he'd already figured out the reason behind his uncle's surprise bequest.

'Yeah,' he said. 'Your brother left me a half-share in the movie theatre in his will. And the rest to Ruby. He must have figured I'd cover the debts. But that's not happening,' he reiterated, for his own benefit as much as his mother's. 'I'm a property developer, not a cinema owner. And I'm not interested in becoming one.'

He braced himself for his mom to attempt to change his mind. She was the queen of emotional investments after all – one of the reasons he'd spent so much of his childhood living out of a suitcase. But instead of commenting, she sat down in the chair opposite him. Not sat, kind of collapsed. Gracefully, because she did everything with grace. But her hands were shaking and her face had gone a sickly shade of grey. For a moment, he tried to convince himself it was another of her acts. But even *she* wasn't that good an actress he decided. Her lucid eyes lifted to his and when she spoke, her voice quivered with emotion – genuine heartbreaking emotion.

'That's not why Matty left you a half-share in The Royale, Luke.'

The tension in his stomach twisted, but he still couldn't prevent himself from asking the obvious next question. 'Then why did he?'

'Because you were Rafe's son. And Rafe was the love of Matty's life.'

The information had Luke's discomfort at the original bequest increasing tenfold, along with his outrage on Ruby's behalf.

'That's kind of an extreme thing to do, even if Falcone was an idol of his ...' he murmured.

What kind of a best friend gave half of what should rightfully have been yours to some random relative just because he looked like the movie icon they'd once had a crush on? He'd always known the Falcone nuts were nuts. But Matty Devlin's bullshit bequest took that insane devotion to a whole new level.

'You don't understand, Luke,' his mother said, still looking stricken. 'Rafe wasn't just the love of Matty's life. Matty was the love of Rafe's life. And I destroyed their relationship, when I got pregnant with you.'

Chapter 11

'I can't believe Devlin didn't come back this afternoon like he promised,' Jacie said as she loaded the hoover back into the supply cupboard after the final clean-up. 'Do you know where he went?'

'No, I don't.' Ruby sighed. 'I'm not his keeper, Jace.' Not even close.

Luke had left before lunch saying he'd be back in an hour and then never reappeared. And she'd missed him. Too much. How had he become such an important fixture after only two weeks? His steady, capable, competent, mostly silent presence, something she had come to rely on? And that was without even factoring in last week's shock hug while she was having her Matty meltdown after his mother's call.

Being able to sink into his strong arms, feel his warm breath on the back of her neck and hear the solid thud of his heartbeat pounding against her ear had been pretty much the best thing that had happened to her for a long long time. Well, the best PG-rated thing to happen to her.

Don't think about Hairgate.

She needed to get over needing him, and missing him,

because sooner rather than later Luke and his strong arms and steel buns and steady, capable presence would be gone. And today had been a timely reminder of that fact, for them all.

'Perhaps we should inform the magistrate's court of his no-show?' Jace said, propping her fists on her hips. 'He *is* supposed to be doing three hundred hours you know.'

Ruby shut the safe where they kept the night's takings and whizzed the dial to lock it.

'We most certainly are not going to be doing any such thing, Jace,' she said as calmly as she could. Jacie's heart was in the right place, but she needed to get over her animosity towards Luke. The guy had been The Royale's very own super-hero so far, working long hours, fixing seats and toilets and a host of other equipment that had been broken for a long time, not to mention starting to return the theatre's infrastructure to its former glory. 'From the schedule Luke's outlined,' she continued, because Jacie still looked like she wanted to argue, 'he's going to be doing five times that number of hours over the next few weeks. I don't even want to think how much money it's costing him to rent a house in Chepstow Villas and keep his business in New York on hold. He probably had a boardroom emergency today he couldn't tell us about ...'

The tickle of anxiety, which had been getting worse ever since Luke had failed to turn up at one thirty that afternoon, clawed at Ruby's throat.

'All I care about is that it's not any other kind of emergency ...' If he'd been hurt, or injured in any way, she'd never forgive herself. Perhaps he'd had to return to America. Was that the real reason his mother had called? To inform Luke of some family disaster? Because Ruby still couldn't get her head around the idea of Helena Devlin ringing The Royale to talk to her. Or why Luke had spoken to his mother so harshly ...

Stop right there, Rubes, not your business.

Ruby steered Jacie through the bar, into the foyer and towards the front door. 'Why don't you head home, I can finish locking up. I've got a long hot bubble bath and a chilled glass of pinot waiting for me before I crash headlong into bed.' Running a cinema and panicking at the same time were exhausting.

'Fine,' Jacie said as they reached the front door. 'But if he's a no-show again tomorrow, we should probably ...'

'If he's a no-show tomorrow, I'm going to start calling hospitals,' Ruby said, as the anxiety sunk its claws into her chest.

Whatever the emergency was, Luke would have let her know, unless he couldn't let her know.

'Now, piss off so I can panic in peace,' she said, as she shoved her assistant manager out the front door.

'He's not hurt, he's just a rich, arrogant, entitled guy,' Jacie said, but even she looked concerned now. 'With great bone structure.'

'Don't forget the buns of steel,' Ruby said as Jacie stepped out of the door.

Jacie nodded. 'I hope we get to ogle them some more tomorrow.'

'Ditto. See you at eleven,' Ruby said, as she closed the door then pressed the button on the inside to engage the outer metal shutters.

Jacie saluted before heading off down the street to the tube.

Ruby listened to the electric clatter of the shutter descending, and swallowed past the ball of anxiety.

Luke Devlin was not lying on a hospital slab somewhere, she told herself. He was probably on a first-class flight to New York, or negotiating some mega-deal at his luxury home in Chepstow Villas. If he didn't show tomorrow, she could always phone his assistant Gwen, and make a polite enquiry as to his whereabouts.

She needed to start looking on the bright side again, and being practical and pragmatic and optimistic instead of heading straight to Death and Destruction Street without passing Go every time something when awry.

Not every unexpected event ends in tragedy.

She was still trying to convince herself, when the toes of a pair of work boots she recognized appeared on the pavement below the descending shutter.

'Luke?' She gasped, all of her fear sucked into a vortex of relief and joined by the shimmer of excitement which always sprinted up her spine when Luke arrived each morning.

'Ruby? Hey, can you open up, I'm here to finish the moulding.'

To finish the moulding … Was he serious? In the middle of the night?

She flipped the shutter button in the opposite direction, excitement rippling across her nerve endings despite her confusion, as his long, rangy, stupidly gorgeous body – broad and dependable in shirt, jeans, T-shirt and work boots – was slowly revealed. Even backlit by the street light, he looked glorious. And upset about something, she realised as his striking face was finally illuminated by the security lighting in the lobby.

'Luke is everything okay?' she said as she unlocked the door and flung it open.

'I missed our date,' he said.

Date? What date? They'd had a date and she'd forgotten about it?

'I should have been here ...' He tugged his phone out of his back pocket, his movements more deliberate and a little less graceful than usual. 'Shit!' He thrust his fingers through his hair, making the silky strands stand up in sexy tufts. 'Ten hours ago. I'm sorry. But I can work through the night.'

Right, he was talking about their DIY date. Ruby's excitement downgraded a notch. But her relief he was not dead from an undiagnosed heart condition was still palpable. Add that to the common or garden sizzles that always occurred whenever Luke was in the building and Ruby was dangerously on edge.

'You don't have to do that Luke, it's okay. I'll see you tomorrow.'

She should get him to leave, before her need got the better of her again and she started to beg.

'But I want to do it, for you,' he said. His hand lifted and he cupped her cheek. 'Jesus, you're so beautiful.'

'*I am?*' she choked. Then wanted to slap herself.

Way to sound like you're shamelessly fishing for a compliment, Rubes.

'Yeah, how come you don't know that?' he said, the rough

calluses stroking her skin making the sizzles become seismic waves. 'Surely a ton of guys must have told you that already?'

'Well, not exactly a ton,' she said, seamlessly switching from shameless to coy.

He lifted his other hand to cradle her face and hold it steady, his wild blue eyes so full of sexual promise she thought her knickers might actually explode.

'Can I kiss you?' he murmured, his breath skimming over her lips as he lowered his head. 'Watching Jake and Heath go for it last week with you sitting right next to me squirming got me so hot. Tasting you is all I've been thinking about ever since.'

Tasting you?

Wait a minute. Who were Jake and—? Oh, goodness, *Brokeback Mountain*.

Embarrassment scorched her cheeks.

So, he'd felt her squirming while they'd watched Jack and Ennis finally release all of their pent-up passion in that pup tent. But the rush of mortification was swift and short-lived.

Had he just said it had made him hot, too?

He had, he definitely had.

The kissing action in that film was so passionate and so urgent. But not as passionate and urgent as the intent in Luke's for once unguarded gaze as he searched her face waiting for her permission.

'Yes please,' she said, before she could second-guess herself.

And then his lips were on hers. Hot, firm, ravenous and tasting of spiced rum.

Was Luke foxed?

The thought occurred to her, but she had no time to engage with it, before he was ravishing her mouth, his tongue licking across her lips to demand entry.

She opened for him, feeling more than a little drunk herself on the pheromones racing round her body.

She gripped his shirt, pressing against his muscular body, feeling the distinct shiver of response.

His fingers delved into her hair and tugged her head back, exposing her neck. His lips fastened on her pulse point, sucking, nipping, caressing, until her rapid pants echoed around the foyer.

She dragged in a shaky breath. Was this actually happening? And did it have any right to feel this astonishing?

He stopped suddenly, lifting his head, and met her gaze.

She waited, seeing the knowledge in his expression. Waited for him to tell her this wasn't happening, that it was a mistake.

If he was drunk, she probably ought to call a halt to it herself.

But he didn't look drunk. Despite the sweet aroma of the rum on his breath. He looked entirely in charge of his faculties, just more urgent, more passionate, more volatile than she'd ever seen him before.

So she waited, his harsh breathing matching her own. And worked out a convincing argument for why they had to take this to its logical conclusion. They could do this, even if it was just for one night, one quickie, one more kiss. It didn't have to be a big deal, a lifelong commitment. She knew he was rich and successful and looked like a god ...

Okay, maybe don't say that.

Luke was touchy about his looks and he still thought she was a Falcone nut, even though she'd been a Luke nut exclusively for a week.

Perhaps she should beg. Mortification was a price she would happily pay if he'd let her jump him, just for tonight.

His hands dropped, and he stepped back. She braced herself, all of her arguments ganging up so fast she couldn't quite spit them out.

But then he grasped her hand and leading her back to the door, leaned over to flick the switch.

The shutter roared down again.

Did this mean what she thought it did? Were Thunderbirds Go?

Anticipation and excitement and panic combined in the pit of her stomach to create a perfect storm of anxiety and need.

The shutter hit the ground and rattled, shocking her out of her desperate conversation with herself. Luke pressed the button to lock it then marched across the foyer towards the door to her flat, her hand still grasped tightly in his. As if he would never let it go.

They climbed the stairs in silence.

The flat was dark, but he didn't stop to turn on any lights, simply headed down the corridor, past her kitchen, the bathroom, the boiler cupboard, to the bedroom at the back.

She had a momentary panic the room might be a tip. But when he opened the door wide, the light from the street outside illuminated the waterfall of throw cushions, and the fairy lights she must have left on when she'd come up to have her dinner during the evening show. The room looked magical, especially when he swung her round and grasped her hips.

She could feel the thick erection she'd felt once before. He glanced around the room, then his gaze landed back on her.

Pressing his hands to her cheeks, tucking her hair behind her ears, his face sunk into the soft skin under her ear lobe and he murmured against her neck.

'Thank fuck you haven't got any posters of my old man in here or I would have had to jump you on the fire escape.'

She laughed, the giddy joy of being wanted, of being needed, of feeling sexy and desired, enough to send her excitement into the stratosphere.

'Don't worry, I would have chucked it out the window if necessary,' she said gasping as his lips worked their magic on her pulse point, and his wide, callused capable hands lifted her dress and sunk into her knickers.

She hissed, as one blunt finger found the slick seam of her sex.

'Jesus, you're so wet.' He groaned.

'I'm sorry ...' she began, not sure why she was apologising.

'Don't be. I want to taste you all over now.'

'Then do ...' she murmured, past caring if she sounded needy. She wanted this to happen before he changed his mind. She didn't know what had upset him today to make him so eager, so intense. Because something had definitely upset him – he seemed different. Urgent, reckless, on edge. Not the smart, stable, painfully pragmatic guy she'd come to know. But she liked the new Luke, a lot, when he groaned loudly, then found the zipper on the back of her dress and inched it down.

The bodice drooped to her waist revealing the red lace bra she'd worn that day – and his groan became a moan.

'Holy shit ...' he murmured, as he traced a reverent thumb along the edge of the half-cup were her ample cleavage swelled against the lace.

Sensation prickled and glowed as her nipples gathered into tight peaks.

Thank goodness she'd upped her lingerie game ever since Luke had become a regular visitor to The Royale. She'd never expected him to see this stuff but it had made her feel confident to wear it around him.

She felt more than confident now, she felt invincible as he stripped off the dress. 'You'll have to turn around,' he said. 'I'm not one of those Bond-like guys who can unhook a bra one handed.'

'I can do it.' She reached behind her back, ready to do the honours.

But he touched her arm. 'No, let me.' The quiver of desperation in his voice pumped her already oversized ego. 'I've been dreaming of unwrapping you since your boiler broke.'

All right, then. She dropped her arms, turned around and waited.

He fumbled for a few seconds, then the tight band under her breasts released. She sighed, the sigh of every well-endowed woman at the end of a long day. Her arms dropped, letting the bra slide down. Then the sigh guttered into a sob, when he covered her full breasts from behind, lifting and caressing them, tweaking the pebbled nipples.

She turned back to wrap her arms around his neck. She

just wanted to hold him, for a moment. She threaded her fingers into his hair and their mouths fused again. More urgent, more desperate.

At last he pulled back, his breath coming in ragged pants. 'I need to get naked,' he said, his gaze devouring her quivering flesh. 'Like, yesterday.'

'Yes, you do.' She grinned, so elated she thought she might burst.

She crossed her arms over her breasts, shivering despite the warm evening, as she watched him strip in the moonlight.

He hopped around on one foot then the other, tugging off his boots without undoing the laces. He wrestled off his shirt, then grappled with his T-shirt and flung it away.

As he bent his head to concentrate on unbuttoning his fly, the shudder of satisfaction echoed through her whole body.

Oh, my. His chest and shoulders were a work of art. The muscles defined, solid but not over pumped. He was tanned all over, a result of his Italian-American heritage she guessed, but the slight darkening on his arms where he wore his T-shirt on a sunny day made her heart lift. Of course, her Luke would have work muscles, not gym muscles.

Her Luke?

He's not yours Rubes, this is probably just a one-time deal.

She dismissed the prickle of pragmatism – nothing was going to dampen her joy tonight, not even her common sense – and followed the happy trail of dark hair that spread across his nipples as it arrowed through his abs.

She watched transfixed and increasingly breathless as he lowered his jeans and kicked them off.

Straightening, he stood in front of her, and her avid gaze snagged on the thick outline of his erection, stretching his boxer briefs.

She choked out a sob as her lung function stalled.

Oh, my days. He's packing some serious heft.

Even though she knew size wasn't really important, because she'd had a boyfriend who was hung like a horse once before and he'd used his penis like a battering ram, the sight of Luke Devlin's enormous erection encased in black cotton was so erotic every one of her pulse points rejoiced.

'Is everything okay?' he said, caressing her cheek, then cupping her chin to raise her gaze back to his, and study her reaction. Was that nerves, insecurity, she could see in his eyes? And hear in his voice? Why did that make him even more delicious?

'Yes ... I ... I ...' she stammered.

Breathe, Ruby, breathe.

'Yes ... everything's good.' She managed at last past the lump of radioactive lust jammed into her throat. 'Everything's absolutely magnificent.' *Actually ...*

He let out a deep chuckle and the concern in his eyes disappeared. 'Good.' He leaned in for another kiss, trapping his magnificent erection against her belly.

She'd never had an orgasm through penetration, but the thought of having that long length inside her made her giddy and wet.

He lifted her into his arms and placed her on to the bed. The soft mattress gave way as he lay down next to her, then plucked her arms away from her chest and cradled one of her breasts.

'Can I kiss them?' he asked.

'Absolutely,' she said and braced herself for the usual mauling. But instead of sucking her nipples into his mouth, as her other boyfriends had always done. He cupped the hot flesh, stroked his thumb under the underside, then leaned over her to circle the nipple with his tongue.

Her breasts had never been particularly sensitive, or so she'd thought. But his attention was so thorough, so careful, so delicate and yet so decisive, as he licked and nibbled, she found herself gripping the coverlet, the darts of sensation hurtling down.

'*Oh … Oh, yes.*' She sighed as he finally licked across the rigid peak.

Capturing the nipple gently in his teeth he flicked his tongue over the now supremely sensitive flesh. She arched off the bed, the darts in her abdomen becoming flaming arrows of need.

And just when she thought she couldn't bear the torture any longer, he reached under the waistband of her knickers and found the slick folds of her sex with his other hand.

She gripped his head, holding him to her breast, bucking against his devious fingers as he located her clitoris and stroked over the swollen nub.

The tight coil of sensation released, triggering an orgasm so strong it swelled for an eternity before releasing her from its grip in a shattering rush.

She lay panting and shaking, in a pool of her own sweat, as the last of it finally swept away.

He rose over her, his smug smile somehow sublime. 'That was awesome to watch, Ruby.'

Her chuckle broke on a sob of surrender. 'Believe me, it was even more awesome to experience.'

Who knew? Luke Devlin was even more delicious than he looked.

He laughed, but the sound was hoarse and strained. 'Can I taste you now?'

Is he serious?

'I don't think I can come again,' she said. Reaching down, she found the impressive ridge in his pants and caressed it. 'Perhaps we should take care of you?'

His erection jerked against her palm, and he groaned as she tugged the waistband of his briefs down and freed him. She explored the magnificent length, her sex twitching and pulsing with renewed enthusiasm.

But then he covered her hand with his and pulled her questing fingers away. After buzzing a kiss into her palm, he adjusted their positions, shifting down on the bed and dragging off her knickers. Suddenly, he was kneeling between her spread legs, her yearning sex open for him.

'We can take care of me later. Just answer this question: do you like oral sex? Because I really want to feast on you right now.'

He *was* serious.

'I ... I don't know,' she admitted.

His brows flattened. 'How come?'

She wiggled against his hold, feeling a little awkward. 'Um ... Well, no man's ever offered to go down on me before.'

'Are you kidding? You're a BJ virgin?'

'Not entirely, I've done it the other way around.' She fidgeted some more feeling a lot awkward now. 'Given guys blow jobs,' she clarified, starting to feel like a bit of a ninny.

'Dammit, Ruby. What kind of guys have you been dating?'

'Selfish arseholes?' she offered, feeling her heart punch her ribs at his outraged expression.

'Dumb selfish assholes would be more like it,' he said. 'Do you want to lose your virginity, with me? Because I'd be honoured to be the first guy to taste you.'

'Are you sure you don't just want to get to the main event?' she asked, not convinced now she'd be able to relax enough to enjoy it. The awkward was still there, not to mention that deep pulsing in her chest which was making his eagerness to give her pleasure feel like more than it should.

'Ruby, I'm so turned on right now, I'm liable to shoot my load about two seconds after I get inside you,' he said. 'And I don't want this to be over too soon.'

Well, all right, then.

The finality in his statement made her early worry, that this was just a one-time thing, ripple over her, but then she grasped what he was saying. He was right, if this was a one-time deal, they should make the most of it. Why miss out on having a single solitary second of Luke's firm body, his clever lips, his devious fingers, his insatiable tongue, or his gorgeous cock at her disposal?

'Go for it, then,' she said, propping herself up on her elbows to watch.

'That's my girl.' He smiled, his fingers flexing on her hips, caressing her thighs, and making the awkward lump in her chest loosen.

She *was* his girl for tonight. And he was her guy. And that was all that mattered.

One of Matty's favourite bastardised quotes rippled across her consciousness and she smiled.

Forget about tomorrow, remember what Scarlet said, it's another day.

But then Luke pressed his face into her sex and inhaled. And all thoughts of Matty and Scarlet, today and tomorrow, flew out of her head.

'Mmm, you smell delicious, good enough to eat,' he quipped.

She laughed. Surely the enthusiasm in his voice couldn't be faked.

'Now relax and tell me what works for you and what doesn't.'

'You want instructions?' she asked, a little astonished.

His lips caressed the top of her mound. 'Uh-huh. Generally, I work better with instructions ...'

She tensed again. Hadn't she just told him this was a new experience for her? And since when did men insist on directions?

'Or, I could go freelance ...' He offered, stroking her thighs, clearly aware the suggestion wasn't working. Her heart sighed, along with her. When had she ever slept with a guy

214

so intuitive and responsive? But then she already knew about Luke's dogged attention to detail from watching him caress wet plaster while repairing the cornicing. 'If that works best for you?' he added.

'Yes, it definitely does,' she said. But he'd already taken her cue.

Spreading her with his thumbs, he swirled his tongue over her clitoris.

She jerked off the bed, the tiny lick exquisite, and enlightening.

'You like that?' he asked.

'I love that, clearly you work very well freelance,' she breathed.

It was all the encouragement he needed. The heat flowed as he settled in to the task of feasting on her.

She wriggled and squirmed as the passion throbbed back to life with each long slow lick, each devious flick. Just when she was convinced she couldn't take any more, one blunt finger entered her, probing, stroking. The passion crested, shoving her towards the precipice that had shattered her once before. She clung to the high, wide ledge, sobbing, begging, but he was relentless, tasting, tormenting, driving her insane.

She soared. Thrusting her fingers into his hair, caressing the thick mane.

Don't stop. Don't stop. Don't stop.

'No way,' he murmured.

Good lord had she just screamed that out loud?

But before she could register the embarrassment, he got back to work. Licking, sucking, probing, stroking.

And sent her soaring again. Higher. And higher. And higher still. Until ...

She shattered into a billion glittering shards of incandescent light.

As she drifted back down to earth, she heard his urgent plea. 'Do you have condoms? I need to be inside you, ASAP.'

'I ... I don't, but I'm on the pill.'

'You're sure?' he said. Cradling her face, his erection pressed against her belly. Long, hard, wonderfully insistent. 'I'm clean, I swear,' he added. 'I have a full medical exam each year for my company insurance and I never have unprotected sex ...' He paused. 'Generally, speaking.'

He was making an exception for her, because he trusted her.

The pulsing in her heart spread up her chest, choking her a little. Why should she find that so romantic?

'I'm clean, too,' she said, stifling the rosy glow in practicalities. 'I had a full STD test ...' Three years ago. She bit off the information. He didn't need to know that Ed, her last boyfriend, had been a cheat. Especially as she could barely even remember what Ed looked like right now. 'Fairly recently,' she lied. 'And I haven't slept with anyone since.' That much at least was true.

'Thank fuck,' he grunted. Then he gripped her hips, angled her pelvis and taking himself in hand, found her entrance.

She circled his neck, her fingers tangling in the hairs at his nape, as the heavy weight slid inside her, the slickness of her two orgasms easing the way. The penetration was immense

216

when he was finally lodged deep, the stretched feeling full and thick.

She gripped his neck, his grunts matching her soft sobs, as the need began to prickle and hum again. Surely she wasn't going to have her first vaginal orgasm, she thought vaguely. That would be too much. Too good.

But he hadn't lied. He rocked his hips once, twice, three times, then collapsed on top of her with a loud grunt.

They lay like that, with his weight pushing her into the mattress, their sweaty limbs entangled. She stroked his nape, refusing to let the doubts in, relishing the feel of his erection still inside her as he softened.

At last, he lifted off her, then positioned himself by her side. Propped on an elbow, he leaned down to kiss her. The touch of his lips on hers was reverent, sweet, the musky taste impossibly erotic, but then the pulse of sadness intruded – because she could already sense him pulling away.

'Sorry, I didn't last,' he said.

She covered his hand on her belly. And smiled back at him. 'Not a problem, there's always a next time ...' she said, then wished she hadn't.

It wasn't a suggestion, it was just a turn of phrase. She didn't want to sound any more needy and insecure than was absolutely necessary.

He didn't say anything, just stroked her cheek with his thumb.

'Plus I got the two best orgasms of my life out of it,' she said smoothly to fill the void. 'So I'm not complaining.'

No other sexual experience had even come close to what

Luke Devlin had just delivered – and she was including sessions with her trusty vibrator in the league table.

But then they'd both been on sexual tenterhooks for over a week, and she liked him. The circumstances had been right for an epic shag. This didn't have to be about anything other than good timing. And excellent chemistry.

Luke was a man who clearly liked sex, and women, and knew how to please them. That said, his formula for success wasn't that complex – he'd put her in charge of her own pleasure and then gotten creative when necessary. The problem with the five guys she'd dated previously, going back to Stan McCormack and the Skoda Octavia Debacle, was they'd not only been dumb selfish arseholes. They'd also been extremely unimaginative.

Pressing a kiss to her forehead, Luke murmured. 'I should probably head back to my place.'

Was that reluctance she could hear in his voice? Or was she projecting?

'You don't have to.' *Really you don't.*

Uncertainty flickered across his face, and she braced herself for the excuses, the polite denials. It wouldn't be the first time a guy had hit on her and run. At least this time she had something to show for it. An afterglow from the two best orgasms of her life which would keep the black bottomless pit at bay till morning.

But to her surprise, he simply said. 'Are you sure? This is kind of a small bed.'

It wasn't that small, he was just a tall guy, but she was too elated at his reply and the willingness in his voice to think of the practicalities.

'Then I guess we'll just have to snuggle more,' she said.

'I can't think of anything I'd rather do,' he replied and the bounce of elation hit her tonsils.

He was going to stay the night? And snuggle? Even without the awesome orgasms, this would be the best date night of her entire life.

She didn't even care that it would be over in the morning. Because tomorrow was a galaxy far far away.

Rolling on to his back, he wrapped an arm around her shoulders. She snuggled against his side, listening to his breathing and loving the feel of him. So warm, so solid, so steady, so sexy, so *there*, beside her.

She found her eyelids drooping, even though she didn't want to miss a thing.

As he petted her hair, he said softly. 'Thanks, Ruby. I needed you tonight.'

She gave him a squeeze, hearing the note of sadness and confusion in his voice again. And tried not to think about where it came from.

'Ditto.'

Chapter 12

When Luke's eyes opened the next morning, he saw the twinkle of green lights above his head, heard a melodic voice singing about lemon drops and chimney tops in the distance, felt the squishy softness of the mattress beneath him and breathed in a lungful of evocative aromas. Rose shampoo and sex and ... was that coffee?

Had he been transported to a triple-X-rated Land of Oz?

He shifted, the twinge in his back from the too-soft mattress protesting. As Ruby's bedroom came into focus, the memories from yesterday flowed back.

His mother's ashen face, the shocking revelation about his father and Matty, the hours spent wandering the streets of West London, re-evaluating his whole childhood and adolescence and everything he'd known about his old man – or thought he'd known – ending up in Brynn's Babes knocking back one too many spiced rums while the crowd went nuts for a queen called Tina Turn You On doing a dead-on rendition of 'River Deep Mountain High'...

And then Ruby.

Her soft smiles and hungry kisses, her incredible rack and

the taste of her – so sweet and exotic – on his tongue. Then the tight clasp of her body as he shot his load in two seconds flat. He would be humiliated, if the memory of that moment wasn't giving him a morning boner.

But then the hours after his titanic orgasm came back too, and the woody wilted. It had taken him until two am to finally fall asleep, and he still hadn't got much straight in his head, but listening to Ruby's soft snores, stroking her lush curves, inhaling that exotic scent, he'd figured out one certain truth from the whole cluster fuck of yesterday. Sleeping with her last night had not been his smartest move.

His whole existence had been crushed and mangled yesterday with his mother's news – like a steel girder under too heavy a load – and sleeping with Ruby had been a way to un-crush and un-mangle it – to feel normal again. To feel better than normal for a few hours at least.

He breathed in the addictive chicory scent of the coffee and detected the salty aroma of bacon. His stomach grumbled. And the guilt and shame threatened to gag him. To add insult to injury not only had he used her for sex last night – mind-blowing unforgettable sex – but then he'd stayed the night.

Ruby was cooking him breakfast. As if they were some kind of a couple – which they weren't, not really.

He rolled, or rather bounced, off the too-soft bed and located the clothing he'd flung off yesterday neatly folded on a vintage armchair in the corner of the room.

After getting dressed, he followed the scent of coffee and bacon down the apartment's hall, his stomach rumbling all the way as he listened to Ruby's soulful voice caress the lyrics of the show tune that had gotten them both arrested what felt like a lifetime ago.

Reaching the doorway of the kitchen, he propped his shoulder against the frame and stopped dead, taking the opportunity to watch her unobserved.

She wore a silk robe decorated with sunflowers, tied tightly around her waist, her bounteous curves jiggly beneath it as she stirred a pan full of eggs. Was it any wonder he'd taken what she offered last night? Not just taken, gorged himself on it. And her. She was so good just to look at. He loved the way she moved, the way her forehead puckered in a frown of concentration, the quick flicks of her wrist to push her wild hair out of her eyes as she worked. Watching Ruby gave him a buzz that went beyond the sex.

Something warm spread across his ribs then sunk low to glow in his empty stomach. Filling it up with ... Comfort? Contentment? Desire? He wasn't entirely sure what he was feeling. But whatever it was, it probably wasn't good news.

Not least because his parents – between them – had managed to screw her best friend over, years before he died.

He cleared his throat.

She startled, flicking some of the eggs on to the countertop and clutched her hand to her beautiful rack. 'Luke? You're awake.'

'Yup.' He stayed where he was, resisting the urge to wedge himself behind her, wrap his arms around her waist, sink his face into that wild spray of hair and breath in her delicious scent. Not much he could do about the revitalized boner though, so he ignored it.

'Good morning, Ruby,' he said, even though it wasn't a good morning. He'd screwed up last night and now he had to fix it.

She laughed, the rich full sound making his woody even gladder to see her.

'Someone woke up very perky,' she said, a little breathlessly as her gaze drifted down to the bulge in his shorts. 'Shall we put this on the back burner?' she asked. 'We've got at least an hour before Jacie gets here.'

He frowned, realizing how simple it would be to jump her again.

'Don't tempt me,' he said, surprised how much he wanted to take her up on the offer. But there was nothing simple or easy about sex with a woman like Ruby. She would have hopes, expectations, which he couldn't possibly fulfil. They were going to be working together until the end of the month and things could get awkward between them if they didn't establish boundaries. 'I could use some food. I haven't eaten since yesterday morning.'

'Oh, okay,' she said, the spike of concern and curiosity in her voice making him realise he owed her an explanation.

'Take a seat at the table, and I'll serve this up while it's still hot,' she added.

She brushed her hair behind her ear, and he imagined kissing the spot on her neck he'd got attached to last night.

Get a clue, Devlin. Not gonna happen.

'Yes, ma'am,' he said, as he strolled into the living room.

There would be questions, questions she deserved answers to, but he would wait until she asked them. He'd never been good at emotional conversations, especially after a hook-up.

His mouth watered as he straddled the chair at the small table in the living room and watched Ruby serve up breakfast.

As he shovelled in the crispy bacon, fat sausages, hot buttered toast, fried tomatoes, and herby eggs, he ignored the continued twist of anxiety in the pit of his stomach.

Ruby was an adult. She could make her own decisions. He'd used her, but she'd enjoyed herself. And like Jake in the cowboy film they'd watched a week ago together, he hadn't been able to quit her last night.

Ruby stirred a couple of sugars into her coffee and admired the spectacular view in her living room, still not quite able to believe Luke hadn't vanished in the night. Or made a speedy exit as soon as he woke this morning.

She'd left him sleeping earlier and started putting together a man-sized breakfast to calm her nerves, totally resigned to probably eating it alone.

She wasn't taking anything for granted.

But her spectacular booty call was still here. Looking buff and built and beyond gorgeous with his 8 a.m. beard scruff, his creased T-shirt and stretchy boxers, eating the meal she'd cooked for him as if it were the last supper.

'*I haven't eaten since yesterday morning.*'

Why hadn't he eaten? What had happened to him yesterday to change him from the practical pragmatic, we-can't-have-sex-under-any-circumstances guy of their hair rinsing date into the rumpled, reckless, and ridiculously hot let's-bang-ourselves-senseless sex machine who had come to her last night?

Not that she was complaining. Now she knew what Luke was capable of in the sack, his hotness quotient had hit the stratosphere. But there was something off about the whole scenario. His unexplained disappearance yesterday, the slight edge of desperation when he'd taken her to bed last night, the frown which contradicted the impressive ridge in his pants this morning. Last night hadn't been the Luke she'd come to know. Luke had always been hot. But playful, insatiable Luke had been scorching.

The old Luke was back now with a vengeance, though. She knew what was coming. She'd had the 'it's not you, it's me' speech enough times before to see the signs. But this felt different. Was it because the sex had been so hot? Was that why she felt bereft at the thought of getting the usual brush-off? It had to be. Because she had known last night, even as it was happening, that Luke wasn't himself and their hook-up was unlikely to be repeated.

She took a long gulp of her coffee watching Luke over the rim as he took his time mopping up the last of the breakfast juices with the final slice of toast.

'Did that hit the spot?' she asked, as he pushed his plate away.

'Yeah,' he said. 'And then some.'

She smiled. 'I'm glad.'

The frown was still there on his forehead, telegraphing what he was about to say. Even so, as he opened his mouth to say the words she had been expecting, ever since falling asleep in his arms last night, her heart did an unfortunate little jitterbug in her chest.

Hello, cock-eyed optimism.

'Ruby, about last night ...' He paused. 'I'm sorry. That wasn't ... It wasn't meant to happen.'

'I know,' she said, keeping the easy smile firmly in place, even as the jitterbug in her chest died. 'But I enjoyed it immensely, so I'm not sorry. And I don't think you should be either.' She crossed her legs, struggling to ignore the pulse of heat between her legs.

Down, girl.

'Unless of course you didn't enjoy it as much as I did,' she added, not caring her cheeks were probably glowing now too.

If a girl couldn't fish shamelessly for a compliment when she was getting the brush-off from the best-sex-of-her-life guy, seriously, when could she?

'You know I did,' he said, but he was still frowning. 'I'm sorry because ...' He looked down at the empty plate, brought his hand up to tap his fingers on the table. She waited, for him to come up with the right words, fascinated despite everything at how hard it seemed to be for him to find them. She would have assumed Luke had given women the brush-off a ton of times before, he'd been so confident and hot last night in bed. She imagined every woman he'd ever dated had probably fancied themselves in love with him at least a little bit. Awesome hook-ups could do that to a woman.

At last, he raised his head, his stare doing interesting things to the glow in her knickers. 'I'm sorry, because I used you last night, to make myself feel better about ... about some stuff. And that's a pretty shitty thing to do to anyone.'

Her heart rate started jitterbugging again at the sincerity in his voice, and the regret. She couldn't tell him that was easily the sweetest most chivalrous brush-off she'd ever gotten, from any guy − or he might get the impression she was expecting more from him than hot sex, when she never had. But she filed the thought away.

She covered his hand, to still the nervous tapping. Then released it again, so he didn't get the wrong impression about that either.

Time to set him straight.

'Luke, I knew something wasn't right, when you arrived here last night looking so lost and alone and smelling of rum. And I took advantage of your awesome oral sex skills anyway, so I'm really not sure who used who.'

'Huh?' His eyebrows popped up, and her smile became genuine.

Men were such adorable dopes sometimes.

'But be that as it may ...' *Moving swiftly on.* 'What stuff was bothering you? Do you want to talk about it?'

It was a risk, she knew that. He'd just told her she had no hold on him, which she totally got. But as a friend, she wanted to help, if she could, by doing something other than just taking advantage of his ninja cunnilingus skills.

'Not really,' he said. The frown was back with a vengeance.

'Then you don't have to,' she said, reaching for the plate. She'd expected that response and she wanted him to know this wasn't about her curiosity, this was about him. If he wanted to talk about it, she was a good listener. If not she was equally good at not pushing.

But as she stood to lift the plates off the table, he grasped her wrist.

'Sit down,' he said, the edge she'd noticed the night before back in his voice.

She sat down, and he let go of her wrist.

'Actually, I kind of do ...' he said, a wary look clouding his expression, 'have to talk to you about it.'

'No, you really don't, Luke,' she replied. 'Just because we hooked up last night. And used each other,' she added, glad when a rueful smile lifted his lips. 'It doesn't make whatever happened to you yesterday any of my business. Okay?'

Luke was a super private guy. She didn't want to make this any more uncomfortable for him than it had to be.

She reached for the empty plates again.

'It's not just about me though,' he said and she let go of the plates again.

She could hear the brittle note which had been missing last night. It saddened her to hear it again, but what saddened her more was knowing that without it, Luke wasn't really Luke.

'It's about Matty and my dad, and my mom ...' he continued. 'And it's kind of about you, too. And The Royale.'

The mention of Matty brought with it the hard hit of grief Ruby had somehow managed to dodge this morning, ever since waking up with Luke's arm thrown over her hip and her clitoris still humming ... But even as her lungs squeezed, and her eyes stung, the grief tugging at her again, she couldn't tear her gaze away from Luke's troubled expression.

'It is?' she said, because he'd lost her, the guarded look on his face only saddening her more. Whatever this was about, it was even harder for him to talk about than finding the perfect break-up line.

'Yeah, it is.' He propped his elbows on the table and scrubbed his hands over his face, then swore softly. He raked his fingers through his hair as he straightened, and finally met her gaze. 'I went to see my mom yesterday.'

Her brain knotted around the logistics. 'You flew all the way to New York and back in a day?' *Was that even possible?*

'No.' He barked out an unamused laugh. 'She's in London, preparing for a one-woman show at the National next month.'

'She is? But that's wonderful,' Ruby said, although she couldn't imagine what that had to do with her and Matty and The Royale. 'How cool. Is that why she rang you last week?'

'It's not wonderful. Or cool.' The furrow on his brow became a chasm. 'My mom brings drama with her wherever she goes, she can't help it. And she didn't call me a week ago, she called you.'

'She was probably only trying to get hold of you though. I mean, why would she ...'

He clasped her hand, squeezed her fingers to silence her. 'Ruby, she called you because she had something to confess to you.'

'She did?'

'To confess to us both. And what she told me explains why Matty left me half of The Royale. It's kind of messed up.'

'What did she say?'

He ducked his head. Whatever his mother had told him he was extremely unhappy about it.

'She told me Matty and my old man were lovers. Not just lovers, hopelessly in love. They met on the set of *The Sorrento Summer*, and had a secret affair while Falcone was filming the scenes in London. They used to sneak into the Serpentine after dark to go swimming, and to make love.'

'*One Summer in Sorrento*,' Ruby corrected him, her mind racing as her chest collapsed in on itself.

Matty had *known* Falcone. Had been *in love* with Falcone. And Falcone had loved him back. *For real*. And he'd never told her? How was that even possible?

She thought of all the nights when they'd talked about their mutual obsession with Falcone over the years, poured over the actor's best movie moments. She could still remember vividly the day they'd both heard about Falcone's death, when she was twelve, and doing her illegal Saturday job manning the ticket booth at The Royale. She'd been hopelessly in love with Falcone, or rather his bad boy persona, ever since she hit puberty. While other girls had swooned over Leonardo DiCaprio and Channing Tatum, she had been enthralled by a guy who was practically old enough to be her granddad.

But she hadn't been as devastated as Matty by his death. Matty had insisted they run a midnight screening of *Boy Blue*, Falcone's B-movie debut from the late-seventies, on the day news of the actor's suicide broke. They'd had a packed house of hipsters, movie buffs, Matty's friends and a contingent of blue rinse matrons who must have taken speed to stay up all night. She'd found Matty in the projection booth before the show, tears rolling down his cheeks as he re-looped the old 35mm projector they'd cleaned up for the occasion. She'd been shocked because Matty never cried. Or certainly not in silence – with real tears and without an audience.

She'd wondered briefly then if he had known Falcone. After all, the actor had once had a world-famous love affair with Matty's sister, when Matty was still talking to her. But when Ruby had asked, he'd simply stared at her for the longest moment, and shaken his head.

Then she'd gotten a grip and realised Matty couldn't possibly have known Falcone, because no way would Matty have kept it a secret. Matty didn't keep secrets, especially not juicy ones concerning himself and one of the most iconic celebrities on the planet. And he'd never kept any secrets from her.

Only he had.

Her throat hurt and her eyes burned.

Matty had kept a lot of secrets. The secret of his will, the secret of the theatre's catastrophic debts, the secret of his feud with Helena, the secret of his love affair with Falcone, the secret of why he'd wanted his ashes scattered over the Serpentine in the hours after dusk ...

What else had he kept from her? And why had he? Perhaps she hadn't been as good a friend to him as she always thought.

'What did you say?' Luke asked.

'*One Summer in Sorrento*,' she repeated. 'That's the name of the movie you're talking about. The only movie Falcone made with your mother.'

'Right ...'

'Do you know what happened? How Matty's affair with Falcone ended?' she asked, not sure she really wanted to know, because it must have ended tragically. But feeling she ought to know, because Matty had been her friend.

Offering solidarity and sympathy from beyond the grave wasn't going to do much good, but at least she could finally quash any of the little resentments she'd felt when she'd first found out about his will.

'Can't you guess?' Luke said, the edge in his voice confusing her.

Was he mad about something?

'No ... I ... Matty never mentioned any of this to me,' she said.

Luke huffed out a breath, the frown catastrophic now. Why was he so tense? Was this the news that had disturbed him so much last night? Turned him into a man she didn't recognise? Made him seem wounded, and vulnerable?

Her head began to hurt because she didn't understand any of it anymore.

'My mom happened,' he said. 'That's how it ended ...'

'I don't ... I still don't understand.'

'Matty found my mom and Falcone in bed together,' he said flatly. 'It was the night she got pregnant with me.'

Oh, no, Matty.

What a blow that must have been. He could only have been nineteen the year that film was made. What a devastating betrayal. Was that why he had never spoken of his relationship with Falcone – because it had simply been too painful?

Was that why he had stopped speaking to his sister? It must have been.

Ruby placed her hand on her stomach, which was starting to hurt. She rubbed the ache, feeling responsible in some weird way for Matty's pain. How hurt he must have been. How devastated. And what kind of friend to him had she really been, if he couldn't even confide in her the truth about his passionate affair with a man they'd both idolised? But then the significance of Luke's inheritance occurred to her.

'He must have forgiven her,' she whispered. 'And your father.'

'What?' Luke said.

'Matty, he must have forgiven them both.' It all made a strange, sweet, symbolic kind of sense, she thought as the knots in her stomach eased. 'That must be why he left half of The Royale to you,' she continued, when Luke just stared at her. 'It's the only explanation, for the bequest. Did you tell your mother Matty left you half of The Royale? She seemed so sad last week when I spoke to her. So devastated by his death. I'm sure it would help her immensely to know Matty forgave ...'

'Ruby, she knows.'

'Okay, well that's good,' she said, glad that he'd told Helena.

'Is it?' She heard it again, the edge to his voice.

'Yes, I think it is, why don't you?' she asked.

'Because I'm not sure she deserves to be forgiven for what they did.'

'Why not?' she asked. He seemed so angry.

'She slept with the guy her own brother was in love with. And if that isn't crummy enough. She kept it a secret from me all these years, that my old man was gay. Or possibly bi.'

She stiffened. She could not have been more shocked with the bitterness in his tone if he had reached across the table and slapped her. This wasn't just anger, it was much more than that. 'Luke, why are you so furious?'

She refused to believe Luke was homophobic, he was far too intelligent for that. But something was going on here she wasn't getting. Why was he so upset about something that had happened before he was even born? He was right, what Helena and Falcone had done to Matty was not cool, and it must have hurt Matty terribly. But people did stupid things all the time. Helena had been so young at the time too, much younger than either of them were now. She could well imagine that if Falcone was anything like his son it would have been far too easy to become infatuated with him. And it was very clear from the way Luke had talked to his mother on the phone a week ago – and the way he was talking about her now – that he had issues with her, but he seemed to be completely missing the most important point. That without that secret affair, he would never have been born.

'Are you angry because your father loved another man?' she asked, scared to hear the answer. 'You're not ... you're not ashamed of him because of his sexuality, are you?'

Luke stared at Ruby. The distress in her face giving him pause.

Was he? Ashamed of his father, because he had a love affair with a man? He examined the question, because it hadn't even occurred to him until this moment. He'd never considered himself to be homophobic. But then people who definitely *were* homophobic probably thought they weren't, either. He'd

235

been shocked when his mother had told him the truth. Shocked and angry. And a lot of that anger stemmed from the fact his father had been living a lie all those years.

He'd never been honest, never admitted to the world who he really was. And after watching that damn cowboy film with Ruby a week ago, he knew exactly how destructive a secret like that could be. But was it really his old man's fault that he had been forced to keep that secret to save his career?

Falcone had been the voice of sex, famous for being able to seduce women at fifty paces. And it was a reputation he'd gone out of his way to uphold. Luke couldn't even remember all the times he'd been dropped off to see his dad as scheduled, and had bumped into some stunning young woman in the kitchen of his father's house in Montecito, usually in their underwear or less. Actresses and models, hat-check girls and barmaids who his father had picked up the night before and then hadn't bothered to get out of the house before he arrived.

How he'd resented those women at first, for taking all of his dad's attention, but when he'd hit puberty, he'd been mortified, realising some of them were not much older than he was.

To discover now they had all been a lie, too …

His dad must have been bisexual, but why had he never had a long-term relationship with any woman, including his mom? His old man had hidden his true self behind a string of casual, careless, indiscriminate booty calls. But it wasn't his father's sexuality that Luke was ashamed of.

'No, it's not the fact he fell in love with another man that bothers me, it's all the lies,' he said at last, in answer to Ruby's question. Because all he felt now was sad and disappointed that Falcone had never been honest about anything.

'I'm glad.' The relief on Ruby's face was palpable. 'It's so important to know that the quality of your relationship with your father doesn't have anything to do with him being bisexual,' she said, sounding so earnest he had the weird urge to hug her. If only it were as simple as that. 'My father was heterosexual,' she added. 'Or at least I assume he was, because I never met him. He disappeared faster than Harry Potter in his invisibility cloak when my mum told him she was pregnant with me.'

'That's tough. He sounds like a dick,' Luke said, and felt the pointless anger scouring his throat again. This time on Ruby's behalf instead of his own.

'Yes, I suppose he was,' she said. 'But I didn't need him in the end. Matty was the dad of my heart, and he made a much better dad than that guy could ever have made, so I consider myself lucky,' she said.

So, Ruby had lost her father a month ago. No wonder she was still struggling with her grief.

'But I don't want to talk about my deadbeat dad right now,' she said. 'We were talking about yours,' she added, neatly changing the subject again. 'Why did you think he was a selfish arsehole?'

He jerked his shoulder. Shit, he really didn't want to have this conversation. He hated talking about his father at the best of times, complaining about him now though – in the light of Ruby's crap dad story – made that even tougher. But as she stared at him, somehow he felt he owed her this conversation.

'My mom wanted me to form a relationship with him. But I don't think he was ever that interested,' he said. 'I lost count of the times as a kid when he'd be due to take me out for the day, and he didn't show. Or I'd get dropped off to spend the day with him in Montecito and he was too hung-over to do much of anything. Eventually I started to resent it and him. But maybe if I had known why he didn't want to see me. Because I was a reminder of what he'd lost. A symbol of the night he'd fucked up what sounds like the one genuine relationship in his life ...' He sighed, and the weight in his stomach from the day before dropped back into his guts. 'I guess I never thought of my father as someone who could be hurt, who deserved my sympathy. He was always so arrogant, so careless. Or so I thought. But to have that secret inside him that he could never acknowledge. It's like Heath Ledger in that movie we watched. It must have destroyed him. I've disliked my father for a large part of my life, because I always thought he was a fraud. Pretending to be cool when he wasn't, but now to discover he was kind of forced to be a fraud ... and he must have been suffering.'

Ruby pressed a hand over his on the table, and the weight in his stomach rose up his torso. He blinked. *Jesus*, he was not going to cry. But the only way to stop the sting from becoming a flood seemed to be to keep talking.

'When I found him that morning, I always figured the over-dose was a mistake,' he said, the words tumbling out. 'I figured he didn't really mean to commit suicide, he was just monu-mentally careless. Or maybe he was looking for attention. A headline. His career was on the skids by then thanks to his addictions. I was sure he had forgotten I'd agreed to come by, because he always forgot details. But now I'm not so sure. What if he meant it? What if he meant for me to find him? What if it was a cry for help? I've been angry with him for so long about the consequences of that day.' The panic attacks, the nightmares that had plagued him for years, and the anxiety which he'd never quite been able to tame completely a result of the emotional fallout from that day. 'But I'm not angry with him anymore,' he continued. 'Because I realise he was never to blame. I guess there's not much point being angry with my mom, either, for taking so long to tell me the truth.'

He sunk into the kitchen chair. Drained. Exhausted. He hadn't meant to say any of that, hadn't even known it was inside him.

But when Ruby knelt down in front of him, put trembling hands on his bare knees he was forced to meet her gaze and saw the emerald green, misty with compassion.

He shifted, supremely uncomfortable at how much he wanted to bask in it. Even knowing he didn't deserve it.

'Luke.' She pressed her cheek to his knees, the sheen in her eyes crucifying him. She looked as if she were on the verge of tears. Who was she crying for? 'I'm so, so sorry. I didn't know it was you who found him.'

Shit! why had he let that slip out? He was seriously losing the plot and it wasn't even noon.

Ruby felt Luke pull away and forced herself to hold in the tears that were making her eyes burn and get off her knees.

Displays of emotion were not the way to go here. He looked

uncomfortable, wary, because he had shared much more than she suspected he had meant to share. She mustn't read too much into it.

Just as she had suspected, last night hadn't ever been about her, about them.

She lifted their used plates from the table. 'Do you want to take a shower?'

His eyebrows lifted a fraction. Then he rubbed his hand over his jaw. 'I should probably head back to my place, before anyone arrives. I don't want you to be accused of sleeping with the enemy.'

No one would think that – not anymore – not even Jacie. But she could see how keen he was to leave, so she nodded and forced a smile to her lips.

'Good thinking, Batman. Do you want to head down the fire escape once you're dressed, just in case?'

'Yeah,' he said. 'You sure you don't want me to help out with the dishes?'

She shook her head.

As much as she would have loved to take him up on his offer, and have him pressed against her hip while they washed the breakfast dishes together in her tiny kitchen, she would just be prolonging the inevitable. And she needed to get her own shaky emotions under control.

'Maybe next time,' she said, then winced.

There won't be a next time.

He nodded, but instead of heading down the corridor to get dressed, he stared at her for the longest moment then said. 'I'm sorry, Ruby.'

'What for?' she asked, hoping he wasn't going to apologise for giving her the best sex of her life again.

'For not being able to save the theatre,' he said, surprising her, especially as she could see he meant it. 'You and Matty deserved better.'

She could see the regret and the guilt shadowing his eyes and she realized that if she pressed, she could easily guilt him into investing in The Royale. Because he felt responsible now, in a way he hadn't before.

But the fleeting thought passed almost as quickly as it came ...

Saving Matty's dream, saving her dream, keeping The Royale open had never been Luke's responsibility, any more than being born made him responsible for the break-up of Matty and Falcone's love affair. And she felt even more ashamed now she'd tried to make it his responsibility.

Tears clogged her throat as she touched her palm to the stubble on his jaw, felt the muscle bunch and flex. 'Don't be sorry, Luke.'

She would just have to come up with another plan ... one which didn't involve Luke.

He dropped his forehead to hers and grasped the back of her neck. His thumb drew tantalizing circles on her nape, making sensation ricochet down to her core. She could hear his breathing, syncing with hers. Even though the hunger twisted and burned in her belly, the yearning all but consuming her, she drew away first.

'You better get going, before Jacie turns up,' she said. 'I'll see you on Monday.'

He nodded, then left her standing in the living room.

She made herself busy, gathering up their empty plates. She could hear him getting dressed in the bedroom, then the soft pad of his footsteps as he walked down the corridor and climbed on to the fire escape. Once the sound had faded away, she stopped rinsing.

Last night had been her and Luke's Brokeback moment, and it had been exciting and wonderful and devastating all at the same time.

She still had at least a month of him working in the theatre and she just hoped their Brokeback moment wasn't going to ruin the time they had left together.

Because she was definitely Jack Twist in this scenario. And he was Ennis. Trying to make this more had the potential to hurt her a lot more than Luke – because she suspected he was a man used to denying his emotional needs. And she was a woman who had always yearned to indulge them, with the right guy.

She had to get it through her head that Luke wasn't that guy.

She went back to washing their breakfast dishes.

'So what's occurring between you and the man of steel buns?'

Ruby jumped and spun round so fast she dropped one of the plates back into the dirty dishwater, splashing her robe. 'Jacie! Give me a clue before you do that,' she said, placing her hand over her racing heart and hoping to change the subject.

'I would have needed a foghorn to wake you up from day-dreaming about you know who.'

'I don't know what you mean.'

'Forget it. I just saw him walk out the back alley, wearing the same clothes he had on when he left yesterday morning to go who knows where. And you have beard burn on your chin.'

Ruby cupped her palm over the sore spot and her cheeks warmed.

Bollocks. Jacie missed nothing. 'Umm.'

Jacie's grin split her face. 'Oh. My. God. You shagged him, didn't you? This is perfect.'

'I did *not* shag him,' she remarked, trying to sound indignant.

'Ruby, you are the worst liar that ever lived. You do know that, right?' Jacie shot straight back.

Ruby swallowed, trying to dislodge the thickness in her throat. 'It was just a one night type of thing.'

'How do you know it's just a one night thing?' Jacie asked. 'Did he say that? Already? That's so not classy.'

And there it was again, the anti-Luke sentiment Ruby thought had been tamed. 'Jace, could you do me a big favour?'

'Sure, what?'

'Could you forget about me and Luke and please don't tell the others. I couldn't bear for this to become a massive issue. For him or for me. It was fun and casual and not a big deal.'

Jacie's brow furrowed. Ruby knew she was effectively asking her friend to swallow a circus elephant by asking her to remain silent about the best bit of gossip since Kim Kardashian released her sex tape. But when it came to something this serious, she knew Jacie would choke down the elephant if she had to.

'Why are you so determined to make this not a thing when

it could be a thing?' Jacie said. 'I don't get it? Don't you want it to be a thing?'

'I'm not sure it can be a thing, even if I wanted it to be,' Ruby said. 'And I'm not sure I do.'

'Why not?'

'Because I'm grieving, Jace,' Ruby stressed, knowing what could have been a convenient excuse to end the conversation was actually the truth.

As much as she had enjoyed last night, and been moved by Luke's revelations this morning, was she really strong enough emotionally to embark on a relationship? A relationship which was full to bursting with complications before she and Luke had even touched each other for the first time. She hadn't been lying when she'd told Luke Matty had been the father of her heart. She was still processing the fact he hadn't told her about his love affair with Falcone, but the more she thought about it, the more it made sense. Would a man talk to his daughter about his failed love affair? Matty's silence didn't detract from the closeness of their relationship, if anything, it enhanced it. Matty had been protecting her, and her dreams, telling her the truth about Falcone would have been too much information.

But she was a grown woman now, and the truth about Luke was he was a complicated, conflicted guy trying to navigate the mistakes both his parents had made. Something she suspected was a lot tougher than he had let on after finding his father's body. And while Luke didn't blame his father anymore for that, she did. A little bit. Suicide was often a result of depression – which was beyond any person's ability to control even with therapy and medication. She knew that, intellectually.

But the thought of Luke as a fourteen-year-old boy going to his father's house to visit with a man who had failed him and finding something so horrific made her want to blame someone. And the only person she could think of to blame was Luke's father. The man who should have loved him and protected him but had been too consumed by his own demons to do either. And that was without even factoring in how Falcone had failed Matty, too.

She let out a breath to release the tightness in her chest.

Anger was pointless and unproductive. Especially anger against a man who had died sixteen years ago.

People were fallible, parents made mistakes, love didn't always conquer all, she of all people knew that. After all, she'd hardly spoken to her own mother since she'd left home at eighteen. There was no law that said you had to understand your parents, or the choices they made, and no law that said you needed to atone for them either.

But she wasn't convinced Luke had gotten that message.

He clearly had a very strained relationship with his mother, but he hadn't bailed on Helena Devlin the way Ruby had bailed on Margie Graham. Did that make him a good man, or a foolish one, or simply a dogmatic one? She didn't know, but what she did know was she had no intention of breaking the confidences he'd given her, or exploiting the heat between them, any more than she had already.

Which meant she wasn't going to force this thing-or-not-thing.

'I just don't have the head space for a grand love affair right now,' she continued, because Jacie was still looking at her as if she'd punched a gift horse in the mouth.

And neither does Luke.

'I'm too busy trying to save The Royale and deal with the fact that Matty is gone forever to think about much else.'

'I think you're missing the big picture here,' Jacie said, still frowning.

'What big picture?'

'If you want Luke Devlin, and he makes you happy, maybe you shouldn't give up on this thing so easily?'

The conviction in Jacie's voice made Ruby's throat thicken again.

'I'm not giving up on anything. If we can keep things casual, I certainly won't say no.' She wasn't ruling anything out, but she wasn't going to rely on Luke either for anything. 'All I'm saying is, I have to put myself first at the moment. And that means not relying on other people to make me happy or to fix stuff – other than my dodgy boiler or the cracks in the cornicing, that is.'

'What about the plan to get Luke to invest his gazillions in The Royale?' Jacie said, pragmatic as always. 'Is that not happening now?'

'No, it's not,' she said, feeling ashamed now she had ever seen Luke as a possible cash cow. 'Saving The Royale is not Luke's responsibility. It's my job to get the theatre into profit and find a way to cover the debts.'

'How?' Jacie said. 'You know as well as I do we can't possibly make enough money to cover that much debt. Not unless you sell the cinema. And if you do that they'll be no business anyway. There's nothing wrong with our business model,' Jacie added passionately. 'Matty wasted money on stuff he didn't have too, like the ten gallons of expired mimosa mix we found in the basement left over from the twenty-fifth anniversary screening of *Steel Magnolias* in 2014.' Jacie huffed out an exasperated breath.

'I know, Matty wasn't the most astute businessman.' Ruby had to agree, in the past month she and Jacie had been able to find a ton savings, and it hadn't been that hard. The mimosa mix debacle was just one of Matty's many sentimental expenditures. She could still remember how much he'd loved dressing up as Dolly Parton that night, though, so she didn't begrudge him in the slightest.

Matty had been a showman first and foremost. Perhaps he should have let her and Jacie take over managing the budget a long time ago, but it was too late to agonise over that now.

'If Devlin could just loan us the money to pay off the debts, we'd be able to pay him back. We've already got the budget for this month and next into the black, especially with all the extra revenue from Matty's Classics,' Jacie said.

'I don't want to ask him, though,' Ruby said, knowing she couldn't.

She placed the last plate on the draining board, dried her hands on the dishtowel, and swallowed past the raw spot in her throat.

'So, we're basically fucked, then?' Jacie said, sounding devastated.

'No we're not ...' Ruby said. 'All we need to do is come up with another plan.'

The kernel of an idea which she had flirted with weeks ago drifted back into the forefront of her brain.

'What plan?' Jacie said, sounding dejected. 'We don't have a plan. Devlin was the plan, remember.'

'You know The Rialto chain?' she said, naming a chain of independent cinemas who had luxury venues all over London.

Jacie nodded. 'Of course I do, the new cinema they opened in Holland Park took a big chunk out of our revenue four years ago according to Matty's records.'

Ruby smiled, the idea gathering pace. 'Before they opened that cinema they tried to buy The Royale, Matty told me.'

'Those sneaky bastards,' Jacie murmured.

'Not necessarily,' Ruby said. It was a long shot, but it might work, if she and Jacie put together a good enough proposal.

And better yet, it would mean working overtime in the office for a while.

What she needed right now was a project not just to save The Royale but also to save her from day-dreaming about Luke and his tool belt and their one night together. And all the things she now knew about him that only made her like him more.

PART FOUR

The Way We Were (1973)

Ruby's verdict: *Everyone when they watch this film falls in love with Robert Redford's Hubbell Gardner, because he's so gorgeous (especially in Navy whites). But Barbra Streisand's Katie is the heart of the movie, with her passion and her purpose, and her determination to make their relationship work no matter what. She has to give up in the end, but the truth is he's not out of her league, it's totally the other way round. She's way out of his league, because she believes in something enough to fight for it, and he doesn't – not even her.*

Luke's verdict: *Streisand's exhausting in this movie, no wonder Redford sleepwalks through the whole thing – and that song has got to be the ear-worm of the century – but you've gotta feel bad for Katie at the end because she still doesn't get it – Hubbell was never worth the effort.*

Chapter 13

'Hey, Ruby, hold up!' Luke dodged past a couple of tourists dawdling by the entrance to Portobello Road Market to catch up with his prey.

Ruby's head swung round and he clocked the pink flags in her cheeks before her gaze darted to both sides. 'Luke!' she whispered as he reached her. 'What are you doing? Is it safe for you to be out here?'

He choked back a laugh at the urgency in her tone. 'I think I can navigate a few tourists without killing myself,' he said wryly as he side-stepped the Japanese pair who were now taking pictures of the Portobello Road sign tacked to the wall.

Really? Even if you filtered the hell out of the shot, wasn't it going to look kind of generic on Instagram?

She grasped his arm and tugged him into a small alleyway off the main drag. Before checking the street again as if they were being followed by the FBI.

'I just ...' Her gaze finally landed back on him, making his heart lift. He'd discovered he liked having Ruby's eyes on him ... Probably because he'd missed them so much over the past week.

'I just don't think it's wise for you to venture out into a tourist hot spot like The 'Bello,' she finally said, her voice barely audible above the colourful shouts of the market traders selling everything from plantains to vintage Indian silk and the back beat of an old-school reggae sound system set up under the overpass by a vinyl record stall.

He tilted the bill on his ball cap down, because he did not want to alert attention, but couldn't resist a grin at her obvious concern for his well-being as her gaze continued to flick back and forth to the road from their hiding spot.

Good to know she still cared. He'd started to wonder, because it had been a week since he'd woken up in her bed and he hadn't managed to speak two whole sentences to her since. She'd either been too busy, locked in her apartment doing taxes, or accounts, or planning something with Jacie, or away from the theatre all together while he was on the premises, running anonymous errands that no one else seemed to know anything about. Such as this one.

But this time he'd gotten the jump on her, spotting her heading out just as he was arriving for his morning shift. So he'd decided to follow her.

And now here he was risking exposure in a West London tourist mecca and he actually did not give a damn. Because he'd wanted to get Ruby alone for a week.

He thought they'd come to an understanding a week ago, that the sex had been awesome but could never be more than that. But he'd decided in the last week – as long as they knew the limitations, which they had both agreed on – that still left some room to manoeuvre.

Stepping closer, he placed his palms on the wall on either side of her hips, effectively caging her in, while also shielding them both from any inquisitive passers-by. Time to test his theory. That he hadn't been wrong about their chemistry. If she wasn't interested, he'd back off.

Her chin popped out, her darting gaze landing squarely on his face, at last.

'Luke, what are you doing?' she said, a little breathless, but he could see the delightful pink flags waving on her cheeks.

'Kissing you?' he murmured, dipping his head.

He took it slow, so she could stop him if she wanted to, but she didn't move, didn't evade him, and his lips arrived at their destination without a hitch.

A gasp came out of her mouth, but then her body softened against his.

He explored, in leisurely strokes, enjoying her murmurs of encouragement as she let him lead their dance.

He broke away, and drew back, before things got out of control again. His own cheeks heated.

Well, that sure as hell settles that.

She was staring at him, her eyes dazed, her breathing thready. He basked in her reaction, while getting his own breathing back under control.

'Have you been avoiding me?' he asked.

So what if it made him sound needy? He *was* needy. One hook-up hadn't been enough to satisfy this hunger. And from the eagerness of the kiss they'd just shared, and the way her pupils had dilated to fill her irises, and her cheeks were rocking a blush worthy of Mary Poppins in a strip joint he didn't think she would disagree with him.

She blinked slowly, her lips pursed, but then she broke eye contact. 'I haven't been avoiding you,' she said, addressing the boxes of trash from the market stalls stacked next to their feet. 'I just ... I've been very busy. And so have you.'

He tucked a knuckle under her chin.

'Ruby,' he said firmly when her gaze finally reconnected with his 'It's a good thing you never wanted to be an actress, because you're a crummy liar.' He tried not to be charmed by her guilty expression. Had he ever met a woman who was easier to read?

'But I *have* been busy,' she said.

'You've also been avoiding me, admit it.'

She swallowed and the blush flared, but this time her gaze remained steady. And finally, she gave a small nod. 'I'm sorry, I didn't know what else to do.'

He straightened, hating the apology, and her sincerity. And the question he was forced to ask next.

'Things got a little weird a week ago,' he said, suddenly feeling like a prize jerk. He hadn't wanted things to get heavy between them, but they had, stuff had been said that couldn't be unsaid. He didn't want her thinking he was coming on to her again to fill an emotional hole. Because the desire he felt was a heck of a lot more basic than that. But he knew what a soft touch Ruby was, and he didn't want her giving him a pity screw either. 'Because of the business with my old man and Matty. But I have no expectations here. You do know that? I swear, I would never pressure you.'

The promise sounded disingenuous, at best, given the kiss he'd just initiated but he refused to regret it.

'Oh, for … Of course I know that, Luke,' she said, the guilty blush spreading up her neck. 'That's not why I've been avoiding you at all. In fact, it's sort of the opposite.'

He should have been relieved, at least she wasn't scared he was expecting something from her no man had a right to expect from any woman, but the end of her declaration didn't make a whole lot of sense.

'Okay, good, but you've lost me. How has you avoiding me got something to do with the opposite of me pressuring you?'

He frowned, because saying that out loud only made it sound like more of a mind fuck.

'It's just I didn't want to pressure *you* into anything,' she said, with complete conviction.

Say, what now?

'Huh?' was all he could manage round the lightning strike of complete astonishment. Was she saying what he thought she was saying? That she had been avoiding him because she didn't want to take advantage of him?

'It felt like I'd taken advantage of you.'

'What?' he croaked. *Jesus, seriously?*

'At a time when you were obviously very vulnerable.'

'Vulnerable how?' he asked, because his brain was starting to knot.

'After everything your mother had told you about your father and Matty that day,' she said and the fog of confusion started to lift.

Shit! Of course. He'd let slip that he was the one who had found his father's bloated corpse hanging from a light fixture in his Montecito bathroom.

Thank Christ he hadn't gone into any of the details.

But even so, he should have figured this might be Ruby's reaction. Because she was that kind of a woman. Unlike most of the people he knew, she took responsibility for her actions, and faced the consequences without complaint. Wasn't that exactly how she'd reacted when they'd gotten arrested after scattering Matty's ashes? Taken all the blame and made no excuses.

He should have realised by spilling his guts she'd somehow feel responsible for his shit now, too.

'What your mother told you had obviously upset you quite a lot,' she continued. 'And given what had happened before, with your father, your emotional equilibrium was shot that night. You needed comfort and support and ...' She sighed, a heavy sigh which reverberated in the pit of his stomach, making the twist of embarrassment and incredulity burn. But beneath the burn was a weird glow.

Sure he'd been surprised – maybe even a little shocked – by what his mom had told him. And, yeah, he'd wanted Ruby that night so he could forget about it all. But vulnerable? Heck no.

He just wasn't the vulnerable type.

You had to grow a thick skin fast – and learn basic survival skills at an early age – to deal with the kind of nomadic rootless childhood he'd been given. And become mature ahead of schedule if both your parents had treated responsibility like a disease. But there wasn't a thing about his childhood he regretted. That thick skin and those survival skills and that hard-won maturity had stood him in good stead over the years. Give or take the odd panic attack, it had made him a wealthy man before he'd hit thirty, put him in charge of his own destiny, given him options and best of all the stability he'd always craved during the chaos of his childhood.

But even knowing he didn't need Ruby's sympathy or her concern, he was still kind of touched she'd offered it so willingly and without any expectation of a reward.

No one had ever thought he needed protecting before – mostly because they knew him well enough to know he didn't. Ruby didn't know him that well, which was why she'd read way too much into his over-sharing the morning after their epic night. Her sympathy and her concern were misguided, but even so the glow in his gut spread, obliterating the burn of embarrassment, and the twist of humiliation until all that was left was the bubble under his breastbone he recognized but hadn't experienced since they'd laid the cornerstone on Devlin Properties first fully funded new build in Manhattan eight years ago.

He'd certainly never experienced this kind of euphoria during his interactions with a woman.

He'd probably be a little concerned about the novelty of that another time.

But as Ruby's gaze met his, so honest and forthright, the bubble of euphoria expanded … and felt way too good to regret.

'And given all that, I totally took advantage of you that

night,' she continued, her transparent expression a picture of contrition and shame. 'And I didn't want to risk doing it again.'

A chuckle formed in his chest. Going with instinct he pressed his palms to Ruby's cheeks. Her eyes widened, but she didn't draw back. And the chuckle worked its way up his torso.

He stroked her cheeks, feeling the guilty heat on her skin, but as she leaned into the caress, he could see the need she couldn't disguise, and the chuckle burst out of his mouth.

'Jesus, Ruby. Do you have any idea how goddamn adorable you are?'

Adorable? Really? What does that mean? Does he think I'm cute? Or does he think I'm special?

The questions whizzed around in Ruby's head.

She'd been trying so hard to steer clear of Luke in the last week while she and Jacie had worked up a proposal for The Rialto in every spare moment in between all the usual chores of running a busy neighbourhood picture palace.

But she'd deliberately scheduled all the meetings with Jacie in the last few days first thing in the morning, when she would usually be checking stock or helping Errol in the projection room transferring any digitally stored films to the main drive and adding the cues in a desperate attempt to avoid the torture of seeing Luke.

Ultimately, she'd been forced to take drastic action, because trying not to notice him, not to objectify him, not to pressure him or pine after him or flirt with him had been absolute agony with him right there, in her movie theatre, in *their* movie theatre, doing amazing things with his strong capable hands wearing a bloody tool belt – especially now she knew what it felt like to have all that focused attention and those strong capable hands on her, instead of the wet rot in the foyer.

As she struggled to process any kind of coherent answer for him now, Luke's lips touched hers again.

She flattened her palms against the worn cotton of his T-shirt. His abdominal muscles tightened deliciously beneath her palms as he licked along the seam of her lips. Tempting, teasing, torturing her ...

On a sigh of surrender, she opened her mouth to welcome him in.

Sod it. There's only so much abstinence a woman can take, especially in the face of extreme provocation.

His tongue thrust into her mouth in hungry, driving strokes, reminding her of the feel of his big body pounding into hers and she thrust back, unable to deny herself – and him – a moment longer.

He lifted his head at last, because breathing was required. But as they both got their breath back, his hand settled on her hip, the thumb rubbing across her hip bone in an absent gesture that felt both easy going and wildly possessive.

The hum of pleasure rose up her torso.

Don't you dare read too much into this. He's just horny and so are you.

But even as she told herself to enjoy the moment and not what it might mean – that Luke was as keen on repeating their wild night as she was, no hidden agendas required – she devoured his relaxed smile. A smile she realised she'd never seen before, but could easily become addicted to.

He seemed amused and in control, nothing like the intense, conflicted, wounded man she worried she might have taken advantage of last Friday.

Perhaps she had read way too much into what he'd shared with her.

After all, she was pretty over-emotional herself at the moment, thanks to the fallout from Matty's death, the revelations about his affair with Falcone, and the stress of finding a way to save The Royale. And she did have a tendency to over-compensate anyway, to be too sensitive to the heartache of others. Wasn't that precisely why she'd ended up cutting ties to her mother, because every time her mum had a bad break-up, Ruby was the one who had felt the need to fix her mother's heartache. Only to eventually realise – with a lot of help from Matty – she wasn't responsible for her mother's mistakes. Or the deadbeat guys she had a bad habit of falling in love with.

'*Excusez-moi!* Do you know Notting Hill Gate, how long away it is?'

Luke's rubbing thumb dropped away as Ruby spotted the man with the French accent standing at the entrance to their alleyway.

Luke tugged the bill of his cap over his face and looked the other way, as she replied.

'It's a good fifteen to twenty-minute walk from here, down Portobello Road,' she said. 'It's a very pretty walk, but if you're in a hurry I'd suggest hopping on a bus,' she hurried on, even though she could see confusion in the man's expression. Usually she loved being asked directions, especially by tourists, proud of the fact she was a local and grateful for the opportunity to get chatting and possibly stick in a plug for The Royale. But for once she did not have any desire to get into a conversation. 'You can catch a number 52 or a 452 bus from Ladbroke Grove, which runs parallel to Portobello Road.'

The tourist nodded and disappeared back into the crowd, probably picking up on her impatience. She dismissed the twinge of guilt at her abruptness.

'Helpfulness is your superpower,' Luke said, his shoulder propped against the wall as he watched her. 'Isn't it?'

Although his expression was shadowed by the cap, she could see the indulgent quirk of his lips.

'Actually, that was me being irritable and impatient,' she said, basking in his approval maybe a bit too much. 'But seriously? He was French? Couldn't he see we were busy kissing? I certainly wouldn't have expected Gerard Depardieu to be so insensitive.'

He chuckled again, the rough sound stroking all the erogenous zones he'd woken up with his kisses, then lifted a forefinger to trail it down her cheek.

He thinks you're adorable.

She chewed her bottom lip to prevent an excited chuckle popping out.

Control yourself, you are a grown woman, not a schoolgirl with a crush.

'Shall we head back to the theatre together?' he said, dropping his finger so he could capture her hand. 'I've already wasted half an hour of my morning shift.'

She nodded, not able to speak without risking another chuckle.

Were they holding hands now? Actually?

He led her down the alleyway, towards Portobello Green and away from any more interruptions.

She probably ought to object, she thought vaguely, as he led her through the small park. After all she'd been on an important errand when she'd left The Royale this morning. But as she could not for the life of her remember what that important errand was, how could she object?

So instead, she gave herself permission to swing her hand in his as they walked in the sunshine back towards Talbot Road.

It was official, she was having a *thing* with Luke Devlin. A hot-sex-only, no-strings, no-ties, no-complications, no-dangerous-emotions-allowed kind of a thing – but still definitely a thing.

Chapter 14

'Go to sleep,' Luke yawned, looking majorly cute to Ruby's way of thinking. 'I've got to get up early to start painting the lobby tomorrow morning.'

But as he flung off the duvet, she grasped his arm. 'Why don't you stay here tonight,' she murmured sleepily, her gaze snagging on the broad expanse of her lover's back as he glanced over his shoulder. 'You could get started sooner.'

'Do you really think that's a good idea?' Luke asked.

'Absolutely,' she said, ignoring the wary tone. 'It's silly, you going back to your house every night.'

She saw him hesitate.

'You sure?' he said as he slung an arm around her and sunk back into the pillows.

'It's no biggie,' she made herself say as she gazed up at his profile from her favourite spot snuggling against his shoulder. The spring rain outside, chiming against the fire escape, only made the moment feel more intimate. And special. 'And it's raining.'

It really wasn't a biggie, she told herself staunchly, it made sense for him to stay.

In the past nine days, ever since their walk back from the 'Bello had triggered a whole new phase in their friendship – which Ruby had secretly titled the shag-like-rabbits phase – he'd got into the habit of appearing on her fire escape after the final screening each night. After making fast furious love, they would eat whatever they could rustle up from the usually meagre supplies in her fridge and then settle in for more sex – after which Ruby had been unable to prevent herself from nodding off in his arms.

Because being madly in lust, she'd discovered, was actually quite exhausting. She'd had more orgasms in the last week than she'd had in her entire life – vibrator dates included. But when she'd woken up again, he was always gone. The bed beside her empty.

Tonight she'd managed to keep her eyes open while lounging against Luke's naked body, the musty smell of sex mixing with the scent of the grilled cheese sandwiches he'd made for their midnight feast while she basked in the sudden, delicious detour her life had taken – and waited for him to sneak out, so she could ask him to stay.

As he leaned down to place a kiss on her forehead – something he did every night before she went to sleep – arousal pulsed.

'It's tempting,' he said, around a jaw-busting yawn, as he played absently with her hair.

She resisted the urge to purr. She adored it when Luke played with her hair, twirling the curls round his fingers, testing the texture, as if he couldn't bear to stop touching her. When had anyone ever been this into her? Maybe it was only on a physical level, but she still found the attention intoxicating.

'But I don't want to take advantage of your hospitality,' Luke continued.

Ruby tried to concentrate on what he was saying, instead of the feel of his thigh brushing against her hip, or the resilient thud of his heartbeat against her ear.

Chillax Rubes. You're both too knackered for another shagathon, anyway.

'But I love it when you take advantage of my hospitality,' Ruby teased, determined to keep things light and noncommittal, the way they needed to be.

She ran her fingers through the three hairs growing around Luke's belly button – hairs she'd become quite attached to in the last nine days – concentrating on why she wanted him to stay. This wasn't about intimacy, it was just about comfort. And practicalities. It made no sense for him to head out now, in the rain, when he could sleep here.

'And anyway the least I owe you is a warm bed on a rainy night,' she added.

Hadn't he ridden to the rescue of the theatre, turned up every single day on schedule and worked his arse off for no reward for close to a month? And wasn't he the best lover she'd ever had, his imagination and enthusiasm in bed only outstripped by his generosity? She suspected – from the few things Luke had told her about his childhood – he'd had so much responsibility in his life, he didn't want to add anyone else to the list. And being indebted to her, would add her to the list, because Luke always paid his dues. But she wanted him to know that didn't apply here because he'd already paid any dues to her a hundred times over.

'How do you figure that?' Luke asked. His hand stopped stroking her hair. 'I hope you're not referring to the work I've done on the theatre.'

'Well, yes, that and ...' She sent him what she hoped was a slutty smile. 'Your services to my sex life.'

His eyebrows shot up, but then he laughed. A deep, rumbling laugh that relaxed his face and only made him more sexy.

His foot brushed hers and his hand trapped her fingers against his belly button. 'Who knew British girls were so naughty.'

His six-pack rippled as he sunk down to join her under the covers. And something stiff and exciting got trapped against her hip.

''Fraid so,' she said, as his callused palm cupped her naked breast – sending endorphins careering through her system. 'So are you staying to help me with my sex addiction?'

'I guess I am.'

He captured her pouting nipple between his lips. She threaded her fingers into his hair and arched into his mouth, a sob escaping as he went to work.

Her sex addiction was nothing compared to her Luke Devlin addiction, she decided. So it was a good thing she only wanted him for one thing.

Luke pressed his face into Ruby's wild hair and inhaled the scent of her shampoo as her body became soft and pliant in sleep. Heat pooled in his lap, even though he'd just had the third of tonight's mind-altering orgasms. Her breathing deepened and he forced himself to let her go and roll on to his back before he got any ideas about waking her up for a repeat performance.

He had to brace his elbow against the bedside cabinet to prevent himself from rolling right on to the floor.

He had a deluxe king-size with a firm orthopaedic mattress in the house he was paying a small fortune to rent less than twenty minutes' walk away from The Royale and as he watched Ruby's fairy lights flicker over the crack in the ceiling moulding above his head he tried to figure out whether he should take her up on the offer to sleep over. She was right, it was raining and he had to be back here first thing in the morning. It really wasn't that big of a deal.

But he couldn't quite shake the feeling that if he stayed the night in Ruby's bed, it would mean something.

He squinted at the ceiling.

'Go to sleep man. It's not a big deal, she said so herself.'

Great, now he was talking to the ceiling.

He scooted closer to Ruby. Why spoil a good thing when they only had a couple more weeks to enjoy it?

The pragmatic thought brought with it a wave of melancholy. Which was just plain wrong. This was a casual hook-up. It had always had a time limit on it.

But as he stared at the rain running in rivulets down the window glass and considered offering to repair the cracked plasterwork on her ceiling, he knew he was lying to himself.

The more time he spent with Ruby, the less time he wanted

to spend apart from her. Which was a problem. Because he would be returning to New York sooner rather than later.

He'd gone over his three-hundred-hour community service commitment a couple of days ago. And he'd be finished all the jobs he'd assigned himself by the end of this week.

All he had to complete was the repainting in the lobby area once he'd reinstalled the baseboards. He could string that out for another couple of weeks, but once that was done, The Royale would be all out of jobs to keep him here – give or take the odd cracked ceiling moulding.

Not only that, but he'd received a text from his mom to invite him to the first preview of her one-woman show at the National on Thursday next. She'd begun bombarding him with texts and WhatsApp messages after getting hold of his British cell number from his kid sister. Once his mom hit town, he would have to head back over the Atlantic. Keeping an ocean between them was essential for his mental health right now.

But at least she'd kept her promise not to contact Ruby directly again.

He shuddered. He didn't even want to think what would happen if his mom ever found out he and Ruby had hooked up.

It made sense to start planning his return Stateside.

But instead of doing that, he'd been thinking of ways to prolong his trip.

What was with that?

This hook-up wasn't serious. They'd even been careful to keep their activities on the downlow so none of The Royale's staff would figure out they were boning each other after hours.

He huffed out a breath.

Although from the side-eyes Jacie kept giving him, he wasn't so sure everyone had been fooled by their no-touching-kissing-or-generally-undressing-each-other-with-their-eyes-during-working-hours rule.

But despite keeping things determinedly casual, what should have been simple and uncomplicated became tougher and more confusing each day he worked side-by-side with Ruby, and each night he crept up the fire escape to make love in her cramped queen bed with the trampoline mattress. And then held her as she fell asleep.

Staying over would only increase his confusion.

Perhaps it was just that he'd developed an affection for The Royale. In the space of a month, ever since he'd first started work on the dilapidated old theatre, he'd become addicted to ripping out the crumbling plaster and rotten woodwork, repairing, re-plastering and repainting. To doing all those odd jobs he figured had been waiting for years. He'd started to join in the staff chatter, learned how to thread an old 35mm projector from Errol, even cashed up a couple of times when Beryl had been struck low with the flu or Claire, the other cashier, had a childcare emergency.

But the more invested in The Royale he became, the more invested he became in Ruby, too. Because more than his addiction to showing up each day at The Royale was his addiction to Ruby's lush curves, her wild rose-scented hair, that dimple that popped up on her cheek every time she smiled, the soft sobs of encouragement she gave him when he touched her, and tasted her, the sleepy conversations they had late at night about everything from installing a new motor for the security gate to whether or not to run the rest of the Matty's Classics season in chronological or alphabetical order.

And the more addicted he became to Ruby and The Royale, the more concerned he became about what would happen to the place and her once he left. He could repair the theatre, give Ruby the orgasms she deserved, but how could he secure her future without becoming a part of it, and prolonging this attachment past its sell-by date?

A clean break was the only way to go, but the more he thought about making that break, the less he wanted to.

Listening to Ruby's gentle snores in the darkness, and the patter of rain on the window casing, he forced himself to switch off his thoughts, and leave figuring out the Ruby conundrum to another night.

Stretching, he snagged the cord for the lights and switched them off too.

Chapter 15

Can you take some time off tonight and meet me @ Brynn's @ six for a date?

Ruby read Luke's text for the second time, and tried to convince herself their first proper date was not a bad thing. But the sinking feeling in her stomach wasn't cooperating.

Luke had finished repainting the foyer two days ago.

They'd had an impromptu staff party yesterday to christen the new look front of house area. Jacie had bought two cheap bottles of fizz from the cash and carry down the road, Gerry had supplied the plastic cups, Beryl had produced some inedible cupcakes – which had a movie theme no one could decipher – and Ruby had given a speech thanking Luke for all of his hard work while trying not to blush knowing his hard work on the theatre's infrastructure wasn't the only work she appreciated. It had been even more of a struggle not to tear up at the knowledge Luke would be gone soon. But when the party had broken up and he hadn't said anything, she'd convinced herself they might still have a few days, maybe even a week left to enjoy each other.

But as she reread the text again, she wondered, was the hammer about to fall?

Why else would he want to take her on a date, somewhere public, unless he had something to say he thought she might get over-emotional about? And why had he disappeared two hours before the pensioners' early-bird screening had started? Was he packing even now, preparing to catch a night flight back to Manhattan?

The hole in her stomach hurt as she tapped out a deliberately nonchalant don't-worry-Luke-I'm-not-going-to-have-a-breakdown reply.

No probs, Jace can cover for me, I'll see you there.

'Hey, Jace, can I ask you a favour?' she shouted above the hoover her friend was using to suck the last of the crumbs from Beryl's rock-hard cupcakes off the newly washed carpet before the pensioners started arriving.

Jace kicked the machine's switch to cut off the noise. 'Yup.'

'I've got to go out, could you watch the fort until ...' She paused, how long was Luke's parting speech likely to take? Would he want to come back to the flat tonight? The questions only made her stomach hurt more. 'Until closing?' she asked.

Even if their break-up drinks didn't last that long, and he didn't fancy a goodbye shag, she was likely to be in bits. No harm in scheduling time for a mini-breakdown until tomorrow morning.

'Sure, where are you going?' Jacie asked.

Ruby pressed her lips together to stop them wobbling. She really needed to get that reaction under control before she got to Brynn's or she was likely to completely screw up the finale of The Ruby Movie.

If she could survive without Matty, she could survive

without Luke. And it wouldn't even hurt as much, once she got over the loss. Because Luke wasn't dead, he just wasn't ever meant to be a permanent fixture in her life.

The Ruby Movie didn't need a man for its Happy Ever After. Because The Ruby Movie was a feminist romcom. No lovesick nonsense allowed.

'Just to Brynn's. I'm meeting Luke for a drink,' she said, the wobble all but undetectable.

Jace propped her elbow on the hoover's wand and studied Ruby. 'Why do you need to go out to meet him when he's going to be scaling the fire escape later?'

Ruby blinked. Fine, she knew they hadn't fooled Jace, or probably anyone else for that matter – the amount of well-meant "bedroom tips" she'd been getting from Beryl was actually scary – but did Jacie have to be quite so direct?

'Because we're just going to be talking, I guess,' she replied, deciding to meet direct with direct.

'What are you going to be talking about?'

'Isn't it obvious?' Ruby said, no longer able to hold on to the wobble.

Dropping the hoover wand, Jacie strode over to the box office counter where Ruby had been busy restocking the popcorn maker before she'd gotten Luke's text of doom.

'Rubes?' She threw her arm over Ruby's shoulder, gave her a comforting squeeze – which managed to hold the wobble back, thank goodness. 'Has Luke done something? Said something?' Jacie asked, her incredulity a sign that even she had discovered Luke's charms. 'You've been so happy in the last few weeks. I thought you guys were having fun together?'

'We are ...' She gulped past the blockage in her throat. 'Or rather we were. But I think he's going to tell me he's flying home tonight.' She brushed her hair back from her face, sniffed loudly, and stepped out of Jacie's hug, feeling foolish now, as well as wobbly.

She'd always known this would happen. Why was she taking it so hard? Perhaps it was just that with Luke gone she wouldn't have him to lean on when she and Jacie did the presentation they'd been working on for The Rialto tomorrow morning. She hadn't spoken to him about it, at all, because they'd both been careful to avoid any questions about The Royale's future.

But without Luke's sturdy, steady presence by her side, as a lover and a friend, and his expert skills in the sack to send her into an endorphin coma, reality just seemed that much more real.

This wobble wasn't really about Luke and his imminent departure, this was about her and all the pressure she'd been busy refusing to acknowledge since they'd begun their nightly bonkfests. Avoidance had been wonderful while it lasted, but she couldn't spend the rest of her life relying on Luke to make her feel good.

'Perhaps you could persuade him to stay?' Jacie offered.

Ruby's heart punched her ribs as she shook her head.

'No, I couldn't. And even if I could ...' And luckily, even *she* had never been that delusional. 'I wouldn't.'

Jacie shrugged, but didn't argue the point.

As Ruby headed upstairs to prepare for her first – and probably last – proper date with Luke Devlin, the hole in her stomach didn't feel quite so bottomless.

Just Like in the Movies

She and Jacie had worked up a brilliant proposal and they'd gotten the green light from The Rialto to make the presentation tomorrow. She didn't need Luke to save her, because she'd always been capable of saving herself.

She was going to make the Happy Ever After finale of The Ruby Movie happen even if Luke Devlin was about to leave the building.

'Hey, Ruby, long time no see,' Brynn wiped down the bar and sent Ruby his sauciest smile when she stepped into the local pub three minutes after six o'clock. The place wasn't too packed yet because it was a week night before ten and Brynn wasn't doing any of his special events to attract customers like Drag Singalong, or Drag Stand-Up or Drag Queens' Quiz Night.

'Hi, Brynn,' she said, waiting for her eyes to adjust to the darker light inside the bar.

'By the way, Ruby, do you fancy some free entertainment for your Babs and Bob night on Saturday? I thought I could do my version of *The Way We Were* for the punters. I know how much Matty adored that song.'

'And your rendition of it,' Ruby added, smiling. 'That would be absolutely wonderful, Brynn, I'll stick it on the poster, if you're sure?'

'Course I am, honey,' he said, then pointed her towards the back of the bar, beside the stage. 'Your man's in the corner booth waiting on you. You want me to fix you a lemon-tini?' he added with a wink.

'Yes, please.'

Your man? Had her and Luke's liaison been a secret from anyone at all?

She hesitated by the bar, not wanting to dash straight over to Luke and give away her eagerness.

'You go on, I'll bring it over,' Brynn said, picking up on her eagerness anyway. So much for subtlety.

As she approached the back of the bar, Luke had his head down, tapping out something on his phone with both thumbs – probably travel plans – and nursing a Sam Adams, which she now knew was his favourite craft beer. Funny to think of all the pieces of useless information you could pick up about a man after sleeping with him every night for close to three weeks.

Spotting her, he clicked the phone to sleep mode and stood up as she approached.

Had it really only been twenty days?

She absorbed his muscular physique in the dark designer suit, the jacket unbuttoned and the perfect crease in the trousers. He looked like the man she'd first seen up close in Ryker's office, rich and reserved, and nothing like the man who had lived in worn overalls and a tool belt doing manual labour for the past five and a half weeks.

'Hi, Ruby, glad you could make it,' he said, touching her arm and guiding her into the seat across from him. 'Is that a new dress? I haven't seen you in it before,' he said, his gaze skating over the green satin mini-dress she'd taken out of mothballs.

'Let's be honest, you haven't seen me in much except my Royale T-shirt,' she said, trying to smile flirtatiously past the ball of misery forming in her throat.

Why did everything seem so formal all of a sudden? And

why was having that hot appreciative gaze on her once more only making this tougher?

'I'm starting to believe in kismet,' he said, his gaze finally returning to her. 'Because the dress is perfect for what I had in mind for tonight.'

'It is? What did you have in mind?' she asked because his gaze had gone past formal straight to feral, and as much as she wanted to keep it there, the not knowing what the heck was going on was not relieving the tension in her tummy.

'I need you to rescue me.' He covered her hand on the table and stroked his thumb across the knuckles, making heat coat the knots in her stomach. 'Please tell me you got Jace to sub for the whole night?'

'I did.'

He lifted her fingers and kissed the knuckles, just as Brynn arrived with her lemon-tini.

'Here you go, Honey, although it doesn't look to me like you need it,' Brynn said with a conspiratorial smile which made Luke chuckle before the bar owner left again.

Lifting the frosty glass, Luke handed it to her. 'Here, drink up, you're gonna need it.'

She picked the lemon slice off the rim and took a quick sip of the citrusy cocktail. 'Why?'

'Because tonight we're going to the preview of my mom's one-woman show.'

Ruby let out a delighted laugh, the burst of relief flooding through her veins with the liquor. 'But that's ...'

Wonderful. Amazing. Awe-inspiring. And not a goodbye. Not yet.

'Likely to be painfully cheesy,' Luke supplied with a playful shudder which made her feel as if she had just landed in Oz. 'I need you with me, to protect me from death by a thousand clichés.'

'You shouldn't talk like that about Helena Devlin,' she said taking a jauntier sip of her lemon-tini. 'I'm sure her show is going to be incredible.'

And Ruby was going to be one of the first people to see it.

'Your mum is an icon,' she added.

But it wasn't Helena's status as an actress, a performer, a personality, even a legendary love goddess that was making Ruby so excited.

Tonight she was going to get the chance to meet Luke's mother. And sleep with him. Again.

After her brief conversation with Helena over the phone all those weeks ago, and years of devouring her exploits in movie magazines, and the few things that Luke had let drop about her, Ruby would always have been curious and excited to meet her.

But what intrigued her most of all now was the thought of seeing Helena with her son, and getting a new insight into the man she'd fallen in— She cut off the thought, hastily reconfigured it ... Fallen in lust with.

'Don't you dare tell her that,' he said, sending her a quelling smile over the neck of his beer bottle. 'Or this is going to be an even bigger ordeal.'

'Bring it on,' she said, clinking her glass with Luke's bottle, and sending heartfelt thanks to whoever might be watching over her tonight.

Chapter 16

'*Devlin? Luke Devlin? Luke? Look this way.*'
   '*Who's the pretty lady with you, Luke?*'
 '*Are you looking forward to your mother's show?*'

The photographers' shouts hounded Luke across the red carpet, which seemed to go on forever, making him doubt his kneejerk decision to bring Ruby to his mom's show every step of the way.

What the fuck were you thinking, inviting Ruby to this shitshow?

He kept his hand anchored to Ruby's hip as he escorted her across the zoned off area toward the entrance of the National Theatre. The monolithic theatre complex's Brutalist façade rose up on the South Bank of the Thames, the stacked grey concrete floors starting to reflect Luke's ugly mood.

If the press figured out who Ruby was, his cover would be blown at The Royale.

A micro-celebrity he didn't recognize stopped to pose for the cameras in front of them and he had to break his stride to stop from barrelling right through the woman.

The shouted questions became more urgent, more insistent, and even more intrusive.

'*Who's your father Luke?*'

'*Why not confirm it's Falcone?*'

Because it's none of your goddamn business.

His heart lurched in his chest. He dragged Ruby past the micro-celebrity – whose posing had finally drawn some of the attention off them.

You're welcome to it, sweetheart.

But then a logjam of guests going through the bag check at the entrance halted their progress again.

His lungs constricted and his palms started to sweat as they were trapped in the glare of the camera lights.

Ruby's fingers tightened on his hand. 'Luke, it's okay,' she whispered, rising on tiptoes to speak in his ear. 'They can't get past the rope.'

He stared at her, the new barrage of noise and light fading as his gaze locked on her face.

How did she know? That he was about to freak out?

But even as the humiliating question echoed through his consciousness, he knew it didn't matter. All that mattered was holding on to her dry fingers like a lifebelt and getting into the damn theatre.

Two seconds later – that actually felt like several lifetimes – they stepped into the lobby area and the cacophony outside was reduced to the hum of guests and critics chatting and the clink of glasses.

His lungs finally released the breath trapped under his breastbone, making him light-headed as Ruby led him to a concrete staircase.

The preview's invited audience mingled on the roped off

mezzanine, sipping expensive bubbles and eating fancy appe-
tizers on silver trays like entitled peacocks. Ruby let go of his
hand to snag them both a glass.

'Drink this,' she said, her concerned gaze searching his face
as she passed him the champagne. The humiliation came back
for an encore but then she smiled and took a sip. '*Mmm.*' She
smacked her lips. 'Just as I thought, free fizz always makes
things better.'

A rough chuckle burst out – part relief, part who gives a
shit – as he took a long gulp of his own free fizz.

He shouldn't have come. He hated these things, especially
if they had anything to do with his mom because it dragged
him right back to being a kid again and having cameras
shoved in his face asking him questions he didn't know how
to answer.

He certainly hadn't intended to come to the show when
the tickets had arrived at the house that afternoon by courier,
followed by a ton of texts from his mom, which he'd deflected
easily enough.

He'd had other plans for tonight, more important plans,
which involved finally breaking the news to Ruby that he only
had a couple more days of snag work to do at The Royale
and he had a flight to JFK booked for Saturday night.

It was a good plan, a smart plan, a plan he'd been working
on ever since the long night he'd spent contemplating the
crack on her ceiling – the first night he'd stayed over, and all
the nights since – and eventually come to the conclusion that
the reason he hadn't been able to walk away sooner was
because he'd needed her.

For sex, for friendship, to appease his guilty conscience over what his mom and dad had done to Matty and for a whole host of other reasons he would probably need a shrink to unravel. That's why he hadn't been able to say goodbye. But he was free and clear again – or he would be in a couple of nights, after he'd finally returned The Royale to its former glory.

He owed it to Ruby, and to his uncle.

His grand plan to finish the work so he could walk away without regrets had all made perfect sense when he'd sent Ruby the text that afternoon.

But everything had changed when Ruby had appeared in Brynn's wearing that emerald dress clinging to every curve, with a look in her eyes that he recognized, from their first merry meeting, in Ryker's office.

Fear. And grief.

And he'd felt the grief too. For a relationship which was never supposed to mean anything.

And in that moment. All he had been able to think was …

I don't want to tell her tonight. I don't want to spoil the last nights we have left together.

And the invitation to his mom's preview had spilled out of his mouth before he could stop it. Kind of like a stealth bomber – wreaking havoc one bad decision at a time.

But he hadn't really factored in the true fallout from that decision until they'd stepped out of the taxi and walked into one of his worst nightmares.

Weirdly though, even getting ambushed by tabloid hacks and paparazzi hadn't been as bad as it could be. Because nothing ever was with Ruby there.

'*Oh!*' Ruby pointed her glass past his left shoulder. 'Is that Ross Barlett? Who starred in *Life's a Bitch* with your mother in 1999?'

He glanced over his shoulder to see a distinguished looking older gentleman wearing a well fitted hair-piece with a much younger woman on his arm. They made eye contact, and recognition flickered into the guy's famous hazelnut eyes before he immediately broke eye contact.

'Shit, yeah it is him,' he said, then grasped Ruby's elbow to steer her to the other side of the bar, as far away from Barlett as it was possible to get.

'Do you know him? Would you introduce us?' Ruby asked obviously picking up on the eyeball tango they'd been doing before Barlett had ghosted him. 'I've seen all of his movies.' She continued trying to sneak a peek over his shoulder. 'I had no idea he was still alive.'

Luke chuckled at the unintentional insult which he knew Barlett would not appreciate, being the vainest man on the planet.

'I do know him,' he said. 'We have history from that shoot. Which is why I'm not going to introduce you to him, to save you from having all your illusions shattered.' He steered her towards the doors to the theatre auditorium as the five-minute call sounded. 'You can thank me later.'

'History? What history?' Ruby asked, her eyes widening with interest like the movie buff she was.

'That's for me to know and you to never find out,' he said, but he couldn't help smiling as he led her to their seats.

As long as his mom hadn't arranged for him to sit within

283

a fifty-seat radius of her former co-star – and even *she* wasn't that Kamikaze – he could actually see the humour in his run-in with Barlett all those years ago for the first time.

He might even tell Ruby about it later tonight – if she really wanted to know. It made a pretty funny story, and what was some movie gossip between friends? He had some juicy goods on Barlett. Goods Ruby would appreciate. And goods she wouldn't rat to anyone else if he asked her not to.

The lights dimmed as the rest of the invited audience took their seats.

All he had to do was survive the next two hours – and get Ruby out of here before she came face-to-face with his mom – and they were all good.

He placed his hand on her knee, rubbed the silky material and felt her shudder.

Response echoed in his groin and he took his hand off her knee.

He had two hours of his mom's anecdotes to get through first.

Dammit, what the hell were you thinking, inviting her to this show? When you've only got three nights left with her?

'Your mum is amazing, she held the audience in the palm of her hand for two solid hours,' Ruby managed as she was dragged through the milling crowd towards the theatre exit.

'She likes the sound of her own voice, that's for sure,' Luke threw over his shoulder as he whisked them past the bar.

Shoving open a fire escape at the back of the foyer, Ruby

was shepherded out into the pedestrian thoroughfare at the side of the theatre.

The musty smell of the Thames was overlaid with the vague aroma of disinfectant. As Luke's grip tightened on her upper arm, he led her away from the Embankment towards the access road at the back of the complex.

'Let's grab a cab before everyone else gets out of there,' he said as they reached the road.

Ruby pulled her arm out of his grasp as he lifted his other hand to flag down a taxi.

'But aren't you going to go backstage?' she asked, confused now and a little flustered.

The show had been incredible. Helena Devlin was a living legend for a reason. She'd told stories of her days in the theatre and on film, performed everything from Shakespeare to Lin-Manuel Miranda and told a host of hilarious anecdotes. Ruby had been awestruck throughout.

'Why would I do that?' Luke said before sticking his fingers in his mouth and letting out a piercing whistle, just like he'd done all those weeks ago in front of Ryker's office.

A black cab appeared from nowhere and braked in front of them. Again.

How the bloody hell do New Yorkers do that?

'To congratulate her? To thank her for the tickets?' Ruby offered as he gave the address of The Royale to the cab driver. 'To tell her how fabulous she was?'

Luke opened the cab's passenger door. 'She already knows how fabulous she is. And the backstage area will be packed with her fans and sycophants. It'll take us an hour to get anywhere near her. And I've got something much better we could be doing.'

The husky tone rippled through her.

Well, okay, then.

'Jump in,' he said, raising his arm towards the cab like Prince Charming directing Cinderella into her carriage. 'Come on, Ruby, scoot.'

A rather impatient Prince Charming.

She climbed into the cab.

'I still think it's a bit rude not to even acknowledge we were there, and we enjoyed it,' she said as Luke climbed in beside her. Although she wasn't sure he had enjoyed it that much. He'd fidgeted throughout, which was unlike him.

'Fine, I'll do it now.' He yanked his phone out as the cab accelerated away from the curb.

Ruby watched, increasingly appalled, as he opened WhatsApp, selected MOM, typed in a string of clapping hands emojis, tapped send, then switched the phone to sleep mode and shoved it back in his pocket.

'Luke! That's not a proper thank you. It's not even a proper acknowledgement.'

'Sure it is, my mom loves emojis.'

'But won't she be hurt? That you didn't go and see her in person?' Ruby asked.

He grasped the handle as the cab turned the corner on to Waterloo Bridge. 'Ruby, if you want to meet my mom, why don't you just say so …'

'B-b-because …' She spluttered, trying to come up with a believable lie. 'This isn't about me wanting to meet her.'

He didn't blink.

'All right, maybe it is a *bit* about me wanting to meet her.' She tried to look contrite. 'But why don't *you* want me to meet her?'

Just when she thought she'd won the argument, he leaned across the seat, captured her cheek and drew her face towards his.

'That's kind of obvious,' he whispered, blocking out the view of Big Ben and the Houses of Parliament and replacing it with a much more exciting one. 'I'm busy.'

His mouth covered hers, his tongue taking advantage when her lips parted on a gasp of surprise and need.

They were all the way to the Palace of Westminster before she had a chance to get another word in edgewise. But by then, she'd completely forgotten what they were talking about.

Glancing at the partition, Luke finally released her and settled into the seat. 'We better chill out before we shock the driver.' Taking her fingers in his he lifted them to his lips and buzzed a kiss into her palm. Her heartbeat stumbled.

'So you liked the show?' he asked absently, not meeting her gaze.

'I loved the show. Didn't you?' she fired back, determined not to ask all the questions she really wanted to ask.

After coming down from the blast of euphoria earlier – when she hadn't been summarily dumped as expected in Brynn's – Ruby had gotten a grip and figured out why. Tonight was an exercise in avoidance.

The mad dash to get to the National in time for curtain-up, and the show itself had made it impossible for them to talk about anything important. And she'd figured out why a while ago.

Their time together was nearly over, maybe not tonight but certainly soon. And Luke didn't want to say so.

She had figured out the truth from Luke's impatience, the fidgeting, the strange decision to invite her to a place she knew he would usually avoid. He'd been photographed by the press, they both had, some enterprising hack was bound to figure out who she was eventually, which meant he wouldn't be able to continue working at The Royale much longer.

But of course, that didn't matter if he was about to leave the country.

As she'd watched Helena Devlin weave her magic over an audience of her peers from the Cottosloe's stage – she'd come to terms with the reality. And promised herself, whatever happened, she wasn't going to ruin the little time they had left together.

The fact Luke seemed so determined to keep things light made her heart stutter as his thumb stroked the back of her hand and they sped along Chelsea Embankment.

This was hard for him, too, and somehow that was enough. All this was ever meant to be was a moment – or rather several moments – out of their real lives. They could never have been a real couple, and not just for the reasons she'd told Jacie.

Luke Devlin was a billionaire property developer, the son of two Hollywood icons. Breathtakingly handsome and a master of the dark arts in bed. He was so far out of her league it was ridiculous. But more than that, despite all the great sex they'd had, all the intimate conversations, all the midnight feasts and shared breakfasts and lengthy discussions about everything from dry rot to flying monkeys, Luke was the most emotionally unavailable man she'd ever met.

She had a better idea of why that might be now. But she wasn't in the right place to change him, and she very much doubted she was the right person.

They'd become accidental bonk buddies. And while she was desperately sad that would soon come to an end – and she knew she would miss him terribly, when no one turned up on her fire escape after dark – she refused to fall to pieces. Which meant no deep and meaningful conversations to make him uncomfortable, or her feel too needy.

He stared out of the cab's window, his thumb rubbing across the knuckles he'd kissed, his profile tense. He was waiting for her to ask about 'them'.

So she searched her mind for something to say that didn't involve 'them'.

'What happened between you and Ross Bartlett on the set of *Life's a Bitch?*'

He turned towards her.

'Is it juicy?' she asked when he simply stared at her.

'Yeah, it's real juicy,' he said.

'Then you need to 'fess up. You owe me.'

'How do you figure that?' he said, but his lips quirked with relief.

'You refused to introduce me to you mum. I could have dined out on my meeting with the great Helena Devlin for decades so I want something to compensate me. Juicy gossip about Bartlett might just cover it.'

He choked out a rough laugh. And her pulse did a giddy little back flip.

'You're such a movie nut,' he said, the gruff affection making her smile. Once upon a time, coming from Luke, that would definitely have been insult. If nothing else, Luke's opinion had softened about a medium she loved and he had been taught to hate, thanks to his association with her and The Royale.

Matty would be proud of her.

'I know,' she said. 'Now cough up.'

She wanted their last nights together to be joyful. And sexy. Not sad and tense. If that meant keeping the conversation shallow, so be it. And to be fair, juicy gossip from the set of a cult nineties romcom wasn't a bad parting gift.

'You're sure you want to have all your illusions about Barlett shattered? Because I'm not taking responsibility.'

'I am okay with having my illusions shattered, now tell the story,' she said.

His shoulders relaxed as he spoke into the darkness, his tone one of jaded amusement. 'Okay, just to give you some background, during a shoot my mom always insisted on having us with her. That meant paid tutors and nannies when I was a little kid, but as Mom's career tanked, the producers were less willing to fork out for that kind of support. When she made *Life's a Bitch* with Barlett her movie career and his were already entering the end zone, which meant she had to pay for the babysitters. It was a micro-budget movie shot on location in the summertime in some podunk town in Georgia.'

He sighed. 'We had been stuck at the location all day watching mom getting tied to a post over and over again and the au pair mom had hired – a local college student called Melanie Schultz – had forgotten to come get us and take us back to the hotel.' He gave a rueful smile. 'Mom sacked Melly the next day when it turned out she'd been getting high with one of the grips and passed out in his trailer.'

'Stop talking about Melly and tell me about Ross Bartlett,' she said.

'It's not *that* juicy, don't get too excited.'

'I'll be the judge of that,' she said, waving him on.

'Okay, so I'd put Jack and Becca to bed in the bedroom of my mom's trailer. And I was reading my *Incredible Hulk* comic in the back, wondering where Melly was and when Mom would be finished shooting so we could go back to the hotel, when I heard a commotion outside. Then both my mom and Bartlett came crashing into the trailer. Not expecting us to be there, they didn't see me. They were arguing loudly, in that theatrical way actors always argue – as if they're on Broadway instead of in real life.'

'Do they?' she asked.

He simply looked at her as if she were impossibly naïve.

Okay, point taken. 'What were they arguing about?'

'Who knows, they probably didn't even know. It was fore-play.'

'Foreplay?' she said, suddenly *feeling* impossibly naïve.

'Sure, my mom's a card-carrying fan of great make-up sex – which means she generally has a lot of shouting matches with the guys she's screwing.'

291

'There's a card for that?'

'Stop interrupting, do you want to hear my juicy Bartlett story or don't you? The press would pay a fortune for this stuff,' he said, then frowned. And she suddenly wondered if he was thinking he'd said too much.

She let out a weighty sigh. 'I would never sell anything you tell me. Ever.' She crossed her little finger over her heart. 'Pinkie swear.' She paused. 'Well, unless it was about Babs and Bob, then I might have to sell just a little bit. Because you know, that's public need to know stuff.'

'I only ever met Babs once.'

'You met Barbara Streisand, why the heck didn't you say so?'

'Which story are we on here?'

'Okay, okay, forget Babs for now, but we will be revisiting that, just so you know.' She gulped. 'Fine, so your mum and Ross are arguing. Foreplay arguing. Then what happened?'

He grinned, the teasing glint in his eye unmistakable. 'Actually I'm not sure I should tell you, it's kind of sordid.'

'How sordid? *Fifty Shades* sordid or *Human Centipede* sordid?'

'Is there anything in your life that doesn't have a movie reference?' he asked, sounding exasperated.

'No,' she said, unapologetically. 'Now answer the question, because *Fifty Shades* sordid I can cope with ... *Human Centipede* not so much.'

'It's sort of between the two.'

'Fine. Go on, I'll cope.'

'All right, so they're arguing, and then he drags her over

his knee, pulls up her skirt, rips down her panties and starts spanking her. I thought he was hitting my mom. I was freaking out. Should I tell him to stop? My mom had always told us never to sass her co-stars, because that was her job I guess.'

'So what *did* you do?'

'I stood there and watched, getting more and more anxious and upset. And then it all started to change. She'd been screaming and then she started moaning. And, well ... he ended up screwing her like a freight train against the sideboard. I thought she was dying, that he was killing her. I finally got up the guts to run out of my hiding place. I kicked him really hard in the nuts, started yelling at him to stop hurting my mom.'

He chuckled, the sound harsh. And her insides twisted.

What a hideous thing for a child to witness.

'Poor Ross,' he said. 'I bet he didn't get an erection for months. No wonder he ghosted me this evening, he's probably still got PTSD from the incident ...'

Ruby pushed out a laugh, trying to see the funny side. 'What did your mum do?'

He shrugged, still smiling at the reminiscent. 'She was furious. After Bartlett ran out of the trailer with his tail between his legs, literally, she didn't stop yelling at me for about twenty minutes.'

'She shouted at you?' Ruby asked, appalled. How could Helena have been angry with her son when he had been a frightened child?

'Yeah, she was royally pissed,' he said, letting out a harsh chuckle. 'And also kind of embarrassed I guess, although not as embarrassed as I was.'

'I can't even imagine,' she replied, trying to see the humour in Luke's story. But she couldn't. No wonder he didn't like the movies or anything associated with them – he'd lived behind the curtain, from an early age, and it hadn't been pretty.

'You know what still bugs me about the whole sorry episode though?' he added, the amusement no longer reaching his eyes.

She could think of about a million things that were bugging her. 'What?'

'I was trying to help her. I actually thought Bartlett was going to kill her,' he said.

'Precisely, she should have given you a medal not gotten mad. You were just a little boy and you were trying to protect her.'

He looked puzzled then he smiled, one of those cynical twists of his lips she recognized from a month ago. 'Yeah, maybe in a Disney movie.' He laughed, the sound so bitter it gave her chills. 'I wasn't a little boy. I was eleven years old. No I meant, why the heck did I try to stop him when I was so damn mad with her that evening? I'd seen a group of local kids shooting hoops on a court across from the set after I'd tucked Jack and Becca into bed, and I'd been jealous and frustrated. I wanted to go hang out with them. But I couldn't because I had to look out for my kid brother and sister. Why did we have to be dragged all over the country when I wanted to stay in one place? Why couldn't I go to a real school? Why couldn't I tell anyone who my old man was? I just wanted to be a normal kid like those kids were, doing normal kid stuff. And it was my mom's fault I couldn't. So why did I intervene when I thought Bartlett was hurting her?'

'Because she was your mother?' she offered, saddened by the confusion in his voice. 'And because you're a naturally protective person? And a good guy.'

His brows lifted. 'Why would you think that, Ruby?' he said, sounding genuinely perplexed by her observation. 'I'm not a good guy, I always look out for number one.'

She thought of his brother and sister, who he'd put to bed that night, even though, like any eleven-year-old, he had been desperate to play basketball with the other kids. And she thought of The Royale, and how much better it looked than it had close to six weeks ago – the new paint and expertly repaired plaster work, the working toilets and no-longer leaky radiators ... Even the boiler in her flat, which hadn't packed up once since the day he'd repaired it.

'And that's never going to change. Because I don't want it to,' he said, and she could hear the warning in his voice.

He wasn't selfish. He shouldered responsibilities rather than shirking them, responsibilities that weren't even his, and had done ever since he was a boy. But she could see by the guarded expression he wouldn't believe her if she told him so.

And anyway, this conversation wasn't really about his mom, or Ross Bartlett or even that little boy who had done the right thing in a trailer in Georgia all those years ago, and been punished for it.

What this conversation was really about was his imminent

departure – the elephant in the cab that had been squeezed between them all night. The one thing he couldn't talk about because if he did he would have to talk about *them*, when he was determined to believe there was no them.

For her, there *was* a them, there would always be a them, these few brief weeks something she would look back on for the rest of her life with joy and affection and no small degree of regret. And for that reason she refused to sour it now with a load of 'what ifs' that would just create more of the melodrama he hated.

She couldn't change his mind about what was right for him, especially as those decisions had been made long before she ever met him.

The cab stopped at the curb outside The Royale and the cab driver hauled back the privacy screen. 'That'll be forty-five quid, mate.'

Luke unclicked his belt and reached into his pocket.

Ruby pulled a twenty pound note out of her purse.

'Don't even ...' He tugged a credit card from his wallet, added a tip into the cabbie's card reader, ran the card down the reader then tapped in his code. 'Tonight is on me.'

She nodded, having lost the will to argue with him. 'Thank you.' She shoved the twenty back into her purse.

He jumped out and took her arm, then slammed the door shut and bracketed her hips with his hands. He pressed his face into her hair, found the rioting pulse in her collarbone as the cab drove away.

'Let's go to bed. Talking about Ross banging my mom has got me horny.'

Ruby laughed, the teasing kisses making her skin sizzle and burn. 'That's a bit kinky.'

'I know, I'm trying real hard not to dwell on how kinky.' He lifted his head, then grasped her hand.

He drew her down the alleyway at the side of the building. Reaching the back, he jumped up and grabbed the fire escape ladder. Levering it down, he began to climb, with her hand still grasped firmly in his.

After they'd reached the first level, he hauled the ladder up behind them and locked it in place. Then he led her to the second level.

Shoving up the window at the back of her flat, he climbed inside and then reached out to help her through.

After closing the window, he flicked the lock. 'I'm going to employ a locksmith to make this more secure,' he murmured. 'I don't want anyone else calling on you late at night.'

Her heart burned at what he had implied without realizing it.

Very soon, there would be no reason to leave her window unlocked, because no one would be calling on her anymore.

Chapter 17

'Ms Graham, Ms Ryan, thanks a bunch for coming in today and for putting together your presentation. Phil and I thought it was really cool,' Jamie Callagher, the CEO of The Rialto indie cinema chain sent Ruby a relaxed smile. With his goatee beard, his messy hair and his more casual than smart hipster clothing, Callagher looked like Richard Branson's geeky younger brother. Or rather, exactly like what he was – a movie buff who had managed to turn his favourite hobby into a money-spinning brand.

Cool? Had he said cool? Was that good, or code for crap?

'I'm so glad you enjoyed it,' Ruby said as the spiced caramel latte she'd been given by the receptionist turned into a spiced caramel nuclear bomb in her stomach. When she and Jacie had gotten the call to come back into the company's head office this afternoon neither of them had been able to eat a bite.

They'd spent weeks working their asses off on the proposal they had delivered this morning, Jacie doing the lion's share of the work on the financials while Ruby worked on a PowerPoint presentation of everything The Royale had to offer.

They'd been brutally honest about the theatre's financial liabilities, but after all the hard work Luke had done bringing the aging décor back up to scratch, the beauty of the theatre had shone through in the series of shots she'd taken over the last week.

Luke.

Just the thought of him had Ruby's anxiety ramping up another notch. Was today his last day of work? She didn't know, he hadn't said anything this morning when they'd had breakfast together, but there had been a moment when she'd caught him watching her as she had laid their plates down on the table in the living room and what she'd seen had made a sharp pain stab under her breastbone. A sharp pain that felt like loss. Perhaps avoidance wasn't so great after all, because not knowing was starting to turn her into a basket case.

'So, Phil and I have got an answer for you ...' Jamie said, and Ruby wrangled her thoughts back from the topic of Luke.

The young CEO glanced at the man sitting next to him, who Ruby had thought for a minute might be his twin when they had arrived to do the presentation that morning – except where Jamie never stopped talking, Phil had yet to say a word.

'When something this hot comes our way, we don't like to mess around,' Jamie said. 'So we have a counter offer for you.'

'You do?' Ruby said.

'Fantastic,' Jacie said at the same time. 'What is it?' her assistant manager asked.

'We totally get that The Royale is special,' Jamie said, leaning forward to emphasise his enthusiasm. 'And the place is looking great. You've got a business we think The Rialto brand can enhance considerably. And from your preliminary numbers we definitely think it's well situated to expand our reach in the West London area. It's kind of close to our venue in Holland Park, but we've been thinking of changing that to a first run theatre so adding The Royale to the portfolio as a venue for classics and retrospectives would totally work.'

'That's wonderful,' Ruby said, letting Jamie's enthusiasm inflate the bubble of hope under her breastbone and push out the pain of Luke's impending parting. Turning The Royale into another Rialto cinema hadn't been what they had offered, that sounded like a takeover rather than the fifty percent buy-in that she and Jacie had proposed so they could cover the theatre's debts. But she was happy to hear him out.

'We thought the name The Rialto Royale would build on your local clientele while giving the venue a hit of extra Rialto cool points ...' Jamie grinned.

But we don't need your cool points, we've got enough of our own.

'Why don't we call it The Royale Rialto,' Jacie said, the flat tone saying exactly what Ruby had been thinking. 'Seeing as it's been The Royale for a lot longer than you've been in business.'

Jamie's grin sharpened. 'That's not going to work for us,' he said easily enough, and Ruby realised Jamie Callagher was nobody's fool. He knew The Royale was in trouble, that he had the upper hand in these negotiations.

'That's okay, Jace,' she said, sending her assistant manager her best cease-and-desist look. 'I think the name change sounds wonderful,' she added.

They needed The Rialto on board as investors, or the only option was to sell the theatre to developers and close The Royale forever – while working on the presentation she had contacted every possible investment prospect she could think of, and she hadn't even gotten a call back from the others.

'Okay, cool,' Jamie said, his silent partner Phil remaining silent but sending Jacie a hard stare which was making the spiced caramel bomb in Ruby's stomach start to implode. Something wasn't right about all this, because she was getting the impression Jamie and Phil were wolves in hipster clothing.

'Now, we'd really like to move on this ASAP. We've spoken to a developer and they think the best use of the space is to gut the upstairs flat and add a floor, so we can create some rental units to increase the theatre's operating profits,' Jamie said, his enthusiasm becoming turbo-charged. 'It'll take a while to get planning permission and do the rebuild.'

Rebuild? They hadn't mentioned anything about a rebuild, or gutting her home.

'So we'd need to finalise the purchase in the next couple of weeks to get going on that and re-open before we hit the lucrative Christmas season.' Jamie was still speeding up. 'We're prepared to be generous to you and your staff to expedite the deal. We're proposing double the asking price you specified plus an extra five percent.' Pulling some paperwork out of a file in front of him, he passed the contract across the table. 'It's all there in black and white for you to look over, but for this to work for us we'd need to close the deal a week from now.'

'I'm sorry? What?' Ruby said, dumbly. 'Did you say you

want to pay me double what I asked for plus five percent for fifty percent of the business?'

Jamie's wolfish grin took on the precision of a killer shark. 'No, Ruby ... Is it okay if I call you Ruby?'

'Yes, of course,' she said, the bubble of hope turning into a lead weight.

'Ruby, a partnership isn't going to work for us. That's not how we roll at The Rialto. We're only interested in purchasing one hundred percent of The Royale and running the cinema with our own team in our own way.'

'But we're not offering you a hundred percent—' Jacie's outraged shout barely registered as Jamie interrupted her, his killer smile making the lead weight in Ruby's stomach collide with the nuclear bomb.

'Plus, we checked out the loan agreements on the theatre, and we know you've got to pay off the theatre's debts by June 20th. So it's not like you've got a lot of time to find a better offer.'

'Jesus, and to think I once thought Luke Devlin was the Antichrist. The man's a fricking saint compared to Jamie and Phil the Evil Hipster Twins,' Jacie stared glumly into her lemon-tini as they sat on the stools at the end of the bar in Brynn's Babes a half hour later. 'What the bloody hell do we do now?'

'We move on to Plan B,' Ruby said, knowing there was no Plan B.

'*Is* there a Plan B?' Jacie asked, the flash of hope in her expression making Ruby want to cry.

'There are other cinema chains, and other possible investors ...' All of whom she had already contacted. They were all out of viable options, but Jacie and the rest of the staff didn't need to know that ... yet.

'You think that's a possibility? Aren't we running out of time to find someone else?' Jacie frowned. Unfortunately, her assistant manager was not an idiot.

'Leave it with me, okay. I can make a few calls. We have a week to make a decision on this offer.' A week during which she might be able to negotiate something to at least save her staff their jobs. Surely Jamie and Phil would have to hire a whole new team, but why bother if the staff were already there? Unless they were planning to rehire on reduced salaries – which she wouldn't put past them. But perhaps Ruby had some leeway there if she offered to take a lower sales price for The Royale, maybe she could guarantee her staff their jobs and salaries. But what about her own job at The Royale? Somehow she doubted she would be able to persuade Jamie and Phil to keep her on. And did she really want to? Taking orders from The Rialto's head office would be very different than being her own boss, or taking orders from Matty.

She took a hefty sip of her own lemon-tini to fill the hole in her stomach left by the afternoon's nuclear explosion.

The thought of being forced to leave The Royale, start a new life, a new job, somewhere else without everyone who had become like a family over the years had been hanging over her for two and a half months. But the possibility wasn't just a possibility anymore ... It was more like an inevitability.

'You're not seriously considering their offer are you? That

would mean the end of The Royale as we know it,' Jacie said, the dejected look back.

Yes, she was seriously considering it, because the alternative was closing The Royale down altogether.

'We've got some bargaining power,' she said. 'I don't mind who owns The Royale as long as we can stay together here and keep the cinema open.'

'You really think those two smug wankers will bargain? They didn't look like the bargaining type to me,' Jacie said.

'We'll see,' Ruby said.

'Should we cancel our Babs and Bob night tomorrow?' Jacie said.

'Absolutely not,' Ruby replied. 'It's a Matty's Classics night.' And they might not have another now, she thought miserably. 'Brynn's offered to do the theme tune in the foyer before the show. Plus, everyone will already have their costumes.'

The dress-up theme was your favourite Robert Redford or Barbra Streisand character to celebrate the penultimate Matty's Classic, the iconic movie in which the two actors had linked up for the one and only time in their careers. She was expecting a lot of Yentls and Funny Girls and probably a few Sundance Kids.

'I've already sourced mine,' Ruby added, because in between working her bum off on yesterday's presentation for The Rialto and having a wild affair with Luke Devlin in the last twenty days, she'd also managed to find a close replica of Streisand's dress in the El Morocco scene at the beginning of the movie.

'Yeah, me too,' Jacie said. 'Okay, I guess you're right. It's not over till it's over.'

Tears stung Ruby's throat at the question in Jacie's voice and her heart weighed several tons in her chest because the end of The Royale wasn't the only ending coming towards her at warp speed.

The door to the bar opened, letting in a stream of sunlight that backlit a tall figure in jeans and a checked shirt she recognized instantly – magically conjuring up the other ending she had been avoiding for days.

Luke waved to Brynn, who was serving behind the bar, then headed towards them. He wasn't wearing his overalls.

Ruby's throat began to hurt. She finished her lemon-tini not sure if she could cope with losing Luke today, too.

Jacie, probably sensing her dip in mood, shifted round. 'Hey.' She lifted her hand in greeting.

'Hi Jacie, Ruby.' Luke nodded. He reached into his pocket and produced the set of keys Ruby had given him nearly six weeks ago now.

The weight in her stomach became a chasm.

'Hey, Jacie, do you mind if I speak to Ruby in private?' he said.

Jacie stared at the keys, obviously figuring out the significance of them too. She sent Ruby a searching look, the stubborn expression on her face telling Ruby that she had her back – if Ruby needed it. For one desperate moment Ruby considered telling her friend to stay, to avoid the inevitable for a few moments more, but she forced herself to nod, the time for avoidance was over.

Jacie took the hint. 'Sure, I've gotta go open the cinema for the evening showing anyway. I'll leave you two to it.' Sending Ruby one more fierce look, she left.

'Your assistant manager is a tough nut to crack,' Luke said as he watched Jacie leave. 'She still doesn't like me much.'

Jacie liked him a lot more than he would ever know. And she wasn't the only one. His calm, practical presence over the last six weeks as he worked his way methodically through the checklist of repairs had endeared him to everyone. He'd become a part of their community without even realizing it. And everyone would miss him. Even Jacie.

'Actually, I think she likes you a lot,' Ruby said, knowing it wasn't just Jacie she was talking about.

Avoiding dealing with his inevitable departure in the last few days had been hard, but not as hard as facing it. After all the qualifying and talking sense to herself she'd been doing in the last days and weeks, ever since this affair had begun, why was she finding it so hard to breathe evenly right now?

He placed the keys on the bar between them and climbed on to the stool Jacie had vacated. 'How did the meeting go, with The Rialto?' he said.

'How did you know about that?' she asked, a guilty flush hitting her cheeks.

The yearning she had been burying for days threatened to spill out of her mouth. She would have loved to ask Luke's advice, to get his take, to lean on him and hope he could find a solution. But she couldn't do that. She had no claim on him, they'd established that without a doubt over the last three weeks. Her ribs began to ache as she had to force the breaths in and out of her lungs.

'Are you kidding me?' he said, a wry smile twisting his lips

She dragged her gaze from his mouth, to find him watching her.

'Gerry and Tozer aren't the most discreet guys on the planet,' he added.

'Hey, Luke, you want a drink?' Brynn asked, having returned from the storeroom. The bar was almost empty at five in the afternoon, which was why Ruby and Jacie had escaped here to debrief after their meeting.

'Sure, I'll take a Sam Adams.' He glanced at Ruby's empty glass. 'You want another?'

She didn't, really. Drinking in the afternoon was not a good idea, especially when you had a ton of heartache to process, and your breathing was already severely compromised. The one thing she could not do was let on to Luke how much she was going to miss him. Because then he would feel beholden, and that was the one thing she didn't want. They'd both gone into this with their eyes wide open. If she went to pieces now in front of him, all that would have been a lie.

But the thought that this was almost certainly going to be her last drink with Luke had the reply popping out of her mouth. 'Yes, thank you.'

Maybe she was pathetic for wanting to prolong the agony, but so be it. And a drink might help her to get through this with her dignity intact.

'You didn't answer my question,' he said. 'How did the meeting go?'

'Good,' she lied smoothly, avoiding eye contact. 'I think we've found an investor. And a solution which will work for everyone. I'm ...' She paused, drawing on all the acting talent she had ever possessed to put the right amount of enthusiasm into her voice. 'I'm excited. This is going to be a new chapter for The Royale, and hopefully a lucrative one. We should even be able to give you something for your share.'

He frowned, his searching gaze only making the blush on her cheeks hit critical mass. And the pain in her lungs more pronounced.

Thank goodness for the dark lighting.

'I told you, I don't want a cent,' he said. 'You can invest my share back into the business if there's any left after the debts are paid.'

'You don't have to do that,' she said. Although she knew on one level he did, and it only made her sadder. Taking nothing from the sale would sever any ties he had to the theatre, to Matty, and perhaps most importantly, to her. And while she knew that's the way it had to be, for both of them, it didn't make the stabbing pain every time she drew a breath any less vicious. 'Matty wanted you to have half,' she added.

'He didn't know me, Ruby' he said gently. 'We both know that bequest had everything to do with Matty's love for my father and you, and nothing to do with me. From what I know about my uncle now, he was big on romantic gestures. But he also loved you like a daughter,' he said with an authority that made her throat burn as well as her lungs. While Luke had spent his days doing up The Royale, he'd come to know what a special person Matty was, and that made her so happy. Or it would once she got over the pain of losing him, too.

'He wanted me to have a stake in The Royale for the sake of that lost love affair and because he wanted me to help you out,' Luke continued. 'I get that. And that's why there's no way I'm taking anything out of the theatre now, when you guys need it. Okay?'

She smiled and swallowed down the tears threatening to spill over her lids. 'You're much more emotionally intelligent than you look,' she said, stupidly moved by his declaration.

'I had a good teacher,' he murmured.

She nodded, knowing she couldn't speak, or all of her best efforts to remain dignified and not desperate would be for nothing.

Don't you dare cry. Don't you dare make a scene. Not now, when you're so close to finishing The Ruby Movie the way it has to be finished.

'Here you go, guys,' Brynn arrived with the fresh drinks. Ruby took a gulp of hers and swallowed. The sweet citrus tang somehow allowed her to ignore the pain in her chest.

Saved by a lemon-tini.

'What are you two going as for Babs and Bob night?' Brynn asked.

Ruby pressed a shaky finger to her nose. 'That's for me to know and you to find out,' she said, hoping no one could hear the tremble in her voice. 'What are you going as Brynn?'

'Dolly Levi, of course,' he said, with a flourish. 'I have a gold glitter ball gown which is absolutely perfect, all I need to do is source some feathers for the headpiece.'

'Wonderful,' Ruby said. 'Are you still okay to sing the theme song before the screening?'

'Darling, just try and stop me,' he said. 'So how about you, Luke. I'm thinking you could pick any of Bob's characters from his prime years.' Brynn gave Luke a careful once over. 'Better known as The Sundance to Waldo Pepper years.'

Luke took a judicious sip of his beer. 'When is this event?'

'Tomorrow night,' Ruby and Brynn said together. Ruby could hear the stupid yearning in her voice and wanted to take the words back.

Had he heard it, that eager desperation? The desire she'd had on lockdown for weeks. It seemed he had, when he placed the bottle back on the bar and the easy smile on his face disappeared. 'Unfortunately, I'll have to give it a miss.'

Oh shit.

The piercing pain swelling in Ruby's lungs scored a direct hit with the confirmation of everything she'd feared his arrival in the bar signified.

Luke had come to say goodbye.

You already knew that, you ninny. Do not screw up all your hard work, not now, not when there has never been anything you can do to change the final fade out of this affair.

'That's a shame,' Brynn said, speaking for both of them. 'You would so have rocked Bob as The Great Gatsby in his Roaring Twenties flares.' Sending Luke a smile, he headed off down the bar to serve a customer that had just walked in.

'So what movie are you celebrating Babs and Bob night with?' he asked. 'Is it another of Matty's Classics?'

She wondered, momentarily, why he was prolonging their conversation. But then she took a deep breath – the painful swelling in her chest threatening to cut off her air supply – and suddenly realized she didn't care what his reasons were.

She wanted all the final minutes she could get with him.

Why shouldn't she grab them with both hands? She could handle the pain later. Today had already been awful enough. Losing Luke was going to be hard, but he hadn't left yet.

'*The Way We Were*,' she said, in answer to his question. 'Matty loved Babs and he always said Bob Redford was at his most bonkable in that movie.' The blush ignited, but she ignored it. *For goodness sake, don't think about how bonkable Luke is, that will just make this even tougher.* 'I know a Streisand obsession is a bit of a gay cliché,' she said, trying to steer the conversation back on to safer ground. Movie trivia had always saved her in the past, and now her life depended on it. 'But Matty always said cliché is cliché for a reason. The film is a wonderful melodrama about two people who fall in love but are total opposites. She's a working-class Jewish spitfire, passionate and determined and believes in fighting for lost causes, and he's a handsome WASP who's laid-back and privileged and doesn't believe in lost causes, let alone fighting for them ...'

Her words trailed off – why on earth was she giving Luke a plot synopsis for *The Way We Were* in their last moments together? And how come she couldn't get over the horrible significance of that plot all of a sudden.

Had Luke figured out the truth? That she was totally Katie in this scenario – destined to be heartbroken and alone – and he was Hubbell – aloof and pragmatic?

The irony helped her even out her staggered breathing a bit. *Get a clue, Rubes.*

This wasn't a movie, it was real life. *Too* real life.

'You think I haven't seen *The Way We Were*?' he said,

surprising Ruby so much she sputtered and nearly choked on her lemon-tini

'You've seen it? *Really?*'

'Yeah, really.' Luke drank his beer, his piercing blue gaze meeting hers. 'It's the longest most turgid melodrama in movie history so kind of hard to forget.'

'No, it's not.'

'You think?' he said and she had the strangest feeling he wanted to prolong this moment as well. Why did that make the moment even more precious and yet even more painful at the same time? 'It's goes on forever while going nowhere ...' He added. 'And that damn theme tune is like the ear-worm of the century.'

'Okay, I'll admit the movie is a bit laggy in places,' Ruby said, managing a smile despite the sadness searing her throat. Just keep talking about the movie and everything will be all right. 'But Robert Redford is beyond gorgeous in Navy whites ...'

'If you like your guys short and squat and with too-perfect hair,' he cut in, as he swept back the dark wave of hair that always flopped over his forehead.

'And Babs is terrific,' she soldiered on while allowing herself to get side-tracked admiring *his* too-perfect hair. 'No way is the theme song an ear-worm, it's beautiful and so evocative. And the whole two hours is worth it for that one scene in the bar.'

'What scene in the bar?' The blank look was back.

'Oh, please? You don't remember it?' Okay, now she was offended. And a bit outraged. But at least she was breathing easier. She could do this, she could definitely do this. 'Close your eyes,' she said, suddenly gripped by an idea. A hopeless, silly, slightly pathetic idea. But one that had the potential to end this affair in the way she had always planned to end it. On her terms, as well as his.

She let the giddy kick of adrenaline flood her veins to cover the lingering pain.

Maybe Luke did not do romance. But when was she likely to get another chance to re-enact one of her favourite scenes from one of her favourite movies with a man who had given her so much in the last six weeks: he'd fixed their theatre and helped her get over the first big emotional hurdles caused by losing Matty, by simply being there when she needed him, and by giving her the best sex of her life. Surely that deserved to be celebrated not mourned?

'Why do you want me to close my eyes?' he said, the suspicious light in his gaze somehow flirtatious. Was this Luke's way of saying goodbye? Letting her have a moment that would make this ending easier, no matter how hard?

'Just close your eyes,' she demanded, enjoying her own assertiveness and the ability to breathe again, if only for a little while. 'I'm going to rewind the scene, so you can remember it.'

He closed his eyes. And her breath slowed in her lungs. Not ending the pain, but easing it, a little.

She studied him in the half light – and savoured the moment he was giving her – determined to remember it always. The fall of hair which had dropped back over his forehead, the lean lines and perfect angles of his face, the dimple in his chin. He was never meant to be hers for the long haul, but he had been hers for a little while, and she refused to regret a single second – which was really the main reason she could not fall apart right now.

One piercing blue eye opened. 'I'm waiting,' he said, then snapped it shut.

She laughed. 'Okay, okay.' She flexed her fingers and then started humming *The Way We Were* theme. Loudly.

'Oh, hell,' he said, but his lips quirked and she smiled, her heart skipping into her throat. However tough this parting was going to be, however poignant, they would always have this moment. And so many more.

'Of course, I really should have had gel nails fitted for this ...' Ruby said as she leaned towards him. The stool wobbled, and she planted her palm to stop herself falling forward, only to have it land on the taught muscle of his thigh.

The muscle tensed beneath her hand. And heat shot through her.

'If this is just an excuse to feel me up ...'

'Shut up,' she said, flustered as she snatched her traitorous hand back, took another sip of her lemon-tini, then rubbed the burning palm on her own thigh.

She started humming again, her heart beating a giddy tattoo when his lips quirked. Then she reached out a nail, and slowly, delicately lifted a thick lock of his hair and smoothed it back from his brow. And all the pain seemed to coalesce into one simple thought.

However much this hurts, it was always, always worth it.

His eyes opened as the song got caught in her throat, her

whole body stilled from the lightning strike of emotion – and possibly one too many sips of lemon-tini before wine o'clock – as she found herself trapped in the sapphire blue, which for once didn't look cynical or pragmatic. He simply stared at her, his gaze pensive and intense. And she wondered what he was thinking.

Her lungs squeezed tight under her rib cage, the moment suspended in time – and she wondered if this hurt as much for him as it did for her.

But then he broke the spell. 'That's it?'

'Yes, you still don't remember it?' she said, appalled and breathless at the same time. 'The scene in the club, where Hubbell's on shore leave in his Navy whites and Babs spots him and he's sleeping and she hasn't seen him in years and she flicks his hair back. And it makes him wake up and their eyes connect.'

Just like ours, now.

Her rib cage contracted so much, she almost couldn't breathe. 'And he hits on her and they end up in her apartment. But the next morning he treats her like a one night stand. It's heartbreaking and awesome at the same time, because she loves him and has always loved him and he doesn't even know it.'

She finally careered to a stop, realizing she had gone too far. Way way too far.

You're not in love with him, Ruby, that is not allowed.

'No,' he said, softly. And she heard the apology in his voice. 'Don't remember it.'

'Oh, well.' She sat back, knowing as she gathered the tattered remnants of her dignity – and her bruised heart – that while it hurt now, she had to carry on breathing through the pain. 'I guess that explains then why you don't appreciate everything that movie has to offer.' She took a sip of the lemon-tini, only to find her glass empty.

She swallowed, knowing what was coming next but suddenly knowing she would survive it, just like she had survived everything else.

Perhaps she would never be able to watch Babs getting touchy-feely with Bob's perfect fringe again while watching *The Way We Were* without seeing Luke but did that have to be a bad thing? Movies had saved her once upon a time, but she'd finally discovered, thanks to Luke, that real life could be so much more exciting than anything Bob and Babs had to offer.

He lifted the keys from the bar and, taking her hand in his, placed the bunch in the centre of her palm. He wrapped her fingers around them as the deep pulse of desire in her abdomen joined her erratic heartbeat and the pulsing pain in her chest. 'The work's finished, Ruby.'

She nodded, staring at their closed fists, unable to speak round the great big wodge of sadness lodged in her throat. If they could have been two different people, this might have worked. But she'd always have the memories.

He let go of her hand, then tucked a knuckle under her chin. 'You look after yourself, and The Royale, okay?' he said, emotion thickening his voice.

She sent him a watery smile and nodded, holding the pain deep inside – letting it sear her lungs and sting her eyes but refusing to let it overwhelm her before she had watched him walk out of the bar.

'Has he left for good?' Brynn murmured having come back down her end of the bar as the door swung shut behind Luke.

Ruby nodded. She couldn't speak, the pain in her lungs too intense to utter a single word.

'Shame, he seemed like a nice guy,' Brynn said, taking her empty lemon-tini glass.

She nodded again and blinked furiously.

He was. But he was never meant to be mine.

And suddenly, Ruby knew what Katie must have felt like at the end of the movie when she had to let Hubble go.

And exactly how much it sucked.

Luke headed out of Brynn's bar into the late spring sunshine of the last day in May. He could hear the cars heading towards Portobello Road, could smell dust and exhaust and the garbage left out in front of the grocery store across the street, could see The Royale on the opposite corner. But all he could really hear was Ruby's sultry voice humming the Streisand tune, all he could smell was the fresh rose of her shampoo, and all he could think about was how much he wanted to turn back and dive into her again, the way he had so many times in the last three weeks.

Dumb. Why would you do that, Devlin?

Especially as the break-up he'd been dreading for days had gone much smoother than he had imagined it would. But as he headed past The Royale, something else about their parting came back to bug him.

She hadn't met his gaze when he'd asked her about the meeting with the guys from The Rialto today. Something wasn't right, he was sure of it.

He shot a look over his shoulder, checked his watch.

No sign of Ruby, perhaps she was having another cocktail. Before six o'clock. Which didn't make a whole lot of sense now he thought about it either. Ruby liked a novelty cocktail, but she wasn't a big drinker, not since he'd known her. So why had she and Jacie been knocking them back at Brynn's before opening for the evening?

His steps paused and he crossed the street to The Royale. He spotted Jacie in the lobby. She looked up from the ticket booth and saw him standing in front of the cinema.

Only one way to find out what had really happened at that meeting.

He'd already said his goodbyes to Ruby, which had been a whole lot harder than he would have thought possible, but he couldn't leave until he knew for sure she was going to be okay.

'Hello?' Jacie said as he pushed open the glass door. 'Come to say goodbye?' she added, the snap of resentment giving him pause. She hadn't liked him at first, but he thought they'd reached an accord in the last few weeks.

'Yeah,' he said. 'And to find out what the heck happened at your meeting this afternoon, because I asked Ruby and I don't think she was straight with me.'

'Why would you want to know that, when you're leaving?' she said.

He bristled, annoyed by the accusation in her tone. What

the hell more did she want from him? He'd worked his ass off for six weeks getting this place back to where it was supposed to be, didn't he get any credit for that? But as he opened his mouth to finally have it out with her, he saw the flicker of distress cross her features ... And suddenly, he knew this wasn't about him.

Jacie was tough, tenacious and a hard nut to crack for sure, but she was also smart and hard-working, she loved Ruby and The Royale and she was fiercely loyal to both.

'What the hell happened in that meeting, Jacie?' he said. 'I can't fix things if I don't know what's going on.'

Her expression softened, and he could see the scared friend behind the tough girl act. 'Do you really want to fix things?' she asked.

Every one of the hairs on the back of his neck stood up, his heart pulsed hard in his chest, and for once he didn't question the wisdom of following his gut. 'Yeah, I do.'

Chapter 18

'Brynn, thanks so much for doing this, you look incredible.' Ruby forced a smile to her lips, determined not to let on to anyone she had an empty space in her chest she was terrified might never be filled.

Watching *The Way We Were* – especially in her Katie outfit from the scene she had relived with Luke yesterday evening in Brynn's Bar – was about to increase the torture.

She missed him, so much, already. He'd walked away from her just over twenty-four hours ago and it had been a titanic effort not to fall completely to pieces in the hours since. Luckily, she and the rest of the team had had their hands full organising tonight's screening. But now the lobby was packed with people rocking their Babs and Bob outfits – just as predicted there were enough Yentls to fill a synagogue – and she could feel the tears queuing up in her throat. How on earth was she going to survive listening to Brynn sing the song she had hummed for Luke yesterday, the last time she'd touched him?

Brynn winked, the gold lamé gown sparkling in the fairy lights Ruby and Jacie had spent the morning stringing across the newly repainted lobby.

'Thanks honey, you look perfect as Katie,' Brynn replied. 'Matty always said you had more heart and tenacity than La Streisand. He wasn't wrong.'

She forced her mouth to curve. 'High praise indeed. Shall I announce you?'

'Oh my!' Brynn's gaze locked on something over Ruby's shoulder and his eyes brightened. 'Your Hubbell changed his mind. How wonderful.'

What? No, it can't be.

Ruby swung round. Her heart stopped beating for two crucial seconds, then started beating so hard she was scared she might pass out ... Or, worse, might be having an out-of-body experience. Because she could see Luke walking towards her.

But this wasn't Luke as she knew him, in his thousand dollar suits, or his paint-splattered overalls and tool belt, or his worn jeans and sweaters as he climbed into her apartment late at night, or his stretchy boxers the morning after, or nothing at all as they spooned in her too small bed.

This was a new Luke, dressed in Navy whites, the black-and-gold epaulettes standing out against the pristine uniform, the officer's cap perched rakishly on his dark hair, his jaw clean shaven, the true blue gaze locked on her face as he ignored the spontaneous applause and headed straight towards her.

He came back.

She was definitely having an out-of-body experience. But if this was an illusion it was the best illusion of her life. She could see Jacie – in her white two-piece suit with sail boat flares from *What's Up Doc?* – grinning at her and clapping, Gerry and Tozer – in their matching pin-stripes from *The*

Sting – laughing too, and Beryl clutching her *Funny Girl* pearls as if she were about to faint with the romance of it all.

I know how you feel.

The piano intro for Streisand's signature song from the film floated over the applause, and Brynn's Dolly began to hum the tune. Just as Dolly's smoky voice caressed the opening lyrics about misty waters and memories, Luke reached Ruby. Taking her hand in his, he dragged her towards him and gripped her round the waist.

'I think this is my dance,' he said, his gruff American accent prickling over her skin and making her heart jiggle in her chest.

'Luke?' was all she could manage, still not sure she could believe this was actually happening.

'That's Hubbell to you,' he said with a smile. And her heart lifted into her throat.

'I thought you were flying home tonight?'

'I've got unfinished business.'

She laughed, the joyous sound matching the gloriously romantic song as Luke – or rather, Hubbell – held her close and led her in a slow dance in the small space the crowd had made for them.

She had no idea why he was here. But he'd dressed up for her as a character from the most turgid melodrama in movie history, and made a spectacle of himself in front of everyone, just to give her this precious moment. Surely that had to mean something ... *wonderful*.

The rest of the evening went by in a blur.

He sat through the film with his strong, supportive arm

slung around her shoulders, and after it ended ... *Finally*, they snuck away upstairs – with him using the flat's main entrance for the first time since the day he had come to fix her boiler.

Leading her down the darkened corridor, he made his way to her bedroom. The fairy lights flickered above the bed as they both got naked.

Within seconds they were falling on to the sheets she'd changed that afternoon because the scent of him in her bed only made the yearning worse.

Skin to skin, sigh to sigh, mouth to mouth, lips to flesh, they devoured each other. He touched and tasted her everywhere he knew would get her to gasp, sigh, beg. The first orgasm flowed through her as if it were a right.

She could feel his urgency, sense his desperation as he plunged into her.

He worked his hips, hitting the sweet spot he'd found weeks ago and ruthlessly exploited ever since.

She clung to his shoulders and rode the storm.

At last, she let herself fall, hearing his deep grunt of completion.

As she lay in the circle of his arms in the dark room, the flicker of lights shining on sweaty skin, she breathed in the delicious scent of him. There were a thousand things she wanted to say to him, a thousand more questions she wanted to ask. But she swallowed them down and placed her hand on his chest instead, scared to break the spell too soon. Happy just to live in this magnificent moment and hope it meant more.

He clasped her fingers in his.

'I told you that was the longest damn melodrama in movie history,' he said.

And she laughed. 'I'd have to agree with you now.'

She snuggled into his side, closed her eyes as his hand settled on her hair.

'Did you iron your hair, too? Like Babs in the movie?' he asked.

She smiled, so he had been paying attention. 'I borrowed Jacie's straighteners,' she said, round a yawn.

'Go to sleep,' he said, dropping a gentle kiss on her forehead.

She wanted to ask him if he would still be here in the morning but chose not to, in case the answer ruined her happy ending.

So she allowed her mind to drift, and let her body float. Accepting the fact that whatever happened tomorrow, she would always have this perfect night for the rest of her life.

PART FIVE

The Last of the Mohicans (1992)

Ruby's verdict: *Love is powerful, even in its darkest hour. And especially if you're trapped behind a waterfall with Daniel Day-Lewis. The most important thing to remember is to be strong, because you will survive, no matter how hard it is.*

Luke's verdict: *Never underestimate the woman you love. However tough you think you are, chances are she's tougher.*

Chapter 19

'Luke, you're still here?'

Luke glanced up from his phone to see Ruby standing in the doorway to her small living room. He steeled himself against the warmth swelling in his chest, making his throat ache.

Damn, but she was gorgeous to look at first thing in the morning. Her hair all mussed, her eyes sleepy, her skin flushed, her body barely covered by the silky robe she usually threw on to make them breakfast.

Her face was a picture of conflicting emotions. Relief and hope and happiness, all flitted across her open features, letting him see every one.

'And you're wearing a suit,' she added, as her gaze roamed over his clothing.

He'd woken an hour ago, tiptoed out of her bed and down the fire escape then walked to his house in Notting Hill in his costume from last night – the house he'd only visited to change clothes in the last couple of weeks until the night before last. He'd packed and changed, arranged to have the costume Jacie had hired for him left with the rental shop and the house keys deposited with the agent, then booked a car and driver for the day. He hadn't planned to return to The Royale. He'd already drafted an email to send to Ruby this afternoon with the details of the settlement he had put together after his conversation with Jacie yesterday afternoon. It had been Jacie's idea he come to the screening, and he hadn't even hesitated. He'd wanted to do it. Ruby deserved that moment of acknowledgement.

But as the driver turned on to Talbot Road on his way to the West End, he'd thought of Ruby still blissfully asleep, and he hadn't been able to drive past The Royale.

As a result, the clean break he'd been hoping for had been screwed.

But right now, absorbing Ruby's glorious bed hair and the jiggle of her curves under the barely-there robe for the last time, he couldn't regret it. He wanted to remember her this way, always.

Although he wished he hadn't put that desperate hope in her eyes.

'I've got a few meetings this morning—'

'You have meetings on a *Sunday*?' she interrupted.

'Yeah.' He forced himself to continue. 'Then I'm catching an afternoon flight to JFK.'

She blinked, and the hope died. He wanted to kick himself. Last night had been a dumb idea – selfish and self-indulgent. He didn't want her to be sad.

'I see,' she said, but then her lips lifted in a determined smile. 'Shall I cook you breakfast before you leave?' she asked.

He lifted the bag of almond pastries he'd picked up from

the bakery next door after deciding to get out of the car. 'I bought supplies, so we could talk.'

The sunny smile which had been way too sunny dimmed. 'What do you want to talk about?'

Surely there were about a hundred things they could talk about. Starting with how he'd climbed up her fire escape for three weeks straight expecting nightly booty calls – and then walked away without a backward glance on Friday afternoon.

'Is this going to be a long talk?' she asked, jerking her thumb over her shoulder. 'Should I make coffee to go with the croissants?' Without waiting for a reply she shot off towards the kitchen. 'I hope you got almond ones?'

'Of course, they're the best ones,' he said. *And I know they're your favourites.*

How many times had he watched her devour the lush treats, then kissed the stray flakes of pastry and frangipani off her lips?

The surge of heat was swift and predictable.

Yeah, not going there.

He shifted on the seat and tugged some plates out from the stack Ruby kept in the sideboard because there was no room for them in her tiny kitchen.

He arranged the pastries on one, placed two other plates in the spots they had become accustomed to using, and waited for her to return.

And ignored the melancholy, at the realisation this would be the last time he'd hear Ruby making coffee in the morning. He'd been prepared for that hit two days ago. How come he was less prepared for it now?

He could hear her puttering around – filling the kettle, switching it on, waiting for it to boil. Then the aroma of coffee filled the small apartment. But unlike every other morning, she wasn't humming a show tune.

At last she reappeared with a steaming coffee pot and a couple of cups.

Before he had a chance to begin the speech he'd planned, she dashed back to collect a carton of milk. And a teaspoon.

He poured himself a cup. Took a sip of the strong brew and waited for her to sit down. At last she compiled.

'Yum,' she said as she grabbed a pastry from the stack. He watched her rip into the flaking confectionary, sprinkling crumbs, and lick the powdered sugar off the top.

The hum in his abdomen became a definite buzz.

He forced his gaze off her mouth – and his thoughts away from the memory of how her lips tasted dusted with almond sugar.

Not helping.

'I've arranged a settlement with my finance team for The Royale. To pay the debts and keep you solvent for the next twelve months. Once the year is up, you can plan a budget with them for the following year.'

The pastry dropped on to her plate. 'What?'

Finally, he'd managed to surprise her. Not just surprise her, astonish her from the look on her face.

The prickle of satisfaction wasn't putting much of a dent into the strange weight pressing against his ribs.

Why did she look so shocked? Surely, the money was the least he owed her? Something he should have done two days,

two weeks, two months ago even. Why had he been so determined not to take this step?

It was only money. And it was money he might even get
back in time. He could be a silent partner.

If he were an ocean away, he didn't need to be involved. He
wanted to do this, for Ruby, and for his uncle. This was the
best way to give back to the guy – for the harm he'd done to
him by being born. And to give back to Ruby for three weeks
he was never going to forget.

'My finance department have set up an investment fund,'
he began again. 'They'll pay the debts as soon as they become
due, then give you access for day-to-day running costs ...'

She lifted her hand. 'Wait! Stop, you can't do that. I won't
let you do that.'

'Why not?' he asked, confused.

This was not the reaction he'd expected. But then maybe
he should have. Nothing Ruby said or did was ever predictable.

'The Royale's not your responsibility,' she said, the finality
in her voice starting to concern him. 'It's mine.'

'If you're worried about the ownership,' he said. 'I'm planning to sign over my share in the theatre to you,' he continued.
'I called Ryker on Friday after I found out what happened
with those clowns at The Rialto; he's doing the paperwork
next week.'

She got out of her seat, but instead of relief on her face,
all he saw was ... What the hell was that? Why was she so
upset?

'When did you find out about The Rialto offer?' Her lips

were trembling. She looked more than upset, she looked devastated.

'Right after I'd spoken to you in Brynn's. I knew something was up, that you weren't telling me the truth. You should have told me what was going on, I shouldn't have had to ask Jacie.'

She sat back down, her face a picture of distress now. He didn't get it.

'That's why you came back?' she murmured. 'That's why you came to the screening? Because Jacie told you we were going to have to sell the theatre? And you thought you had to rescue me?'

It wasn't the only reason.

The truth struck him hard. He'd wanted to see her one last time. Wanted to spend one more night with her. But what would be the point of admitting that now?

Her head lifted and her eyes were dry but he could hear the tears in her voice when she spoke. 'You shouldn't have come back, Luke.'

'I had to,' he said, 'I couldn't leave knowing you were going to lose your home.'

'I can't accept the money,' she said, so simply and firmly that the pressure in his chest became unbearable.

'That's nuts,' he said, leading with his frustration. Why was she being so stubborn? 'Of course, you can.' He reached across the table and covered her hand with his, felt the spark of connection, the sizzle of need.

'No, I can't.' She dragged her hand free, and the weight in his chest sunk into his stomach.

'I figured it out, Ruby,' he said. 'It's what I was always meant to do,' he continued, but he could hear the desperation in his own voice. 'The theatre was in financial difficulties. Matty loved you like a daughter, he didn't want to leave you with nothing, so he gave me half the theatre to save it for you.'

She shook her head, her eyes shiny with unshed tears now. 'That's not true. Matty was never that mercenary.'

'I wouldn't call it mercenary, more like smart.'

'Why did you change your mind?' she countered.

'Huh?' he asked, the weight in his stomach now heavier than a cannonball.

'Why did you change your mind?' she repeated. 'When you first inherited a share of The Royale, you told me you couldn't help us. That it was a bad investment.'

'Come on, a lot has happened since then, you know why I've changed my mind.' Did she want him to say it? Was that it? To make him declare he had feelings for her?

'What's changed?' Yeah, she did want him to say it. He guessed he owed her this, too.

'Everything's changed, damn it. I care about this place now.' He threw his arms in the air, let his gaze roam over the worn couch where he and Ruby had necked while watching a movie he couldn't even remember, because he'd been too into her. The table where they'd eaten breakfast, sometimes with her sitting on his lap. The hallway, the kitchen. Even the poster of his father on the wall, which no longer had the power to freak him out.

'I care about the theatre,' he said. 'And the people in it.'

He closed the gap she'd created between them and took

her hand in his, ran his thumb across her palm – felt her shudder of response. 'And most of all I care about you.'

There, damn it, he'd said it.

But as he lifted her hand to kiss the knuckles, she pulled her fingers free. 'Don't, Luke.'

Chills raced through his body at her rejection.

'Just because you slept with me.' Her voice was dull, flat, contradicting the heat in her face. 'That doesn't make you responsible for me.'

'I know that,' he said. But when he tried to take her hand again, she stood up, and wrapped her arms around her waist.

'I don't think you do,' she said. 'I won't take your money. I don't want it.'

'Don't be dumb,' he said, frustration flaring now. 'You need the money, The Royale needs the money. I've got lots of it. It's the only solution.'

'No, it's not. I can sell The Royale to The Rialto the way I planned.'

'But you don't want to sell it,' he said, starting to get desperate. She was actually serious about this? She'd rather sell than take his money? What was wrong with his money? 'This is your place. It belongs to you. Matty wanted you to have it.'

'Matty was a lot of wonderful things,' she said. 'But a great businessman wasn't one of them. The theatre's my responsibility now and I'm going to sell it. This place isn't my whole life ...' She let her gaze roam around the room, but where he would have expected sentiment, what he saw was steely resolve. 'Not anymore. I've been hiding here all these years. I need to get out and build a new life for myself. A real life, instead of one that only exists in the movies. You taught me that.' Her eyes met his, the pragmatism he saw somehow disturbing.

'But you don't have to do that.' What wasn't she getting about this? 'Why would you sell The Royale? When I can solve the problem? When I'm *offering* to solve the problem?'

'Because it's not your problem to solve, Luke. It never was. Matty didn't leave you a share in this theatre to save it. All he wanted was for you to love it, the way he did, because he loved your father. And now you care about The Royale. Job done. Can't you see that's all that matters?'

Jesus, what crap. Did she really believe this stuff?

'I refuse to be another responsibility you don't want,' she said, her back straightening.

'But I do want this one.' *Almost as much as I want you.*

The thought echoed in his head.

'No, you don't, Luke,' she said. 'Because then you'd have to accept the fact that I love you.'

She said the words so simply, and with so little inflection, he almost didn't catch them. 'What?'

'I love you, Luke,' she said again, clear, precise, and still with that steely determination, as if she were revealing something terrible instead of something wonderful. 'I think I've known it for a while, but until last night, until you came back, I had totally convinced myself I would never have to admit it to myself. And I certainly wouldn't have to admit it to you. But you came back, and you ruined everything.' She crossed her arms over her chest, her ragged breathing making his own chest hurt. 'And now here we are,' she continued. 'I can't take the money because I think the real reason you want to give it to me is you feel guilty, and I don't want you to feel that way about us,' she finished with a huff of breath.

She didn't look as if she expected a reply.

Which was probably a good thing, because he didn't know what the hell to say. He could see she meant it, one hundred and one percent, but he could also see how sad it made her. And he knew why. Because she was right.

He couldn't feel that much. Not for Ruby, not for anyone. Because it would force him into a corner he'd spent his whole life trying to get out of.

'I think you should leave now, Luke,' she said.

He stared at her, the softly spoken words like a blow. He wanted to take her in his arms, to make her take the money. He didn't want to let her throw away everything she deserved, everything she'd worked so hard for. But how could he do that now without hurting her even more?

He closed his hands into fists and shoved them into the pockets of his suit pants to control the burst of need and frustration.

He couldn't argue with her.

Or things might be said he couldn't take back. Emotions exposed that he didn't want to reveal. That he didn't know how to handle.

Emotions he didn't even understand.

'If that's what you want,' he said, giving her one last chance to change her mind.

'I do,' she said, her voice trembling with emotion, but still firm, still sure.

'Then I guess this is goodbye, Ruby.'

She nodded, her face a picture of regret. A regret he could feel in his own gut, and had spent a lifetime learning to ignore. But as he walked away, he felt the knife twist as he heard her murmur behind him.

'Goodbye, Luke.'

Rubes? I'm outside waiting in the rain? Where r u we're opening in half an hour!

Ruby made her way down the flat's staircase, her head aching from a crying jag that had begun as soon as Luke had walked out of her life, for good this time, and would not stop.

Pull yourself together. Tears never solved anything. He's gone. And you'll survive.

'Just opening up now,' she shouted through the metal shutter in reply to Jacie's text.

She flicked up the switch to lift the shutters.

Luke had reconditioned the motor and replaced the tracking last week, so the shutter lifted smoothly in half the time it used to take.

Ruby sniffed loudly, wishing she had those extra minutes now to compose herself. A new boulder swelled in her throat. Every time she worked the shutter she'd think of him.

Until you sell.

With the shutter lifted, Ruby unlocked the door and shoved it open.

Jacie turned to shake her umbrella before ducking into the

foyer, giving Ruby a few precious extra seconds to compose herself. But despite her best efforts to do so, as soon as Jacie's gaze landed on Ruby's face she knew the sixty-second shutter lifting delay that Luke had left her with hadn't been long enough to hide the evidence of her Luke-induced meltdown.

'Ruby, what's wrong? You look like shit,' Jacie said, appalled. 'Is Luke still here? Didn't he tell you he's going to save the cinema? And why aren't you dressed yet, it's almost noon?'

Because I'm falling apart.

Luke had only left an hour ago. So much for being strong, being a survivor, finding a new life, she was an abject failure at all three.

'I look like shit because I feel like shit.' She waved her arm in the vague direction of the door to her flat. 'I'll go get dressed. Could you open up?'

'Wait, where's Luke?' Jacie asked, cutting off Ruby's retreat.

'He's gone. He's not coming back. End of story.' Ruby scrubbed her face and talked around the sob threatening to choke her. 'You shouldn't have told him about what happened at The Rialto meeting. And you shouldn't have persuaded him to come back for the screening, I'm guessing that costume was your idea.'

'He didn't need any persuading.' A blush darkened Jacie's skin, but she didn't relinquish eye contact. 'I thought ...'

'You thought what?' Ruby asked.

'I thought he was going to stay,' she said simply.

So did I, for one brief shining moment of stupidity.

Ruby's face collapsed, the tears rushing back.

Jacie rushed towards her and enveloped her in a hard hug.

'I'm so sorry, Rubes.' Her friend fished a damp tissue out of her raincoat pocket. 'Here, blow,' she said, holding the tissue to Ruby's nose.

Ruby blew, attempting to clear out the sadness clogging her sinuses.

It didn't work. She felt washed out. Exhausted.

'Why don't I ring Beryl and Tozer and get them to cover for the matinee today?' Jacie said. 'We can order in pizza, steal some medicinal Prosecco from the bar and keep working on Plan B.' Her friend examined her tear-streaked face. 'I'm guessing you turned down his offer?'

Ruby's tear ducts threaten to flood again as she nodded. 'I couldn't take his money, Jace. Please understand.'

I told him I loved him, and he had nothing to say.

She had re-considered her decision several hundred times since he'd left an hour ago – had she just done the stupidest thing imaginable by refusing his, what had he called it, his 'financial settlement' – but she couldn't make herself regret it.

Maybe her head was saying she should have accepted the money. But her heart knew the truth. Accepting Luke's money would have confirmed what Luke had always believed: that Matty had left him half The Royale because he expected his nephew to bail them out. When she knew the opposite was true.

But more importantly, this wasn't about Matty, anyway, it wasn't even really about The Royale – it was about her, and Luke.

It was Luke she wanted, not his money. And she couldn't

have him. Because he didn't want her. How could she ever move on if she didn't confront that reality? And while what she'd said about starting a new life had been a desperate attempt to get him out of the flat before she lost the last of her resolve and begged him to want her – like she'd watched her mother do too many times to count – maybe there was some truth in it. She *had* been hiding at The Royale. Allowing Luke to save her, the way she'd once let Matty save her, wasn't good enough. What she needed to do was save herself.

'I *do* understand,' Jacie said, not giving Ruby the argument she had been braced for. 'I wish I didn't. So, what happens now?' she asked, but it was obvious from her expression she knew the answer.

'I'm going to sell.' Ruby looked around the foyer. 'It will still be a cinema, which is the most important thing. And Gallagher has agreed to keep everyone on – on full pay – while they refurbish.' It was a white lie, because she hadn't had a chance to contact Gallagher yet, but she would drop the price to whatever he asked to get that much for her staff.

'Really?' Jacie looked surprised. 'That's incredible, he never struck me as the generous sort. I mean, it would have been cooler if you and Falcone's son still owned it together, but you'll be rich right? There's that.'

Ruby sniffed and forced herself to smile. 'Absolutely loaded.' Hopefully, she'd have enough to put a deposit on a flat, and take some time out to go travelling before finding a new job. The way she'd always planned. Even if that was the very last thing she felt capable of doing right now.

Going to LA was definitely out, because being in the US would be too close to Luke.

'So loaded, I won't have to work for a while,' she added. 'The manager's job is there if you want it.'

'Wait a minute, you're not going to be managing the place anymore?'

'I decided not to,' Ruby said, making sure she sounded jaunty rather than lost. 'I think I've spent too long here. It's just not the same with Matty gone.' And Luke gone. 'And I need a new challenge,' she added. It felt like another lie now, but she knew she needed to make this break. She couldn't stay here, she had to stop hiding, however painful that was going to be.

'Right.' Jacie didn't look convinced, but what could she do about it. 'So next week marks the end of an era?'

'Yes, I thought we could schedule the last of Matty's Classics for the final showing before we shut down for six months.' *Not we, Ruby.* She swallowed past the lump of grief stuck in her throat.

Jacie's brows furrowed. 'But isn't the only one left *The Last of the Mohicans*? Are you sure that's the right choice for The Royale's final film? It's a really dark movie.'

'It's not *that* dark, it's an epic romantic adventure.' Not unlike her romance with Luke, a rollercoaster ride of emotion.

'People get burned alive and take headers off cliffs,' Jacie pointed out. 'And pretty much everyone dies at the end. So I'd have to disagree with you there. Don't you want to choose something more upbeat? Seeing as how you've already had your heart broken by Luke Devlin?'

'My heart is *not* broken,' Ruby said, determined to believe it. She loved him, she'd told him, and he'd confirmed what she had always known to be true: he couldn't or wouldn't be able to love her back. She refused to wallow. 'We were only really a thing for three weeks.' Goodness that was even shorter than some of her mum's grand love affairs.

'Hawkeye and Madeleine Stowe were only a thing for about three hours, but that didn't stop her promising to survive a fate worse than getting her heart cut out and eaten by the acne-faced guy to be with him again,' Jacie said pragmatically, because suddenly, she was the authority on *Last of the Mohicans*.

'Losing Luke is not a fate worse than getting your heart cut out and eaten by Wes Studi,' Ruby said, fairly sure it wouldn't feel that way, eventually.

'It's not me you have to convince, Rubes.' Jacie headed towards the auditorium to grab some medicinal Prosecco. 'It's you.'

Chapter 20

'You're late,' Luke said, as his kid brother Jack strolled into the small bar in Les Halles. Tucked in a side street, the dark interior smelled of stale beer and garlic and was crammed with tiny tables full of burly guys who looked as if they'd just finished unpacking truckloads of fresh fruit and vegetables as Paris's premiere market, probably because they had.

'I didn't come all the way from Manhattan to see you, just to get blown off for ...' Luke checked his watch. 'Close to forty-five minutes.'

He'd made the last-minute decision to come to Paris yesterday, after only five days back in New York, when he'd received the text from his brother saying he was going to be hanging out in the City of Lights for the summer. But now Luke was here, he didn't know why he'd bothered. Sure, his penthouse had felt like a prison the last five nights, and he hadn't seen his brother in a while, but he had a ton of work to do in New York and Jack clearly did not appreciate his efforts to totally rearrange his schedule just to make this meet-up happen.

'Stop pissing and moaning and give me a hug, man,' Jack

said, then tugged him out of his chair and pulled him into his embrace.

Luke hugged him back, the irritation subsiding as he absorbed the smell of motor oil and leather and soap that clung to his brother's standard uniform of battered jeans, T-shirt and biker jacket.

Standing back, Jack gripped Luke's shoulders. 'Good to see you, too, big bro,' he said, still smiling that killer smile, then signalled to the bartender.

Luke sat, fighting the dumb lump of something closing his throat.

Jack was a pain in the butt, he always had been, and after this afternoon he probably wouldn't see him again for another year, because his brother was currently drifting his way through Europe doing odd jobs, as far as he knew.

'What you having?' Jack asked, as if the last time they'd seen each other had been a week ago, instead of close to twelve months by Luke's count.

The barmaid, who'd been super surly when Luke had walked in forty-five minutes ago, hurried over to take Jack's order as if someone had lit a fire under her butt.

Funny that. But then, Jack tended to have that effect on women. The more laid-back he was, the more attentive they became.

'A Stella, I guess,' he said.

'Not a Sam?' Jack asked, surprising Luke by remembering the brand of bottled beer he drank. He shook his head. The last Sam Adams he'd had was in Brynn's, with Ruby crooning to him.

He cut off the thought. *Not going there.*

'They don't have the Boston Lager here,' he murmured, knowing that wasn't the real reason. He was avoiding anything that reminded him of her. Unfortunately, that was turning out to be pretty much everything from his empty minimalist penthouse in the Meatpacking District – because it wasn't her cramped apartment above The Royale – to his favourite craft beer.

'Such a purist,' Jack mocked, then ordered from the waitress. His brother bantered back and forth with the punky girl in perfect French for a moment, then she headed off to get their order, all the time grinning at his brother as if he were cuter than Ryan Reynolds.

'Looks like you scored,' Luke mumbled, as Jack pulled out the chair opposite, flipped it round, then straddled it. What was it about Jack that he could never sit on a chair properly?

Jack watched the woman leave, his gaze lingering on her butt. 'Nah, she was just being friendly.'

'She wasn't as friendly to me,' Luke said.

'You speak any French?' his brother countered.

'Not a lot,' he had to concede.

'Then there's your answer, French women prefer to converse in their native tongue. Go figure,' his brother replied.

They both knew that wasn't the reason for the girl's attentiveness, but Luke had to admit that was one of Jack's few endearing features. He loved women, but he never took for granted all the attention he'd been receiving from the opposite sex since hitting puberty.

Unlike you.

Luke dispelled the unpleasant thought. And the memory of Ruby's devastated face on their last morning together when she'd told him she loved him. And he'd had no reply.

Not your responsibility. She told you so.

'So, what you doing in Paris?' Luke asked.

'Looking for a job,' his brother replied as he popped an olive in his mouth from the dish the bargirl had brought to their table.

'Do you need any money?' Luke asked, out of habit as much as anything else. 'Or a place to stay? I've got a company apartment a couple of blocks from here?'

Jack's smile became rueful. 'Nope. I'm good.'

He bristled at the easy refusal. He had no idea how his brother survived. As far as Luke knew, Jack hadn't had a steady job since he'd dropped out of art college age eighteen. He didn't own any property or have any possessions other than what he could fit on the back of his bike. But he hadn't asked Luke for money for years now. So whatever he was doing, it must be working for him.

'Still no plans to settle down and live a normal life?' he asked, not quite able to stop himself from needling Jack anyway.

His brother just grinned some more, then thanked the bartender for his beer.

'Nuh-uh,' he said, after the girl had left. He took a long gulp of the cold beer, then smacked his lips, still smiling. 'I left that to you, remember?'

'What's that supposed to mean?' Luke snapped.

How the hell did his brother do that, look super smug and

super could-not-give-a-shit at the same time? It was a gift his brother had possessed which reeled in women by the dozen and allowed him to be rootless and without a care in the world. And while he had always tried to take Jack's attitude problem in stride when they met up, today it was bugging him. Big time.

'You did the settling down thing so well, bro, I'd feel kind of outclassed before I even started. And I'm just not the competitive type.'

'You mean you're not the mature type,' Luke countered, knowing he was going to lose this argument, but unable to let it drop.

'That too.' Jack took another sip as if he'd just been complimented not insulted. Another of Jack's irritating life skills: to piss on criticism with charm and bonhomie. 'So enough about me,' Jack said easily, because he was well used to deflecting Luke's attempts to get him to grow up. He dumped the bottle back on the table and stabbed another olive with a cocktail stick. 'How's tricks in the world of property development and gazillionaire-domination?' he said before eating the olive.

Luke gave a strained laugh. The distraction this meet-up had offered yesterday wasn't looking so good anymore.

He usually enjoyed hanging out with Jack. Jack was the original good-time guy, who could make any problem seem small and unimportant. But all he felt was irritable and out of sorts. And Jack seemed to have picked up on it.

Terrific.

'Great, I guess,' Luke said. 'I'm seeing a couple of sites in France, thinking of investing in a new project in Lille to make this trip worthwhile. Then I'm heading home in a couple of days.' Even if home didn't feel like home, anymore.

'So the stories aren't true,' Jack said. 'I figured they had to be BS.'

'What stories?'

'That you were moving to London full time to run a movie theatre with some British chick.'

'Who told you that?' Luke's insides churned, and the vice around his ribs which had been there for days – ever since he'd walked away from Ruby – tightened.

'Mom by way of Becca. For the record, kid sis didn't believe it either.' Jack's gaze narrowed.

'Is that why you got in touch?' Luke said, annoyed all over again. What the fuck? Why couldn't his family butt the hell out of his business? He'd come to Paris to get away from thoughts of Ruby and now he was having to talk about her with his kid brother, who had never even met her.

'Maybe,' Jack said, still nonchalant and unconcerned. 'Okay, now I'm confused, because you're blushing.'

Luke could feel his face glowing under Jack's stare. 'I'm not blushing.'

'Yeah, you are, bro. Then it's true?'

'No, it's not true. I got served with community service over there so I had to ...'

'*Whoa*.' Jack spurted out the mouthful of beer he'd just necked. 'You? *You* got served by a judge? You have got to be shitting me,' he said, looking more animated than Luke had seen him in years. Probably ever. 'What the hell did you do? Lecture someone to death?'

'Is it really that hard to believe I'd break a law?' Luke asked, indignant now as well as annoyed. Was he really that much of a stuffed shirt?

'Hell, yeah. Luke, you're the dude who came out in a rash when I dissed the on-set tutor. What law did you break? 'Cos this I've gotta hear.'

'Trespassing in a Royal Park.' He decided to leave out the part about disturbing the peace, because that would require him mentioning singing with Ruby. And he was not going there. Jack would probably choke. And he wasn't sure his ribs would survive the recollection of Ruby standing on the jetty, her sweet soulful voice drifting into the night as she scattered his uncle's ashes.

'No shit,' Jack said, sounding genuinely impressed with Luke for the first time in his life. 'They have laws about that stuff in London?'

'They have laws about that stuff everywhere Jack. Just because you chose to ignore them, doesn't mean they aren't there ...' He trailed off, because railing on Jack just didn't seem worth it anymore.

'And you broke them.' Jack let out a laugh. 'Awesome. So what does you breaking into a Royal Park have to do with the British chick and the movie theatre?' Jack added, getting straight to the point.

'I was required to do community service at the theatre. Three hundred hours. So I decided to take a break from Mom and relocate to London for six weeks to get it done. The Royale used to belong to our Uncle Matty. He left me half of it in his will. And the other half to a British chick whose name is Ruby. Ruby Graham ...' He paused. Why was it so damn hard to say her name? Would it always be this hard? 'Anyway, the theatre needed a lot of work. It was kind of run down.'

'Hold up. Uncle Matty? You mean Mom's long-lost brother she doesn't speak to? He died?'

'Yes, he died Jack, months ago. How do you not know this?' Exactly how clueless was his brother about family affairs? And why did Jack's cavalier approach to life seem even less charming all of a sudden?

'I guess Mom must have mentioned it in one of her texts,' Jack said, still clueless.

'Ya think?' Luke said, his tone cutting.

'Damn, now I feel bad for never reading her texts,' he said, not sounding that cut up about his complete inability to pay attention. 'But those things are like novels,' he added, as if that was an excuse. Jack really was a self-centred asshole – why had he never noticed that before? 'But anyway, so you own half the theatre now? And the British chick owns the other half.'

'The British chick has a name. It's Ruby.'

'Is Ruby hot?'

It was Luke's turn to choke on his beer. He slapped the glass down on the table. 'That's a dumb sexist question.'

'Uh-huh? You're blushing again. So I'm going to take that as a yes.' Jack's gaze narrowed and Luke's non-blush ignited. 'Damn, you hooked up with her, didn't you?'

He could have lied, he wanted to lie. Whatever he'd had with Ruby was over.

I love you, Luke.

The simple words echoed in his head again. Crushing his ribcage a little bit more.

Totally over.

Talking about the affair with Jack was not going to change that. But somehow the denial wouldn't come out of his mouth. So he sat dumbly in front of Jack as his face incinerated.

'Yeah, we hooked up. But it wasn't a big deal …' The words clogged his throat. 'And the theatre is being sold to pay off Uncle Matty's debts, so we don't own it anymore.'

Being sold off in approximately twenty hours' time, if the timetable Jacie had given him a week ago was still true.

Get over it. She didn't want your help. She said so. You don't love her. End of.

'You were into her, weren't you?' Jack said, the non sequitur throwing Luke off course.

'Yeah.' Why lie about it? 'She was a nice lady. Smart, compassionate, creative, funny …' He took a swallow of beer – why did that description sound so inadequate. 'And yeah, she was hot.' *So* hot. Hot enough to haunt his dreams every night since he'd left her.

'That sounds like a heck of a lot more than nice.'

Luke glared at his brother. So now Jack was intuitive? *Give me damn break.* 'It doesn't really matter whether or not she was nice or more than nice because it's over.'

'Why?'

'Because it is – because it *was* – just a casual hook-up.'

For me, at least. I never lied to her.

'It doesn't sound casual to me,' Jack said. 'The woman made you blush, that's got to be a first.'

'Whatever, it was never gonna work long term.' He took another long swallow of his beer, his throat so dry he could probably sandpaper a wall with it.

'Why not?' Jack asked.

Luke intensified his glare. Why wouldn't Jack drop this? Couldn't he see he did not want to talk about it? 'Because she's a nice person and I'm not.'

'Bullshit.' Jack's forceful reply gave Luke pause. His brother wasn't smiling anymore.

'She needs someone who can settle down,' he replied. 'Who *wants* to settle down. Who can commit to a long-term relationship. Who *wants* to commit to a long-term relationship. That's not me, I'm not the settling down type.'

Ruby had got that much at least. She would never even have told him she loved him if he hadn't made the dumb decision to go back for Babs and Bob night.

'Are you actually serious right now?' Jack replied.

'Of course I'm serious,' Luke said, shocked by the look on Jack's face, because all traces of his usual super-relaxed, couldn't-give-a-shit charm had disappeared.

'Luke, you're the most settled person I know,' his brother said, sounding more serious than a traffic accident for the first time in his life. 'You *live* for fucking commitment. Or you wouldn't have been riding herd on me and Becca ever since we were born ... And Mom ever since *you* were born.'

'That's not the same. You guys are family, I'm stuck with you.'

'You mean like your old man was stuck with us. Like mine was? Like Becca's father was?' Jack's voice had an edge to it Luke had never heard before. This wasn't the Jack he knew, not at all. This Jack sounded angry. And also weirdly supportive.

'What are you trying to say?' he said, feeling like he was seeing the real Jack for the first time in his life. Where had this guy been hiding? And why?

'They all bailed on us, in their own way,' Jack said, his expression tense. 'The men who should have cared about us and kept us safe and put us first. But you never did. Not even when you could have. Even when it was never your responsibility. You shouldered it anyway. Getting me to do my homework and not hang out with the wrong kids, getting Becca to brush her teeth each night and letting her cling on to you when she came back from her dad's place, and keeping Mom afloat when she had one of her wild moods.'

'You were just a kid, you needed someone to guide you and we all knew that wasn't gonna be Mom,' he said. 'Becca's dad was an alcoholic and a massive dick, she should never have had to spend summers with him in the first place. And Mom had issues, you know that,' he said, in his defence, disconcerted to hear Jack of all people talk about him in this way. Jack has always hated it when Luke told him what to do, or how to do it. His kid brother had rebelled against every rule, every suggestion, every offer of help. Had he admired him all along? Because that was so messed up he didn't even know what to do with it. It would change the whole dynamic of their sibling relationship and he wasn't ready to deal with that right now.

Not after Ruby.

'You were a kid too, Luke. You're only three years older than I am,' Jack said, finally winding down. 'And Mom's issues weren't your problem, but you took them on. So don't tell me you're not the settling down type. You are. You always have been. And you want to know why?'

Luke just stared, not sure if he did or didn't want the answer. Getting relationship advice from his kid brother had to be a low point in his life. The fact the advice was actually making some sense made it even lower.

'Tough shit, because I'm gonna tell you anyway,' Jack said, taking the choice away from him. 'You're the settling down type not because you had to be, but because you're good at it. And you like it, or you wouldn't have spent the last ten years making a killing building other people homes. You say this Ruby chick is smart and creative and compassionate and funny? Well, you're all those things too.' Jack gave him a deliberate once over. 'I don't find you hot, but I guess it's not outside the realms of possibility she might think you are. Women can be screwy like that or they wouldn't get crushes on douchebags like Ross Barlett.'

'Yeah, well, it doesn't matter anymore because it's over,' he said, suddenly feeling defeated. 'I left and Ruby decided to sell the theatre rather than take my money to save it, so I think we can safely say she was not that into me.'

It was a lie, because Ruby had been pretty into him. But her being in love with him didn't change anything. Not if he couldn't love her back. Ruby got that, and she was a hopeless romantic, so it was a lie he could live with.

'You offered her money to save the theatre?' Jack asked.

'That's what I just said isn't it?'

'I guess you can add pride to your list of her good qualities then. And self-respect.'

'What?'

'Come on, Luke, would *you* have taken your money? To save something that means so much to you?'

'I wouldn't have said no. That's just dumb. She's gotta close the theatre now and sell it, just because she didn't want my help.'

'You don't get it, do you?'

'Get what?'

'How could she accept your money if she loved you?'

'How did you know that?' Luke blurted out, so shocked Jack had figured it out he felt like he'd just leapt into a parallel universe.

'She told you she loved you, then,' Jack said, but it wasn't really a question, as his eyes narrowed and his lips pressed into a thin line, and Luke said nothing.

'And I'm guessing you didn't say the same to her,' his brother said, reading his mind again.

'No,' Luke managed at last.

Jack took a long draft of his beer. 'Why not?'

'Because I don't love her, obviously,' Luke snapped.

'You sure about that?' Jack said, only pissing him off more.

'Of course I'm sure. Why wouldn't I be sure? I'd know if I was in love or not, wouldn't I?' Luke said.

Why was he having to argue with his brother about this? And why was having to think about what he had, or rather hadn't, said to Ruby, turning the weight in his gut into a super nova?

'Would you? Because you've always been real good at avoiding those conversations.'

'What conversations?'

'The ones where people talk about their feelings.'

'Uh-huh. Since when do you like talking about feelings?' he asked. Getting relationship advice from Jack was bad enough, being told he should talk about his feelings was just plain wrong. If there was ever a guy who didn't talk about his feelings it was Jack. Except now, for some whacked out reason he couldn't figure.

'Since never,' Jack conceded. 'But we're not talking about me. This is about you and Ruby Graham, who is smart and funny and compassionate and super-hot and loves you. And who you've talked about more than I've ever heard you talk about any woman you've ever dated. Even that super model you were hooking up with on a regular basis for two years.'

'Fuck ...' The beer started to bubble in his belly, his throat felt raw and achy and he wasn't going down with anything.

Was Jack right? Why hadn't he even been able to have the conversation with Ruby? Why had he let her tell him he didn't love her. He cared about her, but what if this was more than that, and he hadn't even asked himself how much more? Had he blown it? How did he really feel about her? Did he *want* to go back to London? To figure it out?

Yes, I damn well do.

And how could he let her lose The Royale when the reason she was selling the place was nothing to do with the theatre, but simply because she didn't want to leave him beholden to her?

'Fuck and double fuck. She's selling the place. Signing the papers tomorrow morning, the final screening is tonight.' He leapt out of his chair and pulled his wallet out of his back pocket, then checked his watch. 'I've got to get back to London, talk to Mom, and then get to The Royale before the final screening finishes.'

'Hey, what about our bar crawl through Paris?' Jack asked, but he was grinning.

'We'll have to take a rain check.' Leaning over the table he grabbed Jack by the cheeks and planted a smacker on his brother's lips. 'Thanks, bro. For once, I think you actually might be talking sense.'

Jack laughed as he scrubbed his lips with the back of his hand. 'I always talk sense – you just don't listen.'

Luke whipped his jacket off the back of his chair.

'What's the final show?' Jack asked.

'*Last of the Mohicans*,' he murmured, as he clicked through the apps on his phone to book a ticket on the next Eurostar train. 'It's the last film in the Matty's Classics season, apparently it was one of our uncle's favourite movies.'

'Sounds like the guy had great taste,' Jack said. 'I loved that movie as a kid. All the running and shooting and shit – although it's kind of a downer, doesn't everyone end up dead?'

'Not everyone …' He clicked the pay now button, then tucked the phone back into his jacket pocket. 'Not this time. I'll see you around Jack, keep in touch.'

Jack saluted him as he turned to dash off, then shouted. 'Go for it Hawkeye, go save your girl, before she saves herself.'

'Hi, I'm trying to locate Helena Devlin's dressing room.' Four hours later, Luke stopped a young man laden with an armful of evening gowns in dry-cleaner bags in the busy backstage area behind the Cottosloe's stage.

The guy stopped, then did a double-take.

'I'm her son,' Luke added, although from the young man's heightened colour he suspected the information was unnecessary.

'Oh my, yes you are,' the dresser said with a purr that could mean only one thing. He was a Falcone nut. 'Wow, you really are the spit of him, aren't you?'

For once, Luke didn't find the provocative stare or the unfiltered comments uncomfortable. He'd figure out why that was later, much later. He had to talk to his mom about saving The Royale before he saw Ruby. And while that should be fairly straightforward, getting his mother to cooperate was never a walk in the park.

'I can't imagine why Hell on Wheels ever tried to deny it,' the guy said.

Hell on Wheels? Was that what the backstage crew called his mom?

Luke would have laughed, if his guts weren't tied in knots.

'Me, either,' Luke said.

As soon as the words came out of his mouth, it occurred to him, it was the first time he'd ever acknowledged his relation to Falcone to someone he wasn't closely related to … or

Ruby. He tensed, bracing for a backlash. But the guy just grinned, as if they were sharing a particularly naughty joke.

Hell, maybe they were. Why had he always been so scared to talk about his father? His mom had always refused to talk about Falcone to the press when he was a kid, and now he knew the reason why was much more complex than he'd ever thought. She hadn't done it to be coy, or stoke the gossip, but because she'd always been conflicted, maybe even ashamed, about having a child with the man her brother had loved. But he could have owned the truth about his parentage himself as an adult. And he never had.

'Mind you, Helena is nothing if not capricious, right?' the young man said, sending Luke a conspiratorial wink. Juggling the garments in his arms, he pointed towards a hallway at the back of the stage area. 'Her dressing room is that way. You can't miss it. It's got a star on the door the size of a small planet.' Giving Luke a wave he rushed off in the opposite direction.

Luke headed towards the dressing room feeling weirdly deflated by the encounter.

Jesus, he'd been kind of a jerk about his old man. And the Falcone nuts.

What was so terrible about being Falcone's son? And dealing with his battalion of fans? After all, Ruby had been one of them. If it weren't for this face – his father's face – she might never have wanted him. So when he thought about it that way, he had quite a lot to thank the guy for.

He reached a door at the end of a corridor with a large gold star on it. Scribbled underneath on a chalk board in his mother's handwriting were the words:

Helena Devlin aka Hell on Wheels.

Do Not Disturb unless you're bearing gifts or uncritical adoration. Preferably both.

Both was underlined twice.

So his mom had embraced her nickname – possibly even coined it.

He tapped his knuckles above the star, oddly charmed by the sign. How come he had never realized his mom had a sense of humour about her diva-ishness?

Perhaps because he'd never had a sense of humour about it himself.

'Danny, if that's you run away and get us both a quick curtain-up mimosa, I'm gasping, sweetheart. And beg Megan for a new pair of stockings but don't tell her I've laddered another pair though or she'll probably chop my legs off.'

His mother's voice rang through the door, rich and fluid, professional and yet full of affection. He'd always known she loved the sound of her own voice – funny that he'd never realized he liked the sound of it quite a lot, too.

He opened the door to find her sitting at a dressing table laden with powders and perfumes and a host of other potions, the traditional light bulbs surrounded the mirror's frame. The room was small for a diva, crammed with rails full of clothing, a day bed, a spray of potted plants and flowers and a huge basket of cellophane wrapped fruit. It looked like a thousand other dressing rooms he'd visited her in over the years.

But for the first time, instead of feeling tense and on edge, the knots of stress in his stomach relaxed.

She glanced round, her hair tied back in a wig net, her face covered in the sculptured foundation she used to make her look a least ten years younger than she actually was.

'Luke? You came to see the show again, how marvellous.'

She bounced off the chair and crossed the room to give him a hug.

She enveloped him with her signature perfume and he took a deep breath in, for once appreciating the exotic scent of wild flowers and patchouli.

'Hi, Mom,' he said, having to clear his throat as she held him.

She stepped back, holding his shoulders, and smiled a guileless smile of pure pleasure, that wasn't faked. 'I'm so pleased you're here,' she said, the genuine affection in her voice tearing at something inside him.

He swallowed.

Jesus, why was he suddenly choking up?

'I can't stay for the show, I came because I need your help with something.'

'You do?' She seemed astonished. And it occurred to him he'd probably never said those words to her before. She'd asked for his help a million times, but when had he ever straight out asked for hers? He guessed that was pretty messed up, considering who the parent was here.

'Yeah, I do,' he said, trying not to dwell on the novelty of the situation.

'Tell me what you need me to do?' she said, without even blinking.

Taken aback by the eager, unequivocal response, he forced himself not to dwell on that either.

'I want you to buy my share of The Royale. Ruby's gonna have to sell the theatre to pay the debts – and she won't take my money – but if you'll agree to buy it, I could give you a loan. No interest, no need to repay it.' It was the only solution he could come up with, that would save The Royale and give him a chance to figure things out with Ruby at the same time.

His mother's eyes took on a curious gleam.

'That sounds a bit sneaky,' she said. 'If you're loaning me the money to pay for your share and I don't have to pay it back, how is it even mine?'

'Mom, could you just not argue about—'

'Why won't she accept *your* money?' she interrupted him.

'Because she's got some dumb idea into her head that it would be going against Matty's dying wish.' Which wasn't completely a lie. Maybe this situation was more about them than Matty, but his mom did not need to know that. 'But I figured if you offered to become The Royale's patron, it's benefactor, she'd accept that.' He sunk his hands into his pockets, feeling exposed under his mother's inquisitive gaze, but determined to make this happen. It would work, it was a great plan. He couldn't work things out with Ruby if she lost The Royale because of him.

'You want me to lie to Ruby about your involvement?' his mother said. 'You want me to trick her into defying Matty's dying wish?'

'What? No, dammit, that's not it at all.'

Why was he not surprised his mom was going to make this perfectly simple plan complicated?

'That wasn't Matty's dying wish,' he said.

Just this once. Please don't let her flake out on me.

'Ruby's misunderstood it,' he continued. Shit, he *had* to make this happen. And to do that he *had* to get his mom on board. 'He left me half The Royale because he wanted me to help her out. And now she won't let me. But if you help me I can still save the movie theatre for her— For Matty,' he corrected himself.

Too late.

His mother's eyes took on a speculative gleam. She'd figured out the truth. About him and Ruby.

She took his elbow, led him to the day bed. 'I think you better sit down, Luke, and explain everything.'

He perched on the edge of the mattress. He was shaking, he realized, as she sat beside him on the bed and touched his knee. 'It's okay, Luke. Everything will be okay.'

The softly spoken words propelled him back in time. To another day.

The smell of perfume and hydrangeas was replaced with the hideous scent of death. Cloying, vulgar, suffocating.

He stared at her fingers on his knee, the heavy rings she wore, the skin still smooth in her fifties but speckled now with sun blemishes, and remembered her sitting beside him that day too, sixteen years ago, in his father's open-plan living room in Montecito. The patrolman's questions that he couldn't answer. The panic tightening around his throat, threatening to choke him. And her voice, like now. Rich, resonant, reassuring, answering the questions for him and dragging him back from the edge.

Funny he'd never remembered that until now.

She had been there beside him through the very worst of that day. She'd arrived like the cavalry, before the cops and the EMTs, minutes after he'd called her to tell her what he'd found.

He shoved the memories back, made himself breathe. *In One-two-three. Out one-two-three.*

For fuck's sake, Devlin. Don't start reminiscing about the worst day of your life. You don't have time.

He took the breaths he needed to stave off the panic attack. His palms remained clammy, the tension and stress still there punching a hole in his ribcage.

But all he could really feel now was the fear.

That he could never deserve Ruby if he couldn't give her The Royale.

'Tell me about Ruby?' his mother said gently.

He glanced at his mother's face. He didn't want to talk about Ruby.

'There's not much to tell,' he murmured, evasively.

'Are you sure?' she said, not buying the denial. 'It seems to me she matters to you quite a lot. Or why would you be so determined to save her cinema?'

She had him there.

If he wanted her help he was going to have to break one of his golden rules – and talk to her about his love life. *Great.*

He rocked back, the knots in his gut tightening, then stood and paced over to the chair she'd been seated in, buying time, trying to figure out what to say without encouraging too much intrusion. He wasn't sure there was a way to do that anymore. And maybe talking to her would help. He'd never asked for her advice, but she was the queen of surviving messed up relationships.

'She's nothing like any of the other women I've ever dated,' he said, sitting down in the chair his mother had vacated. 'She's smart and sweet and so hot it hurts.' He cringed inwardly. Jesus, he was losing it, had he just told his mom his lover was …

'How long have you been dating?' his mother asked.

'For three weeks.' Did it even qualify as dating? 'We broke up nearly a week ago.'

'And you want her back,' his mother said. 'And that's why you think you have to save The Royale?'

'Yes … No,' he said, he tugged his fingers through his hair, feeling like a total dumbass. 'I don't know.'

Jesus, could he sound any more clueless about his own life? How could he not know if he loved her? His mom was going to have a field day with this.

He stole a look at her, expecting to see a gleam in her eye because she was finally going to get the 'deep and meaningful' conversation about his commitment issues she'd been wanting to have with him ever since he could remember – and which he'd been avoiding just as long – but instead of the gotcha expression, what he saw was something else.

She didn't look happy or smug – she looked devastated.

And all he felt was more confused. How could every single thing he thought he knew about his relationship with Jack and now his mom be so screwed up all of a sudden?

'Oh, Luke,' she said, the pity in her tone scrambling his guts. 'I'm so sorry I failed you so spectacularly.'

He blinked. And for once he had not one clue what to say

to her, or how to avoid this conversation, or even if he wanted to anymore.

'Mom, I never said you failed me—'

'But I did, because you wanted stability,' she said. 'And I didn't give it to you. And for once I'm not being melodramatic. I knew how anxious you always got, even before ...' She stopped. 'Even before what happened with your father.'

He searched his mother's face. And realized she *was* serious. This wasn't her 'serious moment' face, the one she wore when she was playing Anna Karenina.

And suddenly, he wanted to know, seeing as they were definitely having this conversation now, something that had always bugged him.

'Then why did you keep us, Mom? Why did drag us all over creation with you? Jack could have stayed with his dad, so could I. I liked Bill, we got along, he was a steady, dependable guy.' *Unlike Falcone.*

'I kept you with me, because I loved you to bits. Both of you. And Rebecca when she came along. You were my babies. And I was selfish. But it hurts now to know you were so scared of stuff I never even thought about.'

She sucked in a heavy breath.

'Love is a wonderful gift, Luke,' she said. 'Mostly because it's never ever what you expect it to be. Sometimes it's fleeting, sometimes it lasts, sometimes it can't. But each time you unwrap it, it's entirely unique. Ruby wants to give you that gift, and it breaks my heart to know that something I did – and all the things I didn't do – makes you think you have to save Ruby's theatre to deserve it.'

He frowned. He wanted to be angry with her, wanted to dismiss her little speech as his mom at her cheesy, melodramatic best. But he couldn't say anything, because all he felt was numb.

'You were forced to be old before your time Luke, long before you discovered Rafe's body.'

He didn't feel numb anymore, he felt fragile. And still so confused.

'You had to keep everything in order to cope with all the disorder I threw at you. But now you have to let go of that and let the chaos in a little bit. I promise it won't hurt you again. Not this time. Not if she really loves you. Do you think she does?'

He nodded, feeling choked, but weirdly not caring. Ruby did love him, that wasn't in any doubt. Because Ruby knew what she wanted and what she needed. And she wasn't afraid to say it. Unlike him.

But it hurt, he discovered, to know his mother understood. May have always understood.

Had he really let all this stuff from his childhood have such a hold over him that he couldn't see what was right before his eyes?

'Are you saying you think I'm a control freak?' he asked.

His mother smiled, moisture making her eyes sparkle. Either she was giving the performance of her career, or she was on the verge of tears. And for once he could see it was definitely the latter.

'Maybe a little bit,' she said on a huff of breath. 'But thank god for it, or I'm not sure Jack and Rebecca would ever have kept all of their teeth, let alone learned how to function in the adult world.'

'I'm not sure Jack does, actually.'

They both laughed, the dry ripple of amusement easing the tension in the room.

Reaching over, his mother took his hands in hers and smoothed her thumbs over the skin, stroking his wrists, and the pulse which had started to beat double time.

Suddenly, he felt like crying, too. For a guy who was not emotional and tended to shun any kind of melodrama, it was not a good feeling. Especially in the presence of his mom, who would never let him forget it.

'Would you do me one favour Luke?'

'I guess, as long as it isn't illegal,' he said.

She laughed again, the sound bright and full-bodied, suddenly reminding him of all the times during his childhood when she'd been the one to make it better.

How had he managed to forget that, too?

For all of her irresponsibility and her selfishness, his mother, like Ruby, was an irrepressible optimist. She was always willing to see the good, the bright, the best in any disastrous situation.

The fact that Helena Devlin had been the cause of most of those disasters didn't seem to matter so much anymore.

'Don't nit-pick and over-analyse this situation,' she said. 'Just tell her how you feel and take your chances. You're actually quite a catch, you know. Ruby has already figured that out, now all you have to do is figure it out, too.'

'Five minutes to curtain, Ms Devlin.' The loud rap on the

door and the shout from the stage manager startled them both.

His mother smiled and shook her head, then released his hands.

He missed the connection instantly.

'Now scoot,' she said, as she nudged him out of her chair. She sat down and lifted a powder puff to finish off her make-up.

He planted his hands back into his pockets. 'So you won't front the deal to save The Royale?' he asked, remembering why he'd come.

She glanced over her shoulder. 'Of course not, darling. That would be dishonest,' she said. 'And anyway, it's not the theatre Ruby needs, now is it?'

He wanted to say more, to push her, to beg if necessary. Still not entirely convinced he could be enough, not without The Royale. But he could see from the stubborn tilt of her chin she wasn't going to budge on this. And he'd been trained never to distract her when she had only minutes until curtain-up.

He headed towards the door. 'Break a leg, Mom, I'll see you around.'

His mother lifted her hand in a dismissive wave, but as he shut the door, he heard her murmur: 'Listen to your heart, Luke. Everything else is white noise.'

Chapter 21

'Oh. My. God. I love this bit of the movie,' Jacie whispered to Ruby as Daniel Day-Lewis's Hawkeye shouted above the thunderous sound of the waterfall to Cora about staying alive and not giving up no matter what occurred.

Ruby nodded in the darkness. She had always loved this part of the movie too because she'd believed, like Hawkeye, that Cora could survive anything.

But as she watched the drama unfold on the screen, The Royale packed with all of their regulars, the community Matty had made and she'd nurtured for so long as riveted as she would once have been, Hawkeye's declaration didn't seem quite so magnificent anymore.

He was abandoning Madeline Stowe's Cora, quite possibly to a fate worse than death. And while that was empowering for Cora, it also sucked.

Survival was tough enough without the man you loved beside you.

And as nuts and delusional as it was, she had fallen in love with Luke Devlin. Because if he had stayed – if he was here right now, beside her – surviving the end of The Royale would be so much easier to bear.

As Hawkeye and his adopted father and brother dived into the waterfall and disappeared and Magua and his angry band arrived to capture Cora and her sister and the dull British guy, Ruby didn't feel empowered, she felt scared and inadequate and so far out of her depth it wasn't even funny.

Would losing The Royale really have been easier with Luke here? Probably not, but the truth was that somehow, in a ridiculously short space of time, he'd come to mean so much more to her than the theatre. She hadn't wanted the theatre, if she couldn't have him. It was as simple as that. Which she supposed was a powerful lesson to learn and an important one.

The Royale had never been what gave her life meaning. Or any of the films she had adored watching within its walls.

It had been her friendship with Matty, with Jacie and Gerry and Tozer and Beryl and Brynn and everyone else in the community they'd built.

But even if she'd been able to keep the theatre, Matty would still be dead and eventually everyone else here would have drifted away too. Because they all had a life outside it, unlike her. Jacie had her granddad Errol and her mum and a huge circle of friends from school and college who she hung out with when she wasn't working. To Jacie this was a job she enjoyed, but it was still just a job. Brynn had his bar – not to mention his partner Thérèse. Beryl had her children and grandchildren and all of her fellow septuagenarian film buffs at the Pensioners' Club screenings. And so on and so forth with every other person here. If nothing else, Luke had opened her eyes to the truth, that she'd spent too much of her life hiding.

I don't want to own The Royale if it means spending the rest of my life here alone.

'Ruby,' Gerry hissed from behind her. 'There's someone in the lobby to talk to you.'

'Who?' she murmured. She did not want to miss any of The Royale's final screening, even if the film was making her feel miserable. Jacie had been right, it was a total downer.

'I think you'll want to find out for yourself,' he said. 'He couldn't come into the auditorium, he's soaking wet. It's pouring with rain outside.'

He?

She left her seat and headed out of the auditorium, just as Cora's wannabe fiancé Duncan – the dull British guy – got strung up over a burning fire.

Luke turned as she rushed into the lobby. Elation surged up Ruby's torso.

His dark hair was plastered to his forehead, those cool blue eyes hot on her face. But as soon as the joy exploded in her heart, leaving her light-headed, the adrenaline fizzled out. Luke wasn't back to declare his feelings, because he'd convinced himself a long time ago he didn't have feelings.

'Luke, what are you doing here?' she said.

If Luke had come back to torture her some more, she would survive it.

I'm stronger than I look. I'm at least as strong as Cora.

Water dripped from his suit on to the new carpet.

'I'm not leaving,' he said. 'I can't.'

Her heart leapt at the passion in his voice, the purpose – only to sink back into her abdomen. He was here to save The Royale for her, to try to persuade her to take the money again. But that wasn't what she needed.

'If you've come back to save the theatre ...' She stepped towards him, placed her hands on his cool cheeks, felt the muscle bunch and tense. 'The answer's still no.' She took a deep breath, determined to keep going when all he did was stare at her the way he had before – conflicted, unsure. But there was something else there now, something open and less guarded.

So she told him everything she now knew to be true. After almost a week without him. A week she had survived, and would keep on surviving even if it killed her.

'The Royale isn't what I love,' she said. 'It's just a building. The reason I came here after school, and every weekend, was to hang out with Matty. And the main thing that helped me get over that huge loss ...' She sucked in another unsteady breath. 'Or at least begin to get over it ... was *you*. You've already helped me so much more than you know. The Royale will be fine without me because, ultimately, without someone for me to love inside it, it's just four walls, a new bar, lots of seats in desperate need of re-upholstering and a projector. And loads of other people's dreams. I think it's way past time I started making my own dreams, don't you?'

Luke stared, shell-shocked, cold to the bone, and struck dumb all over again. He'd been trying to figure out what to say all the way here, had even jumped out of the taxi and into a thunderstorm to give himself extra time to think up a couple of good lines. And she'd beaten him to the punch, opening her heart all over again. All he wanted to do right now was drop to his knees in front of this insanely hot, sweet, honest, capable, smart woman and thank her. But he knew he had to be straight with her first, and it was killing him.

'I'm scared ...' The words choked off in his throat. 'I'm scared I can't give you what you need, that I'm not that guy. That's why I wanted to save The Royale. Because I guess, underneath everything else, I wasn't sure I could give you more than that.'

Her smile was sweet and sad, but also confused as she tilted her head and stared back at him. 'Oh, Luke. Can't you see what I'm trying to tell you? You've already given me everything I need.'

'Like what?' he asked, because he still didn't get it. But the damp from the early summer rain, which had started to seep into his bones, didn't feel so cold anymore.

Probably because of the naked tenderness in her expression, which was full of hope and understanding, uncomplicated truth, compassion instead of judgement, and something more ...

Something he wanted, more than anything else he'd ever wanted in his life. And he'd wanted a lot of stuff once. Stability, security, a house with a picket fence, a dad who showed up when he said he would and didn't look through him like he wasn't there, a mom who didn't draw the attention of every photographer within a twenty mile radius and would tell Becca to brush her teeth and Jack not to jump off that roof so he didn't have to. Funny to think that none of that stuff seemed to matter so much anymore.

'Well, orgasms.' Ruby's cheeks lit up brighter than the fairy lights in her bedroom. 'You gave me lots of orgasms. And then there's your amazing DIY skills.'

'DI-what skills?' he asked.

'Repair skills,' she clarified. 'And having your arms around me when I needed a hug ...' Her smile quivered and he knew she was thinking of Matty. 'And I've needed a lot of those lately. You got me almond croissants in the morning because you knew they're my favourites. You cooked me grilled cheese sandwiches, and gave me the sexiest hair wash I'll ever have. You fixed my boiler and sat all the way through *The Wizard of Oz* even though you hate singalongs and flying monkeys. You watched *About a Boy* even though you don't fancy Hugh Grant and ...' She leaned into him, bringing her rose scent with her and whispered: 'And there was a scene in it that reminded you of something absolutely terrible.'

His gaze got stuck on the lush, sexy mouth he'd feasted on for days, and dreamed about often, but had never gotten enough of.

It was what came out of it next, though, that was the hottest thing he'd ever heard.

'You don't have to save me, Luke. I can save myself. Just like Cora under that waterfall.'

'I know,' he said, even getting the movie reference. For once.

She dropped her head. Examined the puddle forming at his feet.

'I could get your suit dry cleaned, before you go?'

She was giving him an easy out. But he could hear the courage and the strength it was taking her to make the offer sound casual. When he knew it was anything but.

And it was the only thing he needed to finally break the seal on all of his insecurities. And step up to the plate.

His mother was right. Love was a gift, and he'd be nuts not to grab it with both hands – simply because he was too scared he might not be up to the job.

Taking her arms, he dragged her towards him, dampening her T-shirt and making her eyes pop wide.

'Fuck the suit,' he said.

And then he kissed her, like he meant it. Deeper than Babs and Bob, more desperate than Jake and Heath, curiouser than Judy, and even more selfish than Hugh the asshat, because he'd finally found his own Cora under her waterfall. But he'd be damned if he was ever going to let her go.

Epilogue

Three hours later.

'I spoke to Gwen. I figured I could relocate to London, leave her in charge of the New York office, buy that house in Chepstow Villas, seeing as you'll need a new place to live ...'

'But Luke, are you sure?' Ruby asked, leaning up on her elbow, the sight of the man she loved lying casually in her bed making her heart race into her throat. Surely the choking sensation would eventually ease once she got used to the wonder of everything that had happened in the last three hours?

They'd gone straight to her flat, and after striping Luke out of his wet suit they'd made love – fast and furious at first, as if their lives depended on making up for the six lost days, and then slow and languid. Her body was still humming from the orgasms, but more than that, her heart was humming as if he'd somehow plugged her into an electric socket charged with happiness.

The only problem was all the happy hormones and

humming heartbeats – not to mention the sight of his naked chest and those dark blue eyes searching her face so full of sincerity – were making it next to impossible to have a coherent conversation about practical considerations. Such as their future plans.

But Luke being Luke, he was insisting on having that conversation now.

She loved how he needed to have order in his life. But right now she loved his left nipple a bit more. And she was finding it super hard not to give into the urge to kiss it.

'Of course I'm sure,' he said, wrapping his arm around her shoulders and pulling her back against his side so she couldn't give in to her nipple fixation.

'But we don't need to stay in London,' she said, yawning, as she snuggled against his chest. Was there anything more glorious than having him in her bed and knowing he wanted to stay?

'You relocating to London seems pretty extreme,' she added.

'Not really,' he said, his fingers playing with her hair in that absent way he had that made her feel so cherished. 'I'm doing a lot of business in Europe. It kind of makes sense for me to open an office this side of the Atlantic.'

'But I won't be tied to the city, anymore,' she offered. 'Not after I sign the sale agreement with Rialto tomorrow.'

He tensed, and she knew he was having to bite his tongue to stop the offer to save The Royale coming out of his mouth again. But she was proud of him when he asked instead. 'Do you have to sign the deal tomorrow? There might be a way to find other financing so you can keep the theatre.'

'Financing that isn't yours?' she asked, just to be clear that they'd had this argument already and she'd won.

She tilted her head up, and the joy exploded in her heart when he nodded. 'I still think you should accept my help. But yeah, financing that isn't mine.'

She smiled and pressed a kiss into his left pec. 'I don't know if I can hold them off,' she said, honestly, pushing away the pang of regret. 'Gallagher has agreed to keep all my staff on and he wants to redevelop the site for a big relaunch in December.'

'But if we could find other investment, you'd want to keep The Royale?'

She swallowed, the emotion making her eyes sting at the passionate intensity in his gaze. Luke didn't do things by halves, and she was his responsibility now, whether she wanted to be or not. And she realized she did want to be. As long as they both knew that didn't come with strings attached.

So she nodded. 'Yes, I'd want to keep it.'

'Okay, then,' he said, leaning closer, his lips skimming hers. 'Then we need to investigate and come up with a financial plan you can accept.'

'Uh-huh,' she murmured against his lips, feeling her happy hormones turn hot and achy. 'But maybe we could do that tomorrow,' she said. 'I've got other things I want to investigate tonight.'

He chuckled, the sound low and deep and gloriously self-satisfied, but just as they sunk further into the bed, his lips finally connecting with hers, there was a sharp rap on the bedroom door.

They both jumped.

'Ruby? Luke? Sorry to cock block you both but you need to come downstairs.'

'Jace?' Ruby felt her face ignite at her assistant manager's shout.

What on earth? What time was it? She had assumed Jacie and the rest of the crew had packed up and gone home hours ago. The whole theatre had ended up witnessing her and Luke's reunion, and it had been wonderful to have everyone there, but they'd gone back to watch the rest of the movie, while she and Luke sneaked upstairs.

She scrambled out of bed as Luke let out a rueful chuckle and rolled on to his side, muttering: 'I always knew that woman hates me.' But it was said with wry affection.

Ruby grabbed her robe, slung it on, then opened the door. No way would Jace have interrupted them unless there was a real problem.

'What is it, Jace? Is something wrong?'

'Not wrong, exactly,' Jace said, leaning round her and then sending Ruby a cheeky smirk at the sight of Luke lounging in her bed. 'I just thought you should know, Helena Devlin arrived approximately half an hour ago. And now she's asking to see you and Luke.'

'What the hell! You have got to be kidding me?' This from Luke, who suddenly wasn't lounging anymore. 'What the hell is my mom doing here?'

He didn't sound pleased. But as Ruby slipped out of the room and closed the door behind her so he could get dressed, she couldn't help the grin that spread over her face.

She was finally going to meet Helena Devlin. The stage legend ... and Luke's mum. 'I can't believe it,' she said to Jace, not quite able to keep the awe out of her voice. 'Helena Devlin's in The Royale?'

Her throat got a little raw. Somehow she knew Matty would have been so pleased to have his sister here at last. The place he'd built out of the wreckage of his relationship with Rafael Falcone. And Helena. This was huge.

'She's not just here,' Jace said, beaming back at her. 'She's been holding court since she arrived. Beryl and Brynn are practically genuflecting. Gerry has had several spontaneous orgasms and even gramps is charmed,' she said. 'But I couldn't hold off coming to get you any longer. Sorry,' she said, not looking all that sorry. 'I hope I didn't interrupt anything important.' She all but chuckled.

'You know perfectly well you did,' Ruby said, grabbing a set of sweats from the airing cupboard and dropping the robe to tug them on. 'But it's nothing we can't take a rain check on,' she added, grinning back at Jacie.

'I'll bet,' Jacie said, lifting her eyebrows.

Ruby checked her hair in the hall mirror. Balls. She looked as if she'd been electrocuted. But it would have to do. She didn't have time to get it in any semblance of order. And she wanted to get down to greet Helena before Luke got dressed and started giving his mother a hard time.

Helena was Matty's sister. And Matty had forgiven her, she knew he had. Whatever Luke's issues were with his mother – and she didn't doubt he had them, and there was a good reason for them, and they were probably deep and complex – she still wanted Matty's sister to know she was welcome at The Royale.

Not least because Ruby was bursting with so much happiness right now, she wanted everyone to be happy.

But even so, as she made her way down the stairs to the foyer, the doubts set in. If only she could have met Helena after her stage show, when she had been wearing her green silk dress and had her hair properly tamed and her wits about her, instead of in shapeless sweats with bed hair, her mind still frazzled from shagging Helena's son to within an inch of his life.

Awkward, much?

But as she stepped into the foyer, and Brynn and Errol and Beryl and Gerry all turned, to reveal the woman in their midst, Ruby's heart rammed her throat.

Helena stood in the newly redecorated foyer, her dark red hair piled on top of her head in an elaborate chignon, her face one Ruby had seen so many times, but somehow different. Not regale, or reserved, but warm and soft and full of joy when a smile spread across it and she marched over the faded carpeting towards her.

'My dear,' she said, her clipped smoky voice bringing back a thousand beautiful movie memories for Ruby. 'You must be Ruby, I'm so so overjoyed to meet you at last.'

She grasped Ruby's fingers and tugged her into a hug, which

felt so natural, the silly sting of tears returned. She became enveloped in the scent of patchouli perfume and the warmth of affection, and acceptance.

For goodness sake, get a grip.

Ruby sniffed as she hugged Helena back and the older woman whispered, for only her to hear: 'I don't know how you did it, my dear, but I will always be in your debt. Luke has needed someone like you his whole life, and I'm so glad he's found you at last.'

Helena knew, she realised, about her and Luke, and she approved.

And suddenly, Ruby's bed hair, and the sweats and what she'd been doing with Helena's son not five minutes ago didn't matter nearly as much as all the wonderful emotions suffusing her heart.

She'd always known she couldn't have Matty back, but having Helena here felt almost like the next best thing.

Helena stepped back and smiled. 'Your wonderful team have been showing me round the theatre,' she said, switching from intense emotion to practicalities in a heartbeat, like a pro. 'It really is such a marvellous place. I can feel Matty here in every nook and cranny. And I know this is where he healed. So, I have a proposition for you that I hope you will accept.'

Ruby wiped her eyes, the tears having welled over at some point. 'You ... you do?' she said, still struggling to get a grip on the conversation.

Clearly Luke and his mother had one crucial thing in common that she really needed to learn: how to be pragmatic when your heart was overwhelmed.

'Mom, what are you doing here?'

Ruby swung round to see Luke standing behind her, leaning back against the concession stand, his arms crossed in a stubborn gesture over his broad chest, his damp suit trousers and shirt and the wary frown on his face only making him look more gorgeous. And more hers.

Strangely though, she couldn't feel the animosity pumping off him she'd noticed before in his conversation with his mother on the phone all those weeks ago.

Her heart did the giddy little leap it always did when Luke was near.

Jeez, she was going to have to get that under control, too.

Had Helena said something about a proposition? What could that mean?

'Actually, my darling boy,' Helena said, with all the pomp and circumstance of a woman who had made a living being a legend. 'I've come to buy your share of The Royale.' She took Ruby's trembling fingers in hers and squeezed, before turning back to her son. 'So Ruby doesn't have to sell it, and I hope ...' Her gaze shifted back to Ruby. 'I hope I can help her run it, as a silent partner of course, the way I'm sure Matty would have wanted.'

Luke jerked upright and released his arms.

What the actual ...? His mom was coming through with the finance *now*, after she'd told him she wasn't going to?

Even though they'd come to a definite understanding in her dressing room four hours ago, and the end result had been nothing but good, he couldn't help being kind of pissed by her contrary decision and her terrible timing. So he blurted out the first thing that came into his head.

'You're gonna let me loan you the money after all to buy Ruby out?'

He knew it was the wrong thing to say as soon as it had come out of his mouth. Because the look of pure joy on Ruby's face turned quizzical. It wouldn't take her long to guess what he'd tried to do, but before he could correct his mistake his mother stepped in to rescue him.

'No, I'm not letting you loan me the money, because that's not what Ruby wants.' She glanced at Ruby. 'Am I right, dear?'

'Yes, yes you are. I can't accept Luke's money, he knows that,' Ruby said, sending him a glance over her shoulder that told him she would be having words with him later about trying to trick her into accepting his help, and then staring at his mother as if she were a legend.

And, okay, maybe she was – but she was still his mom and now he had no idea what the hell was going on. And what she was even doing here.

'So, how are you going to get your hands on the two million pounds The Royale needs to pay off Matty's debts?' he asked, because everyone else seemed to be frozen in place, waiting for an explanation.

He knew how that felt, because he'd been dealing with his mom and her grandstanding gestures for a lot longer than they had.

'I've spoken to my financial team and I made a few calls,' his mother said, sounding more practical and forthright than he'd ever heard her. 'It actually wasn't that hard putting the finances together once I set my mind to it. Does that satisfy you, Luke?' she said, snapping slightly.

He blinked, realizing he'd been put in his place. Okay, maybe he *had* underestimated her. But before he could get up the guts to admit as much, Ruby had intervened.

'Ms Devlin, if you'd like to invest in The Royale, we'd love to accept you as an equal partner.'

'That's all settled then, my dear,' his mom said, positively beaming. 'And don't you dare call me Ms Devlin, it's Helena.'

The theatre's crew – Jacie and Errol and Gerry and Brynn and Beryl – all stepped up to congratulate them both on the new partnership, Jacie making a pointed comment that she couldn't wait to tell Gallagher where he could shove his buy-out offer tomorrow, which Luke *had* to agree with.

He crossed the foyer, propelled by the need to rope his arm around Ruby's waist and anchor her to his side as he turned to his mother and said, 'Just in case anyone's interested, I'll agree to sell to you, Mom.'

He felt an odd wrench in his chest as he took his mom's hand to shake on the deal. Glancing around the theatre, he took in the moulding he'd spent hours repairing, the new baseboards he'd hammered into place a week ago, the fresh paint and gleaming brasswork on the concession stand, and sighed.

It would actually be kind of hard not to have a part of this place anymore. But as Ruby leaned up to kiss his cheek he could feel the joy vibrating through her, and she murmured, 'Thank you.' He had no regrets.

Matty Devlin had given him half of his dream.

And by some miracle, it had morphed into him finding his own dream – to live with Ruby by his side for the rest of his life – and then finally figuring out how to make it come true.

He would buy that place in Chepstow Villas, and set up an office in London to develop his business in Europe. And Ruby could run The Royale.

But he also intended to prise her away from time to time so they could travel, and he could give her the adventures she'd missed out on.

The Royal wasn't her whole life anymore. And his business wasn't his whole life anymore either.

They had each other now, and there was nothing they couldn't do together. He was sure of it. Just as he was now pretty sure Auntie Em and Uncle Henry had managed to rescue Toto from the abattoir for Dorothy after all.

Ignoring his mom's laugh of encouragement, and the murmur of excited conversation from their eager audience, he gripped Ruby's cheeks and said, 'You're welcome.'

Before sinking into the kiss.

Selling his half of The Royale wasn't an end, it was a beginning.

For them to get started on the rest of their lives.

THE END

**If you enjoyed *Just Like In The Movies*, be sure
to follow Heidi Rice on Twitter @HeidiRomRice,
on Facebook @HeidiRomRice25, and check out
their website at heidi-rice.com for all the updates
on their latest work.**

**You can also find us at @0neMoreChapter_ on Twitter
and @0neMoreChapter on Facebook where we'll be
shouting about all our new releases.**

Acknowledgements

Firstly, I need to say a big thank you to Charlotte Ledger and her team at One More Chapter.

Thanks Charlotte for being so enthusiastic about this rather sketchy idea when I first pitched it to you over burgers and curly fries one rainy February night in Five Guys in Soho ... I can't help thinking at the time that my pitch and your enthusiasm might have had something to do with all the Prosecco (aka dutch courage) we'd necked before 'having' to watch Magic Mike Live (totally for work! Honest) but thanks for sticking with it and even coming up with the 'high concept' which turned it from a sketchy idea to a fully fledged labour of love.

Big thanks also to my writing support posse – Fiona Harper, Iona Grey and Susan Wilson – and most of all my best writing mate Daisy Cummins. Without you guys, I'd probably sink into a puddle of writer's angst every time I switched on my computer (instead of just every other time)!

Heidi Rice

I should also say a special thanks to Alice Roberts at the
Everyman Screen on the Green for answering all my stupid
questions about how to manage a cinema. And also running
my favourite local cinema which has turned movie-going into
an all round fabulous night out.